NO ESCAPE

NO ESCAPE

N. J. Cooper

SIMON &
SCHUSTER

w York · Sydney · Toronto

CBS COMPANY

First published in Great Britain by Simon & Schuster UK Ltd, 2009
A CBS COMPANY

Copyright © N.J. Cooper, 2009

1 3 5 7 9 10 8 6 4 2

Simon & Schuster UK Ltd
1st Floor
222 Gray's Inn Road
London WC1X 8HB

www.simonandschuster.co.uk

Simon & Schuster Australia
Sydney

A CIP catalogue record for this book is available from
the British Library

ISBN 978-1-84737-414-1

Typeset by M Rules
Printed in the UK by CPI Mackays, Chatham ME5 8TD

In memory of Susanna Yager

Acknowledgements

I have lots of people to thank, including Professor Bernard Knight and Doctor Anthony Bateman, both of whom gave me the huge benefit of their professional experience, then said in almost the same words, 'But it's a novel; you can do what you want.' Fidelis Morgan helped with Island information, which I have adapted to suit my fictional purposes.

Many others provided information, inspiration, advice and useful criticism. They include Elizabeth Atkinson, Suzanne Baboneau, Mary Carter, Emma Dunford, Jane Gregory, Isabelle Grey, Stephanie Glencross, Peter McKay, Sheila Turner, Libby Vernon and Julie Wright. I am grateful to them all.

Naturally all the characters in this novel are imaginary and bear absolutely no relation to any real people, living or dead, on the Island or on the mainland. And in the year in which I wrote this novel, there was no powerboat race in the Solent.

N. J. Cooper, 2008

Prologue

Dan lay back on the rug and let the August sun warm his face. His left hand idly stroked the sheep-cropped grass of Chillerton Down, near the old chalk pit, while his right became a plaything for his eighteen-month-old son. The sensations of gummy bite and sticky dribble on his fingers added an unlikely charm to this perfect day.

'I've got your picture, Daddy. I've got your picture.'

Dan opened his eyes to smile up into his daughter's face. Foreshortened like this, it had the plump sweetness of some putto on the ceiling of a Tuscan church.

'Let Daddy sleep, Anna,' said Izzie. There was the cosy sound of amusement in her voice. 'He's worn out with eating so many chocolate biscuits.'

Dan switched his attention from the squashed oval of his daughter's face to the long bony perfection of his wife's. The mixture of mockery and protectiveness in her eyes was so much part of her that he wanted to reach up and pull her towards him, as though they were in bed.

'Where would I be without you?' he said.

'Locked to your desk by obsession, duty, and unspeakably awful ambition,' she said, pushing some of the soft dark hair away from her face.

'I've got your picture, ladybird. I've got your picture,' chanted Anna, clicking madly at the camera as she stared towards the ground.

'Your sister has a lot to answer for, Izzie.' Dan pointed a lazy finger towards the budding Cartier-Bresson, who was now dancing away towards the trees at the edge of the field. Her pink dress dwindled to a single bright spot in the centre of his fuzzy vision. 'Just because she didn't want her camera any more, that's no reason to turn our life into a perpetual slide show.'

Izzie screwed the top on the old honey jar that had held vinaigrette, raising one finger to suck the gleaming gold oil drops off it.

'Anna will be bored within a couple of days and forget it. Just as she's forgotten to look for the fossils we came here for. I suppose we should be thankful it's a digital camera and we're not faced with paying to get film developed. This way if she does manage a shot without putting her thumb in front of the lens we can save it and tactfully delete the rest.'

'We could even print the odd one,' Dan said, regaining his fingers from his son, who promptly rose to his feet and performed his latest trick of flinging his now considerable weight straight down onto Dan's diaphragm. 'Ough! Family life.'

Izzie had finished packing up the picnic and scooped Jake away, tucking him between her arm and ribs.

'You love it,' she said, looking down. 'Is your gut OK?'

'Sure.' Dan prodded himself experimentally, then added: 'At least it will be once I've recovered from major surgery to my abdominals and had a year or so of physio.'

'Wimp!' Izzie kissed her fingers and bent forward to lay them briefly on his forehead.

He was impressed by her ability to hold their squirming toddler under her arm without breaking a sweat, or interrupting anything else she might want to do. But then she'd always managed the superhuman trick of making motherhood look as though it were an enchanting sideline to an easy life. He couldn't imagine existing without her now.

'Where's Anna?' she said, her voice sounding as near sharp as it ever did.

'Photographing worms and midges I should think,' he said, pushing himself up onto one elbow to look in the direction their daughter had taken.

A shot sounded in the trees, cracking through the warm air.

'Anna!' Izzie dumped Jake on the rug and ran towards the straggly copse at the end of the field.

'It'll only be someone after rabbits,' Dan called after her, surprised by the overreaction.

Another shot smashed through the still laziness of the afternoon. It sounded even nearer. He listened. There were birds, and the buzzing chuntering background sounds of any bit of empty countryside. But there were no voices.

In the calm after the shots, the lack of human noise spooked him. He was on his feet in seconds, picking up Jake and feeling for his phone with his free hand, even as he, too, ran towards the copse, shouting his wife's name and his daughter's.

His own panting was so loud and his heart was banging so hard in his chest and Jake was crying so loudly that it was far too long before he noticed the sound of heavy, trampling feet coming through the edge of the scrubby little wood ahead of him.

He dumped Jake on the ground and forced his phone out of his pocket. His fingers seemed to have swollen and sweat made them slip off the tiny keys. He swore and cancelled the first attempt at 999, then tried again.

'Daddy! Daddy! Monster!' Jake was tottering on his feet, one hand clamped to Dan's trousers, and pointing.

Dan followed the line of Jake's finger and saw a truly monstrous figure in a tattered brown overcoat that came nearly to its feet. A tight black woollen balaclava covered its face, with ragged holes cut for the eyes. Unbelievably it held out a short stubby shotgun between its gloved paws. The two-eyed barrel was absolutely steady.

'Who are you?' Dan said, just as something ferociously heavy hit him in the chest.

Boiling heat drove tracks all through his body. As his knees buckled, he turned to shield his son and fell. The last sight he had was of the rough edges of the gun barrels pointing past his face straight into Jake's eyes.

Chapter 1

Ping. Ping. Ping.

Rain fell from the loft under the leaky shingle roof to hit the base of the bowls Karen had arranged all over the kitchen floor when she'd arrived late yesterday afternoon. Confronted then with fast-spreading puddles, she'd remembered the chipped enamel bowls at once and found them at the bottom of the kitchen's only cupboard without even thinking about it.

What she hadn't remembered through the eighteen years of absence was the shabbiness of this small holiday chalet on the unfashionable side of the Isle of Wight. Her last sight of it had been through a fog of tears at the age of fifteen, when she'd come to the Island for her beloved grandmother's funeral.

Ping.

Granny had once used these same bowls to catch similar drips until the roof had been replaced two years before her death. Karen hadn't expected it to need doing again so soon.

Ping.

She braced herself for the next drop, rather as she'd once braced herself for each new bout of her husband's snoring. There'd been a hideous pattern to it: seven snores rising in pitch and intensity until they'd peaked in one tremendous snort, before stopping for at least two minutes. At first she'd lain beside Peter, silently screaming with frustration. Later in their five-year battle of a marriage, she'd often sat up to watch his sweaty, stubbly face and thought about putting a pillow over his nose and mouth and leaning on it until he was dead.

Ping. Ping. Ping.

A distant bellow interrupted the drops' rhythm and her worst memories. This was a trumpeting kind of sound she'd been warned to expect whenever the rain was especially heavy.

Her nearest neighbour in these weird and muddy woods apparently believed he was descended from elephants and liked to greet the rain with a triumphal roar. According to local gossip, he'd been sent to live here decades ago, when his family had finally admitted they found him too embarrassing to keep with them on the expensive side of the Island.

Ping.

'He's utterly benign,' Jan Davies, the most ordinary of the few other neighbours, had told Karen yesterday. 'Got a fantastic memory, a wrinkled kind of skin that looks too big for his body, even though that's fat enough, and this habit of trumpeting in the rain. He won't bother you in any other way.'

Ping. Ping.

Now the noise of the drips made Karen think of war films, with tense young men using sonar to listen out for enemy submarines and the torpedoes that could kill them in seconds.

She turned back to her laptop and the email she was composing to her boyfriend to stop herself thinking too much about the very different sorts of danger she was facing. The chalet had no broadband – it didn't even have a phone line – but she could save the text on a memory stick and take it with her to the nearest Internet cafe on her way back from the prison tomorrow.

Talking to Will, even at several removes like this, always cheered her up. Sometimes it was better doing it at several removes because she could include all the things she would never actually tell him, whole paragraphs she could delete before sending the email. She typed:

I keep reminding myself, that in my family we don't make mistakes. Ever. Sometimes our plans 'just don't work out'. But that just opens the way to new plans and new achievements.

Trouble is, the reminding doesn't always work. If I were to list all the things I've got wrong, apart (maybe) from coming back here, they'd look like this.

'Fuck it,' she said aloud, determined to be more positive. 'Don't be pathetic.'

She grabbed her phone and drove halfway up the road that led out of the woods, to the point where she could make and receive calls. She pressed the speed dial for Will's mobile.

'Hi,' she said when he answered. 'You busy?'

'Never too busy to talk to you,' he said, and she could tell he was smiling from the sound of his voice. 'How is it?'

'Grim. Dank. Full of memories I don't need right now.' She thought of adding: so I wanted to talk to my resilient, untouchable, unworryable, brilliant bloke. 'How was today's list?'

Will was a neurosurgeon at Brighton Hospital, with a long queue of patients waiting for his skills.

'Fine. Nothing too hard. But we've got a five-year-old whose glioma isn't going to be safely accessible. I've got to talk to the parents tomorrow to tell them why we won't operate.'

'Awful!' Karen said, knowing she'd find that kind of encounter impossibly hard. 'For them and for you do.'

'Part of the job. Easier in some ways than interviewing murderous psychopaths in prison like you do.'

'Maybe. Are you going to be able to get away at the weekend and see my eccentric refuge? I should warn you there's nothing here but the kitchen/living room, a couple of small bedrooms and a ramshackle shower.'

'I hope I can make it,' he said, and the smile was back in his voice. 'I'll let you know for certain as soon as I can.'

'Great. And I hope I'll have found a way to fix the leaking

roof by the time you come. Otherwise you'll be falling over bowls full of rainwater.'

'Don't let the leaks distract you.' His voice was still light, but there was an unmistakable note of authority in it, which she didn't like at all. They'd been together for three months now and just occasionally he seemed to forget that she wasn't one of the junior doctors on his team. 'They don't matter and your work does.'

'But you don't believe in my work,' she said, hoping she sounded confidently amused.

'That's not fair. I don't myself see how you could ever find enough evidence of the formation and causes of Dangerous Severe Personality Disorder from interviewing any number of individuals, however psychopathic, to come up with an incontrovertible diagnostic test, but . . .'

Will paused in his measured counter-attack for long enough to make her understand that sometimes cool rationality could be even more irritating than thoughtless prejudice and shouting. She still didn't know why she found him so irresistible, when his unshakeable self-control, long sinewy torso and short spiky blond hair made him so completely different from every other man she'd ever fancied.

'But,' he went on, 'that doesn't mean I don't think it's worth the attempt. Or that any other psychologist, forensic or otherwise, could do any better. You're as good as they come, Karen.'

'Aaah,' she said, forgiving him. 'You do know how to make a girl feel good about herself. I'd better go, Will. Sleep well.'

'I always do. Take care. Bye.'

She sat in the car, holding the hard little phone and thinking of all the differences in the way she and Will approached their work.

For him, the brain was a collection of differently shaped masses with the texture of very lightly scrambled egg, a neat arrangement of regions named by ancient scholars and surgical explorers: the hippocampus they thought looked like a sea horse; the amygdala, so called because it was almond-shaped; the corpus collosum; the cerebellum; the ganglia; all clustered around the brain stem that reached down into the spine and ordered movement, thought, speech and behaviour by electrical impulses; each part of the whole subject to lesions and disease and tumours that his scalpel might be able to excise and correct.

For her, in spite of what she knew about its physical characteristics, the brain was a mass of anguish and delight, container of memories of punishment and despair, generator of impulses to excitement, awe, dread, hope and terror; and occasionally a terrifying labyrinth, in whose dark heart lurked a monster that had to be found, named and, with luck and courage, slain. Or at least neutralized.

Realizing that she'd spent at least five minutes staring at the raindrops that were chasing each other down her windscreen, she put away the phone and drove on to the junction with the main road, where there was enough room to turn the car and so get it back to its little parking space outside the chalet.

As soon as she opened the door, she realized the pings had stopped. Inside she saw why: water was now cascading over the edges of the enamel bowls. They'd have to be emptied before the floor was flooded all over again. And she'd better climb up into the roof space to empty the deeper buckets she'd put up there. This rain might go on all night.

After that, she'd have to make serious plans for tomorrow's trip to Parkhurst Prison and her first encounter with Spike Falconer, who had blasted a husband, wife and two small children to death with a shotgun at point-blank range for absolutely no reason anyone had yet been able to establish.

Chapter 2

Next morning Karen stopped her rattly car at the place she thought of as Reception Point, where she'd phoned Will last night, pulling off the narrow road in case of other traffic.

Only one message had been left and no texts. She put the phone to her ear and heard his voice again, as crisp and light as usual, saying: 'Great to talk last night, but you sounded rather down. I hope you're more cheerful now. Go for it today and ignore everything negative I've ever said about psychology. If you can get anywhere with Dangerous Severe Personality Disorder, you'll have the world at your feet. Bye.'

A smile stretched her cheek muscles and banished half the doomy thoughts that had been in her mind since she woke. Will was exaggerating, but, if she did make a breakthrough, her career would get a much-needed boost, Max Pitton – the head of her department at Southampton University – would be pleased, and the prison governor would feel justified in allowing her access to his most notorious inmate.

Parkhurst had been turned into a Category B training prison after some embarrassing escapes in the mid-1990s and now usually held only those lifers who weren't considered too high risk in terms of either escaping or reoffending if they did manage to break out. Spike Falconer was most definitely a Cat A killer, but the maximum security prisons were all full. He'd been chosen for Parkhurst because he'd grown up on the Island and was assumed to have a good support network here, which might help keep him quiet as he served out his life sentence.

Karen stowed the phone in the glove compartment and turned the ignition key. The engine fired, faithful as ever, but when she put her foot on the accelerator the car didn't move. Looking over her shoulder out of the window, she saw the wheels spinning in the soft mud, flinging gobbets of it behind, like a terrier after some tasty prey.

Shifting into reverse, she tried again. It would be absurd to drive the car further back into the mud, but if she could just get the wheels to grip, she might be able to get it moving forwards with a fast enough gear change.

The wheels didn't grip. The screech they made as they spun uselessly through the surface of the mud set her teeth on edge. She turned off the engine, left the hand-brake down and got out to see whether she could push the car back onto the road. One of her shoes slipped in the mud and she cracked her knee on the bumper, messing up the loose black linen trousers she'd ironed with such care this morning.

'Shit!'

Karen righted herself and fumbled for a tissue so she could clean some of the dirt off her hands. At least she hadn't got mud on the cream linen of her jacket.

Thank God the phone worked here. She should be able to get help. Even so, she could have done without this. Calling out a pick-up truck would make her feel like a fool and cost a fortune, and she hadn't any slack in her budget. *And* it would make her late for Spike, which could be fatal to her chances of persuading him to talk.

Her encounters with the five other killers she'd interviewed so far made it clear that Spike would never tell her anything useful unless he trusted her, which wasn't going to happen if she let him down so early in their dealings.

'Can I help?' said an authoritative male voice from behind her.

Karen whipped round in relief and saw a tall but squidgy-look-ing man dressed in old-fashioned tweed breeches, army-surplus sweater and shooting stockings. He repeated his offer of help, peering at her with bright brown eyes. His sparse grey hair was brushed back over a domed and shiny forehead and his wrinkled skin was reddened by broken veins and long exposure to weather. He looked as though he could be in his late sixties or early sev-enties, but she found it hard to be sure.

Over his arm was a shotgun. Karen was glad to see the breech was open. Shotguns had been very much in her mind since she'd reread every version of the story about the picnic massacre last night before she turned off her light.

She tried a smile and was relieved to see him smile back.

'You see what I've done,' she said. 'I pulled over to make a phone call and I'm stuck. I tried to push, but it didn't work.'

With his spongy pendulous body he didn't look strong enough to do any better.

'Don't worry,' he said. 'Wait there.'

He turned and lumbered off between the thin trees. She'd reinvented her memories of these woods during the eighteen years she'd been away, making herself believe they were like a kind of Disney landscape, with sunny clearings full of glossy moss banks and tumbling streams, and crystal-clear air full of blue birds and butterflies. The dank reality could hardly have been more different.

The undistinguished, unbeautiful alders and scrubby conifers grew close together, and many were being slowly throttled with ivy. The ground consisted of grey mud, made even more slimy by years of half-rotted fallen leaves, and probably dead slugs too, and worse. The only punctuation in the dreariness was provided by the few isolated holiday chalets like her own.

She saw a thin thread of smoke drifting upwards and made out the lines of a tin chimney. That must be where her eccentric res-cuer had headed. She heard his crunching, shuffling footsteps coming back before she could distinguish his sludge-green clothes from the surrounding vegetation.

He'd left the shotgun behind, and now carried a pile of thick, ancient sacking. The smell hit her from yards away, a mixture of damp, mould and something pungently animal. He hurried forwards, saying:

'These should do the trick.'

She couldn't imagine how, and watched without much hope as he shook out one sack after another, making the stench even worse. She tried not to gag. He laid them in heaps stretching out in front of her wheels towards the safe hardness of the road's tarmac.

'Get in again,' he said, 'and build up the revs before you move, then go. The sacking should give you just enough traction. Go on – try it.'

'OK,' she said, smiling again, even though she was still not convinced. 'But keep out of the way in case I skid. I don't want to hurt you.'

'You won't. Go on. Have a go.'

She pulled up the handbrake in case of accidents, turned on the engine, pumped the gas, then slowly let the brake out again. Miraculously the wheels gripped the heavy sacking and were back over the edge of the road in moments. When she'd made certain the whole car was properly supported, she stopped, wound down her window and leaned out to thank him, adding:

'What's your name?'

He grinned, with a rictus of a smile that didn't seem to fit his jowly wrinkled face, and said quite seriously: 'Round here they usually call me the Elephant Man because I'm descended from elephants, but my family called me Roderick.'

'Thank you, Roderick,' she said. 'You've saved my life.'

'Don't exaggerate,' he said, as severe as any schoolteacher.

He bent to collect his sacks, which were marked now with the mud from her wheels, then trudged off with them towards his home.

She watched him in her mirror as he disappeared into the murk of the trees, thinking he was more like a gigantic Hobbit than an elephant. She'd have to get some sacks so she could do the same trick for herself next time. A piece of old carpet might be even better.

Pausing at the junction with the main road for a gap in the straggling line of cars and trucks, she saw Jan Davies emerging from her chalet at the sound of the engine. Karen waved and saw Jan coming towards her, so she pulled up the handbrake again and opened the window.

'How was last night, Karen?' Jan said, balancing her arthritic hand on the edge of the window. 'I worried about you in all that rain. Your grandmother would've hated the thought of you suffering on your own down there like that. She always took such trouble to make things nice for you and Aidan when you came to stay.'

'I know she did,' Karen said, smiling. 'And I know how good you were to her when she got so ill. I wish I could stay and chat but I'm going to be late if I don't get going.'

'Of course, dear.' Jan stood up straight. 'You get off and have a good day. We'll have a cup of tea one day when you're not so busy.'

'I'll look forward to it, Jan. Thanks so much.'

The slight traffic had passed while they were talking and Karen turned left into the main road, heading towards Newport, the main town on the Island. Turning left again, she followed the signs for Cowes and Parkhurst Prison.

The prison's origins as a military hospital were clear only in the elegant nineteenth-century brick and large windows of one building. The rest varied between barn-like Victorian wings and a forbidding slab of modern red brick. Karen parked as she'd been instructed, left her phone and made her way to the reception area.

She was searched politely but firmly by a woman officer, who ran her hands up and down Karen's legs and felt all round her waistband, as well as in her pockets.

'Good clothes,' she said with a smile as she stepped back. 'Loose. Easy to manage, too.'

Karen gave her a brief smile. She'd had enough experience of the atmosphere in male prisons to make sure her clothes did not cling to any part of her long body. The olive-green T-shirt she wore over her trousers was big enough to conceal her breasts, and the long jacket hid the curves of her narrow waist and hips. Her thick, shoulder-length blonde hair had been tugged back and twisted up into an informal cockade, held together with a basic rubber band.

'Now,' said the officer, 'have you got any maps, keys, or umbrella?'

All Karen had were her keys: a big clattering bunch on a metal ring. They opened not only the chalet, but also her flat in Southampton, her office at the university, her filing cabinet of confidential records, and her parents' London penthouse. Her car keys followed, on their own separate plaited leather strap.

'These must weigh you down,' said the cheerful officer as she took them all from Karen. 'Now, if you'll just put your bags through the scanner. Great. Jim Blake will be down for you in a minute. He'll explain procedure and take you along to Spike.'

'Jim Blake?' Karen said, letting her voice rise at the end to invite more information.

'He's the officer best placed to help you. Spike responds better to him than anyone else. Likes him too. Ah, here he is.'

He was a big man with a shock of unruly red hair and a childish splurge of freckles over his nose, which made it look as though someone had showered his face with cayenne pepper. But his height and broad shoulders gave him an air of authority. Karen thought he looked sensible, and his smile was friendly.

'Is it Ms Taylor?' he said in a deep voice with the long vowels she suddenly remembered were characteristic of the Island.

They sent her right back to childhood, even more efficiently than Jan Davies or the rain-drip bowls had done. She could almost see her grandmother's face and smell the powdery, denture-fixative, *old* scent that had always clung to her.

'It's Doctor Taylor really,' she said, bringing herself sharply back to the present, 'but it doesn't matter. And "Ms" does stop people telling me about their itches and digestive problems. Thank you for coming down.'

'How much d'you know about Spike? It's this way,' Jim Blake said, reaching one large hand past her to unlock and push open a gate to let her through. Then he locked it behind them both before ushering her on to the next one.

In spite of her experience of other prisons, she was taken aback to find that this one smelt of nothing but disinfectant, which suggested a general cleanliness that could have belonged in any modern hospital.

'Only that he was adopted at the age of eighteen months by a well-established Island couple,' she said, looking over her shoulder at Jim's face as she answered his question.

He unlocked the next of the cream-painted steel gates and followed her into the usual broad, vinyl-floored corridor lined on both sides with blank, locked doors.

'That he exhibited strange behaviour almost from the start,' she went on, 'which became worse once his adoptive parents' own son joined him at school. That he'd dropped out by the age of fourteen, took drugs, drank too much, and was eventually thrown out by the family when he was eighteen, when the first vague diagnosis of "some kind of personality disorder" was upped to Anti-Social Personality Disorder, then later to full-blown Dangerous Severe Personality Disorder.'

'That's more or less it. He lived in hostels for a while, then slept rough all over the Island and gave everyone a lot of trouble. Have you seen any recent pictures of him?'

'Only the ones in the papers and files his solicitors sent me,' she said, surprised by the question. 'Why?'

He caught up with her and pulled the chained keys forwards

from his belt to unlock the next of the gates. 'Because now he's off the drink and drugs, and super-fit from all the time he spends in the gym, he's just about the most beautiful man you're ever likely to meet.'

Karen thought back to the blurred face that had stared at her out of newsprint and lawyers' photocopies. Spike had looked pleasant enough, except for the bad skin, angry staring eyes and twisted lips, but nowhere near beautiful.

'That's unexpected,' she said. 'But is it important?'

Jim paused with the key already in the lock, then he turned it with a decisiveness that surprised her.

'I'd say so. It's why . . . why some people hate him so much. Makes them judge him more harshly than an ugly man who did the same things.'

'Interesting,' she said, surprised to find him so analytical.

'Haven't you noticed how beautiful people are supposed to be better than the rest of us? Like children are supposed to be inno-cent. That's why people get so angry when they offend.'

Karen wished she'd had her tape recorder running. She knew by now that only a few prison officers fitted the stereotype of thick-as-pigshit, unimaginative petty tyrant, but she was always glad to find ones as perceptive as Jim.

'But *you* must know that,' he said, with an emphasis she took to be a reference to her profession rather than her own looks.

Although she was tall, not remotely fat, and had the kind of skin that takes on a smooth tan at the first hint of hot sun, she disliked her small round face, blonde hair and hazel eyes, in which she could see nothing appealing at all. She'd much rather have had Titian hair and emerald eyes, or raven black and dazzling blue.

'How long have you known him?' she asked.

'Four years. Ever since he was sent here on remand after that family was shot.'

Karen noticed that he didn't refer to 'the Picnic Massacre', which was another point in his favour.

'Does he give you trouble?'

'Not much. He seems to feel safer here than he ever did out-side. He knows what he's supposed to do and mostly he does it.'

'That's characteristic of DSPD. It's interesting you've seen it so clearly, working with him like this.'

'I've been reading up about personality disorders, so I've been looking out for symptoms. Now, you'll be alone with him, as you requested, but there's a panic button on your side of the table. Press it the moment you're worried. I don't think he'll go for you, but so far no one's been able to work out what makes him flip, so you need to be prepared.'

'Thank you,' she said, ignoring the roughness in her throat that was her body's familiar response to threat.

'Then there's the ordinary bell beside the door to ring when you want to leave. If you haven't pressed it in thirty minutes, we'll come in and get you out.'

He pushed open the door.

Chapter 3

Karen was glad of Jim's warning. She had never seen anything like the unearthly perfection of Spike's face. Botticelli's angels mixed with Hollywood action heroes and the best complexion she'd ever seen in a prison.

'Hi,' he said in a voice with no trace of the Island in it. 'My lawyer tells me you've come to get me out of here.'

Then he smiled, stretching his lips wide apart, like any PR-trained celebrity. Unlike them, though, he had horrible teeth: stained and chipped. They were the only ugly thing about him. Karen smiled back and noticed his expression didn't change even when she moved. His features could've been stuck in the same position with superglue.

'That's not exactly why I'm here,' she said.

Jim was hovering by the door. She wondered if he was going to say something and glanced over her shoulder at him. He was watching Spike intently, as though assessing the quality of his self-control this morning.

Karen turned back and ploughed on: 'I've come because I'm making a study of people diagnosed with various kinds of personality disorder so that I can understand exactly what's happened to them, and why. I did make that clear to your lawyers when I asked if I could meet you. I hope they told you?'

Spike nodded, still with the smile fixed to his face. Karen heard Jim step backwards and close the door. He must have satisfied himself that his charge was calm enough for her to be safe alone with him today. She registered the position of the big round red panic button. The heavy steel door clanged as the automatic lock activated, and the hard surfaces all round threw the sound back at her.

Spike didn't react. The noise must have been too familiar to bother him. Nor did he let his face relax. Karen thought he looked like someone who had been told what smiling was but had never understood the point of it. Which would fit. Empathy was almost impossible for any severely personality disordered individual.

'I've had two,' he said, at last allowing his lips to contract back into their perfect resting shape.

'I'm sorry?' she said, moving away from the door, towards the chair that had been set for her, directly opposite Spike. 'Two what?'

'Diagnoses. Personality disorders. Two for the price of one!' His voice was rising in excitement. 'That should help you, Doctor Taylor, shouldn't it? My two diagnoses, Doctor Taylor. They'll help, won't they?'

'Probably,' she said, keeping her own voice very calm. 'There are lots of things I'd like to ask you. Is that OK?'

He put both hands in the pockets of his jeans and leaned so far back that his chair tipped until it was balanced on only two legs. She noticed how slim he was, and how muscular.

'I didn't shoot those people, you know,' he said in a mechanical way, as though repeating something he'd learned by heart. 'I was asleep. Fast asleep. So I didn't know why the police were yelling at me and shaking me when they woke me up.'

He waited for her response, but she hadn't anything to say yet.

'My lawyers must've told you what really happened,' he said. 'They were supposed to.'

'They did.' Karen kept her voice light and hoped it would express nothing but unthreatening good humour.

She knew from the files that he'd been sleeping off a heavy

intake of skunk when the police had found him after the shooting. He'd been only about half a mile away from the place where it had happened.

Later they'd found his tattered old brown tweed overcoat and black woollen balaclava mask, dumped in a ditch. Scientists had soon established that the splatters on the cloth matched blood they'd taken from the body of little Anna Sanders. The position of all four corpses suggested she'd been Spike's first victim.

The tweed coat had been wrapped around a sawn-off shotgun with his prints all over it. There had been four cartridge cases in the pocket, also covered in his prints. In spite of all his denials that he'd ever had access to any kind of gun and hadn't left his sleeping place that day, no one involved had ever had any doubt that he was guilty.

But his disorder meant he would never be able to accept responsibility and so there was no point trying to make him do it. Instead Karen wanted him to tell her about his perceptions of himself and the world from inside his head. She knew she had to make him like her enough to want to cooperate.

'They also warned me you don't always like answering questions,' she went on with a friendly smile.

Spike laughed, which would have been encouraging if she hadn't caught a hint of spite in the sound. She waited for more.

'Sometimes I answer because I get so bored in here.' His speech had slowed down a little, as though to emphasize the malicious undercurrents. 'And sometimes I don't. You'll never know what it's going to be like each day when you get here.'

'I see.'

'Good. Because this is how it goes, Doctor Taylor: you're allowed to ask me whatever you want; and I'm allowed not to say anything.' He laughed again, hunching his shoulders together as though he could hardly contain his pleasure. 'It'll be like going to the bookies. You make a bet, and you don't know if you're going to win or the bookies are. OK?'

'Fine,' she said. 'It should be fun.'

All her research subjects so far had exhibited similar attempts to manipulate her. None of her interviewees had been anywhere near as sophisticated as fictional psychopaths such as Hannibal Lecter, or as successful. Some had been intelligent; others not. But each had had an ability to show supreme disdain for everyone around him.

As she pulled out her chair to sit down at last, she made sure she'd be able to reach the panic button.

'It works, too,' Spike said from the other side of the table. 'The panic button.'

'Right,' she said, determined not to give him the satisfaction of seeing he'd disconcerted her. His ability to follow her thoughts was unexpected. 'Thanks. D'you mind if I tape our session?'

'Not at all. So, what are we going to start with? How come I was born evil?'

She made herself smile back at him again, shaking her head When she'd taken a pen and large white ruled pad out of her briefcase, just in case the recorder failed, she said:

'What I'd like you to tell me this morning is the story of who you are.'

He frowned, the gesture pulling his face out of shape and making it more interesting. The clouds must have moved outside because a shaft of sunlight came down through the small window high up on the wall opposite her and gilded his smooth fair hair for a second or two.

'Story? What story?'

'Most of us,' Karen said, drawing an intricate key pattern at the top of her pad, to give him an illusion of privacy while he worked out what to say, 'have a story we tell ourselves to make sense of what we do and what other people do to us. We add to it when-ever something difficult happens – or doesn't happen in the way we wanted.'

She looked up to make sure he understood her. He nodded, as

though he thought she needed encouragement, but he didn't speak. Her so-far unpublished theory held that if you could tell a credible story to explain your own actions and motives you had a chance to overcome anything that had been done to you, however bad it had been.

If she was right, no one with a severe personality disorder would be able to do it because an inability to accept responsibility or reason from past experience was part of the condition. So far none of the interviews she'd conducted in prisons around the country had made any holes in the theory. She hoped it would stand up long enough to become part of her recommended diagnostic process for DSPD.

'Some religious people,' she went on to encourage Spike, 'tell their stories in terms of ideas they've been taught by their priests. Others do it with what their parents used to say about them. You know, "She's the untidy pretty one, and her little sister is the neat clever plain one, who never breaks a rule." D'you see what I mean?'

'That's what it's like for us.'

Karen waited, smiling encouragingly, but he didn't go on.

'What *did* your family say about you?'

He shrugged. 'I'm the special, bad one and Silas is the dream kid, who always does what he's supposed to.'

'Did you believe it?' she said, fighting a dangerous surge of sympathy.

If she were to produce usable research, she'd have to keep her own feelings right out of these sessions. They would muddle her intellectual response to what she heard and, perhaps, make her see things that didn't exist and invent her own stories about him, which would distort the whole project.

Spike laughed, with a high teetering sound like a drunk giggling to pretend that his brain wasn't shutting down as he failed to decode what other people said.

'Then there are the lucky ones,' Karen said when the creepy noise had stopped and Spike had made it clear he wasn't going to volunteer anything else, 'who make up their own stories, using only what they themselves have seen and thought about the world.'

'Lucky or clever?' Spike said, suddenly sounding quite ordinary again and as though he was interested and able to follow her ideas without difficulty.

She knew from the files how he'd messed around in every class at school, truanted and caused endless trouble, before dropping out completely. But no one who'd ever tried to teach him had had any doubts about his IQ.

'Maybe lucky and clever are the same thing,' she answered, ready for the moment to let the conversation flow in whichever direction he was going to allow.

'What's *your* story, Doctor Taylor?'

Karen chose her words even more carefully, wanting to say enough to give him a sense of equality in the conversation without revealing anything he could use against her.

'I'm lucky enough to have a good qualification that allows me to be paid for work I enjoy. And I'm a survivor. That makes me even luckier.'

Spike's interest sharpened at once. 'What have *you* survived?'

'Nothing but childhood and adolescence and the kind of frustrations everyone has to deal with,' she said, smoothly covering the unintended hint of weakness. No way was she going to tell a research subject like Spike about the wars she'd fought with Peter.

'Even with that kind of ordinary stuff,' she went on, 'if you tell a story in which other people do things to you, you become a victim.'

He nodded wisely, as though he knew all about victims. But he still wasn't offering her anything from his past.

She plodded on: 'If your story is about how you fight back, you become a survivor, a winner.'

She paused, then added with a deliberation at odds with her usual light tone: 'And *no one* can do anything to you then.'

'Unless they kill you.' Spike's face was as angelic as ever.

She had a sudden, splinteringly vivid vision of the way Peter had died and closed her eyes for a second.

'Why won't you look at me, Doctor Taylor?' Spike giggled. 'I'm not going to kill *you*. Not while Jim's right outside the door ready to come in and save you anyway.'

'Of course, you're right,' Karen said, ignoring his taunt with the utmost calm. 'No one survives being killed. Now, what about your story? What can you tell me about what happened to you?'

'It's easy,' he said, sounding very superior, as though he felt he'd scored some kind of victory over her.

He let his chair fall back onto all four legs so he could lean forwards across the table. The surface was too wide for him to reach out and touch her, but the effect of his movement towards her was to suggest an intimacy between them that was almost more disturbing than the giggles.

'I'm the Island Freak, Natural Born Killer. Monster of Depravity. Time Bomb Waiting to Explode.'

He laughed and swung himself away, tipping back his chair again. Karen recognized the tabloid headlines. She was interested to find him so articulate, so easily able to decode some things about her and yet so completely unable to understand what she wanted from him in terms of a narrative of his life. It was a sad but useful confirmation of all her assumptions about Dangerous Severe Personality Disorder.

But it still wasn't enough. She wished he and his lawyers hadn't put a ban on the psychometric tests she'd wanted to give him. Even better would have been a combination of tests and a parallel series of brain scans that would have shown all the different areas of his brain lighting up in response to her carefully designed stimuli.

At the end of her half-hour, she got to her feet to ring the bell beside the door, planning to pack up her stuff while she waited to be released.

'You know what you should have asked me?' Spike said chattily.
'No. What?'

'What it feels like to stare into a toddler's eyes and then blast them out through the back of his skull with a shotgun.'

Karen didn't press the bell. This was, of course, one of the many things she wanted to hear, but on her own terms and not delivered as part of one of his games.

'Why should I?' she said, moving back to the table so she could look into his eyes.

The irises were a clear grey-green, and the whites had all the gleam of perfect health. Her recorder was still running.

'Because that's what interests you.' He let his chair swing back onto all four legs again, with an echoing bang as the metal hit the concrete floor. 'This stuff about stories is just an excuse. You're like everyone else. You want to know what it's like to kill, how it happens, how it feels, how it changes you for ever, how *exciting* it is.'

'What would be the point of asking you anything like that?' Karen asked with an air of wholly fake innocence. 'You've just told me you didn't do it.'

For an instant he looked dumbfounded, then he giggled again, sounding wild and skittering off to the outer edge of self-control. When he spoke his voice rose with every quick and breathless word:

'I see I'm going to enjoy our talks, Doctor Taylor. Like I say, I get bored in here. Same time tomorrow, Doctor Taylor? We can talk about more stories and more killings then, can't we, Doctor Taylor? That's what you'd like, isn't it, Doctor Taylor? Lots of killing.'

This time she did press the bell for freedom, while her ears rang with the high insistent repetition of her name.

Chapter 4

Karen was too pumped up by the encounter to go straight back to the gloomy chalet. The mixture of adrenaline, ebbing anxiety, and even sharper curiosity than she'd felt before she met Spike, made her feel as though she'd overdosed on Red Bull.

She walked towards her car, rummaging in her loose brown-leather shoulder bag for the note Professor Pitton had sent her when he'd been urging her to produce some startling and therefore career-building research.

Dangerous Severe Personality Disorder's a good choice. There's a lot of non-professional interest in it right now. Highly political too, with the government planning to imprison men who have been diagnosed with it before they have committed any crime whatsoever. Outrageous. It might be acceptable if there were a diagnostic tool as definitive as a blood test, but, as you know, there isn't. Until the Oxford study is completed, there's only the list of assumed symptoms. Find something better before they do, and you'll have made your career. MP

Good enough as an idea, Karen thought as she passed the other parked cars, but studying my first five subjects hasn't got me anywhere and if Spike goes on playing games like today's, he's not going to be much more use. What will the Prof do to me if I fail?

Knowing nothing of her real reasons for turning to academic

psychology after Peter's death, Max Pitton was always trying to make her want more than she had: good, if belated, qualifications, an interesting job that provided her with a modest living, and a possible future sideline as an expert witness in criminal trials.

He liked to mix encouragement with some pretty savage goads, as though he thought insult might drive her on towards the kind of career success and public recognition he had. One day he'd stormed into her office at the university, asking why she'd written 'such a bland, banal, little paper' for one of the professional journals.

'I know you worry about being such a late starter,' he'd said, 'but you're potentially very good and you could really go places, but you keep sabotaging yourself, making your talents look bog standard at best. Whatever it is, get over it, Karen.'

If only I could, she thought, as she unlocked the car and made plans for the rest of the day.

People who'd heard she was coming back to the Island after so long had told her how weird she'd find it, what a throwback, how amazingly polite everyone would be from bus drivers to passers-by, how cut off from the hurly-burly of real life. The few inhabitants she'd met so far had confirmed all of it. Even the Elephant Man had been the epitome of old-world courtesy.

In the old days, when she and Aidan had been children sent here for holidays, the place had seemed like heaven. Looking back to the charms of toffee apples, dodgems, ramshackle canoes bucketing about in the surf at Totland Bay, and fish and chips in steamy cafes, she wondered how much of the bliss had come from the sensation of absolute safety provided by her grand-mother.

Her parents had never offered any safety at all, too distracted by work to pay much attention to their children. Sometimes, when their advertising business had been doing well, there'd been glam-orous family trips to DisneyWorld in Florida, or skiing in France. But there'd been other times, too, when clients hadn't paid and bills had poured in and bailiffs had come banging on the door.

The children had had to learn to pretend they didn't need anything then, just as they'd had to learn to hide with their parents, silent and unmoving, until the debt collectors had decided there was no one at home and given up.

Karen would never forget the first time she'd seen her father under the bed, cowering and in tears. She must have been three or four. Finding the most powerful adult in your life lapsing into a pathetic heaving heap did things to you.

Aidan had cut and run for the States as soon as his last term at school was over. Karen had never told him how deserted she'd felt then, in spite of all his letters and the promises he'd made to bring her over to join him 'as soon as I can afford it'.

Her loneliness and fear had made Peter seem heaven-sent when she'd met him only days after she'd finished her A levels. They'd married four months later and Aidan had been so angry with her he'd stopped writing altogether until after Peter was dead.

It had taken the two of them a while to get back on the old easy terms with each other, but now, ten years on, talking to Aidan was almost like talking to herself.

She reached the outskirts of Cowes, passing the low grey-stone cottages and half-timbered Edwardian horrors, searching for an Internet cafe. Soon she was near the centre, much older and prettier than the rest, and much more crowded too.

Some of the buildings had facades of the same untouched grey stone as the cottages; others were stuccoed and painted white or yellow. Cheery flags were strung across the side streets in preparation for one of the many races and festivals, and in every gap between the buildings she could see the white sails of expensive yachts pottering about the Solent and the bare masts of others still attached to their swinging moorings and pontoons.

She wound down the window and tasted the familiar salty tang in the air, somehow not at all spoiled by being mixed with petrol fumes, and heard the wild cries of the gulls that wheeled and swooped on any tiny bit of edible matter dropped by passers-by.

Once she'd spotted a suitable Internet cafe, she swore silently at the new pedestrianization of the High Street and all the ugly double-yellow lines, but eventually she found her way to a parking space and locked the car. Eight minutes later, with a tall cardboard cup of coffee at her side, she settled at a free computer. The email to Will could wait until she'd given Aidan all the latest news.

He was making a name for himself now in Boston, Massachusetts, as a defense attorney. He hadn't yet met Will. She hoped it would work when they did. If not, Will would have to go. Aidan's loathing of Peter should have warned her of what might happen. She'd never ignore him again.

Having logged on, she waited for the system to crank itself open, taking up the time by pulling the rubber band off her ponytail and letting the shoulder-length blonde hair fly free. Except for prison visiting she always wore it loose, in the hope it would do something to disguise the small round face she'd inherited from her mother, Dillie.

Topping Dillie's five-foot-three frame, the size and shape were fine; quite pretty even. Karen, who was five-nine, thought they looked absurd on her.

She found the expected email from Aidan in her in-box. All it said was:

I envy you being back on the Island. Is the chalet the same? Does Granny's ghost walk the rooms? Have you had a crab tea at Freshwater yet? And is there anywhere you can get your beloved sushi? Somehow that doesn't fit my memories of the Island. Axx

She hit 'reply' and quickly typed:

No ghosts. Might feel less empty if there were a few. The chalet's tiny and dark and damp. Not at all as I remember it, although the rain-drip bowls are. Did you realize there wasn't even a proper kitchen? No wonder Dillie's always hated the place. I keep wondering why she never tarted it up for holiday lets – or even flogged it in one of the financial crises. Although I can't imagine it would raise much, and she may have hung on to it in case they ever did lose the business completely and needed a hideaway. They could live on very little here – provided they never tried to take a car on one of the ferries!

Anyway, the kitchen: just a calor gas cooker, an old pot sink on legs, a table, a kind of meat-safe cupboard thing with a chicken-wire front, a few shelves of cracked plates and mugs, and a motley collection of bent cutlery. Not a single sharp cooking knife to be found. I'd have to restock it if I were going to be here long, but for six weeks? Not worth it. The fridge is vile.

How's life in Boston? Still spending all your time fighting injustice wherever it rears its ugly head, or do you get a few minutes for friends . . . for romance? I'd love you to meet someone.

Karen paused with her fingers on the sticky keys, then, even though the email was far too long already, quickly added:

Especially if she's English. We have lots of injustice here, too, you know. Kxx

When the screen had cleared, she wrote in much the same terms to Will, adding a description of her rescue by the Elephant Man. Her half-hour at the terminal almost up, she checked her in-box again and found a new message from her professor.

How did it go? MP

She had only fifty-nine seconds left and quickly typed:

Fine. Nothing useful yet. But a start. K

And then she saw he'd added a second line below his initial, which she hadn't noticed on first reading:

PS Had a strange phone call from your ex-mother-in-law last night. Rather not send details by email. Phone me.

The screen went blank in a neat reflection of her mind. The last thing she needed now was any kind of encounter – even at one remove – with the woman who had hated her for so long.

A familiar, bouncing, tinny tune distracted her. For a second she couldn't identify it, then recognized the ringtone on her own phone. Helen's re-emergence in her life shouldn't cause this kind of amnesia. Karen pushed both hands down into the big bag and got to the phone before the voicemail cut in, which she didn't often manage, and gave her name.

'Oh, hi,' said a brisk confident male voice. 'DCI Charles Trench. You were at Parkhurst this morning with Spike Falconer.'

He paused.

'That's right,' Karen said. 'How did you know?'

'We need to talk.'

She noticed he hadn't answered her question so she asked it again.

'Nothing on the Island's a secret,' he said casually in a voice that sounded as though he came from somewhere much further north and east than this diamond-shaped blip floating off the very bottom of the UK. 'Can we meet?'

'Why?' she said.

'Spike claims he's innocent of the killings on Chillerton Down.'

'And you thought . . .?'

'That you need to hear his history here on the Island before you buy into those claims.'

'That sounds as though you think I might try to get him

exonerated. Don't worry, Chief Inspector. I've no interest in his next appeal. I made that clear to the prison governor when I first applied to interview Spike.'

She remembered the governor's open-minded and helpful response. He had said that she was welcome to come if Spike himself was prepared to talk to her because the prison authorities needed all the insight they could get into Dangerous Severe Personality Disorder as they worked out how to manage their most difficult inmate.

'Don't you *want* to know about his background, Doctor Taylor?' said Trench down the phone. 'And about what else he's done here on the Island?'

'Of course I do.'

'Then talk to me,' Trench said.

'Are you inviting me to come to the police station?'

He laughed, sounding younger. 'Don't be so suspicious. Let's meet in a pub. Where are you now?'

'Finishing a cup of coffee in Cowes.'

'Then you're about eighteen minutes from the best pub on the Island.'

'Why so far away? My guidebook says there's one pub to every square mile here.'

'True enough. But this one's worth a drive. Got a pen? I'll give you directions.'

Twenty-two minutes later, Karen was parking the car on a small asphalt square beside a whitewashed building that looked like a drawing by Beatrix Potter. There were even a few geese drinking from an old stone trough in the corner. A swinging sign announced that this was the Goose Inn. Only one other car spoiled the view, a highly polished dark-blue Ford that could have belonged to any law-abiding middle-aged driver.

Even so, it must be the cop's, she thought, pushing open the pub's creaking door.

Inside she saw a man wearing jeans that had once been black
and an ancient leather jacket. It was hard to judge his height
because he was leaning on the rough wooden bar talking to a
woman who would have been beautiful if she hadn't been so
tired. Dark-brown hair was looped back from a perfectly oval
face. Her skin was pale and a bit spotty around the chin and
nose. Big dark-grey half-moons disfigured her eye sockets.

The two of them looked as though they were involved in something private and important. After a moment the man glanced
round.

A slight smile widened lips that were full and mobile enough to
suggest an easy enjoyment of any pleasures life offered. He looked
to be in his early thirties like Karen, but she wasn't good at judg-
ing men's ages. He might have been older.

'Chief Inspector Trench?' she said, a little doubtful.

'Yeah. You must be Doctor Taylor.' He looked her up and
down, as though assessing the careful, colourless clothes she'd
picked for her visit to Spike.

'Not what I expected at all,' he went on. 'Nothing about the
"Doctor" or the "forensic psychologist" made me expect a tall
blonde off of a magazine cover. What can I get you?'

As suspicious as she'd be of any stranger who paid exaggerated
compliments, Karen thought she'd better keep her head clear for
whatever was coming next and said she'd have something soft.
The woman behind the bar looked insulted but offered orange
juice, tomato juice or pineapple juice, pointing to a row of tiny
dusty bottles behind the bar.

'Don't miss out on Peg's bitter,' DCI Trench said. 'It's a home
brew and great.'

Peg, Karen thought. Who's called Peg nowadays? Only on the
Island.

'I'm not really a beer drinker,' she said aloud. 'Tomato juice,
please. With Worcester sauce, if you've got it.'

Both sighed, as though at the cussedness of visitors, and Karen made sure she got her money on the bar before DCI Trench could pay for her drink.

He straightened up and revealed himself to be an inch or two taller than she was, which would have made him a little less than six foot. He had broad shoulders and big hands and, as he scooped up their drinks and led the way to a small round table by one of the tiny windows, she saw that he moved like someone who knew his own strength and what to do with it. He dumped the glasses on the table and turned to face her.

Karen inspected him, checking out his clear dark eyes and rough shave. With his biker jacket and the tattered jeans that did nothing to disguise his powerful thighs, he looked more like an undercover sergeant in some inner-city drugs squad than a DCI who owned such a matronly car.

'What do you really want from me?' she said, smiling at him for the first time.

'Have a seat and I'll tell you.'

She dropped the brown leather bag on the floor and sat, noticing that he waited until she was settled before pulling out his own chair. He had clearly been infected with the Island's old-fashioned customs.

The toffee-coloured beer looked horribly sweet to her, but he swallowed a huge mouthful with pleasure, then took a photograph out of an inside pocket and laid it face down on the table, hiding whatever it might show.

'Are you squeamish?' he said.

Chapter 5

'I'm a forensic psychologist,' Karen said. 'I study murderers and rapists and paedophiles. Of course I'm not squeamish.'

That wasn't true, but DCI Trench didn't need to know.

'OK,' he said. 'Just before the Sanders family were shot, we had another murder, down at Alum Bay.'

Alum Bay, she thought, distracted by memories of collecting the coloured sand that had formed in stripes over the millennia. All the beach-side shops sold souvenir test tubes and glass models of lighthouses filled with layers of the sand. Pink and blue and buff and green. More memories flooded back.

'Doctor Taylor?'

She blinked the past away. 'We saw a porpoise once in Alum Bay, and I was reminded of that. Who was killed?'

'A swimmer. Young woman; visitor to the Island. Reported missing by her husband when she didn't come back from her usual early-morning swim. Presumed drowned. Body rolled up four months later.'

'What's it got to do with Spike?' Karen said.

Trench turned the photograph face up, without answering the question. Karen saw a woman's body, already partly decomposed and eaten away. Whatever had fed off the dead flesh had cut right through to the bone in the woman's left leg. Enough of her head and neck had been left to show she'd been strangled with something sharp, and the remaining skin on her body showed regular slash marks from the shoulders to the feet. They were neat lines, precisely the same distance apart, horizontally cut into her flesh and looking surprisingly like the striations in the cliffs that could be seen in the background.

'The pathologist says the slashes were made after death,' DCI Trench said. He pointed to dark dents and pits in her skull. 'But even after all those weeks in the water, there were minute traces of brick dust pushed deep into these wounds. The theory is that the mess made of her skull wasn't the result of the waves mashing it against the sea floor. They think her head was beaten in with a brick before she was strangled. Then she was slashed. Then she was thrown into the sea. I think Spike did it.'

'Alum Bay's a popular beach,' Karen said, maintaining her professional distance from the woman who had suffered all this. 'Wasn't there anyone to see what happened? Or to find footprints in the sand? Or blood.'

'No reason to think he did it on the beach itself. He probably nabbed her on her way from the hotel, killed her in a quiet spot and chucked her in somewhere along the coast. We've reams of stuff about the tides and the likely throwing-in points that would bring a body up on shore at Alum Bay, but you don't need all that.'

'Still, whoever did it took a hell of a risk of being seen.'

'Isn't that how psychopaths work? Not thinking about risk; just grabbing a chance when they see it. That's what *our* shrink said anyway.'

Karen didn't think Trench would appreciate a long explanation of the difference between the kind of killers who enjoyed meticulous planning and postponement of gratification and those – like Spike – whose behaviour was so chaotic their violence was unpredictable, often triggered by an incomprehensible mixture of stimuli.

'It's why they're so hard to convict,' Trench went on, with surprising bitterness.

'I don't see why,' Karen said, wondering what was driving him, what past experiences had sent him into a job where he had to stare at photographs of mutilated corpses like this one.

'No obvious chain of events for us to reconstruct,' he said with an impatience that suggested she shouldn't have had to ask. 'No pattern for us to follow; no *reason* for them to do any of it. So even when we do get one of them convicted, the bloody lawyers have all this scope to bring the case back to the appeal court, arguing away the few scraps of evidence we have got.'

'So what are your scraps of evidence for Spike's involvement with this Alum Bay swimmer?'

'That's my problem. The body'd been in the water too long for forensics to get anything that could prove he was there. But there's this.' Trench took out another print, creased and much older-looking, of a Labrador that had been split open from back legs to chin, lying on its spine with its guts in a pile to one side.

'I've read about that,' Karen said, wishing she had chosen any drink but blood-coloured tomato juice. She pushed her glass away, reminding herself that she was not squeamish, and that she cared more about human beings than animals. It didn't help. 'Hard though it is to believe, Spike did it when he was seven and still too small to dig a proper grave. The family gardener stumbled over the half-buried body while it was still warm. How come you've got the photo?'

'Spike's old man called the police at the time. Our photographer took this and it was kept on file. We were like you and couldn't believe a seven-year-old would do it. The family got hold of an expert from the mainland. He gave us chapter and verse on kids who mutilate animals – and what most of them go on to do later, all the way from arson at school to murder. Could've been a clairvoyant. Spike's done the whole lot since then.'

Karen frowned. 'You say "we" and "us", but you can't have been here then.'

'Nope. It's just shorthand. But I've read the files.'

'Why? What's driving this obsession? Spike's safely in prison. Even if he gets another appeal, it'll fail. You must know that, even if you do hate lawyers. Were you here when he shot the picnickers? What's your interest in all this?'

'I don't like big unsolveds on my patch,' Trench said, reverting to the casual tone, which didn't disguise his determination for a second. 'Now, look at these.'

A third photograph joined the other two. In this the Labrador had been turned onto its eviscerated belly. Across its back could be seen a single straight horizontal cut that was so neat it might have been made by a machine.

Karen ignored it. For the moment she was more interested in DCI Trench's motives for showing her these pictures than in the earliest manifestations of Spike's personality disorder.

'So, you're hoping against hope you can find some way of pinning the swimmer's death on Spike, because it would be a convenient way of getting an unsolved crime off your books: have I got that right?' she said.

'What's wrong with that?'

'I don't think you're going to do it this way.' Karen pointed towards the photograph of the dog, with all its sickening evidence of human cruelty. 'There are no connections between this, the swimmer and the Sanders family.'

'Look closer.' Trench moved his forefinger along the black-and-white photograph of the Labrador's back, pausing every so often.

She peered right down into the photograph, noticing that his fingernail was very short and very clean and that his hands smelled of old-fashioned Pears soap.

'I can see a few indistinct marks,' she said as she pulled back and looked at him again. 'But you can't tell me they're deliberate parallel cuts like the ones on the swimmer's body.'

'Why not? Look harder.'

Karen was reminded of dodgy art dealers telling restorers (or fakers) what they could 'see' in an undistinguished canvas they wanted repainting to lift into a higher price range. She glanced towards the bar. The exhausted-looking woman was sipping a glass of water.

'Are you sure you should be talking like this in public?' Karen said.

Trench also glanced at the woman behind the bar, then shook his head.

'Does she look interested?'

'Not particularly,' Karen said.

She picked up the print and peered into it again, forced to admit she could see hints of regularly spaced horizontal lines. But they were very faint and, from the little she knew of photography, could probably have come from poor storage of the print or damage to the original negative.

'Even if these are the same kind of cuts,' she said, 'so what?'

When Trench didn't answer, she added with some mockery: 'No more photographs to show me? No more crimes it would be convenient to lay at Spike Falconer's door?'

'Plenty. I thought these would be enough to make you help us. I didn't know you'd behave like all those fucking lawyers and defend him.'

'As I keep telling you, I'm not in the business of defending him.'

She wondered why Trench was so sure she would be Spike's champion and put it down to natural antipathy between their professions. She'd had no personal experience of police mistreatment of psychologically vulnerable suspects, but there were more than enough anecdotes from her colleagues to make her wary. Maybe he'd picked that up.

No one interested in justice could ever forget what had happened in the worst cases, such as that of Stefan Kisko, who had been 'helped' to confess to a crime he'd been physically incapable of committing. He had served sixteen years in prison before his case had eventually been reviewed. Tragically he had died soon after his release.

'If I can help you without prejudicing my research or my independence,' Karen added, reminding herself that just as Trench was probably quite unlike the officers in the Kisko case, so Spike had nothing in common with their victim. 'I can't see any reason not to. But doing what, exactly?'

'Helping me get a confession for this,' Trench said, touching the print of the Alum Bay swimmer's body.

Karen opened her mouth to refuse, but she didn't have time to say anything because Trench was talking again.

'We've had officers interviewing him about her several times now. But they get nowhere. He just laughs and won't say anything.'

'Maybe because he's got nothing to confess. Maybe he doesn't know anything about the swimmer,' Karen suggested. 'Have you thought of that?'

'Then why not say so? I told you: he won't talk; he just giggles, like he's having the time of his life; then begs the officers to come back again because he gets so bored in his cell.'

'You know,' Karen said, recognizing the picture of Spike's behaviour with an unpleasant jolt, 'if you *are* right and there is some kind of link between the dog and the swimmer, which I still think is highly unlikely, there would have been other slashings too. Not necessarily murder, but definitely cutting. More animals first and then people, in a steady escalation of violence until he did kill a human being. Without that, your theory hasn't the faintest chance of holding up.'

Trench grinned at her, as though she'd just told him he'd won the lottery instead of throwing professional cold water over his ideas.

'At last!' he said. 'I've been trying to make people see it for months, and they won't. But you're an expert so maybe we can get somewhere now. The way I see it, no law-abiding bloke wakes up in their late twenties and thinks: Ooh, I'd like to kill someone today. We . . .'

His phone rang. He looked at the number on the screen, grimaced, and looked as though he was going to put it back in his pocket.

'Go on, answer it,' Karen said. 'I don't mind.'

'Sure?'

'Yes.'

He half turned away from her, which made it impossible for her not to listen.

'Eve?' he said. 'What's up? I'm in the middle of something.'

A faint tinny bizzing issued from the phone. Karen couldn't hear anything, except an impatient-sounding sigh from Trench.

'No. I'm fine . . . Of course I'm not. What d'you mean? She's a pro, for fuck's sake.'

A pause, during which Karen couldn't help assuming the 'she' he'd been talking about was her. She wondered who Eve was.

'No. Drop it,' Trench said. 'I'll see you when I get back. Haven't you got work to do?'

He clicked off the call and turned back to Karen with a rueful but laughing expression, which made her realize suddenly that his face was like a rougher version of Robert Downey Jr's.

'Christ! I hate kindness sometimes,' he said, still laughing. 'Now, where were we? Yeah. Spike's other victims. We haven't found them yet, but I know they must be here, buried somewhere on the Island with slice marks all over their bodies.'

Karen didn't like the idea of her sunny childhood paradise as a graveyard for a string of murdered, mutilated women.

'Why buried?' she said, switching to her professional mode as fast as she could. 'The swimmer wasn't buried. And who could the other victims be? Have there been any reports of likely women going missing from here?'

'Several,' he said, 'and hundreds more from the mainland.

They don't have to be Islanders. They could've come here from anywhere before they crossed Spike's path. And even if he didn't bury the swimmer, or the Sanders family, he did try to bury the dog.'

'But that's hardly . . .' Karen began.

'I've picked out four possibles from the misper lists,' Trench said, clearly determined to explain the whole of his theory while he had the chance. 'But my budget won't stretch to an investigation. If I had a confession from Spike, even a hint of it, I'd get funding. I mean, it's clear he went for visitors, and . . .'

'Hey, wait a minute. You're making another huge leap here. *How* is it clear he went for visitors?'

Trench looked at her as though she was a mindless worm leaving a muddy trail over his lovely clean theory.

'The swimmer was here for a second honeymoon with her husband. Dan Sanders and his wife were here with their kids in the school holidays. It's obvious.'

'And what inference do you draw from that?' Karen knew she sounded like Max Pitton at his most irritating, but she thought it might make Trench reveal what was really behind this obsession.

'That Spike enjoyed killing but avoided locals. Maybe he thought it'd be easier to get away with killing tourists. Like all those serial killers who go for runaways or sex workers. Doctor Taylor, I *know* Spike's done other women. You know it too. You must help me find them.'

'I don't see how I could. And there's a problem with your theory in any case. Solitary murder and mutilation of a woman like the swimmer is about as far as you can get from a spree shooting like the one on Chillerton Down,' she said. 'Most studies have shown killers enjoy one or the other, but not both. It's much more likely someone else killed your swimmer.'

'Two psychopathic killers operating at the same time on one small island? Come on, Doctor Taylor. Doesn't make sense. Now, look at these.' Trench fished two more photographs from his wallet, both showing tall slender women with long dark hair flying about their good-looking faces.

'Horses,' Karen murmured without thinking.

'Sorry?' he said, puzzled.

'Human faces are divided into currant buns and horses,' she said quickly, not wanting to sound as though she was making jokes about his idea of a string of slashed and murdered women. There was nothing remotely funny about it. 'These are both horses. You're a currant bun.'

'Thanks for that,' he said, his dark face lightening as he grinned again, revealing teeth that were uneven but a brilliant white. 'I used to think I wasn't half bad when it comes to looks.'

'Nothing to say currant buns can't be ravishing,' she said, taking her tone from his. 'It's just that horses are usually thought of as cleverer and more important than us.'

He considered her, head on one side.

'Us? I like it. OK, I'll go along with the idea of a couple of ravishing currant buns.' He paused for a second, then pointed to one of the photographs. 'Back to work. This woman is Isabelle Sanders in life. And this is the swimmer before Spike got at her.'

'I concede the similarity,' Karen said, retreating to absurdly formal language because she realized he thought she was flirting with him. 'But couldn't it just be coincidence?'

'Why should it be? I've read the FBI profilers' books, too,' he added before she could make any more objections. 'We all know serial killers get off on one particular type of woman. What if Spike saw Isabelle Sanders, fancied her for his next victim, and was disturbed by the rest of the family before he could slice her up?'

'Except that she was shot, not bludgeoned or strangled. And m.o. is even more characteristic of serial killers than how their victims look. Any of your other possibles look like these two?'

He nodded. 'The four I've picked from the misper lists do. That's why I chose them rather than any of the others. The likeliest is called Claire Wilkins. She phoned her parents from Bristol, where she was at uni eight years ago, to say she wasn't coming home because she'd run out of money and had got herself a job waitressing here on the Island, in Freshwater. There are no records of her here – which is why there was never any kind of investigation – but she could've worked for tax-free cash and so been off the books. Anyway, whatever, she never went home.'

He put his hand in his inside pocket and brought out yet another photograph. Karen looked down to see a much younger version of Isabelle Sanders, with the same long, fine-featured face and smooth shoulder-length dark hair. Her smile wasn't as confident as Isabelle's, and there was something very appealing in her vulnerability.

'Eighteen,' he said, watching Karen's face, 'when she disappeared.'

'And you want me to ask Spike if he killed her and how and why and where he put her body?'

Could Trench be that naive about her role and capabilities?

'No,' he said, without any histrionics. 'I want you to draw me a roadmap of the best way *I* can get him to confess.'

'Why does it matter so much, after all this time, when he's already serving life without much chance of ever being given parole?'

Trench's thick black eyebrows twitched together. 'Of course it matters. Think of the Wilkins parents, still waiting for their Claire to come home. She was their only child.'

'And that's what motivates you, is it?' she said. 'Nothing to do with your targets and crime figures and career prospects?'

'Cynic!'

'I'm right, though, aren't I?'

'Maybe.' His stubbly face changed, as though some force had wiped all the humour out of it. 'There's also the reputation of the Island. We don't do murder here.'

'Except for the picnic massacre. Not many tourist spots can

boast anything like that. Why d'you care about the Island's reputation? You could work anywhere, and you're not a *caulkhead*. You're an *overner* from Newcastle,' she said, using the local terms for natives and incomers.

'How d'you know?' he said, picking up his beer.

She laughed. 'Oh, come on! I may not be Professor Higgins, but I can recognize a Geordie accent when I hear one. I used to live in North Yorkshire when I was married, and I heard voices exactly like yours on every train I ever took.'

'I must be off.' He pushed forward a business card and stood up. 'Let me know how you get on with Spike.'

Karen took the card and saw it held his office details and a mobile number.

'If there's anything I can pass on, I will,' she said, glancing up at him. 'But I can't work *for* you.'

'I know. If you need anything while you're here, give me a call,' he added, sounding warmer.

Then he was gone, without waiting for her to comment. Karen thought of asking the woman behind the bar what made him tick and how the Islanders thought about him. But she looked even more ill and exhausted than before, so Karen left her alone.

Chapter 6

Karen emerged from the pub into watery light with only a hint of sun creeping out from behind dense black clouds. The geese were huddled together beyond their trough as though they expected rain again.

More like March than full summer, she told herself, shivering. She knew she ought to follow up Max's postscript about her mother-in-law and hated the idea.

Luckily there were more important things to think about first, such as the idea that Spike might have killed other women who looked like Isabelle Sanders and dumped or buried their bodies around the Island.

Karen thought of the soft clinging stickiness of the ground where her car had foundered this morning and gagged. She fought the nausea in the only way she knew, distracting herself with rational analysis. There was nothing – not even one of DCI Trench's wild speculations – to suggest anyone had ever buried anything near the chalet, so it was absurd to feel so queasy.

Back in the car and heading towards Cowes again, with her mind full of the sliced-up Labrador and the lost women who might have followed it in Spike's killing career, Karen found it hard to want to buy food. But she would have to eat something later and there was nothing in the chalet except bread, milk and yoghurt. Given the state of the fridge, the milk and yoghurt would probably have gone off by breakfast tomorrow.

A small supermarket offered a fairly good range of dried and tinned stuff, so she loaded up a basket. The only fresh things she could make herself add were more milk, a loaf of wholemeal bread, and a big lump of basic Cheddar.

She glanced at the refrigerated cabinets full of pre-cut slabs of meat and fish. None of it tempted her. The only fish she really liked was sushi, but that needed the freshest, best quality, and these pieces of plaice and bright-yellow haddock looked as though they might have been sitting on their plastic trays under their plastic wrapping for a long time. The meat wasn't much more appealing.

She found a real butcher a little later, but today that was worse. Staring through the open window at the ranks of chops and liver and kidneys, separated from each other only by plastic parsley, she tried to remember how unsqueamish she was. But the smell of blood was too strong and the faint whiff of urine from the kidneys made her cough in disgust.

Besides, she thought, if I'm going to the prison every day, I can always pick up fresh food in Newport as and when I want it.

Newport was the shopping centre of the Island, according to the guidebook, as well as being home to Parkhurst Prison.

Tonight she'd eat tinned sardines, mashed up with lemon juice so that they didn't look like anything that had ever lived, and follow them with oranges. That would be plenty. Cheap, too. And healthy. Lots of omega-3 in sardines. Calcium as well, so long as you didn't discard the bones as you mashed.

A panoply of glittering kitchen equipment in the window of a shop in the centre of Cowes was easier to enjoy than the array of dead flesh. She felt like a Dickensian child, pressing her nose to the window of a toy-filled nursery, as she gazed on gleaming machines and shining towers of matching stainless-steel bowls. A huge chinois strainer, like a coolie hat, hung over a tower of silvered Cuisinox pans, which she knew from experience would probably last for the rest of her life. She'd had eight when she'd been married to Peter. Helen had produced them as a wedding present, and then taken them back again after Peter's death so that the creditors couldn't get anywhere near them.

Karen forced herself away and wandered down to the pier, where the Red Jet catamarans zoomed in from Southampton every half-hour, with their special speed-limit exemption. It would be so easy to catch one, see Max Pitton in his office at the university or his nearby flat and find out exactly what Helen had been saying to him.

In normal times, Karen would then have taken the familiar journey to her own flat, high under the eaves of an old warehouse on one of the now disused wharves. She missed its bright, clean emptiness and the way the light that reflected off the sea bounced from one of the big white walls to the next.

From the moment she'd walked through the door with the estate agent she'd known she had to live there. The developers had let her haggle a little, but she'd still had to raise a scary mortgage to pay their price. Even so, it was worth it to have a place so huge, so light, and so absolutely hers. Before the builders had done their work, the only permanent inhabitants of the place would have been the rats that must have fed off the cargoes stored there while the docks were still in use.

The thought of the rats had never worried her. They'd been banished long before she'd ever seen the place, and these days every surface was hard and gleaming and pristine. Everything was visible. There was nowhere to hide secrets or contain unknown horrors that might one day ooze out all over her.

But for the moment she was exiled. Keeping up with the mortgage payments had become seriously hard after the last interest-rate rise, and she couldn't waste a single pound, so she'd rented it out for the whole summer to a visiting American friend of Aidan's. The money he paid would see her through, provided she didn't give in to any kind of extravagance. But she didn't like the idea of someone else – even a friend of Aidan's – touching her few things, messing up her space.

Don't get sentimental, she told herself, as she turned back towards the car.

A junky antique shop lay between her and the free parking space she'd found. Outside it stood two bins of tattered prints, protected from any risk of water damage by a thick plastic sheet. With the rain no worse than spotting at the moment, she thought it fair to lift the plastic and riffle through the pictures. Anything to put off the call to her professor a little longer.

Most of the pictures had been cut from books and were the usual poorly printed botanical and costume illustrations owners of shops like this seemed to assume people would buy in any tourist hot-spot in the country. A bigger, more expensively reproduced sepia photograph of Osborne House, Queen Victoria's vast Italianate seaside house on the far side of Cowes, caught on the edge of the plastic and she had to put down her heavy bag to use both hands to free it. Behind it she found a much smaller picture, which had once illustrated Kipling's story of 'Toomai of the Elephants'.

Karen remembered it well. Her grandmother had been a fan of Kipling as well as Shakespeare and Aesop, whose works provided her entire library at the chalet. She'd read and reread *Just So Stories* and *The Jungle Book* to Karen and Aidan all through their childhood, and they'd both chosen favourite sections for her funeral eighteen years ago.

This picture showed little Toomai being honoured by a line of elephants, raising their trunks and trumpeting in the official salute they were trained to give only to the Viceroy.

The pencilled price on the back of the frame seemed so small that Karen raised the picture to look more closely. Reassured, she took it into the shop and handed over £8.25.

'Would you like it wrapped up?' The assistant looked about thirteen, with spiky blue and black hair and a stud in her nose.

'Yes, please. It's a present.'

'I'll see if we've got any nice paper. Won't be long.'

Karen leaned against the counter and phoned Max Pitton.

He didn't answer, so she had to leave a message and tried to keep it light. 'Hi, it's me. Karen. Your email said Helen had been weird on the phone. Tell me more. I can't get reception at the chalet, but you can leave a message, and I'll ring again round about this time tomorrow.'

'Will this do?' asked the assistant, coming back with a fluttering sheet of purple foil wrapping paper. 'It's all we've got except newspaper.'

'It looks great,' Karen said. 'Thanks.'

There was no sign of the Elephant Man when Karen knocked at the door of his house to give him the picture as a way of thanking him for this morning's rescue, so she tore a sheet off her pad and wrote a brief note, folded the paper around the top of the parcel and leaned it against his front door. The rudimentary corrugated iron porch should keep the rain off it.

Her own chalet was no more welcoming than it had seemed last night. She unpacked her meagre provisions, emptied the rain-drip bowls, then took a bunch of notes with her to the bedroom she and Aidan had always shared.

The sagging divans were still covered by the same old blankets. They were made up of multi-coloured squares of wool left over from whatever Granny had been knitting at the time. Karen could date the progress of the blankets from the jerseys and cardigans that had arrived as Christmas and birthday presents.

There were the pink and white and lavender mohair squares from her earliest cardigans, which had always had tiny difficult pearly buttons, and a few later ballet wraps. Heavy red and navy-blue wool came from Aidan's tough, boyish jerseys. There were even a few squares made up of the delicate, miraculously silky, sea-coloured yarn left over from the last thing Granny had ever knitted for Karen: a lovely slippery shawl she'd worn whenever she'd been ill until it had actually fallen apart. She could remember the feel of it on her bare shoulders even now.

Blinking, she took the pillows from one bed and piled them up on the other. They gave her neck and back just enough support to make reading the files possible, and with both blankets spread over her clothes she should be warm enough. How could anyone believe this was summer?

Tomorrow, after her trip to the prison, she was going to cross the Island to the grand side to meet Spike's adoptive parents. She needed to know exactly when they had first noticed something odd about the boy they had taken on twenty-eight years ago.

Luckily for her, Max had good contacts in high places and had got her some information that should never have been made available. She'd been able to read the informal notes one of the original social workers had written after his first meeting with the colonel and his wife.

V sure of own stdng. Fmly ownd chnk IoW snce long bfre Q.Vic & Osb'ne. Career not mch cop. Ret'd as soon as mde Col. No mdls.

Karen was amused to see that at this point the prof had scrawled: 'No wars during his service, ergo no medals. Fool.' She was amused at the familiar impatient tetchiness and went back to the original notes.

Mrs = chming. Wrm. Shd be OK. Only ? is her stmina. Hve expld adptd kids ofn uncoop; dshnst. Esp w. his bckgrnd. Wsh c'd hve gvn egs of pst cases, but how cd I? Dn't knw 4 sure wht'll hppn ths time. And wd they tke him if all rsks splld out? Hs only hpe, poor lttl bstrd.

'Poor woman' said Max's scrawl on his covering note. 'She's the key. If you can get her to talk freely you'll have a chance of unpicking the chain that led to Chillerton. Mothers always notice first signs of damage and the confident ones try to make it good.'

Yes, Karen thought, looking up at the cracked ceiling and the cobwebs that hung there like ghostly decorations. Which is why the 1950s and 1960s theories about refrigerator mothers were so cruel. Their coldness was assumed from the existence in their children of conditions such as schizophrenia and autism, which were later found to be mainly genetic in origin and nothing to do with the mother's behaviour.

A playground taunt about farts suddenly danced into her mind: 'He who smelt it surely dealt it.'

'Rubbish!' she said aloud.

The pathways of ideas into and through communities had always interested her nearly as much as the difficulties and dangers of adoption. And she was very conscious of the responsibility she carried. She wasn't the first psychologist to pick the subject as a way to sort out her own emotions, and it bothered her that so many theorists in her own and related fields had laid immense burdens on other people by publishing ideas that may have helped their own distress yet had no general application.

Ideas about refrigerator mothers were only one example of the problem. For Karen, Freud's theories about the incestuous sexual fantasies of children were the first and worst. According to his disciple Ernest Jones, Freud built the entire theory of the Oedipus complex on a childhood memory of being sexually aroused by the sight of his naked mother. Some subsequent commentators had refuted Jones's claim, but if it was true, hundreds of people had suffered because of Freud's rationalization of that one disturbing moment.

The invention of the Oedipus complex had had two pernicious effects in Karen's view: the first, that genuine victims of sexual abuse were assumed for decades to have invented the abuse as part of their own fantasies; the other, that anyone suffering any form of neurosis must have been suppressing sexual desire for his or her parent.

Ever since she'd heard the Ernest Jones claim, Karen had been aware how easy and how dangerous it would be to generalize from her own experience. That should have no bearing on anything to do with her work. Peter's death just before her twenty-third birthday, her guilt, and his mother's hatred were all things she had to ignore. If she were ever to have true peace of mind again, she would have to go back into all that darkness and pain and deal with it. But not now. Now she had other minds and other emotions to explore.

Karen shifted uncomfortably beneath the squared blankets, thinking: Maybe Will's right and the only safe way of assessing anyone is to look at the physical structures and connections within the brain because those are the only scientifically measurable factors in all this.

Psychometric tests could provide statistical probability, and scans taken of brains during practical and mental tasks could show up damage in a way no one could refute. But any theory a psychologist produced could be challenged by anyone who had a different idea.

Had anyone ever examined Spike's brain?

Leafing through the file, she found nothing to suggest there had ever been any scans. And there were plenty of other gaps, too. Somewhere in some archive would be his original birth certificate and other, more official and even less accessible, files to explain why the local authority had taken the baby into care in the first place.

The Falconers should have been given all the details, of course, but adoptive parents often weren't. Sometimes the social workers didn't have all the information, or hadn't been well enough trained to evaluate it and pass it on in usable form. Sometimes it was deliberately concealed because adoption was thought to be the baby's only hope and unlikely to take place if the full risks were laid out.

They must have known, though, that their new son wouldn't have had the perfect start. Very few babies in the UK were adopted straight after birth. Most had a traumatic period of temporary fostering after they were removed from their natural parents. The lucky ones were then parcelled out to hopeful families. Sometimes the adoption worked. Often it did not.

Karen had learned when she was working for her first degree ten years ago that the way a baby was treated before it was even two had an impact on the development of the prefrontal cortex, the area of the brain that dealt with all the skills of empathy and learning from past experience that were such a problem for men like Spike Falconer.

Some psychiatrists believed therapy could make good the original lack of care; others that it could never be put right. Will and his fellow surgeons knew no action of theirs could help. Not even the maddest of mad scientists had yet suggested transplanting an effective pre-frontal cortex into a man with an inadequate one.

Thinking of mad scientists made her smile as she remembered her first encounter with Will.

One of Max Pitton's many contacts, he had come to Southampton University three months ago to give a lecture about the effects of a particular kind of tumour on one of his patients. The growth had been pressing down on the pre-frontal cortex, causing severe behavioural problems, which had originally been ascribed to a whole range of psychiatric disorders. Once the tumour had been removed, the patient's mood and behaviour had become absolutely normal. There had never been any psychiatric problems at all, and all the experts who'd diagnosed everything from depression to schizophrenia had been made to look like idiots.

Will had given his lecture in the coolest possible style, displaying huge knowledge, lightly carried, a dry acerbic wit, and a range of non-work references that had made it clear he was no nerdy obsessive.

Karen had gone out to dinner with him and Max after the lecture and had suddenly found herself boiling with a scary anger she had thought she'd overcome. Something about the way Will had rubbished her profession had lit all the old fuses, and she'd exploded.

As far as she could remember now, her main charge had been that his contempt for psychology was such that, had he been working as a neurological surgeon in the 1950s, he would have been happy to perform life-ruining lobotomies on young women for no better reason than that they'd defied their parents, had sex before marriage, or given birth to illegitimate children.

Her final accusation had been that if he refused to admit the existence of purely psychological problems, he was not only dangerous but about as much use as a badly programmed robot.

In a way she still couldn't quite understand, her rage and Will's astonishing absorption of it had led them to abandon Max and go first to a bar she liked and then back to her big, almost empty flat, where, with the thin blue light from the stars leaking round the edges of the blinds, she had embarked on her first relationship since Peter's death.

Looking back to that first argument, Karen saw how Will could so easily have retaliated with accounts of the wilder excesses of psychiatrists and psychologists. Refrigerator mothers and troubled children weren't the only ones to have suffered from batty ideas dreamed up by her predecessors, particularly the sort who, so short of sex themselves, ascribed every form of human misery to some kind of erotic dysfunction.

Even Winnicott, whom she still revered, had published a paper in which he'd written that nose-picking was a substitute for anal masturbation.

She scratched her own nostril, pushed herself up off the bed and went into her grandmother's room. All the furniture was still covered in dustsheets. Karen twitched off the one over the bookshelf to see not only *Aesop's Fables* and the collected works of Kipling in their cracked green bindings but also the old Shakespeare. Leafing through the sonnets, she found the one that seemed to fit Will so well:

They that have power to hurt and yet do none . . .

Chapter 7

'I've been thinking about my story,' Spike said as Jim Blake ushered Karen into the interview room on Tuesday. 'D'you want to hear it?'

Karen paused for a second. To encourage him or not? Would it be better to frustrate his intention to communicate and so, perhaps, jerk him into telling her the truth instead of some well-rehearsed farrago he'd invented?

No, she thought, you can't ask him for something and then choke him off when he tries to cooperate.

'Great. Yes. Thank you,' she said.

'I'm in here for something I didn't do.' He looked smug and superior, in exactly the same way as all her other five interviewees had done when they thought they'd beaten her in some way. 'I'm getting another appeal. It'll all be OK. How's that?'

'Great. Interesting,' she said, although his interpretation of what she'd wanted was yet more confirmation that he wasn't going to be able to provide it. 'But actually what I was hoping you'd tell me today is how your brother fits in to your story.'

She watched the cockiness of Spike's smile shrink a little and liked it more.

'Why?'

'I was thinking it must have been hard for him to be the younger sibling of the Island Freak. Isn't that what you called yourself yesterday?'

He looked sulky, then produced a brilliant smile that was not remotely convincing. 'Only sometimes. Sometimes it helps him.'

'How's that?'

'If he ever had a reputation, it'd be the Island Wimp, so he needs me. I bash a few of his enemies and they know I'm looking out for him. And I'm dangerous so they let him alone.' The smugness was back. But he wouldn't meet her eyes.

Karen bent her head as she made a note, aware that he was watching her. She tilted up her pad so he wouldn't be able to see what she was writing, even if he could read upside down.

There was no sun today. Black clouds stopped any extra light entering the room, and Spike's hair looked almost mousecoloured instead of radiantly blond.

'Was he grateful when you took on his tormentors?' she asked, looking up and noticing the way his eyes slid sideways.

'What do you think? He's scared of everything, so when he knows I'm around he can relax.'

'What scared him?' Karen asked, wondering whether the vulnerable baby brother could have been a helpful repository for some of Spike's own inadmissible fears. In her experience, even the cruellest and most ruthless of killers had great wells of fear they couldn't bear to admit even to themselves.

'Mainly Pa.' Spike grinned, but still would not meet her gaze. 'D'you want to know what he did to us, Doctor Taylor?'

Karen nodded. She was about to meet the colonel; she needed anything Spike was prepared to give her.

'He wanted us to be good at sport – what he calls games – and Silas couldn't catch a ball from two inches away. So he was made to practise on and on all day, every day, without any food till he could catch – or till he fell over because he couldn't stand up any more.' Spike tipped his chair back in the familiar way and giggled. 'He learned.'

Karen sat and watched him until he controlled his mirth – or realized it wasn't having the effect he wanted.

'And what about you, Spike?' she said with extreme coolness, not at all sure she could believe in the scene he'd described. 'What did he do to you?'

'Nothing.'

'Really? Even if he didn't make you practise catching a ball until you collapsed, he must have done something.'

'You want me to say he beats us and rapes us, don't you?' Spike was looking over her shoulder. When she moved a little, hoping to make him meet her eyes, he shifted his gaze and stared down at the floor instead.

'Spike?' she said gently.

'Pa doesn't do any of that.' His voice was petulant. Then he sent her a tight little smile and added: 'He scares Silas. But he can't ever scare me because I'm much scarier than he is.'

'That's interesting,' she said, surprised Spike wasn't taking the obvious route of making himself into someone else's victim. 'Did you like him when you were a child? Or were you too busy making yourself scary for him?'

For a tiny instant of time, a tenth of a second perhaps, he looked disconcerted, then he let his lips part in a much weirder smile, baring those ugly, neglected teeth.

'He's the first grown man I ever spend any time with. I think everyone's like him. What's to like or dislike?'

'Do you now?'

'Do I what?'

'Know what it is to like someone.'

'I like Jim.'

'Only Jim?' Karen said, bending her head as she wrote her notes to hide her increasing interest.

'Yeah.'

'Why d'you like him?'

She could see why someone with a life as chaotic as Spike's would enjoy being with a man as reliable as Jim seemed to be. For a moment she thought about how much she enjoyed that herself with Will.

Spike made her wait for his answer. Either he had no sense of time or he lacked most people's urge to fill conversational gaps. He said absolutely nothing. Nor, she discovered as she looked up again, did he let his eyelids drop this time.

'He's fair,' Spike said at last. 'Always the same. You know where you are with Jim, Doctor Taylor.'

'You value fairness, do you?'

'Sure.' He looked surprised, which seemed genuine. 'Doesn't everyone?'

'So, who have you met who wasn't fair?'

'The teachers at school.' His expression held some contempt now, as though she should have guessed. 'They always blame me for everything that happens. Like everyone else always does.'

'Blamed you for what?'

He shrugged. 'Peeing in corners, beating up smaller kids, breaking things, drawing in textbooks, starting fights, starting fires, hurting animals.'

'And none of that was really down to you?'

'The only people I ever beat up are the ones scaring Silas. And I never pee in corners. Or set fires. Just like I never hurt Lara.'

'Who's Lara?' Karen asked and watched him hunch his shoulders and turn away. Was this the first hint that Trench's suspicions were justified? She made her voice a little warmer than the usual professionally detached tone. 'Tell me about Lara, Spike.'

'She's a Labrador.'

'The one who was . . . killed?'

'And ripped up. And half buried. Yeah.' His eyeballs swivelled forwards for an instant, then shifted sideways again.

'Are you saying you didn't do that?' She had regained her professional voice now, keen to be sure she didn't lead him into anything he would not have said without her suggestions. Or the ones Trench was hoping she'd pass on for him.

'Of course not. I *love* Lara. She's mine, Doctor Taylor.' His voice was rising with every word; speeding up, too. But he wasn't giggling yet, so she might get something useful. 'Given to me on my fourth birthday when she's a puppy, Doctor Taylor, when Silas is beginning to walk and getting in the way all the time and messing about with my cars.'

'So who did kill her?' Karen could see the list of DSPD symptoms in her mind's eye, as though she had the textbook pages in front of her.

The inability ever to admit guilt was high up there, along with violence, manipulation, anti-social behaviour, undermining of authority, difficulty in forming and maintaining relationships, substance abuse and much more.

'Pa prob'ly, trying to look scary. Or maybe some stranger, Doctor Taylor,' he said, laughing wildly now. 'Lot of weirdos on the Island, you know. I may be the Island Freak, Doctor Taylor, but I'm not alone.'

Karen tried not to think of the Elephant Man. 'How do you know?'

'Met them when I was living rough, didn't I? There's one who dosses outside Sandown.' Spike was calming down and his smile looked more natural, more convincing. 'He's a creeper.'

'A creeper?' This wasn't a criminological term Karen had met so far.

'Creeps around watching and wanking, exposes himself to little kids. Filth. And then there's Batty Betty, who uses mud and ground-up leaves for camouflage on her face. Like a commando, you know. And some of the crack-heads from Yarmouth . . . You wouldn't believe what they're like.'

'Is Yarmouth where you usually bought your drugs?'

His smile widened, but still seemed real. One of his incisors was so pointed it looked almost as though someone had taken a file to sharpen it.

'Sometimes. And sometimes from tourists.'

'Did you meet many of them?' Karen asked, thinking of Trench's idea that Spike specifically targeted women visitors to the Island.

'Not a lot. I scare them off. They don't expect a walking scare-crow to come bursting out of the woods in a long raggy overcoat with a balaclava over his face.' He inclined his head towards her, not threateningly but like a friend chatting in a bar. The hysteria was gone from his voice too. He looked and sounded completely rational. As before, this was more disturbing than the wild gig-gling.

'Sometimes I do it on purpose, rushing out to see how they run. Like in the "Three Blind Mice". You know?'

Karen nodded.

'And sometimes after I scare them, I pull off the balaclava and give them my best smile. Like this.' He tipped his face up a little, softened the expression in his eyes and made his lips quiver.

Karen had never seen anyone look quite so vulnerable. She found it hard to imagine that Spike hadn't at some time experi-enced the feeling he was acting for her now. And it seemed clear enough that it was his father who had made him feel it, however fervently he might deny it.

'And I'd say, "My girlfriend's hurt herself. I need to get a taxi to take her to hospital but I haven't any money."'

'Did it work?'

'Usually.' His voice had a note of complicity. They could've been planning some scam together. 'But I have to scare them first; else they feel too safe, which gives them time to think about whether to believe me or not. Then they don't.' He laughed again.

'Was that what you were planning to do when you met the Sanders family?' Karen said.

'Who?'

'The picnickers at Chillerton, who got shot.'

'Wasn't me. I *told* you.'

He checked his watch, nodded towards the door and tipped back his chair, signifying the end of today's interview.

'That's it?' Karen said after a few moments' silence.

'That's it. Think up an interesting question for tomorrow. Else

I might get so bored I stop cooperating. Then where's your research, Doctor Taylor?'

She waited again, before collecting her dignity and preparing to press the buzzer for Jim Blake. Before she reached for it, she decided to risk one last question:

'Did you ever get into any fights with the "weirdos" you met sleeping rough?'

'Who's been a naughty gossip now?' Spike's voice was lightly amused, but she thought there was a hint of strain in it, as though he was hiding something rougher, more dangerous. 'Who told you? Have you been talking to the police? You're supposed to be on *my* side. Nobody else is, except Jim, and he doesn't count because Pa pays him to spy on me. I need you. That's why I'm letting you talk to me. And why I'm telling you things. I don't talk to anyone else.'

She smiled without speaking, a slow, uninterested smile that had precisely the effect she wanted. Spike started to talk, and the words poured out so fast she had to work hard to disentangle each from the general gabble:

'Just because I woke up when he was pissing over me, Doctor Taylor. You couldn't blame me. Anyone would have reacted like I did. He was pissing on me, Doctor Taylor. You'll understand if you think about it. You'd have done it too.'

'What did you do?'

He giggled. 'Grabbed his cock, didn't I? And twisted. And felt for my knife with the other hand. I was going to cut it off in little slices like salami and stuff them down his throat.' His face tightened and all the laughter went out of his voice. 'Then a cop came and arrested me. But they couldn't keep me. I hadn't done anything and when I got out I went back to look for the pisser and he'd gone. I was going to stuff the slices down his throat, Doctor Taylor. You would have too. Anyone would, Doctor Taylor. Stuff them down his throat.'

*

'How was it?' Jim said as he walked her past the endless closed
doors and through the long series of locked gates on the way out
to the real world. He sounded as though he cared what her
answer would be, which was interesting in the light of Spike's
combination of affection and contempt for him. Karen wondered if Jim really was being paid by the Falconers to report on
Spike.

'He's hard to read,' she said mildly. She was still processing the
images he'd planted in her mind.

'You're telling me? But it's good to know even experts can't
make sense of him. So, you're off to Sandown now?'

'Does everyone on this island know my business?' she said,
remembering how DCI Trench had been aware of precisely when
she'd left the prison after her first visit.

'Mostly.' Jim Blake reached across her to unlock the last of the
gates. 'It's a small place and you're a real novelty. People ask
questions and anyone who knows anything gives them answers.
And a few people who don't know anything make them up. The
governor's pleased with you though.'

'Is he? Why?'

'Because Spike was easy to manage yesterday. Sometimes when
he's had a visitor he's a right pain, causing all sorts of aggro. But
he was sweet as a lamb after seeing you. The governor thinks you
could be doing him good and should be encouraged.'

Karen thought of reminding him that she wasn't offering Spike
any kind of therapy and that, even if she had been, a single session
wouldn't have wrought any kind of change in anyone.

'Does he have many visitors?' she said.

'Only his cousin. She comes on the third Tuesday of every
month, in the afternoon. Sometimes afterwards he's OK, but
sometimes he's a right monster, causing all sorts of trouble. The
governor was worried it could be the same after your sessions.'

'Well, I'm glad he's pleased,' she said. 'Thanks, Jim. I'll see you
tomorrow.'

'OK, Doctor Taylor. Take care.'

Karen's appointment at the White House, Sandown, was not until half-past three so she had plenty of time to eat first, which was lucky. Spike's accounts of his father might have been exaggerated, but they'd made it clear he wasn't going to be an easy proposition.

She could try Cowes, of course, where there were plenty of pubs and restaurants and cafes in every price range. Sitting in one of them, looking out at the sea and the yachts would be good, provided she could dodge the predatory gulls.

Or she might go back to the Goose Inn. She'd caught sight of a handwritten menu there yesterday, with some enticing dishes on it that cost very little. And she wasn't likely to run into Trench. However small the Island might be in terms of gossip, it must be quite big enough to avoid that kind of coincidence.

His dark-blue Ford wasn't in the car park when she drove in. A couple of mountain bikes were chained to the fence, and two mud-splattered cars squatted beside them. Both looked completely unfamiliar, so she parked beside them.

When she pushed open the inn's door she was greeted with the sound of cheerful voices, instead of the intimate low-level buzz she'd interrupted the previous day. The landlady, if that's what she was, still looked tired and showed no sign of recognition when Karen ordered half a pint of her home brew to placate her and some chicken and green-olive pie.

'Great choice,' said one of the mountain-bikers, pointing to his own plate. He was obviously inviting conversation.

Karen smiled and took a seat at the furthest table, pulling out her notes to show she was not up for any casual encounters.

Her standoffishness wasn't only self-protective. She had a puzzle to solve. Nothing in the reports she'd read on Spike had suggested the kind of humour he'd displayed when he'd been talking about Batty Betty with her commandoesque make-up and all the other eccentric islanders he'd met in his years of living rough.

Nor did his straightforward confession of deliberately frightening tourists before soothing them with fake vulnerability fit
with the kind of chaotic personality-disordered man who, having
blundered into a picnicking family, would have shot them all for
no reason. The confession showed far too much awareness of
both himself and other people.

The facts that he'd apparently lost it at the end of the morning's
session and produced a textbook excitement and brutal fantasy
weren't enough to settle her doubts.

After all, he was intelligent. His vocabulary and ability to switch
voices and personae made that clear enough. And Jim Blake, who
brought him books, had told her that he'd been reading up on
personality disorders. Maybe Jim had passed on some of that
information to Spike, even though prison rules forbade any medical texts for inmates. And maybe Spike had absorbed enough
from the current technical literature to know how to suggest the
DSPD diagnosis wasn't as straightforward as the various psychiatrists and lawyers had assumed. Maybe his agreeing to see Karen
and producing all these contradictory symptoms were part of
long-range planning for his appeal.

In which case, maybe the Sanders family *had* died because of
the way Isabelle Sanders looked, just as DCI Trench had suggested. If that were true, then he would definitely be right to
worry about all the long-faced women with shoulder-length dark
hair who'd gone missing. Like eighteen-year-old Claire Wilkins.

An insistent tune and an irritating rhyme bounced round and
round Karen's mind:

> *Three blind mice, three blind mice.*
> *See how they run, see how they run.*
> *They all ran after the farmer's wife,*
> *Who cut off their tails with a carving knife.*
> *Did you ever see such a sight in your life*
> *As three blind mice?*

Was there a link between the nursery rhyme Spike had instinctively chosen to illustrate the way he'd scared tourists into running away from him and his fantasy revenge on the man who'd pissed over him? Or was she over-interpreting a quite ordinary coincidence?

If there were a link, could it also have a connection with the neat slices that had been made in the flesh of the dead swimmer and, perhaps, Lara the Labrador? Knives and slices were clearly an important part of Spike's interior life.

'Here you are,' said the landlady, laying a steaming plate in front of Karen and adding a rolled-up paper napkin with cutlery inside it.

Belatedly Karen realized why the other woman seemed so tired: she was pregnant. Four or five months by the size of her small bump.

'You shouldn't have brought it over,' Karen said at once. 'I could have come to the bar to fetch it if you haven't got any help. Are you on your own here?'

The landlady smiled and shook her head. Some of her hair slipped out of its pins and fell down the side of her cheek in a loose dark cloud, making her even more beautiful.

'Only on weekdays,' she said, sighing. 'My father helps out every weekend and my husband when he can, but he drives a taxi so he's in demand whenever we are and I don't see much of him. I've a couple of students booked to help me through Cowes Week. But on ordinary weekdays, we're never very busy, so I do it myself.'

'The cooking, too?' Karen said with easy sympathy. It sounded like hard work even for someone who wasn't weighed down by pregnancy.

'Yes.' The woman leaned down towards her and whispered. 'But in big batches that go into the freezer. I microwave the lot. Don't tell.'

'I won't,' Karen said, understanding why the pie was covered with potato rather than pastry, which never crisped properly in any microwave. 'This smells really good. Thank you.'

'D'you want another drink?'

'Better not. I'm driving. And I wouldn't want your police friend to give me grief.'

'He's no friend of mine. And from the questions he asks, I don't think he's interested in traffic,' Peg said bitterly. 'But you're right to take care.'

The pie was a good enough reason to come back here. Karen finished every scrap, then drank the last half-inch of beer, which was a lot less sweet than its toffee colour had suggested. After that she had no other reason to put off phoning Max Pitton.

This time he picked up the call, sounding brisk and busy.

'Hi,' she said, without bothering to give her name. He would recognize her voice without difficulty. 'You were going to tell me about my ex-mother-in-law's latest.'

'Ah yes,' he said in the familiar deep voice that sounded as though it was made by someone grinding stones together in a metal bucket. 'She phoned me at a tricky moment when I was entertaining the vice chancellor and his wife so I didn't have time to cross-question her. But she did tell me you should have been prosecuted for all the frauds you forced her "poor son" to commit before he killed himself as the only way he could get free of your wicked wiles.'

He paused, but Karen didn't comment, instead conjuring up a vivid image of Max's heavy face with its double chin and the expressive eyes that could switch from the familiar sneer into a wonderfully wicked smile with almost no notice.

'I thought you ought to know,' he added.

'Thanks. It's not as bad as the last accusation, which was that I'd bludgeoned him to death before covering my crime by hauling him out into his car and ramming it into the tree.' Karen heard echoes of the old resentment in her own voice and added more patiently: 'She'd always adored him and he was her only child so it's understandable that she needed someone to blame when he died, but I thought she'd got past it now. Did she give any idea of what could've set her off again?'

'Drink, I assume,' Max said with all the ruthlessness Karen had come to know.

She wondered how his wife had coped with it and whether it could have had something to do with their divorce. Not that he was always so tough. There had been a few times when he'd been exceptionally kind to Karen.

'She sounded as though she'd been at the bottle for a good while before she phoned me,' he went on. 'But you ought to do something to stop her if you can. Doesn't matter what she says to me, but you don't want anyone else getting the idea you could be a fraud. You need a clean reputation in our world.'

The tip of Karen's tongue caught between her teeth and she bit down hard. After everything else living with Peter had made her do, the idea that his ghost could ruin her professional future as well was unbearable.

'There's been so much flak over iffy expert witnesses in the past,' Max added, 'they're now having to be very cautious about who they pick. If there's the slightest whiff of dishonesty, no reputable lawyer will touch you, and you won't have to sabotage your career in the courts because it'll be over before it's begun.'

'It's not exactly easy to control Helen,' Karen said, refusing to rise to yet another challenge about her supposed self-destructive tendencies. 'How did she choose you as the target this time? Did she say?'

'Only that she'd been googling you, seen a report of your latest success, picked up the fact that I'm more or less your boss and "felt you ought to know the kind of woman you're giving prizes to".'

'Charming! Thanks, Prof. I'll get on to it.'

'How're the sessions with Spike Falconer going? Is he telling you anything helpful?'

'I haven't got very far. He's playing games, as you'd expect: all vulnerable and reasonable one minute, then a hysterical jittering mess the next. He's hiding something, probably something big.' She paused, wondering whether to tell him of DCI Trench's suspicions, then decided to keep them to herself.

Max could be overwhelming at the best of times, and she wanted to form her own views about the possibility that other slashed bodies might be buried around the Island before she let him anywhere near the idea.

'I've got a few ideas but nothing solid yet.'

'Par for the course. Everyone's always agreed that Spike's got a high IQ, so he's probably messing you about to ease the boredom of life in there. Stick with it, and don't go and screw up or fudge anything. You can do this, Karen, if you let yourself. I must go. Bye.'

'But . . .' she began and heard nothing but the buzz of the empty line.

He'd already gone.

She was putting the phone back in her bag when she realized this was as good a time as any to ring Helen. She wasn't likely to be drunk at lunchtime.

But Helen didn't answer, and there was nothing to say that could be left as a message other people might hear. Karen switched off the phone and stuffed it in her pocket, half relieved but frustrated, too.

The White House was a serene two-storey building, set on its own small banked plateau and probably dating from the late eighteenth century. Two long windows punctuated the facade on either side of the pillared front door, and there were five along the first floor. The slate mansard roof had a single round window in the centre, which looked like an all-seeing eye.

Smooth green lawns, mown in precise diagonal stripes, swept towards the bank below the house, accentuating its height above the rest of the landscape, and specimen trees were artistically placed at intervals around it. A great copper beech away to the left was balanced by a cedar of Lebanon in the foreground. Its dark layers somehow made the pristine whiteness of the classical facade seem even more detached from the rough and tumble of real life.

This is the English dream, Karen thought.

She didn't want to spoil the symmetry with her tatty car and so drove on round the side of the house, hearing the gravel chatter and crunch beneath her tyres. This was clearly the right thing to do. In a separate quadrangle, bounded on two sides by walls and on the third by a row of greenhouses, she found three cars and a Land Rover neatly parked. She edged her ancient Fiesta in beside them.

A back door opened as Karen locked her car, and a tall thin woman dressed in a pale-grey linen shirt dress beckoned. Her hair was more or less the same colour as the material, and her skin tone only slightly warmer. The hair was drawn back into a severe French pleat, which showed off antique pearl earrings and a matching necklace.

Unlike pearls worn by the successful lawyers and bankers Karen had met during her marriage, these were not evenly matched gobstoppers ringing the base of their wearer's neck. Sylvia Falconer's consisted of a long graduated string, with the largest pearl only about a quarter of an inch in diameter, reaching right down to the breastbone and almost disappearing into the vee of her dress.

'You must be Doctor Taylor,' she said in a gentle voice that held none of the arrogance Karen had expected. 'Do come in. My husband won't be long.'

She showed Karen into a drawing room as quiet and perfect as the exterior of the house.

There's still money here, Karen thought, lots of money and a very traditional taste.

Well-padded chintz curtains kept out the draughts from the long windows. The carpet looked old and French, with no pile of any kind, and the furniture was delicate and spindly, made of various kinds of gleaming wood. China stood on display behind the glass doors of matching cabinets, and the paintings were softly coloured landscapes in florid but unburnished gold frames. A small fire burned in the grate beneath a white fluted marble mantelpiece, even though it was nearly August.

'Who would believe in global warming with a drenched and chilly summer like this?' said Mrs Falconer, shivering. 'I hope it clears in time for Cowes next week. A lot of businesses will suffer if it doesn't.'

'Isn't it awful?' Karen recognized an effortful attempt to make this meeting into a social occasion. If she'd been facing a psychologist as the mother of an uncontrollable killer, she'd have been nervous herself.

'I hate the rain,' Karen added. 'But, you know, I'm glad to have this opportunity to talk to you on your own. D'you mind if I ask a question or two before your husband gets here?'

The delicate grey eyebrows drew together and the unexpectedly vivid brown eyes beneath them slid sideways towards the door.

'It's just,' Karen said cosily, 'that mothers always notice more than anyone else. I wanted to ask what it was that alerted you to Spike's . . . difficulties in the first place?'

Mrs Falconer relaxed visibly, as though she'd expected a much more difficult question, and she sat down in a deep chair on the left of the fireplace, arranging her full skirt neatly around her knees.

'I had no experience of babies or little children,' she said, 'so I'm not sure I'll be of much use to you. The first thing that surprised me was that he never cried. He was only eighteen months old when we got him, and I'd expected him to be tearful and show signs of trauma . . . homesickness, at the very least.'

Karen nodded. 'And he never did? I agree, that is odd.'

'And he was always such a compliant boy . . . so easy. To start with anyway.'

'How did that make you feel?' Karen didn't see any point in explaining that severely neglected or damaged babies learned not to cry or make any kind of demands, having been taught in the hardest possible way that their needs would be met by nothing but pain or abandonment.

'Relieved at first,' Mrs Falconer said, with a sweet, tremulous smile. 'I'd been so nervous. I mean, I'd wanted a child so badly for so long that I was sure when he came I'd mess it up somehow. Break him, even.' She shivered again, this time much less elegantly, then pulled herself together to smile and say: 'D'you know what I mean?'

'I do. Of course I do, even though I haven't had any children yet. But then you did have one of your own, didn't you?'

'Wasn't it odd? After failing to conceive for so long. But my doctor said it can sometimes happen like that. I mean, you'd understand, I expect, being a psychologist, but I was surprised when he told me it had probably been nerves that had stopped me having one in the first place.'

She flinched, which surprised Karen until she, too, heard the sound of footsteps in the corridor outside the room. They both looked expectantly towards the door and Karen was astonished to see Mrs Falconer stand up and move quickly to greet her husband, as though he was a guest in her house.

He patted her shoulder absent-mindedly and walked right past her to shake hands with Karen.

Her first thought was that he must often have been mistaken for Lord Lucan, the long-missing aristocrat. Like Lucan, Colonel Falconer was tall, with swept-back dark hair, a conventionally handsome face and a small moustache above his full lips.

She knew from the files that Falconer was seventy-four and assumed he must dye his hair and moustache, which was odd, considering that his wife had kept her natural silvery grey.

How well Spike would have fitted with these two, Karen thought. As tall as they, quite as good-looking, if not more so, and just as slender. Physically he'd have been their ideal son.

Was it their age that had made the adoption society offer them only a damaged child? The colonel must have been in his mid-forties when they got Spike, and his wife at the upper end of the permitted age range.

'Good afternoon, Doctor Taylor,' Colonel Falconer said in the kind of brisk masterful voice she'd have expected from a man who looked like him. 'You come highly recommended, but I have to warn you that I doubt you'll be able to help us. Spike was a walking time bomb from the time he was born. Nothing will change him now.'

She smiled her thanks and looked down in the kind of submissive gesture she assumed he would enjoy. When she raised her eyes again, she saw that he was still looking at her, concentrating on her in a way she would once have found flattering. In those days she'd felt as though she would always be on the edge of life, of no use or interest to anyone. She smiled again, this time apologetically, and said:

'I wish I could offer help, but that's not why I'm here, Colonel Falconer. My brief is to discover more about the formation of DSPD. No more; no less.'

'Quite. There's not much my wife and I can tell you. The damage was done long before we even saw the boy.'

'Damage?'

'There must have been damage, what? I *won't* believe any child becomes wild and violent like that without harm having been done to him first.' The colonel sounded gruff and uncomfortable. 'But we were told nothing about his life before we got him. Nothing.'

'Never?' she said, looking from one to the other. Mrs Falconer pressed herself further back into her chair, as though leaving her husband to answer all the difficult questions came naturally to her.

Abnormally compliant, Karen thought, as usual unable to avoid categorizing the people she met according to various psychological theories. She remembered how Max had been sure that Sylvia Falconer held the key to Spike's problems.

'Not enough,' the colonel said, making Karen concentrate on him as carefully as he on her.

She saw his facial muscles quivering, as though he was fighting to keep some words unsaid.

'That must have made you angry,' she suggested, probing, and saw the quivering intensify.

She also caught a very slight movement from Sylvia Falconer. Turning to look more closely, Karen saw that her arms were rigid at her sides and her hands were gripping the edge of the cushion on which she sat. Her lower lip was caught between her teeth and she was looking up at her husband with the expression of a child dreading an adult's outburst. When his voice barked out the answer to Karen's question, Sylvia Falconer looked away.

'I persuaded one of them to tell me more in the end,' he said to Karen, ignoring his wife completely. 'Drug-addicted mother, father god-knows-where, semi-starvation, neglect. Brought to an end only by a responsible neighbour reporting the woman to social services. Even when I got that much out of them, they wouldn't admit there'd been any actual abuse, physical or sexual. Although the little bastard had cracked his skull when he fell off the table on one of the few occasions when his slut of a mother bothered to change his nappy.'

'In fact, persistent neglect *is* usually more damaging than actual abuse,' Karen said, feeling sorry for them all.

'Is it? Well, in Spike's case it was certainly a recipe for disaster.

He should never have been offered for adoption and if I'd had my way they'd have had him back at the first sign of trouble.'

'But he never gave any tr . . .'

'Sylvia!'

'I'm sorry, Fergus.' She hung her head.

Karen waited. When neither of them said anything more, she applied a prompt:

'And yet you said, Mrs Falconer, that he'd been such a good baby when you first had him here. What happened to change that?'

'I don't know,' she whispered, sending a pleading glance at her husband. He ignored it.

'My wife finds this hard to discuss,' he said to Karen, 'so I'd be grateful if you'd keep it short.'

'I'm sure it's hard,' Karen said with absolute sincerity. 'But what was it that first made you aware there was something seriously wrong with Spike?'

'When he killed the dog. Labrador bitch.' The colonel could have been dictating a shopping list for all the emotion he was showing now. 'Good pedigree. Good animal altogether. He ripped her open, you know. Stole a knife from the kitchen and ripped her open behind the greenhouses, before trying ineffectively to bury her in the vegetable garden.'

Karen saw that Mrs Falconer had closed her eyes, as though only by withdrawing completely could she bear to hear the story again.

'Yes, I did know,' Karen said. 'What I'm not clear about is how you knew it was Spike who'd done it.'

'Knife hidden in his room. Blood all over his clothes. Admitted it when questioned.'

'Not much doubt then,' Karen said carefully. 'I see. What else happened; I mean, what else did Spike do to worry you so?'

'He terrorized the local children, the boys at school, anyone whom Silas, my son . . .'

'Our *younger* son,' Mrs Falconer said, still with her eyes closed.

'. . . brought home from school,' Colonel Falconer added as though there had been no interruption. 'Spike stole from everyone, without any sign of conscience. As you can imagine, after the Labrador died we watched him pretty closely, but we couldn't always nip the trouble in the bud. Other animals suffered, though not pets. Small wild animals. We never took the risk of having any more pets in the house after Lara. Couldn't. What?'

'It sounds as though you did everything you could and were very patient,' Karen said, wanting him to feel comfortable enough to tell her everything she needed to know. 'What made you ban Spike from the house in the end?'

'He was eighteen. Adult. The trick-cyclists. Sorry. As you were. Shouldn't call them that. Your colleagues. They had diagnosed DSPD and we'd reached the end of our tether. We could tell it was only a matter of time before he did something terrible to a human being, and waiting for it was making my wife ill. It was also threatening to ruin any chance my own boy had to succeed, and . . .' The colonel smiled suddenly, as though he hoped to suggest a more appealing personality than he'd revealed so far. 'And driving me potty, if that's not too frivolous a term to use to an expert.'

'We trick-cyclists often use words like it in private,' Karen said with a short laugh and heard an answering guffaw from him. 'You must have had a hell of a time.'

'We did,' he said grimly, banishing all signs of amusement. 'And it's hard to have to bring it all up again, so if there's anything else you need to know, please tell me now so we don't have to do this again.'

Karen had thousands of questions she wanted to ask and knew she'd have to settle only for the most obvious.

'Are you satisfied that the Sanders family were Spike's only victims?'

'Yes.' The single syllable that issued from Sylvia Falconer's mouth came with such passion that the sound actually throbbed.

'Everyone's always tried to make us say that atrocity was merely one in a whole series. But it's not true. Something happened, must have happened, to Spike that day to make him kill them. It wasn't like him. You must believe that. They must have terrified him or threatened him in some way. They *must*.'

'Now, Sylvia, don't talk nonsense. You'll only confuse Doctor Taylor,' said the colonel, 'and make yourself ill. Doctor Taylor, if there's anything else . . .?'

'How did your other son respond to Spike's activities?' Karen asked, wondering how much of what Spike had told her about his brother's fears could be true.

Now that she'd met Colonel Falconer, she found it just about possible to believe he might have forced his younger son to practise catching a ball until he was so exhausted he collapsed. But it still seemed unlikely.

Sylvia Falconer swallowed hard as though she was about to speak, but her husband forestalled her.

'Silas was terrified of Spike throughout his childhood. Never told us so. Too self-disciplined, of course. But we could see. Fear came out in nightmares. Night after night he'd wake screaming. He was often sick, too, for no reason at all. After a while he was so scared of what Spike might do to his friends that he stopped bringing anyone home and had to be more or less forced to have birthday parties and what-have-you. The only way to do it was to send Spike to stay with someone and have the party while he was away. And even then sometimes Silas would lock himself in the lavatory. It was intolerable for him and for us. What?'

Sylvia looked at Karen with an expression she couldn't read. Before she could ask a question that might have given her a clue, Colonel Falconer was away again:

'So we sent Silas to boarding school. Woefully homesick at first, but it was his only chance. And he's made good. Done really well in the City. Respected. Successful.'

From the little Karen knew about traditional army families, she would have assumed any sons would be sent away to school.

'But you never let Spike board?' she said, keeping any hint of comment out of her voice.

Mrs Falconer got up, straightened her skirt and murmured something about having to check the contents of her oven. When she'd gone, her husband made his confession:

'To be perfectly frank, Doctor Taylor, I was not prepared to waste money on Spike's education. Had he shown any aptitude for either books or games I'd have done it, whatever it cost, but since he couldn't be bothered to cooperate with any teacher, I decided the local school was more than good enough. Now, as you see, my wife can't take any more. If you've any more questions, please let me have them in writing. That way, she needn't be bothered, and I'll do my best to tell you anything you need to know. Thank you for coming.'

Karen obediently got to her feet, hoping for the chance to slip into the kitchen on her way out to find out more about Mrs Falconer and everything she hadn't managed to say. But the colonel insisted on accompanying her all the way to the front door and then stood on the step, waving as Karen drove away from his beautiful unhappy house.

Somehow she was going to have to get round his ban and achieve another solo interview with his wife. And she might have to go to London to engineer a meeting with Silas, too.

Did he ever come home, Karen wondered, or had he made himself safe in the only certain way by creating a wholly separate life away from the Island?

Chapter 8

Karen dreamed of dead bodies and crashed cars and broken skulls and blood. But she woke into a sensation of wellbeing that astonished her. She lay for a moment, wondering what was making her so comfortable.

The rain had stopped. Its continual drumming on the roof had gone. Now, she could hear birds singing outside and the rustling of small animals in the undergrowth. And adult footsteps approaching her front door.

She flung back the checked blanket and reached for her kimono so she'd be decent if she were summoned. But there was no knock or call. She waited, sitting on the edge of the bed, listening. A soft thump sounded, as though something had been dropped on her porch, then the footsteps started again, moving rapidly away into the distance.

Her jeans were lying across the chair at the foot of her bed. She grabbed a clean pair of knickers, pulled on the jeans after them and added a sweatshirt from the pile waiting for a trip to the launderette. Respectable enough for any encounter, she ran in bare feet to open the front door.

There was no sign of anyone moving down the narrow road or through the trees. Whoever had been here had disappeared completely. She stood for a moment enjoying the warmth and the way the sunlight sparkled through the softly shushing leaves, lightening even these dismal woods.

Remembering the small thump she'd heard of something being dropped on the porch, she looked around and suddenly retched, backing away until her heels had hit the wooden shingles of the house and she could go no further.

At the edge of the porch lay a large knotted transparent plastic bag, containing something pink that glistened. She made out two rounded spines; a tangle of limbs; flesh. Very young. And very small.

Last night's dreams of dead bodies rushed back into her mind and she moved her hand up over her mouth.

'You're not squeamish,' she said aloud, knowing that she lied to herself as she'd lied to DCI Trench three days ago.

Then she saw there was a piece of paper with writing on it, tucked under the bag. Reluctantly pushing forward one naked foot, she pressed the big toe down on the corner of the page, then pulled it back towards her. As she bent to pick up the note, she saw the contents of the bag for what they were.

Rabbits. Skinned, headless rabbits. Meat, not babies' corpses.

Sweating, and ashamed of herself, she fought for control. At last she unfolded the note. It was unsigned, but the handwriting was easily legible, the kind of upright old-fashioned style that had once been called 'educated':

I don't know if you like rabbit, but they make good eating stewed slowly with onions and thyme. Wild garlic's good too. I cut their heads off when I skinned and drew them because I know ladies don't like dealing with heads. There shouldn't be any shot left, but take care in case I've missed a pellet or two. They can break your teeth.

Karen leaned against the wooden shingles of her house and thought of the times when Peter had taken her to Michelin-starred restaurants in London and she'd ordered rabbit. Never again. However delicious it had been, never again.

She picked up the bag by one of its knotted corners and took it into the chalet. These rabbits were presumably a present from Roderick, the Elephant Man, in return for the Kipling picture she'd given him.

What on earth could she say if he ever asked her how she'd liked them? If she pretended, he might well give her more. But the truth would be unkind. Maybe the best thing would be to drop them in some inconspicuous rubbish bin on one of her trips to other parts of the Island.

Pulling open the door of the ever-humming fridge, she dumped the bag in there to deal with later.

A lump of coarse grey olive-oil soap stood by the kitchen sink. Karen turned on the hot water and scrubbed at her hands until they were puckered and very clean, wishing the soap would fluff into a proper lather.

'What's happened to you?' Spike said as she came into the interview room.

'What d'you mean?'

'You look shocked. Hurt. Has someone been horrible to you?' He sounded concerned, and there was a kindly aspect to the way he was looking up at her.

She shook her head, interested and wondering whether this was the start of a new game or whether he was actually capable of empathy.

'I made a stupid mistake this morning,' she said, wanting to know more about his intentions. 'Someone gave me a couple of rabbits he'd shot and skinned for me. I thought they were . . .'

'Dead babies? They do look like that, don't they? But they make good eating, stewed with onions and wild garlic,' Spike said, laughing and sending her stomach tightening into a painful knotted mass.

He'd repeated the Elephant Man's words exactly. Only coincidence, she told herself, but enough to explain the recurrence of this morning's disgust.

'And the brains are good too when you're really hungry. Different from the meat. Different texture. But good. You suck them out of the heads.'

'Have you shot many rabbits?' she asked, recovering her composure so fast she hoped he wouldn't have noticed the momentary loss.

'Shot? How would I shoot them, Doctor Taylor? You shouldn't try to trick me, you know.' Now his smile had not the smallest iota of kindness anywhere in it. 'Like I've said all along, I've never had a gun, which is why I couldn't have shot those people. Which is why I'll get another appeal and this time I'll get out of here.'

Karen made a note of what he'd just said, in order to remind them both that she was a professional, here to study him and the workings of his mind.

'But I have killed *lots* of rabbits,' he went on. 'You do when you live rough in a place like this. There're thousands of them, all over the Island, and easy to catch. You snare them, you see. Wire round their necks. It's easy and quick. Well, usually quick; sometimes they struggle.'

He paused, watching her and licking his lips. She didn't react, making him work for it.

'If you bring me in a piece of strong fine wire tomorrow, I'll show you how to do it, Doctor Taylor. It'll have to be a good eighteen inches long. And it's best if it's that garden wire with the green plastic casing.' His voice was rising again in the way she'd come to know.

She made another note and saw how her switch of concentration away from him added to his determination to provoke a reaction.

'When there's that plastic on the wire you've got less risk of cutting their little furry heads off and making a mess,' he said, speeding up his delivery. 'You wouldn't want that kind of mess, you know, Doctor Taylor. Too much blood. And you wouldn't like the way the head looks, ripped off. You will bring me some wire tomorrow, won't you, Doctor Taylor?'

'No,' she said, without elaborating, waiting to see what she'd get next.

He didn't say anything, just sat with his hands laid out in front of her on the edge of the table before lifting them a little, with the wrists balanced on the edge so that he could make a circle with his bent fingers. Then he rammed them together with such speed he cracked one knuckle. The sound sent her stomach back into spasm.

He was far too intelligent to have expected her to agree to put anything as dangerous as a length of wire in those hands. She waited again.

'Doesn't always work first time,' he went on more calmly, as though trying a different tactic now the first hadn't worked. 'But if the snare hasn't broken their necks, you just hit them over the head with a stone on and on till they're dead. A stone. Or a brick.'

She thought of the swimmer, who had been garrotted and had her head smashed in with a brick, if DCI Trench's information could be believed. Was this the moment to ask questions on his behalf?

'Jim says you met my parents yesterday,' Spike said, smiling his most charming social smile and switching persona again. 'How did you get on? Did Pa tell you how growing boys need discipline and games to develop team spirit and ambition?'

Karen shook her head.

'Oh, so it's still "Jolly unfair of social services to wish a mad psychopathic baby on me", is it?' He'd put on a voice of rich round arrogance, even more pompous than his father's actually was.

'That wasn't quite what he said, Spike.'

'It's what he thinks. Which is why I hate him.'

'How old were you when you first decided that's how he saw you?'

Spike tipped back his chair with even more speed than usual. Karen had to stop herself putting out a hand or warning him to be careful. If he overbalanced, he could crack his skull open on the hard floor. And then she'd get nothing from him.

'When he blamed me for Lara's death.'

'Lara?'

'You're not concentrating, Doctor Taylor. Or are you pretending so you can trick me again? I told you about her yesterday. She's my Labrador.'

'Why did you call her Lara?'

'I didn't.'

'So who chose the name for her?'

Spike shrugged. 'Someone who's read *Doctor Zhivago*, I suppose. D'you know, they think the real Lara was KGB and spying on Pasternak all the time, poor bastard? Jim lent me a book about it only last month.'

'I think I read that somewhere, too.' Karen was intrigued at this glimpse into the twisty pathways of his imagination. 'D'you believe it?'

'Makes more sense that way, doesn't it?'

'Why?'

'All those coincidences. They keep meeting up all over Russia and fall in love all over again and it looks like chance. Much more likely she was always being sent after him to check up on him, keep an eye on him, watch him, report on everything he did.' Spike looked across the table at Karen with a serious expression, as though he wanted to show he was being straight with her now. 'Like I say, poor bastard.'

'Is that how you felt, growing up? Watched and reported on?'

His wide unconvincing smile was back. 'Of course.'

'What did you do about it?' Karen drew another pattern at the top of today's notes, as before hoping the illusion of privacy might tempt him into giving her something real.

'Play along. Give them what they want. Then I had enough.

Got sick of it. That's why living rough is better. You can do whatever you want and not have to listen to all those voices.'

'Voices?' she said, too quickly. Nothing in any of the files she'd read had suggested internal voices had ever been one of his problems.

'Voices on the phone, voices whispering to each other, reporting, asking questions. Where's Spike? What's he done now? Is he dangerous? Is he psychotic? Is he ill? Is it something I did? Can he be treated? How can we stop him hurting anyone else? How can we get rid of him?'

He let the chair clunk back onto all four legs.

'They can't have said all that,' Karen protested. 'Not where you could hear them.'

'Course they did. All the time. And when they didn't say it they thought it. Like in cartoons, you know, with a bubble over their heads. Why can't we recycle Spike? Pa never wanted to adopt me in the first place. And when Silas was born, ready to be him all over again, carry on his genes, I was superfluous to requirements.'

Surprised by his fluency as much as his insight, Karen looked receptive and hoped for more. But he laughed.

'You can't have asked the right questions, Doctor Taylor,' he said. 'And you a doctor of psychology! Did you really let him make you believe he was a do-gooder?'

'What's the worst thing you've ever done?' she said very fast, hoping to get him to respond as quickly and without thinking.

He stared at the wall above her head, as though concentrating hard. His lips moved, and he smiled like someone revelling in a secret pleasure.

'Wanked in church,' he said, looking at her with a challenge in his eyes, as though daring her to disbelieve him. 'Pa was *dis* . . . *gusted*. That's how he said it, like it was two words with a great huge gap in the middle. I've never seen him in such a frenzy.'

'What did he do?' she asked. When Spike didn't answer, she tried again: 'Were you punished?'

'He didn't hit me, if that's what you mean. He says he's disgusted, like I say, that I'm not fit for normal human society. He sent me to my room for three days. That was the longest it ever was, Doctor Taylor. I heard him telling my mother I'm like an animal that can't ever be socialized and she's a mad sentimental fool to believe I can.'

He stopped, his face blanked, then he started to play with his fingers, interlacing them, bending them, straightening them out, winding them into the old English children's game that went with the rhyme about the church and steeple.

'How did that make you feel?' Karen said at last.

Spike flattened his hands on the edge of the table and checked his watch, like someone impatient for the end of a tedious business meeting.

'Bored,' he said, looking up again to smile at her. 'Three days is boring on your own when you can hear them downstairs. I get my meals on trays, but she's not allowed to talk to me when she brings them. We can't go into it all now, Doctor Taylor. You have to go. The half-hour'll be up in a minute. Ring the bell. And don't forget to pick some wild garlic on your way home; it helps rabbit stew a lot.'

Turning her back on him was hard now that he'd started to give her the first hints of what she needed, but he was right: her time was up. The officer who answered her summons was a stranger.

'No Jim?' she said, when he'd locked the door behind them.

'He's filling in on duty in reception now. You can see him there if you need to talk to him.'

'Thanks.'

She waited by the glassed-in desk until the visiting chaplain had handed in his penknife and umbrella, then she collected her keys and nodded to Jim. He looked as though he'd like to talk, but she'd had enough for one morning, certain now that Spike had a great deal more control over his thoughts and speech – and, presumably, his actions – than he pretended. He could tell perfectly good stories of incidents from his past, too, and reason his way through the theory that the real-life model for Lara had been a KGB plant in the life of Boris Leonidovich Pasternak.

There was no way he was the straightforwardly bumbling psychopath who'd killed a family for no reason other than that he'd come across them unexpectedly one hot summer's day. So maybe Spike *had* picked Isabelle Sanders because she fitted his fantasy of the perfect victim and turned what should have been a solo murderous indulgence into a spree killing because he'd been disturbed by the rest of her family.

Karen could see how she owed Trench a phone call and a more serious discussion of his ideas, but she wouldn't make it yet. She needed time first to get her own mind clear.

On the way home she drove into Newport so that she could replenish her supplies of food and drink.

A man was sitting on her porch when she rounded the last bend. Without thinking she rammed her foot down on the brake. The tyres skidded on the mud that still lay like an oil slick over the tree-shaded tarmac, in spite of today's dry weather.

Fighting the slipping sliding sensation, turning the steering wheel into the skid as Peter had taught her in the days when she'd still been his adoring acolyte, she felt the car whirl round in a complete circle before coming to rest, with the bonnet once again facing her chalet.

The male figure was standing now and revealing itself to be Will Hawkins, who should have been in an operating theatre fifty miles away, on the other side of the Solent, slicing into someone's brain.

Karen's hands were gripping the steering wheel and her mind was full of Spike's references to coincidences that weren't pure chance, and people knowing all about her and what she was doing on the Island and leaving her repellent packages of dead rabbit flesh.

Not wanting to engage with any of the ideas for the moment, she waited for an explanation. Will descended the two low steps onto the sticky path and came towards her. Karen opened the car door and leaned out, one hand still on the steering wheel and the other elbow balanced on the back of the seat.

'What the hell happened?' he said, his voice tight with either shock or anger.

'I skidded,' she said unnecessarily, beginning to notice more than her own sensations.

He was wearing his favourite loose low-rise blue jeans and a beautifully made pink cotton shirt that showed off his long lean torso and made him look much younger than his real age of thirty-nine. His fair hair was its usual spiky self, looking as though he'd just emerged from the shower and given it a rough rub with a harsh towel.

Getting out of the car, she was glad to find her legs were absolutely firm and her breathing steady.

'I've had a crash course in my body's reactions to unnecessary fear this morning,' she added. 'You were just one more footnote, in case I'd missed the point. What the hell are you doing here on a Thursday?'

'We had a patient who tested positive for MRSA after a routine operation yesterday. All the theatres have been shut for super-cleaning, so I swapped my shifts. I left a message on your phone. Didn't you get it? I can stay till the last ferry back on Saturday.' He paused, looking wary, then added: 'If that's OK.'

'Sure. Great. Come on in.' Karen felt in the pocket of her jeans for the big clattering bunch that included her house keys.

Much as she'd longed for the weekend with Will, this unex-pectedly early visit was making her uncomfortable, resistant. She'd organized her own plans for today and they hadn't included anyone else. She'd never been easy with disruptions to her routine.

'Why don't you keep them with your car keys?' he said, point-ing to the heavy bunch.

'Because if I lost one lot, I'd lose both,' she said, hoping to hide her reluctance to have him here today. 'This way I can keep spare car keys in the house and spare house keys in the glove compartment of the car.'

'I've never known anyone take so many precautions against her own possible failings,' Will said as he picked up his familiar weekend bag, an affair of khaki canvas and strong brown leather straps, almost a parody of sub-military masculinity, quite unlike what she hoped was his real character.

It could have been made of tissue paper and contained nothing but feathers for all the effort he had to expend on lifting it. Even if she hadn't known how much work he did with weights, that movement would have told her. He dropped the bag just inside the door, out of the way.

'Tell me about the crash course,' he said with some of the stiffness leaving his voice. 'Who's been scaring you? Your psychopath?'

'In a minute,' she said, handing him the strong cotton shopping bag of fresh milk and chicken she'd bought after she left the prison. 'Could you put these in the fridge for me?'

She heard the horrible ripping sound as the perished rubber of the door seals pulled apart.

'Ough,' he said, 'what have you . . .? Oh, I see. It's just a couple of rabbits. I thought . . .'

'So did I.' Karen was beginning to relax. 'I'm glad it wasn't just me. It was mistaking them first thing this morning that started me off. I could almost feel my amygdala light up like a beacon.'

'You haven't been having brain scans, have you?' He sounded worried.

'No. But I've studied enough to know what fear looks like.'

'And to know about the floods of cortisol that are produced while the amygdala's lighting up, I expect,' he said with an academic formality she assumed was designed to calm her down. 'Which, if they're not dissipated in some urgent physical action, linger to generate ever-increasing stress and lead ultimately to migraine, gastric disorder, depression, and probably plenty more. No wonder you're spiky.'

'Which is why I had been planning a long, long walk this afternoon to wash the chemicals out of my system.' Karen pushed aside all her plans for solitude. Will was here. She couldn't send him away now. 'Are you up for that?'

'Sure. Then we can come back and cook the rabbit to take away any residue of irrational fear by rediscovering how good it tastes when it's carefully cooked and . . .' He paused, as though to give her time to comment or finish the sentence for him.

She didn't, bracing herself instead to hear him tell her to stew the corpses with onions and wild garlic.

'And in the meantime,' he said, 'have you had any lunch?'

'Not yet.'

He flicked open the weekend bag and pulled out a pie wrapped in cellophane and tied up with red ribbons, and a long narrow brown-paper parcel. He laid the parcel on the cluttered table she used for both work and eating and offered her the pie, as though making a ceremonial presentation.

'I had time to waste in Lymington while I was waiting for the ferry, so I bought this,' he said. 'Traditional pork pie. We could have that and some of your apples. No cooking. No hassle.'

'Great,' she said, although she didn't feel much like eating anything quite as pink as the filling in a pork pie. 'And there's some wine. If you're off duty until Saturday, you can let yourself have a glass, can't you?'

He nodded. She could feel an unfamiliar sensation driving her towards him, as though her subconscious wanted her to fling herself into his arms and beg him to make her safe from everyone for ever. Silently she told her subconscious exactly what it could do with itself.

'You know your prof thinks your shell is the toughest he's ever encountered,' Will said over his shoulder as he peeled the cellophane off the pie and put it on a large cracked white plate. 'Before we even met, he told me he wasn't sure anyone would crack you.'

Karen paused, with the corkscrew partly driven into the cork of a bottle of basic claret. 'Is that some horrible male sexual metaphor?'

'If it is, I haven't heard it. Do we eat in here?'

'I was beginning to wonder if he'd challenged you and that's why we ended up in bed that first night. Yes. I'll move my books off the table. Hang on a sec.'

'As far as I can remember,' Will said, sounding more relaxed as he put down the pie plate and touched the back of her neck with his forefinger, 'it was your suggestion that we went back to your flat that first night.'

Enjoying the familiar smell of his skin, a mixture of pure soap and the cedarwood balls he'd once told her he used among his clothes to keep moths at bay, she turned to kiss him, still holding the bottle by the corkscrew.

'Doesn't sound like me,' she said, as she drew back.

'Well, *I*'d never have dared suggest it after your ferocity in the restaurant.'

'But you weren't reluctant?'

'Not reluctant at all.' He put both hands on her shoulders. 'Who would be?'

She laughed, but she couldn't get the picture of him and Max Pitton out of her mind, with Max trailing her supposed invulnerability in front of his visiting celebrity speaker. Taking bets, maybe, over how long it would take Will to 'crack her'.

Don't be paranoid, she told herself.

'What's in the other parcel?' she said aloud, determined to flick her mind back into the present.

'You told me in your first email that the knives here are useless.' Will pulled open the drawer in the old dresser and withdrew one bent, rusted specimen. 'And I can see what you meant. So I brought you one. But I don't think you should attack the pie with it. We'd better make do with this for the time being.'

Curious, she put down the wine bottle at last and reached for the package. He'd packed it with sticky tape so neatly cut and firmly pressed into the brown paper that there were no lifting corners. She had to scrabble at the edge with her nails until she'd raised enough tape to grip and pull it back. Inside the brown paper, she found a slip cover made of white card and inside that a long box, covered in the darkest blue matt silk and secured with tiny bone toggles.

'My God!' she said, looking up at him. 'It's a sushi knife.'

'I know you love the revolting slimy stuff, and I thought being on an island, you'd get properly fresh fish, so you should have a decent knife to deal with it.'

'But one like this!' she said, flicking open the box to see, just as she'd expected, the most desirable of all the knives in the world: a Japanese chef's knife with a pure ceramic blade. 'They cost a fortune.'

'And they're pretty hard to get over here. But they said it was the best. That's all I cared about.'

'We must get some fish tomorrow.'

'Only if I can have mine cooked. Can you really skive off to play on a Friday?'

'Why not? I'm doing this in my time; no one's paying me. Unfortunately. I'll phone the prison and say I won't be in again till Monday. It's no problem,' she said, closing the silk-covered box and putting it in pride of place on the shelf over the sink. Unless one of them toppled it into the washing-up water, it should be safe up there.

After lunch, they set off down the road towards the beach. Karen was certain they'd have it to themselves. There was nothing welcoming about the shore on this part of the island. Barely three or four feet wide, it consisted of large round pale-grey stones, which made for uncomfortable walking, and the looming woods blocked any view of the countryside.

The sea itself was a muddy grey today, sloshing up on the stones in a lackadaisical way, as though there was no energy in it. The water smelled of rotting seaweed and the dead birds that flopped in the sulky ripples, some already half-eaten by the crabs and shrimps.

On the far side of the Solent, the soft green Hampshire countryside looked normal, easy, safe. A few yachts made their way up and down the narrow stretch of water, too far from the bleak beach to offer any inconvenience.

Will slung an arm around her shoulders and kissed her ear. 'You're not unhappy here, are you?'

'No. Frustrated by my talks with Spike. Puzzled. Not sure I'll ever get anything useful out of him or his parents.' She turned towards him, as always surprised by the devastating effect he had on her.

The open neck of his pink shirt revealed the twin bumps of his collar bones and made his neck seem even longer and smoother than it was.

'And I was feeling twitchy,' she added, trying to keep her mind on the conversation rather than his body.

'So I saw.'

'It's been quite interesting to monitor my state of mind.' Karen didn't want Will to think he'd broken through her supposedly impervious shell. 'I know that as soon as Spike tells me anything real or my brain turns up some useful insight, I'll be fine. This is no more than the foggy start of any project.'

'And being back in your childhood holiday house? Hasn't that been hard?'

'In a way.' She was glad she didn't have to explain all her mental processes to him. 'That's probably the chief ingredient of the twitchiness, apart from missing you, of course.'

'Of course,' he said, pretending to laugh, as though he knew just how hard she was having to work to deal with his invasion of her privacy.

'There was always Aidan here before,' she added, 'and now I can't even phone him without driving halfway up the road, or email without going into town. We were such a unit, he and I. It felt like us against the world.'

'I guessed it might have been like that. Now, how's the cortisol? Can we go back yet?' Will said, his hand slipping both arms around her waist.

She leaned back against him and felt him brace his feet against the round grey stones to take her weight.

'If it weren't for these pebbles . . .' she murmured.

'Hussy!' he said, using one of her grandmother's favourite words and turning her round so that he could kiss her properly. At five-nine, she was only an inch shorter than he was. 'Come on. Forget the walk. We've got more important things to do. Let's go back.'

Chapter 9

On Friday Karen decided to take Will sightseeing since he'd never been to the Island before. She wanted him to see everything that was good about it as well as the bleak north shore and the gloomy woods. They went first to the Needles, the line of three chalk spires marching out to sea beyond Alum Bay.

Families clustered on the beaches here, building sandcastles, paddling, shrimping, just as she and Aidan had done nearly thirty years ago. There were still toffee-apple sellers, she discovered, and candy floss. And wasps now the temperature was rising.

'D'you remember,' Will said, pointing to a small boy who was carrying a clear plastic bag filled with pale-pink fluff, 'how that gets impacted into a nasty hard red mess when you suck it?'

'I do. Vile!' Karen said, wondering whether that sensation was at the root of her dislike of sweet things. 'But I can't remember the taste. Odd. Toffee apples, yes. But not candy floss, and there must have been something in it besides sugar. Now, ready for lunch? I thought I'd take you to a pub I've discovered on the other side of the island, where the cooking's good and the welcome's civilized.'

'Won't it be very crowded, on a sunny day in August? We could just pick something up and take it back to eat at home.' Will grimaced. 'I don't much want to share you when we've got so little time.'

'Do you have to go back so soon? Will you really be operating on Sunday?'

'If they've got the theatres sterile again, yes. All the patients who had to be postponed on Thursday.'

'Is it a big list?'

'One granuloma and two meningiomas. One very tricky to access. We're going to have to go in through the cheek.'

When he talked of his work, which wasn't often, Karen could understand why he found so much of hers absurdly imprecise. When there was a tumour to be excised from the brain, everyone could agree what the problem was, even though no one could guarantee that surgery would be perfect or avoid causing unexpected damage. With her profession, everything was much fuzzier, much more susceptible to argument and interpretation.

'And you?' he said. 'Will you go to the prison to make up for missing today's session?'

'I doubt it. I'll listen to my tapes of Spike talking and write up my notes and reread all the latest stuff on DSPD and try to see which of the textbook cases most resembles his. And I want to see if I can find anyone local prepared to talk about his parents.'

'Hence the pub,' he said with a smile. 'Which will be less crowded today than on a Sunday just before the start of Cowes Week. I see. Let's go then.'

'Sure?'

'Absolutely. Much easier to fall into conversation when you've got cover like me. My presence should stop you looking like a private eye.'

'Precisely.' Karen laughed. 'But I think you'll like the publican.'

The car park was much fuller than usual, but the first person Karen saw when they pushed their way in was DCI Trench, propping up the bar as before, dressed in the same tattered jeans. In concession to the heat, he had a black polo shirt over them instead of the leather jacket. He raised a hand and asked if he could get her a drink.

'This is Will Hawkins,' she said. 'Will, DCI Trench, who's also interested in Spike Falconer.'

The two men shook hands and she watched Will's reaction with interest. He had once claimed to have a good radar for the untrustworthy, and she was glad to see his narrow face relaxing as he smiled at the detective.

'How's Spike?' Trench said, turning towards Karen. 'They say you've got him eating out of your hand already.'

'The gossip on this island is atrocious!' she said. 'And wrong. He's trying to play me, but so far we're still circling round each other. Wherever you're getting your information, it's wrong.'

Trench laughed. 'I never listen to gossip; only to snouts. And this one always knows what he's talking about when it comes to Parkhurst.'

He looked her up and down, making her very conscious of the close-fitting cropped black trousers, picked specially to impress Will with her long brown legs. She'd painted her toenails too, a rich dark-red like raspberries.

'I hope you don't go to Parkhurst looking like that. You'd start a riot. Never seen a currant bun with better legs. What can I get you both?'

'Let me,' Will said, sounding amused. 'Karen tells me the bitter's special here. Another pint for you?'

'Great, thanks.'

'Karen?'

'I can't decide. Why don't you take your drinks into the garden? We haven't had enough sun this summer. Mustn't waste it. I'll join you in a minute.' Karen waved towards a door marked 'Toilets'.

'Sure. DCI Trench?'

'Charlie. Fine.'

When Karen came back, she was glad to see the two of them amicably chatting in the garden. Peg was wiping down the bar.

'Hi,' Karen said. 'You look a bit less tired.'

'Thanks.' The woman smiled. 'They say the first three months are the worst, so I'm overdue for feeling better.'

She stroked her bulge.

'Will it be your first?'

'That's right. We'd been trying for so long I'd begun to give up hope. Which is why I took over the pub when my uncle died. No one else in the family wanted it, and I thought if I couldn't have children I'd better have a job, so . . . Then, straight away. This.'

'I didn't realize it was a family pub. So are you a caulkhead?'

Peg smiled at Karen's use of the local term. 'Me and both my parents and all four grandparents.'

'You'll know all the local families then.'

'Most of them.'

'Like the Falconers?'

'What can I get you?' Peg said in a frigid voice, making it clear she resented the question as every muscle in her body stiffened.

'Cranberry juice, if you've got it,' Karen said, accepting the ban for the moment. Then she remembered the limited selection of soft drinks and corrected her request to tomato juice, with a good big slug of Worcester sauce to disguise the sweetness.

She paid for her drink, and carried it out to the garden. As she sat down, she said to Trench:

'Did you bring me here in the first place to pump her because she wouldn't talk to *you* about the Falconers?'

His dark-stubbled face split into a wide smile. 'More or less. I thought not being a cop would help for starters. And being a woman.'

'Then you should have briefed me. I'd have gone in with much more open questions if I'd known. Why won't she talk? Everyone else round here does.' Karen thought about his earlier comment about Spike's response to her and quickly added: 'Even if they get it wrong.'

She flashed a quick apologetic glance at Will, who shrugged as though to express equal measures of irritation and permission to spoil his break with her work. He tipped his face towards the sun, as though determined to get whatever satisfaction he could from the session.

As he streched his neck, the tendons were pushed forwards through the pale skin, like a body builder's. She hoped he would not burn.

'She's Sylvia Falconer's niece,' said Trench.

'*What*?' said Karen, completely distracted from Will's neck by memories of the big serene white house and the air of wealth and status that hung about it, along with the chilliness and misery. 'That woman's from a family who run a pub?'

'Why not?' said Trench, enjoying her surprise.

'Because Colonel Falconer's such a crashing snob. How come he married her?' As she asked the question, Karen thought of the way Sylvia had risen to her feet to greet her husband of thirty-five years. Did she feel she was in some way inferior, or on sufferance in his life? Surely not.

'Fuck knows!' Trench said cheerfully. 'They say he fancied her because she and her family were so different from all the chilly, formal, snotty bunch he'd grown up with. In those days, they say, she was warm. Sexy. Even confident.'

Karen thought of the bleached, submissive woman she'd met. None of the adjectives Trench had picked would fit her as she was now.

'He was such an arrogant wanker,' Trench went on, staring down into his beer as though he hated it, 'he thought a girl like her would screw him at the first opportunity. Or so they say. When she wouldn't, he lost it. Made a right tit of himself, hanging round the place, until *her* family got arsey. In the end he married her and tried to turn her into an ice sculpture. Then they couldn't have kids . . .'

'Just like her niece,' Karen said, imagining the misery of a woman removed from the friendly cosiness of the Goose Inn to the lonely grandeur of the White House, married to a frightening man she hadn't fancied much, only to discover that she was going to be alone with him for ever because she couldn't get pregnant.

What could that kind of experience make you do? Karen asked

herself, but she didn't have time to consider the idea because Trench was talking again.

'Except the Falconers gave up and adopted Spike. Peg won't talk about how he was when they were kids. Which is a right pain. She's more or less the same age so she must know where all the bodies are buried.'

'Unfortunate phrase to pick in the circumstances, if what Karen tells me about your theories is true,' Will said drily, without opening his eyes or turning his sun-basking face towards them.

'It's a perfectly ordinary Freudian slip,' Karen said, defending Trench without thinking about it. 'You don't really think she knows anything useful about his crimes, do you, Charlie?'

Trench drank some beer, then wiped the thin line of froth off his upper lip with the back of his hand.

'She's the only member of the family who ever goes to Parkhurst to visit him. She must know something.'

Chapter 10

'He fancies you, you know,' Will said, as he slid his hand between her thighs.

'Who does?'

'Charlie Trench, Ace Detective,' he said, keeping his hand moving, trailing his fingers all the way up her body, making her shiver as they pushed aside the flaps of her white shirt. He kissed her, his tongue flickering against hers.

'Nonsense,' she said against his lips. When he pulled back, she added: 'He saw me as a useful chisel to get at some information; that's all.'

The rare sunlight was barely muted by the thin checked curtains they'd pulled across the window. Its glow slid over Will's face, lightening the shadows in the dip below his cheekbone and the tiny compression in his chin. He looked even younger than usual as he stood in front of her.

'It's not nonsense.' His lips followed his trailing finger, pausing below her collarbone, moving on to touch first one nipple, then the other. He pulled her shirt down over her shoulders and she shrugged it off, feeling the caress of the fine linen sliding down behind her. 'I watched him. He kept making excuses to lean towards you, brush against you. He could hardly keep his hands to himself.'

'What else did you see?' she said, putting her own hands either side of Will's body, feeling his prominent ribs expand as he breathed, knowing that nothing they actually said was what they were really telling each other. The length and sinewy strength of his torso had always amazed her.

'That you're gorgeous and no one but me is getting anywhere near you if I can help it,' he said, breathing hard.

She let her fingers splay and stroked her thumbs downwards. He gasped and guided her back, towards the bed.

Later, when they'd admitted how hungry they were, he left her lying in bed and went to the kitchen. The chalet was so small that even from the bedroom she could watch him as he laid ten rashers of bacon into the black enamel roasting tin, before placing it squarely across the two Calor-gas burners of the rickety stove.

The crisping salty meat smelt delicious. Karen lay back, enjoying the sight of Will moving about her makeshift home, with a dark-blue bathtowel tied low, just above his narrow hips. He cut thick slices off a fresh loaf of white sourdough bread and spread them lavishly with butter.

Strange, she thought, how such a straightforward domestic moment can seem so sexy.

They'd never had time to spend like this before in the three months they'd been together. One or other had always had to catch up on sleep before an important day or rush off to a meeting somewhere. Lying like this, watching and noticing and getting to know him, seemed unutterably luxurious. She couldn't think why she'd wasted time taking him sightseeing or to the Goose Inn.

'Except that it heightened anticipation,' she murmured aloud.

He cocked his head, as though he'd caught a vague sound, then turned, saw her watching and looked back with such undisguised affection that she was winded. After the disaster with Peter, she'd sworn never to let anyone matter enough to make her care what they did or said. Now she didn't know if she could stop herself.

For a long moment Will looked at her, then turned back to his cookery. The precision of his movements didn't surprise her, but the muscles did until she remembered how much physical work any surgeon must do.

Karen had become so used to exploring her subconscious and analysing all her most difficult impulses that she had to make a deliberate effort to stop, to let sensation and emotion overtake her. By Saturday evening, she felt as though she had peeled off at least five layers of protective covering. Which scared her for both of them.

Watching Will board the last ferry of the day was horrible. He turned and, having dropped his bag by his feet, leaned against the rail so that he could look down into her face.

'Come to me next weekend?' he called, sounding urgent enough to tell her she wasn't alone in her feelings. 'I won't be operating then. Please, Karen.'

'OK.' She smiled suddenly. 'OK. I'll come.'

'Great.' The ferry's hooter blasted, drowning all other sounds. When it stopped, he shouted: 'Phone me when you know what time you'll get to the flat.'

She waved, blew him a kiss, and then turned away, desolate at the thought of being on her own again with an empty Sunday in prospect.

That night she couldn't sleep. The bed seemed to have grown lumps wherever she tried to lie. The pillows were like chunks of concrete. And every time she closed her eyes, there were noises that dragged her back into full wakefulness. She knew it was her own mind tormenting her with little pinpricks to distract it from the loneliness she'd been determined never to feel again.

Why does being with someone always cost so much? she asked herself, pummelling her pillow into shape again. Why can't you just keep your head down and live your life in peace and quiet, without taking any kind of risk?

She could hear Max Pitton's voice in her head, urging her on.

Taking risks was essential, he thought. If you didn't, you stagnated, and your mind turned to misery and mush.

'So you'll fail sometimes,' he'd said once. 'And offend people. Make them angry. Make some of them hate you. So what? Failing and being criticized are marks of any real human being. Only a rag doll escapes both.'

An animal padded along the ground outside, brushing against the thin wooden shingles that covered the external walls. Karen shrank away from her side, as though the animal might get at her. A heavier, noisier creature walked past.

She grabbed her dressing gown and wrapped it tightly around her. If she couldn't sleep, she might as well get up, make a cup of tea and do some work. And do her damnedest to forget Max and the way he dug virtual spurs into her. He obviously had a Pygmalion-complex, she'd told him once. At least that had made him laugh and let her alone for a day or two.

As the kettle boiled, she surreptitiously checked that she'd bolted the front and back doors, telling herself it was absurd to give in to such neurotic behaviour. The sense of unease was merely a distraction, a displacement anxiety that her mind would find easier to absorb than all the ones aroused by Will and the feelings she didn't want to have again.

The dark-blue silk box containing the amazing sushi knife he'd given her lay on the scruffy Formica shelf. She brought it down to the worktop and let her fingers trail along the top, surprised by the roughness of the silk. Then she slipped the two bone toggles out of their loops and opened the lid to look at the cold white ceramic. Somehow she couldn't imagine laboriously creating a masterpiece of raw fish and sticky rice for herself alone, here on the Island. But it was a magnificent offering to receive, and the generosity of his picking something entirely to her taste and against his own reassured her.

Peter had charmed her from the start and given her increasingly lavish presents, but they'd always been things he liked, or clothes or jewellery selected to make her look more like the kind of woman he wanted. She couldn't imagine Peter ever buying something like the sushi knife, designed to prepare food he didn't like.

Maybe Will would be safe even if she did let herself love him.

A human footfall outside sent a deep shudder through her body. She reached for the heavy torch she kept on top of the fridge in case of power cuts, then fumbled with the back-door bolts. Outside, with her bare feet flinching from the hard sticks and pebbles of her apology for a garden, she swung the narrow beam of light this way and that.

A running figure, bent low and ducking even lower under the branches, showed for a moment in the light. But he swerved and disappeared into the woods. However carefully she moved the torch beam, she couldn't find him again in the darkness.

'It's probably only Roderick,' she said aloud, then walked all round the outside of the house in case he'd left her another dead animal, tiptoeing in the hope of avoiding nettles and crap of one sort or another.

There were no scary gifts, nothing to explain the presence of the running man. Alarmed now, rationally alarmed rather than neurotically anxious, she told herself, she went back inside to push her feet into a pair of shoes. Returning to the garden, she made a much more systematic search for evidence of a prowler.

She found some flattened grass outside the kitchen window and when she shone the torch right down to the ground and peered into the puddle of light she thought she could make out the marks of footprints, with regular ridges and studs, like those made by a pair of trainers. Some were clear, others blurred, as though whoever had been here had spent some time, moving within the very small area just outside the window.

Roderick wore old-fashioned brogues or wellies. Who else could have been watching her? And why?

'If he could be scared off by the sound of the door opening and the sight of a bare-footed woman holding a torch, he can't be much of a threat,' she said aloud, bolting the door again.

She washed her grubby feet, noticing that some of the red varnish was already chipped, and took her tea back to bed, along with a copy of the latest edition of her favourite professional journal. In no time she was absorbed in a soothing account of the gender differences that could be found in deliberately inaccurate witness statements.

Next morning she reached for more bacon from the fridge before she caught the impulse and checked it. Will wasn't here. Making sexy, butter-dripping bacon sandwiches wasn't going to bring him back. And it would pile on the pounds. Instead, she took half a grapefruit as usual and set about making a pot of coffee.

As she spooned up the sharp yellow segments, she thought again about the different ways in which she and Will saw the brain. Their ideas coincided, of course, with the effects of malformation or chemical flooding. Where they were not yet in agreement was over the precise causes of poor development or overactive secretions. Will clung to genes, maternal diet in pregnancy, and pollution. Karen was convinced that emotion itself could help shape the developing organ.

Her job was to map the labyrinth and find the monster, the source of the agony that led to the crimes men like Spike committed. For her, it was an absolute – the only absolute she would ever admit – that violence always followed agony of some kind.

Had Spike's monster really been the neglect of his drug-addicted mother? Or had it been terror of the man who had adopted him? If so, it was a terror he still could not admit, she thought, remembering the way Spike had boasted of being even more 'scary' than his father.

Chapter 11

Jim was on reception duty again on Monday.

'What happened?' he said, as he took Karen's keys from her and watched while she put her bag through the scanner. 'You didn't come on Friday.'

'Didn't they tell you? Something else came up. I phoned and left you a message.'

'I was off duty till this morning.' His voice was heavy with something she couldn't immediately understand. He sounded critical, but a little sympathetic too.

'What are you really telling me?' she asked.

'Come back when you've seen Spike. We can discuss it then, if you want. How long will you be?'

'Half an hour.' She was surprised that he should need to ask. 'As always. See you.'

One of his colleagues unlocked the six gates between reception and the interview room, then the door of the interview room itself.

Spike was sitting in his prison uniform of blue jeans and dark-green T-shirt, with his golden head bowed in a shaft of sunlight from the high window.

'Hello,' she said.

He raised his head and she gasped.

Down one perfect cheek were four dark-red parallel lines, each about one inch long. Someone had cut him. Unless he'd been indulging in bizarrely visible self-harm.

Most of the people who found relief from psychiatric problems in the pain from self-administered cuts attacked their arms, where the marks could be easily hidden, or occasionally their thighs. Karen couldn't remember seeing any cases that included deliberate mutilation of the sufferer's own face.

'What happened, Spike?' she asked when she'd got her voice under control.

He tipped his chair onto its back legs and smiled at her. The movement must have hurt his face because there was a minute clenching in the muscles around his eyes, but he made no other sign.

'Some young newcomer thought he'd get respect from slicing up the Island Freak,' he said in his smugly disdainful fashion, as though she was stupid not to know the answer to an unnecessary question. 'It's nothing.'

Except that it's a miniature version of the cuts in the swimmer's body and, possibly, the Labrador's back, she thought. Has someone been winding up dangerous prisoners in here with information designed to punish you for crimes they think the law can't touch?

It wouldn't be the first time in the history of the police and prison services, but Karen hadn't expected such low sneakiness from Charlie Trench or Jim Blake.

'D'you want to talk about it?' she said.

'No.'

'Does it hurt?'

'Why do you care?'

She paused to control her immediate response to check it for both accuracy and safety, then decided to let it out.

'Because I like you. I don't enjoy the idea of you being hurt.'

He frowned, then smoothed out his clenched eyebrows and shrugged, letting the chair clang forwards onto all four legs again.

'Then why'd you leave me sitting here like a lemon on Friday, Doctor Taylor? Everyone was laughing at me.'

'Didn't they give you my message?'

'What message?'

'I was held up. Something came up that I had to do on Thursday evening and I knew I couldn't finish in time, so I phoned and left a message here to explain and say I'd see you this morning.'

'And I'm supposed to believe you?' he said, staring at her with a harshness she found disturbing.

'Why should I lie?'

'Everyone else does.'

'Who?'

'Everyone.'

'Give me a specific example, Spike. Who lies to you?'

'Who doesn't?'

This wasn't going to get them anywhere. Karen pulled out her tape recorder and notebook and said:

'Tell me what happened on Chillerton Down, the day you were arrested.'

He shrugged again. 'I'd had some great skunk. Great. Best ever. I was off my face and asleep when they started pulling at me, shouting. I didn't know what they were after, who they were. I lay there, smiling up at them. It was hot, you know. And I was sleepy.'

He paused, as though giving her a chance to comment, but she merely made a note, then looked up to nod in encouragement.

'And the sun was right behind them. Dazzling. I couldn't see anything. Just felt their hands: big and hard and uncomfortable. Then I heard some of the words they were yelling: "Where's the gun? Where's the fucking gun? On your feet. What have you done with it?" On and on and on. Made my head ache. Wasn't till I got to the nick and was standing in front of the custody sergeant that I even knew what I was supposed to have done.'

Karen had read more or less exactly the same words in the file. He wasn't going to tell her anything she could use. Or not yet anyway.

'Who came to support you?'

'What, to the nick?'

'Yes. When you'd been arrested. Didn't you phone home to ask someone to come?'

Spike blinked once. Then shook his head. She was surprised. The police record distinctly said that he'd phoned the White House. Had he asked for support and been denied? If so, he must have spoken to Colonel Falconer. Karen couldn't imagine that Sylvia would have refused Spike anything, however submissive she might be when her husband was ordering her to stop defending him.

'Who'd I have phoned?' Spike said, sounding bleak. Then he smiled widely. 'What would've been the point when I hadn't done anything wrong? I'd never even seen those people who got shot.'

'So, if it wasn't you who killed them up there near the wood, who was it? Have you ever wondered?'

'Am I bothered? I don't have to prove who else did it, just that they haven't proved I did. And I didn't. So they can't.'

'And yet your DNA was on the gun when they did find it and on the coat that was wrapped round it. How do you explain that?'

'Cock-up,' he said, smiling again and sounding both sane and confident. Superior again, too, like someone with access to arcane knowledge denied to ordinary people. 'Or conspiracy. But cock-up's more likely. Labs aren't run by gods, you know. They're full of busy bored underpaid ordinary people, who make mistakes. They had all the swabs the cops had taken from me and all the evidence. Who's to say they didn't screw up and muddle the two, Doctor Taylor?'

'There are plenty of procedures to ensure that doesn't happen,' she said, surprised by his air of tolerance.

Unlike the tone of disdainful superiority, tolerance was not a feature of many personality disordered people.

'Will you be here tomorrow?' Spike said, crossing his arms in the classic gesture of defence.

'Yes.'

'Even if something else comes up?'

'Yes.' Only for Will would she have interrupted her work and then only once.

'I'll see you then.'

He couldn't have been more different today from the hysterical, giggling psychotic of some of their other encounters. Had he discovered he couldn't spook her by playing that part and so was now trying a different tactic?

Or was this the real man and the giggling other a persona he'd assumed she wanted until she showed so little interest that she didn't even bother to turn up for Friday's performance?

His narrative skills had increased, too, in a way that made a nonsense of her theories about severely personality disordered people. Were they fundamentally wrong? Or was Spike's disorder more complicated than anything she had so far encountered in her own work or in any of the reports she'd read?

How calculated *were* the games he played with her? Lying about something as straightforward and easy to check as his phone call to the White House, suggested he had very little insight into the way other people would react to him and the things he said. And yet he could also be rational, tolerant, even occasionally sympathetic. Nothing about him made sense.

Oh, for some straightforward, impersonal psychometric tests, Karen thought.

Downstairs, she found Jim waiting to tell her the truth about the cuts in Spike's face.

'He was upset, I tell you,' he said. 'He's come to rely on your visits.'

'Honestly, Jim, that's nonsense. It's more likely that he was pissed off at such a clear sign of my refusal to play his games.'

'You're wrong. Even though he learned long ago that he couldn't trust anyone, he'd begun to trust you. And then you went and let him down.'

Karen shook her head. But Jim's expression was unyielding. Now she understood the source of the heaviness she'd heard in his voice this morning: criticism of the way she'd failed the man in his charge, the man he cared about far more than she'd realized.

Jim said: 'After I'd taken him back to the wing, when it was clear you weren't coming here, he went out of his way to wind up the most dangerous of the other inmates at feeding time. Spike went on and on at him till the other one dug his fork into Spike's face and dragged it down. Blood everywhere. Must have been agony.'

Karen thought this part of the story sounded all too likely to be true.

'What did Spike do then?' she asked.

'Stood there with the blood streaming down his face and neck, laughing his head off.'

The picture was disturbing.

'I'd better be off,' Karen said.

'You going straight home?' Jim said, handing her the big bunch of keys.

She shook her head. 'I can't ever take the silence straight after a session with Spike. And today I need time to get my ideas in order. I usually go into Cowes, but . . .'

'You don't want to do that now all the yachties and their totties are there for Cowes Week.'

'Exactly. So I thought I'd buy a sandwich and take it up to Chillerton Down to see for myself where it all happened.'

'Good idea.' Jim grinned, then his expression hardened. 'Not that it'll tell you anything. Nothing to see there now except the radio mast and the grass and rabbits.'

Rabbits, she thought. Bloody rabbits. Why does everyone talk about bloody rabbits all the time?

'Oh, while you're here, Doctor Taylor . . .?'

'Yes?'

'We're collecting, some mates and me, for a mental health charity. Will you . . .? I mean, is it a cheek to ask for a contribution?'

'Not at all,' she said, needing his cooperation too much to refuse him anything as easy as this.

She dug in her wallet and found three twenties and a ten-pound note. She gave him the tenner, and hoped it didn't seem too mean. With the picture she'd bought for the Elephant Man this made just over eighteen pounds more than she'd budgeted to spend. She could manage that without too much trouble, but she hoped there wouldn't be many more unplanned calls on her purse.

'That's great,' he said, handling the note with unexpected delicacy as he slid it into an envelope he'd taken from his pocket.

Had he expected her to hand over a few pathetic coins? Did he know how humiliatingly short of money she was? Everyone in the place seemed to know everything else, so he probably did.

Chapter 12

A chalk track, very white against the green grass either side of it, led away from the isolated farm above Chillerton. Karen parked on the verge beyond the farm, changed into trainers, and rolled her black linen trousers up above her knees. In the boot was her linen book bag, filled now with a bottle of water, the cheese-and-pickle sandwich she'd bought in Newport, notes of all her conversations with Spike, and the original report of his arrest. She folded her jacket and laid it on the floor of the boot, before slinging the bag over her shoulder.

It made a heavy load, but she had an idea that rereading the notes and files here, in the place where the shooting had happened, might bring her some new insight that everyone else had missed. She locked the car, and, with the radio mast behind her, set off down the chalk track, watching the fat sheep scatter in front of her.

Reflected sunlight shot up from the whiteness and nearly blinded her. She wished she'd brought sunglasses. Squinting down to make sure she wasn't going to trip over one of the ridges and rick her ankle, she had a sudden vivid memory of the way harder lumps of chalk would skitter away from her feet across the soft white surface. Had they come this way, she and Aidan and Granny? Or were there other places just like it? She couldn't remember.

But the smell of the grass and the flowers, with the faint salty scent from the sea and the lanolin in the sheep's fleeces moderating the sweetness, seemed very familiar; as did the sound of buzzing insects backed by a machine clanking somewhere in the distance. Small hard round black sheep's droppings sprinkled the short grass wherever she looked. She could remember them, too, and the astonishing day when Granny had told her that they weren't hibernating insects after all, and Aidan had laughed and laughed at the way he'd taken her in and persuaded to watch, very carefully and quietly, for the first sign of movement.

The Sanders family had spread their picnic blanket on the nearer edge of the chalk pit. Karen couldn't think why parents of a toddler would have chosen anywhere so risky, but they had. They must have had extraordinary discipline over their son to stop him running over the edge and crashing down. Maybe they'd just been being good citizens, determined to make sure they didn't spoil any crops.

The track divided into three. Karen took the southernmost of the possibilities, which looked from her walkers' map as though it led most directly to the chalk pit.

On the far side of the top track was a field of some kind of grain, a little squashed after all the rain, but still gleaming gold in today's sun. There was a sizeable copse beyond it, but the wooded area in which Spike had hidden before he emerged for his shooting spree looked surprisingly small. What had he been doing there, if he had not been lying in wait for the family? Why had he chosen to be there in that tiny scraggy wood of all the possible places on the Island?

When Karen got nearer to the few trees, she saw that they'd have given him hardly any shelter and not much cover either. The coat he'd been wearing before he'd wrapped it around the shotgun and dumped it had been made of brown tweed, according to the files. Karen had always assumed it had been the bright coppery colour of Harris tweed, like the branches of dried bracken. But if it had been darker, the same colour as the earth between the trees, then maybe it had made him invisible to the Sanders as he lay there. And if he'd been off his head with particularly strong skunk, as he'd claimed, he wouldn't have been thinking about his surroundings, just retreating to a remembered place where he could lie down and sleep it off.

So what had made him flip and embark on his killing spree? Had the drugs sent nightmares curling through his sleeping brain so that he'd woken into a sensation of threat? Had the Sanders family just been in the wrong place at the wrong time? Who – or what – had Spike thought he was killing here when he'd grabbed his sawn-off shotgun and fired?

And why had he had the gun in the first place?

Karen turned away to look around the rest of the landscape, still having to narrow her eyes against the glare, even though it was now reflected off grass rather than the dazzling white of the chalk.

She crossed the grass to the first of the trees and settled down, with her back against its trunk and her legs stretched out ahead of her, to reread the solicitor's file. When she'd got to the end, with all the details fresh in her mind again, she shoved the papers back in her bag and looked around once more.

The day the Sanders family had died had been rather like this: hot and dry and sunny. Dan and Izzie and their children must have smelled these same smells, felt the short crisp grass under their feet. Karen kicked off her trainers and then her socks to let her soles and red-tipped toes spread against the cool sharpness of the grass stalks. A ladybird laboriously climbing one in front of her stopped as her toes moved and then it opened the spotted red casing of its back to reveal gossamer-thin black wings, before flying off. That too was utterly familiar.

Karen tried to imagine what the victims must have felt during the attack. The files told her the pathologist thought the six-year-old girl and her mother had been killed first, then Dan and the toddler later. Why?

Even if Spike had woken out of a nightmare and grabbed the
gun instinctively, why had he gone on killing? For pleasure? Or
because he'd thought if he got rid of them all there'd be no one to
give evidence against him?

Or was it all a lot more subtle than that?

Given his ability to mock and act all sorts of different parts, she
was prepared now to consider something more complicated,
something that might explain the otherwise bizarre differences
between these killings and that of the swimmer. Could Charlie
Trench be right about the whole case hanging on Spike's fasci-
nation with long-faced women with clouds of dark hair?

There was nothing here in this ravishing place to help Karen see
into the labyrinth of his mind. Dispirited, vaguely ashamed of the
sentimentality that had made her think there could be, she put her
shoes back on and walked between the trees, thinking they added
up to more of a big hedge than an actual wood. Even covering the
length and breadth of it twice revealed absolutely nothing.

The linen bag over her shoulder banged into her side as she
swung round, reminding her of the water and the sandwich it
held. She didn't want to eat here among the trees, so she made her
way back to the chalk pit. Sitting on the edge, with her legs dangling, she ate her small picnic.

Sheep moved slowly across the grass beside her, unbothered by
her presence, chewing their way to satisfaction. A few dark birds
wheeled silently in the sky above her, while gulls shrieked and the
agricultural machine clanked on. There were no humans anywhere in sight.

Karen tipped back her head, eyes closed, to feel the warmth on
her face and the peace of knowing no one was going to interrupt her.

Maybe that was what Spike had come here for in the first place.
The Island was small, not much more than 26 miles at its widest
point and 12 miles across. Although there were still pockets of
open country like this, there weren't many places where you
could be certain of being absolutely alone.

Had his motive for the killing been nothing more than rage that his sanctuary had been invaded while he slept? Could it be as simple as that?

Had this been the one place where he'd thought he could never be found and punished by his father or pissed over by other rough sleepers? Had all he wanted been an escape from the outside world because he knew he'd never get away from whatever tormenting ideas and fantasies rattled about in his mind?

Karen finished the sandwich, brushed the crumbs off her linen trousers, and stuffed all the rubbish back into her bag with the files and her unread notes. Then she moved north-west across the two other arms of the track and over the fence into the cornfield. Carefully skirting the edge of the crops, she walked round towards the bigger wood where Spike had been discovered by the police.

The distance didn't look far, but as she plodded along, with the hairy grain stalks irritating her smooth bare brown legs, it seemed to go on and on. Something bit her calf, leaving a smear of blood and an aching itch in the skin. She stopped to roll down her trouser legs and tuck them into her socks. Sweat was pouring off her back and through her hair.

Shade seemed more and more appealing. Tempted to cut across the crops, she resisted, speeding up. Eventually, breathing heavily and aware of a blister forming on her right heel, she rounded the last corner before the wood.

This one definitely gave far more cover than the little copse where he'd hidden before the shooting. She stood in the shade, catching her breath and revelling in the coolness. A fallen trunk lay across a small clear space ahead of her. She sat down, grateful for the rest, and examined her surroundings.

The shape of the wood was long and narrow, but she could see how Spike might have camped out here. Remains of small fires were obvious, and a smell of human waste told her he hadn't been the only person who used it.

Emerging at last into the sunlit field on the far side, Karen saw four rabbits scampering away across the grass and thought of the lesson Spike had wanted to give her in how to snare them without cutting off their heads.

She remembered the moment he'd asked her – oh so innocently – to bring some wire into the prison so he could demonstrate his technique. Maybe the man who'd sliced those straight parallel lines into his cheek was lucky she hadn't.

Chapter 13

Karen vaguely heard the sound of knocking through the pounding of water on her head. The shower was the only thing in the chalet that worked as it should, so she decided to ignore the summons until she'd finished rinsing the conditioner out of her thick hair.

An urgent voice called out: 'Doctor Taylor! Doctor Taylor! Please come.'

Added to the non-stop banging, that plea did make her turn off the tap. She shook water out of her eyes and twisted the wet hair back behind her head, reaching for a towel with her free hand. Relatively decent, she stepped out of the bathroom, crossed the living-room floor, hoping she wouldn't pick up a splinter in her bare feet, and opened the front door.

A young uniformed police constable stood there, with sweat all over his white face. At the sight of her, he whipped off his cap.

'Doctor Taylor?'

'Yes.' She became aware that the dark-blue towel was slipping and hitched it higher.

'DCI Trench sent me,' he said, keeping his eyes firmly directed towards her face. 'I'm PC Jenkins.'

She tightened the towel even more.

'He needs you in East Cowes. Right now.'

East Cowes was the old working part of the town, separated from the yachting paradise by the River Medina. A few grand residences had been built on the outskirts, but most of the place was too redolent of its industrial past to be much of a draw.

'Why?' Karen said without finesse.

'Spike Falconer's escaped from Parkhurst.'

'*What*?'

'And he's got a hostage. You've got to come. Please. DCI Trench said I was to bring you quick. And he's . . .'

'OK. Come in and put on the kettle, while I dress.'

'No time for tea, Doctor Taylor. He said "Quick".'

'Wait here then. I won't be long.'

Karen ran into her bedroom, slamming the door behind her as she ran, and rubbed most of the water off her body. The sun was already high. Soon, she thought, it would heat up. And she didn't know whether Trench wanted her for a calm interview with Spike or some kind of physical exertion. Pulling on knickers and bra, she felt them rasp her damp skin.

Jeans would cover most eventualities. She dragged them from the cupboard, along with a T-shirt and a hoodie to wear over it until the temperature did rise, then reached for her trainers. Bits of grass from Chillerton Down clung to their sides.

Ready two minutes later, she emerged from her bedroom, combing her wet hair with her fingers as she went. She paused for a second by the front door to grab her keys, change and phone and stuff them into the pocket of her hoodie. She could feel water from her hair dripping down her neck.

'I'll drive you,' the PC said as she veered off towards her car. 'It'll be quicker and I can bring you back as soon as DCI Trench has finished with you.'

'Who's the hostage?'

'Three-year-old girl,' he said, sounding as though his throat hurt. 'Blonde. Visitor called Ellie Bridger. Looks like the six-year-old he shot four years ago.' He seemed almost ready to cry.

'Have you got kids yourself?' Karen asked as he revved the engine and whipped the car round onto the road.

He shook his head. 'My sister has though.'

'A young daughter?'

'Yeah. Same age as the hostage. Can't stop thinking about her.'

'I can understand that. But the hostage isn't your niece, so you need to try to keep the two separate in your mind. Otherwise you'll lose it and make mistakes. What has Spike done with her?'

'He's got her tied up in full sight of the first-floor windows of an empty house. He didn't gag her, so she screams. All the time.' His eyes filled, but he kept them directed at the road ahead and drove carefully enough. 'Like someone pushing screwdrivers into your ears.'

'In which case,' Karen said, determined to make him stick to reality, 'she's probably in more danger of choking herself than anything else. Are her parents there?'

Karen thought she saw Roderick, the Elephant Man, hovering at the edge of the trees near Reception Point, where she could get a signal for her mobile, but when she turned her head over her shoulder to make sure, he'd disappeared.

'Yeah. DCI Trench is trying to get them moved.' PC Jenkins swung the car left onto the main road, just missing Jan Davies, who was walking her new puppy. 'They're in the way. Everyone feels sorry for them, but having them there makes managing the scene even harder.'

'Is that what Trench wants me for?'

'I don't know.' PC Jenkins put his foot on the gas and then swept through the countryside, past Parkhurst Forest, ignoring the road that led down to West Cowes, into Newport and on to the next turning.

Karen almost hit the door as he slung the car left and speeded up towards East Cowes. Just beyond the entrance to Osborne House, he turned left again.

Even this far from all the Cowes Week action, every parking space was taken. Cars had been driven up onto the narrow pavements and left on the corners, hiding road markings and generally making life difficult for everyone.

'Something like this would happen in a week when the town's bursting and we haven't any spare manpower,' Jenkins said, sounding tougher, even though he still had tears in his reddened eyes. 'Here we are.'

He drew up by some blue-and-white police tape. Two other uniformed officers were keeping a crowd of civilians at bay. Within the cordon were three distinct groups of people.

As she got out of the car, Karen saw that one group consisted of fire officers, heads down as they stood in a tight circle, conferring; another, an obviously hysterical couple, presumably the parents, being talked down by two women in civilian dress.

Trench was in a group nearest the house, a biggish, yellow-painted neoclassical villa. In the middle window of the first floor, right over the front door, stood a very small fair-haired child in a pink cotton dress, with her arms outstretched, screaming. Karen thought Jenkins's description of the sound was remarkably accurate. She wanted to press her hands over her ears to shut it out.

'They think the cords round her wrists must be tied to hooks in the window frames, which is why her arms are stretched out like that,' he said from behind her, but she hardly heard him because his boss was striding towards them with his hands clenched into fists at his side.

'DCI Trench,' Karen said as calmly as possible. 'What can I do to help?'

'Doctor Taylor. At last. We need you.' His face was moving constantly as the muscles below the skin jumped each time he tightened his jaw. He'd shaved today, so she could see every tiny movement of the bones and muscles under his tanned skin. 'Come here. Jenkins, get over to the parents and do what you can.'

'Where exactly is Spike?' Karen asked.

'Somewhere in the house, keeping well out of sight. The only witness says he's armed. He's probably booby-trapped the place, too.

Otherwise, why have the kid in full sight like that, tempting us to rush in? The negotiator can't get Spike to show himself or answer any questions. So we're stuck. Can't go in till we know more.'

'So what *do* you know?'

'Only this.' Trench handed her the first of two crumpled, dirty pieces of ordinary white paper, of the sort sold in reams for laser printing and photocopying. 'Transcript of a call made to the nick at seven-thirty this morning.'

Six short lines of print ran across the centre of the sheet:

I've just seen a tall fair-haired man dragging a small child in a pink dress into a house on the edge of East Cowes. She was screaming. I went to see if I could help but he yelled at me to keep off and waved a sawn-off shotgun at me. I legged it. But you've got to help her. He had straight scars on his face. Four I think. They looked new. The house is at the corner of . . .

Karen looked up, frowning.

'Are you sure this is genuine? Spike's waiting to hear about his next appeal. He's not going to get anywhere if he does something like this. He's not stupid. Far from it, in fact. He'd know anything like this would keep him in prison for ever.'

'Spike's never been consistent or rational. You know that. Here's *his* note. Copy of it anyway. He left the original here, on the front step, weighted down with stones. That's at the lab now.'

She took the second piece of paper, again a copy of what looked like bog-standard laser printing.

When you give me the date for my appeal I'll let her go. I haven't hurt her yet. If I have to I will. Get me the date and I'll let her go.

Karen looked up at him, still holding on to the note. 'Perfectly spelled. But . . .'

'Don't waste time. I need an assessment of his psychological state – what he'll do to the kid if we get it wrong and piss him off – and a plan for making him talk to the negotiator. And how . . .' Trench hesitated for a second, his round dark eyes very bleak between the long lashes, then added: 'How we can get her out without having to shoot him first. Myself, I don't care if he lives or dies, but the press get antsy when we kill these fuckers.'

Karen was still frowning over the note. 'His state of mind's impossible to assess without knowing more about what's been going on this morning. First of all, how did he get out of Parkhurst?'

Trench looked uncomfortable, chewing his bottom lip. Then he shrugged, as though getting past some kind of inhibition.

'Dressed as an officer, along with Jim Blake,' he said briskly. 'Jim took an extra night shift, saying he needed the overtime pay. They walked out together just before first light this morning. It's all there on the CCTV.'

'Someone must have seen them.'

'Yeah. But they were both in uniform, so the blokes monitoring the gate and the CCTV didn't realize who Spike was. On the film you can see Jim walking ahead of him – few inches away. They think Spike got hold of a weapon and forced Jim to get him out.'

'"They think",' Karen quoted, 'that sounds as though you disagree. Why?'

'Spike was behind Jim. If Spike had a weapon, why didn't Jim look at the cameras and signal for help? Wouldn't have been hard.'

The wire, Karen thought. *This* is why he wanted it.

Thank God she hadn't been stupid enough to bring it to him. Had someone else? His mother's niece, Peg, maybe, from the Goose Inn? No, it couldn't have been her; she visited only on the third Tuesday of every month. Maybe he'd got it from the spiral binding of a notebook. Would anyone let such a thing into a prison?

It didn't seem possible, but if Spike had got hold of a loop of wire from somewhere, he could have put it round Jim Blake's neck, ready to be tightened at any sign of resistance or movement in the direction of the security cameras. No one under such threat would risk making faces at them or calling for help in any other way. Karen was about to tell Trench about the wire when he said:

'Another theory is that Jim did it for . . .' He hesitated, then added with clear discomfort, 'affection.'

'Oh, nonsense,' Karen said. 'Jim must be, what, forty-five? Fifty? He's a career officer. He's not going to throw up his pay and pension for a man like Spike Falconer.'

'Close, though, weren't they? Jim's looked out for him since his first day on remand. We didn't know before, but we're getting information through now that says Jim's life outside his job is bloody empty. No family; no animals; no one. It's not unknown for one of the screws to . . .' Trench's loathing of the idea got the better of him, and he shook his head like someone attacked by clouds of midges.

'I don't think you need worry too much about that scenario,' Karen said. 'From the way Jim talked to me it's clear he'd never risk putting any kind of trust in Spike.'

'I hope you're right. Spike's always been a devious shite.'

'But . . .'

'Oh, I don't know, do I? And it doesn't matter now. What matters is getting that kid out alive, and . . .'

'Then someone needs to go into the house,' Karen said, suddenly boiling hot. She pulled off the dark-blue hooded sweatshirt. Its hem caught some of her long wet hair and tugged it painfully. 'If you're not prepared to go in, I'll do it.'

'. . . and not getting anyone else killed,' Trench finished. 'That includes you. No one's going in till we know he's not sitting inside that door with his shotgun across his knees. That's why I need you. Not for stupid heroics. What do you . . .?'

A loud bang, like two cars crashing head on, made them both

step back. Smoke billowed up from behind the house. A woman screamed, 'Ellie! Ellie! Let me go.'

'Get the parents out of here,' Trench yelled, beckoning to one of the fire officers.

Three of the others ran in the direction of the explosion. The panting red fire engine began to reverse towards a side road that ran up the hill and presumably gave access to the back of the house. More bangs, much less loud than the first, and then silence, except for the child's drilling screams.

Karen smelled burning wood and something acrid, chemical. She couldn't hear the sound of any water.

'Why aren't they using hoses?'

Trench looked at her, contempt pushing aside all the other ingredients of his expression. 'The explosion could've been electrically triggered. Water could make it worse.'

Karen wasn't listening to him. All she could hear were the screams. And all she could see was the figure of the child, straining against the ropes that held her arms up as though she was being crucified. Even without the noise, her panic would have been unmistakable.

'Even if she doesn't choke herself, she can't be left like this. Every minute she's in this much fear is causing damage to her mind that may be permanent. And maybe her brain too. She's young enough for that. Someone's *got* to go in, whatever the risk. You have . . .'

'Not now, Karen.' Trench turned away to talk to the chief fire officer.

If you didn't want my input, why the hell didn't you leave me out of this? she thought, looking at his broad back and weighing up her options.

Intensifying screams made Karen's decision for her. She ignored Trench and his colleagues and quietly walked in the wake of the fire engine, up a small steep side street and then left, following the line of a tall garden fence. She saw the gap the fire team had made as they crashed through and she followed them. Two officers passed her, returning to their chief.

'Doctor Taylor,' she said crisply to the one who waited, as though on guard. 'What was the explosion?'

'We're still not sure. Something chemical.'

'No sign of the perpetrator yet?'

'Not yet.'

'Fine,' she said, stepping past him towards the swinging back door. They'd obviously rammed it open.

'But you can't . . .'

'DCI Trench sent me.' She flashed the young officer a smile over her shoulder. 'Don't look so worried. I'm fully trained. Here, take this.'

Karen handed him her hooded sweatshirt. He took it automatically but he reached for his radio, too, so she ran inside. Even if Spike were here, and she didn't believe he could be, she thought she would be able to talk him down.

He wasn't sitting guard at the foot of the staircase as Trench had feared. Not letting herself think of guns or booby traps, or trip wires, she ran on up the stairs and headed for the door that must give access to the room where the child was tied up.

Gently knocking, calling 'Spike? Spike? It's me, Doctor Taylor' she turned the handle.

There was no resistance. The door wasn't even locked. Karen pushed it open and shot a glance to left, then right. There was no sign of any adult, although there were marks of large feet in the dust that covered the bare floorboards. The ropes tying the child were too tight to allow her to turn, but at the sound of Karen's footsteps, her screams grew louder still.

'It's all right,' Karen said, at her calmest and most professional. 'I'm here to help. My name's Karen. I'll have you out of here really soon. Hold on. I've just got to undo these ropes.'

The knots near the child's wrists had been pulled so tight by her struggles that Karen couldn't get her nails between the different strands of the tight cord. Holding down every thought that didn't have to do with the practicalities of the knots, and ignoring all the shouts from outside, she ran to the wall and found the other end of the rope, which had been tied around a large staple driven into the plaster. This knot wasn't nearly so tight. She broke two nails but had it undone in seconds and ran to the opposite side of the window.

Another nail cracked agonizingly far down and drew blood, but the knot yielded at last. Karen picked the child up, the cords still trailing from her excoriated wrists, and felt how hard her heart was pounding. Her small body was shaking, too, and she was clammy with sweat and worse. The strong ammoniac smell of urine rose from her clothes. The poor child had wet her knickers.

Who wouldn't? Karen thought, holding her more closely.

Murmuring meaningless but soft words over and over, Karen ran with her down the stairs, praying she wouldn't trip over the trailing ropes.

The fire officer was still jabbering into his radio as she ran out of the house.

'She's got her, sir,' Karen heard him say as she ran on. The ropes were wrapping themselves around her legs like snakes by the time she reached the fence. When she saw Trench she held the child out to him.

'What the fuck do you think you were doing?' he shouted.

The child cried out again, this time producing only a high keening sound that was full of absolute terror.

'Take her and shut up,' Karen said, keeping her temper with difficulty. 'There'll be time to talk later. I need to get these ropes off her wrists or someone's going for a burton.'

She forced the child into his arms and set to work on the knotted ropes. The flesh around them was puffy and the reddened skin had been scraped raw in several places. Using only the tips of her fingers so that she wouldn't make the child's pain worse, Karen tried the first of the knots.

'Leave it!' Trench ordered, spitting out the words. He bent down, still holding the child, and sat her on the low garden wall. Keeping his hand on her shoulder, he added: 'We've sent for a medic. Should be here any minute. He'll deal with everything here. Did you see Spike?'

'No. And no one tried to stop me getting her out. There's no furniture in the house so nowhere to hide.' Karen paused and let some of her anger emerge in mockery: 'I didn't go beyond the first floor – or down into the cellar – but I don't suppose any bogeymen are going to jump any troops you send in now.'

Trench's dark eyes blazed and between his lips she could see his bright white teeth jammed tightly against each other. From the sound they made he must be grinding down their pristine surfaces. His hand tightened on the child's shoulder. She screamed again.

'Let her go, Trench. *Let her go.*'

He looked down, saw what he was doing and pulled his hand away at once. The child's eyes were rolling so far back in the sockets they looked as if they might turn right over. And she was panting heavily. Her lips were working, too, and saliva dripped from the corner of her mouth.

'Don't be frightened,' Karen said quietly, ignoring the rage that was coming off Trench like waves of white heat. 'You're all right now. This man is a policeman. He's not angry with *you*. He'll keep you safe. OK?'

The child stopped rolling her eyes. Then she choked, turned her head slightly to one side and spewed out a horrible mixture of half-digested food and blood from where she'd bitten her tongue.

'Get hold of yourself and find the fucking doctor,' Karen hissed at Trench. 'And her mother. And some water.'

As he ran, his powerful thighs pumping like pistons, Karen turned back to the child, trying to remember the name Jenkins had used. At last it came to her.

'Your throat must be hurting, Ellie, so try not to scream. It just makes everything more sore. Can you breathe all right through your nose?'

After a while, the child nodded again. She was still shaking, but eventually a little colour seeped back into her face and her breathing became more regular; deeper, too. Karen cradled her as though she were a baby, stroking her hair and murmuring a repeated litany of comfort and safety until she was relieved at last.

Through all the bustle of doctor, child-protection officers, and desperately relieved parents, Karen was aware of Trench and his burning animosity. When they'd all gone, and the garden was empty, he had his chance and yelled at her, quite out of control, accusing her of lunatic irresponsibility in risking the hostage's life.

'You could have been killed, too, you stupid bitch. Not that that would have mattered.'

'Nor is it very likely,' Karen said, hardly even hearing his stress-driven insults because she was quite as angry as he.

She gathered her thick blonde hair together with both hands and twisted it into a self-restraining knot at the back of her head, as though she couldn't bear to have it flying free while he insulted her.

'The child was in far more danger than me and you were leaving her to suffer. Couldn't you see there was no time to fuck around with bloody health and safety crap?' Anger – or maybe fear – had always made Karen's language lapse into what Granny would have called 'filth'.

'Irresponsible. Dangerous and fucking unprofessional.'

'You're not used to having your orders disobeyed, are you?' Karen said more moderately.

She felt retrospective fear rush through her as the adrenaline that had kept her going drained away. But she wasn't going to let him see any hint of weakness.

'I don't work for you, so I don't have to do what you tell me,' she added. 'Now, your PC Jenkins said he'd drive me home as soon as you'd finished with me. I'd like to go. And I need my sweatshirt.' She could see it chucked into a shrub beside the back door.

'He's too busy,' Trench said, gesturing towards the house, from which issued the sound of many pairs of feet trampling on uncovered wooden floors. 'We've got more important things to do than get you home. Like collecting any evidence you didn't corrupt, trampling around like a stupid amateur. Wait here. I'll let you know when someone's free to drive you.'

'Don't be so childish,' she said. 'Just because I showed you up by getting Ellie safely out. I'll make my own way home.'

When Karen had rescued her sweatshirt from the hedge and started to walk down into the town to find a taxi, she felt as though her legs were made of wet spaghetti. If it hadn't been for the tightness of the denim around her thighs, she thought she might have fallen over. The small pain of yesterday's blister on her heel increased with every step. Forcing herself on, she made it down to the old chain ferry floating bridge to cross the River Medina into West Cowes.

Even when she'd disembarked and was leaning against a blessedly sturdy supporting wall, she looked back to make sure Trench hadn't followed.

He hadn't. Still sulking presumably. She reminded herself that no one was dead and the child was safe over and over again until she'd controlled the trembling in her legs. Then she went on into the crowds milling all over the town and forced her way through the pedestrianized High Street towards the point where she thought she'd once seen a taxi rank.

The air was thick with the smells of suncream and burgers and frying onions. People were yelling in dozens of languages, calling out to each other, screaming with laughter, fighting the gulls for the most piercing sound of all. In the distance, between the buildings, over the bouncing shifting heads of the crowd, she could see

the tall white sails of the rows and rows of expensive yachts waiting for their races.

Her memory had let her down and she couldn't find the taxi
rank. Surely somewhere there must be a cab to take her home,
even in this nightmare of noise and colour and smell.

'Hey, why the long face? Isn't it great?' shouted a half-drunk
woman in the crowd, waving an ice-cream cone in Karen's face.

How could anyone be jaunting and roistering like this? They
were only a short journey from the scene of Ellie Bridger's trauma
and yet they obviously had not the slightest idea of what had
been happening to her. Or that a highly dangerous man could be
moving among them.

Presumably Trench's team and the town's authorities were keen
to keep it that way. Mayhem would follow any announcement
that a man known to be responsible for four killings and suspected of many more could be anywhere on the Island, probably
with a pocketful of wire snares as well as a sawn-off shotgun.

A spree killer on the loose.

Trench's lack of control seemed a little less outrageous as Karen
recognized everything he was facing now. Her own anger cooled
a little.

Conscious of the pound coins rattling against each other in her
sweatshirt pocket, she knew she needed to control her stress and
turned into a sandwich shop to buy some carbs for calm. It was
nearly twelve and all the morning's events had made her hungry.

Chewing on brown bread and cheese a few minutes later, she
made her way slowly back across the river and up the hill to the
yellow house, hobbling slightly because of the pain from her blister and planning to apologize to Trench.

When she got back there, she found he'd already gone, and
most of his team with him. Now there were only SOCOs, who
could be seen through the windows working methodically to pick
up all the dust and fibres that would one day prove who had been
in the house.

Most of it would be irrelevant. With a house for sale like this, estate agents and prospective purchasers would have been trampling through it for days, weeks probably, leaving evidence of every step and breath they'd taken. And Karen herself must have left all kinds of traces of her dash to rescue Ellie Bridger. But somewhere in the samples that were being so painstakingly collected would, presumably, be some of Spike's hairs, or a thread or two from his clothes, to prevent any defence lawyer trying to suggest that Spike had never been anywhere near the hostage or this house.

Outside, there was nothing to be seen except the 'For Sale' board and the marks of feet and tyre treads in the thin gravel of the forecourt.

Karen looked up at the windows and watched one of the officers delicately pick something from the wall with a pair of tweezers and drop it into an evidence bag. There was nothing for her to do here, and no point going into the house again. As Trench had already told her, she'd probably messed up most of the evidence they were hoping to find.

Discouraged, she tried to think herself into Spike's mind for some insight into why he had taken Ellie in the first place. As Karen had said to Charlie Trench, even before she'd discovered that Spike wasn't in the house guarding his hostage, he must have known today's kidnap would screw up any chance of a successful appeal. So what could he possibly have thought he'd get out of it?

Chapter 14

Roderick, the Elephant Man, was waiting outside the chalet when the taxi drew to halt soon after half past three. Just what I need now, Karen thought, fumbling in her pocket for money to pay the driver.

There wasn't enough change left and she couldn't find her wallet. Working through her memories of this morning, she realized she'd picked up her keys and her phone from the shelf by the door but hadn't taken the time to get her wallet from her bag.

'Can you hang on a minute?' she said to the driver. 'I've got plenty of money inside. Won't be long.'

She tried to open the car door, but he'd activated the central locking.

'I can't pay you if you don't let me out,' she said with forced patience. 'And I'm hardly going to run off into the woods. Come on. Let me out.'

He unlocked the doors with such a grudging, disbelieving grunt that she was sure he was a new arrival. No caulkhead would behave like this.

'Hi, Roderick,' she said, as she strode across the ridged dry mud. 'I'll be with you in a minute. Don't go.'

Not wanting either of them to follow her into the chalet, she kicked the door shut behind her and ran, hopping at every other pace to save the blister from worse abrasion, into her bedroom for the wallet. It was still at the bottom of her linen bookbag, exactly where she'd left it yesterday. She extracted a twenty-pound note and took it back to the car, holding out her hand for the change.

When the driver had completed an unnecessarily laborious three-point turn, she sat on the top step and stretched out her long legs in their now bagging and crumpled jeans, trying to smile at her unwanted visitor.

'How are you, Roderick? I haven't seen you for days. Sit down. It's lovely to be able to sit in the sun after all that rain, isn't it?'

'There was someone asking for you this morning. I thought you ought to know,' he said, still standing. He seemed very large as he loomed over her.

'Who? What did they look like?'

'Big. Red-haired.'

'Man or woman?' she said, thinking at once of Jim Blake. Had Spike let him go once they were away from Parkhurst? If so, why not go straight to the police for help? Why come here? There was nothing Karen could do for him that the police couldn't have done better.

'A man,' said Roderick. 'I said I'd seen you drive off with that young policeman first thing and that I didn't know when you'd be back. Was that all right?'

'Sure.' Given there were no secrets on the Island, it didn't much matter what he'd said.

'Then I told him to keep away and not bother you any more; that you were fine with your boyfriend here.' A surprisingly sly smile slid across Roderick's face. 'I didn't tell him your boyfriend had gone and that you were all alone again last night.'

Karen levered herself up off the step. She'd always known he watched her, but this was too much. She had a right to some privacy.

'Right,' she said briskly. 'I see. Thanks for telling me. I must work now. Goodbye.'

'That's all right. You haven't had any more trouble with your car, have you?'

'No. No, it's going fine now. And I won't get stuck in the mud again.'

'Good. I'll be shooting again tonight, so I'll bring you more rabbits in the morning. I know you don't usually get up till after eight, so I'll wait till then. Goodbye, Doctor Taylor.'

He waited a moment, as though he was expecting something from her, but she wasn't going to give him any encouragement. He turned and clumped down the steps in his old-fashioned brogues and eventually melted into the woods.

She licked her lips, working to tease out the various strands of her unease. Failing, she told herself the sensation of the terrified child panting in her arms and clinging to her had aroused all her own flight-or-fight responses and that there was nothing seriously wrong with Roderick's knowing everything she did. She went to finish the morning's shower and get rid of the smells of sick and urine that had impregnated her clothes. But before she took them off, she checked that all the windows were locked and the front and back doors bolted.

The thought of leaving the Island to stay with Will for the weekend was even more alluring than when he'd first suggested it. And now there was no Spike to visit in prison, she had no reason to delay. Maybe she should go first thing in the morning. Or even later today. Except that the afternoon and evening car ferries from Yarmouth were usually fully booked, and if she went back into Cowes to catch one of the Red Jets to Southampton, she'd have to leave her car behind. Better to stick to her original plan.

A shower, some strong tea, a large sticking plaster over her blisters and a siesta, and she'd be herself again.

Five minutes of hot water drumming down on her head wasn't nearly long enough to wash out all the morning's rage and fear, but it was all she got. Once again a tremendous banging on the front door wrenched her out of the shower. And once again, clad only in a towel and fat drops of water, she opened it to the police.

This time she was faced not with a nervous uniformed constable, but with DCI Trench himself, standing beside a scrawny-looking woman in her late twenties.

'Can't this wait?' Karen said, gesturing to her water-splattered shoulders. 'As you see, I'm busy.'

'No, it can't.' Trench's jaw was clenched so tight that the words were hardly comprehensible. 'Get some clothes on.'

'As I told you this morning, I am not under your orders.'

'Get some fucking clothes on. I can't talk to you in that state.'

Don't let the interviewee's tension or emotion make you display any of your own, Karen thought of telling him, as she remembered the advice of one of her first tutors. But it wasn't her job to help anyone who shouted at her like that, so she smiled with unusual languor, first at Trench then at his sidekick, whose gaunt face registered nothing except contempt and dislike.

'Give me a minute,' Karen said, addressing the woman rather than Trench. 'Make yourselves tea. The kettle's there by the sink, already hot so it won't take long to boil again. Teabags in the box on the shelf above. I won't be long.'

But when she came back four minutes later they were still standing where she'd left them.

'Even if you don't want tea, I do,' she said, moving towards the sink to fill the kettle. She saw that her long bare feet had left wet marks on the splintery wooden floor. Keeping her back to the unwanted visitors, she reached for the least stained of the old mugs and dropped a teabag into it. 'It's been a tough day so far.'

Then she did turn and, smiling again, asked what they wanted.

'The whole story,' Trench said, still through clenched teeth.

Karen worried about the stress chemicals his brain must be generating and the ailments to which they would probably give rise.

'Sit down, won't you?' she said. 'What story?'

'About why you helped Spike Falconer escape, what he is intending to do next, and where he is now. And why the fucking-hell you ever got personally involved with a psychopath like that.'

Karen laughed because the accusations were so absurd. Trench's skin looked as though it was thickening and darkening around the resurgent stubble, and his round dark eyes were like red flags warning of danger. His sidekick obviously thought so too because she moved uncomfortably and said:

'This is serious, Doctor Taylor. We're going to have to take you in to answer some questions.'

'Arrest me, you mean?' Karen was still incredulous.

'If you don't cooperate, yes.'

'But why?' All temptation to laugh had gone. Karen had even forgotten her thirst for tea.

'Because you knew Spike wasn't in the house this morning when you burst in to "rescue" that child.' Trench was still too angry to moderate his voice. 'You knew you'd be in no danger. Otherwise you'd never have gone in. Therefore you knew about the kidnap in advance. Therefore you probably know where Spike is now.'

Karen couldn't believe what she was hearing. She opened her mouth to explain the obvious – that no professional in her position would ever contemplate helping anyone escape from prison.

'What can you tell us,' said the sidekick suddenly, 'about a ceramic sushi knife?'

Trench flung her a glance of furious reproof, but Karen didn't mind answering. She thought the distraction might give him a chance to cool down.

'Plenty.' She flicked a glance towards the dark-blue silk box, still standing on the shelf over the sink. 'But shouldn't you introduce yourself if you're going to interview me?'

The other woman nodded impatiently and said: 'DS Eve Clarke. Now: the sushi knife.'

'It was a present from the man who came to stay with me last weekend. Will Hawkins. He's a neurosurgeon based in Sussex. DCI Trench has met him. But how do you know anything about the knife, and why would you care?'

DS Clarke's eyes gleamed with satisfaction and, when she spoke, her voice was full of fake sweetness:

'So you've had it only a few days, have you?'

'That's right. Again, why are you interested?'

'Did you ask him to bring it here from the mainland?'

'No. It was a complete surprise and nothing to do with you,' Karen said, before she remembered Spike's request for a loop of wire. 'Unless you're mad enough to think that I . . .'

Trench came right up in front of her, to stand so close she could feel the warmth of his breath on the skin around her eyes. He smelled of powerful peppermint. Either he'd just washed out his mouth or there was gum stashed somewhere under his tongue.

'We found a sushi knife an hour ago, covered in Jim Blake's blood. There are prints on it, too. The SOCO thinks they belong to at least two separate people.'

'Well, they won't be mine,' Karen said. 'If you've found a ceramic knife, it can't have anything to do with me. Mine is here.'

'You had it in your bag when you saw Spike on Monday, didn't you?' DS Clarke said, hectoring and obstinate, without even fake sweetness in her voice now.

Karen felt as though making them see reason was like trying to pick up a needle in boxing gloves.

'You knew you'd fool the scanner because there's no metal in those knives,' DS Clarke went on. 'That's why you asked your boyfriend to bring one, wasn't it? No shop on the Island sells them. We checked as soon as we found it. So you *had* to get it from the mainland.'

'Oh, don't be ridiculous.' Karen moved away, glad of the instant sense of freedom, and reached up for the box. 'I haven't taken *my* sushi knife anywhere. Look.'

Pushing the tiny bone toggles out of their loops, she lifted the lid and saw only the smoother silk of the lining and the shape of the knife pressed into it.

'Oh, shit!' She looked back at the pair of them, almost forgiving their suspicions of her. 'Someone's taken it. A burglar.'

'Don't make me laugh,' said Trench, with his jaw so tight that the words were barely recognizable. 'The oldest excuse in the fucking book.'

'Have you had a break in?' said DS Clarke, pretending innocence. 'I don't remember seeing any reports.'

'I didn't report it because I didn't know the knife had gone. But it's more than possible. I've heard prowlers around this place several times. And one night when I went out to investigate, I saw a man running away. I put it down to a shy weird neighbour prowling about, but maybe it was someone who'd been watching me and assessing my things. What is it you call it? Casing the joint?'

'Not any more.' Trench was talking through tightly closed teeth, which made his Geordie voice sound very odd.

'Reported the prowler?' said DS Clarke, sounding as though she expected the answer no.

Karen shook her head. 'I didn't want to be or look pathetic. And what harm was some sad watcher likely to do me?'

'Then have you found any signs of a break-in? Smashed window maybe? Forced lock? Isn't there anything you can give us to support your story? We're going to need something you know, Doctor Taylor.'

'I haven't looked, DS Clarke. Why don't you? The chalet's not exactly big. Search wherever you want. Bring in a scene-of-crime team. I don't care.'

The sergeant looked towards Trench as though for permission. He nodded, then flung himself down in the bigger of the two easy chairs.

'Why'd you choose Falconer to research?' he said, pretending he was calm again.

His moderate voice didn't trick Karen for a second. His vocal chords might have relaxed a little, but there were still pumping bumps on either side of his jaw, and the rest of his body language was as aggressive and suspicious as it had been since they arrived.

'A mixture of things,' she said, keeping her own voice calm. 'As you probably know, I've already interviewed five convicted murderers with Dangerous Severe Personality Disorder and I was looking for another subject. My professor picked out Spike as one of several possibles, and I was keen to come back to the Island so I agreed. I told you I used to holiday here as a child. I knew this place was available and free – my mother inherited it and, even though she never uses it, she hasn't bothered to sell it.'

Karen looked around the damp unwelcoming chalet and wasn't surprised to see scepticism in Trench's hot eyes.

'As I don't have much spare money, that was a lure in itself,' she went on. 'All I had to do was get the electricity and water switched back on. And I was interested in Spike's story, even outside my research into DSPD. I've always been curious about the effects of adoption. His case seemed to me an extreme example of the possible drawbacks for both child and adoptive parents.'

Trench chewed his lower lip, still watching her with hostility.

'You know,' she said casually, 'you're not going to find my fingerprints on that knife. I've never taken it out of the box. I may have rested one fingertip on the blade, but I've never held it. If there are prints on the handle, they're not mine.'

'Will you let us take your prints?'

'Sure. Why not?'

'Not that it'll change anything. Smears show someone handled the knife in gloves.'

'It may not prove my innocence,' she said, enjoying herself for the first time since PC Jenkins had wrenched her from her morning's shower. 'But that doesn't matter unless you can prove my guilt. Much more important than all this is: how's the child, Ellie Bridger?'

'Traumatized, of course. Why d'you need to ask? Who would not be traumatized if they'd been kidnapped by a murderous psychopath, tied up so tight their arms are going to take weeks to recover, and screamed non-stop for nearly an hour?'

Karen waited for him to thank her for saving the child from even worse, but he was far too angry for that. Angry and almost certainly humiliated too because she'd done the obvious thing while he and his men had hung back, pleading health-and-safety regulations.

DS Clarke came back. 'What's in the roof space above the twin bedroom? There's a trapdoor I can't open.'

'Boxes, damp, cobwebs, stuff,' Karen said. 'Nothing important.'

'Then why's it locked?' said Clarke.

'It's not.'

'So how d'you access it?'

Trench was jittering with suspicion now. Karen made a face that was supposed to tell him not to be so stupid, then turned towards DS Clarke.

'There's a long rod under the left-hand bed. You push the end of that into the small round catch at the side of the trapdoor. It flips up and a ladder descends. I'll show you.'

When she'd brought down the ladder, she left DS Clarke to search the mildewed dusty roof space on her own. Back in the kitchen-living room, Karen saw that Trench had abandoned the easy chair and was prowling about, opening cupboard doors and peering behind the few large pieces of furniture. He looked round at the sound of Karen's step.

'You mentioned blood on the knife,' she said. 'Jim Blake's blood. How do you know it's his? You haven't had time to get the samples to the lab yet, let alone expect results, even if you've got the money to pay for extra-fast tests. And it didn't sound to me as though your budget's over-generous if you couldn't even search for the bodies you're sure are dumped around the island.'

His jaw clenched again.

'Probability.'

'Is there much blood? Do you think he was badly hurt?'

'A man like Jim Blake isn't going to release a dangerous offender without a fight. A hard fight. We need to find him.' Trench glanced upwards, as though he couldn't stop himself. 'I just hope he's still alive and not lying in some hidden place with slices cut all over him.'

'You're not really telling me you think I've got his body in my roof space, are you?' Karen said, tempted to laugh in spite of her knowledge of what Spike could be doing, at loose on the Island. 'That's absurd! You're wasting time. If Jim has been badly hurt, he'll need help. Have you talked to any of my neighbours yet? Roderick, in the nearest chalet, told me he saw a large red-headed man hanging around here this morning while I was with you. Sounded a lot like Jim Blake to me. And Jan from the bungalow nearest the main road is a bit of a watcher, too. Talk to her. If there was anything to see, she'll have seen it.'

'I already know he was here. Both your neighbours confirmed it. Why d'you think we came to talk to you? What's Spike done with him now? And where is *he*? Come on, Doctor Taylor. Give it up. We'll get the truth in the end. Save us all a lot of hassle and tell me now.'

'There's no point talking to you if you won't listen to me,' Karen said with more patience than she felt. 'I have no idea where Spike is or what he's doing. But if I were you I wouldn't be talking to innocent bystanders, I'd be out there searching until I'd found him, hoping I'd get to him before he killed someone else.'

'Christ! You're hard.'

'Hard? You must be joking.' Karen was now so angry herself that the words came out of her mouth like lead pellets exploding from a shotgun cartridge. 'Right now I'm so hacked off I can't think about anything except getting you out of here.'

Trench turned his face away, as though he couldn't bear even to look at her.

'What about all those CCTV cameras around the prison?' she

went on, a little more calmly. 'I don't mean the ones by the gate you talked about this morning, but the rest. There has to be something to see if you can be bothered to get past your loopy ideas about me and do something practical to find Spike. And Jim.'

'Don't take the piss.' Trench stood up, moving out of the low chair in one smooth movement. 'Of course we've got people looking at the CCTV tapes. You better come down to the station now. Identify the sushi knife and make a full statement.'

'Fair enough,' Karen said, holding on to her temper only because she could at last see signs of the anxiety that must be driving his aggression. 'But can't it wait until tomorrow? I told you: I'm hacked off. Exhausted, too. And I've got blisters the size of dinner plates on my feet. I was just beginning to wind down. Give me the rest of the day and I'll do whatever you want tomorrow.'

She looked around the dismal chalet. 'After all, I'm not going anywhere.'

He paused long enough to show her who was boss here. 'It can't wait. We'll take you.'

'I'll drive myself,' she said. 'I'm not giving you the chance of keeping me hanging about again. I hope you've got people searching every boat at Cowes that could be ready to remove Spike from the Island.'

He didn't comment, even though she paused to let him speak, so she went on again.

'And interviewing Peg at the Goose Inn, who sounds like his one support here. And the child, Ellie, too. However little you think you need her to tell you anything, she'll be bound to have information that could help – if you go about asking in the right way.'

DS Clarke had returned and was fastidiously washing her filthy hands at the sink.

'The child's refusing to talk,' she said, rubbing at the olive-oil soap as though determined to make it foam.

'Oh, for God's sake! Why didn't you say so?' Karen said. 'I could help there. Really help. I'm trained to interview difficult subjects. Use me for something productive, instead of playing stupid games of cop and suspect.'

'You are a suspect. You don't get to talk to witnesses,' said Trench.

'That's ridiculous. Just because someone's stolen a knife from here, you . . .'

'Like I said when we first got here, you knew you weren't in danger when you got the kid. You'd never have gone in if you thought Spike was in that house like I said he was. You . . . Fuck it!'

He swung round on one heel.

'Go in her car with her,' he said to DS Clarke just before he stormed out of the chalet, banging the door behind him. The whole thin wall shivered under the impact.

A second later he slammed his car door even harder and revved the engine. Karen hoped he'd skid off the road and get bogged down in the still sticky mud of the woods. But she was afraid he was too efficient for that.

'OK,' she said, turning to DS Clarke, who was now drying her hands. 'We'd better get this over with. Is he always so uncontrolled?'

Satisfaction seemed to plump up the sergeant's face, making it less cadaverous. 'No, but he'd been telling everyone how wonderful you are and how with your help we were going to clear up all the Island's unsolved violent crimes. Now he's discovered you're even worse than we all warned him you would be, and he knows he looks like a tit.'

Chapter 15

Karen assumed she'd be interviewed by DCI Trench himself, given that she was not under arrest, and thought she could make him see reason, so when she was asked if she wanted a lawyer she said no. But in the interview room, she was confronted with DS Clarke and a strange man in plain clothes, who introduced himself as DI Baker from the mainland.

He reminded her that she'd declined legal representation and asked whether she'd changed her mind. Knowing of her own absolute innocence, and not prepared to wait out the hours it would take to get a lawyer here, she said calmly:

'I don't need a lawyer. I have nothing to hide.'

'Very well,' said DI Baker. 'Can you identify this?'

He pushed forward a plastic evidence bag containing a sushi knife with some brown smears defacing the pristine whiteness of the ceramic blade. If they were blood, it had dried a while ago.

'It is a sushi knife,' she said deliberately, looking at the spooling tape in the recording machine. 'I was recently given one just like it. My own has gone missing. I cannot be certain this is the same one, but it could be.'

He led her through all the questions Eve Clarke had already asked about possible intruders to the chalet, then said:

'Tell me about your relationship with Spike Falconer.'

'He agreed to answer the questions I wanted to ask for a paper I'm writing about men who have been diagnosed with Dangerous

Severe Personality Disorder. He hasn't yet told me anything of any significance and we've barely touched on his crime. Each time I've raised the subject, he has denied having anything to do with it.'

She paused to pick the right words to express precisely what she wanted to say, then carried on:

'One day last week when I was with him, he was describing how he used to snare rabbits when he lived rough. He volunteered to show me how it was done and asked me to bring him an eighteen-inch length of wire. Naturally I declined, but I wonder now whether he was planning his escape then and wanted to make a garrotte so he could force Jim Blake to . . .'

'That's absurd,' said Eve Clarke in a voice of blistering contempt.

'May I ask,' said DI Baker in a much cooler tone, 'why you didn't mention this at any time today when you were talking to my colleagues? You had plenty of chances.'

He shuffled through some sheets of paper lying on the table in front of him.

'I have reports here of your discussions with DCI Trench alone this morning and with both DCI Trench and DS Clarke this afternoon. There's no mention of you telling either of them that Falconer wanted a garrotte. Did they forget what you said when they wrote these up for me?'

'No,' Karen said, still in control. 'Each time I thought of it something else took over and I was distracted.'

'Or else you've just dreamed it up in an attempt to make yourself look innocent. When did Falconer ask you to bring this knife into the prison for him?'

'He never did. As I've said before. Even if he had asked me to, I wouldn't have agreed, just as I didn't agree to bring him any wire. I'm not a fool, Inspector. Nor a criminal.'

'Can you explain why Spike Falconer has been so cooperative with you when he has never spoken to anyone else who has tried to interview him in prison?'

'No.'

'Can you explain why he was so upset by you missing one appointment that, I'm told, he nearly started a riot in the prison and could have been injured?'

'No.' Karen folded her arms across her chest.

'Doctor Taylor, this attitude is not going to help.' DI Baker's cool voice was becoming tighter, as though he was impatient to get some revealing reaction from her. 'We need . . .'

'There's nothing I can give you,' she said, clutching at her fast-dwindling patience. 'You can ask me questions all night, but the only answers will be the true ones: that I had no part in Spike Falconer's escape and that I have no idea where he is now. Or what his plans are. Incidentally, have you identified the caller who rang in to say they'd seen Spike with Ellie Bridger this morning? Presumably he – or she   would be able to give you useful evidence. And what about the footprints in the dust of the house where he tied her up? They must tell you something.'

Eve Clarke flinched, as though she couldn't bear the way Karen had pinpointed an obvious weakness in their investigation. But DI Baker showed no reaction at all. In an instant he was boring away at Karen again, repeating his earlier question:

'Why was Spike Falconer so cooperative with you when he has never spoken to anyone else who has tried to interview him in prison?'

Pain was biting at Karen's head and she knew she must be dehydrated, but she was too angry to ask for water or tea. If she lost her thread and let herself become distracted, she might say something stupid, something that these two officers would latch on to and use to make her look shifty.

She wished she had Trench here. In spite of today's rage, he was a reasonable man, and they had established real contact. She'd have been able to reach him, to make him understand what she'd been doing with Spike and how she could never have done anything to help spring him from prison.

The risk Spike represented to everyone in his family and everyone who had ever been involved with him was big enough, but, if he were the type of serial killer Trench suspected, he would also be a danger to every woman on the Island. Karen still wasn't sure she believed in Claire Wilkins and the other victims, but she would never have . . .

'Doctor Taylor!' DI Baker's voice was sharp, angry, demanding.

'Sorry. I missed your question. What did you say?'

The only sensible thing to do now was to say 'no comment' to every question and every spiteful dig they used to try to make her react. She hoped Trench *was* combing the Island for Spike.

DI Baker's voice went on and on: 'Where have you arranged to meet Spike? Is he coming to your chalet? Have you made arrangements with a yacht-owner to get him off the Island? Or are you intending to escort him onto one of the ferries?'

Karen didn't want to dignify such stupid questions with any kind of answer, so she just looked at him. He repeated them, word for word.

'Don't be stupid,' she said at last, rubbing her sweaty forehead.

The skin felt gritty and she knew she must be smearing dirt over her face. Words flittered into her mind, swooping and disappearing like flies. She couldn't catch any of them. Somehow she had to say something sensible.

'He's a research subject.' She squeezed out the words, feeling as though her tongue was twice its normal size. 'Killer of four people we know of and probably many, many more.'

'What do you mean many more?' DI Baker's voice was even more insistent, acting like hot wires penetrating her aching head. 'Has he told you of other crimes? Why haven't you reported them?'

'Ask DCI Trench. It's his idea. He asked my opinion.' Karen didn't care whether she was dropping Trench into it. He deserved anything he got after doing this to her.

*

After three hours, Karen could feel her balance going. Thirst had made her throat not only dry but sore, too, and the headache was distracting her. At times she couldn't work out what she'd actually been asked, although now that she was answering nothing but 'no comment', it didn't really matter.

To ask for a break might give them the opportunity of locking her up, and she didn't want that. Her only hope was to wear down their patience so far that they gave in first. But there was an expression in Eve Clarke's eyes that was disturbing. Eve showed more than contempt now; there was a kind of satisfaction in her face, as though Karen's exhaustion and heavily suppressed distress gave her real pleasure.

And all the time Spike was out and running free with God knew what weapons available to him.

'Thank you, Doctor Taylor,' said DI Baker suddenly and for no apparent reason, 'that will do for the moment. You're free to go.'

Karen felt numb. Her brain had slowed to a hedgehog's pace, and every joint was aching. She sat dumbly on her chair, looking from one to the other.

'We have no more questions for the moment,' DI Baker said, speaking very slowly as to a young child or a foreigner, 'and so you may return home. I understand you came in your own car. Are you fit to drive?'

'What?' she said, before running her swollen tongue around her sandpapery mouth. 'Yes. Yes, I'm fine to drive.'

Energy was returning and with it a consciousness of how awful this process must be for anyone less confident, less certain of their innocence than she. Presumably anyone at all worried wouldn't have rejected the offered legal assistance, but she was surprised to find how disturbed she was, how unsettled.

'Thank you,' she said, regaining some of her self-respect. She could feel a faint hint of energy returning as she stood on one foot, shaking the blood back into the other, and rolled her head on her neck to ease some of the stiffness.

'We'll be in touch. DS Clarke will show you out. Oh, by the way, are you planning to leave the Island?'

'Only for the weekend,' Karen said, prepared to be professionally cooperative. 'I can leave you my phone numbers.'

'I'd rather you stayed.'

'No chance. I need some time off.'

'I could arrest you.'

'I doubt it.' Karen checked her watch and was amazed to find it was still not quite half-past six. She felt as though she'd been on the go for twenty-four hours already. 'But try if you like. Then I will get a lawyer, and it'll be an outsider you can't bully.'

'That's slander,' he said and left her with Eve Clarke.

A large blue plastic tub of cooled drinking water stood just outside the interview room. Karen paused there to fill cup after cup with water, draining them so fast she almost choked.

DS Clarke looked on with amusement, which was unbearable.

'Presumably,' Karen said, 'since you're so sure I'm in league with Spike, you'll have someone watching my chalet tonight?'

DS Clarke shrugged. 'If it was down to me I would.'

'Then tell them if my lights are on I'm good for a cup of tea whenever they want it.'

Back in the chalet four hours after she'd been wrenched away, Karen opened the fridge door, wincing at the scrawching sound the ancient seals made as they let go, and wished she had some sushi ready prepared. The lightness of the raw fish and the sharpness of the accompanying pickles would have cleared her palate of all the stuffiness of the police station.

But there was nothing in the fridge except the remains of the bacon, which she didn't fancy, the end of a brown loaf, a wilting lettuce and some basic mousetrap cheese. They'd have to do.

She assembled a sandwich, thinking that some mayonnaise would make it slipperier and easier to swallow. The memory of

Ellie Bridger, roped and screaming, made Karen choke as she tried to get the food down.

When she'd washed up the plate and knife she'd used, she felt so wiped out she decided to go to bed, early though it was.

DS Clarke had left the trapdoor open and the sight of the black hole in the ceiling seemed threatening. Karen grabbed the torch and climbed the squeaking metal ladder.

Shining the light around the space, she saw it was the same as it had been when she and Aidan had played up here in defiance of all Granny's rules. Old boxes of photographs and papers were ranged against the walls. They must be pulp now, after decades of damp air and the recent flooding from the leaky roof.

Smells of many different moulds tickled her nostrils. Cobwebs hung from the rafters in festoons of sticky threads. And something scuttled away from the light. Too big to be a beetle, but luckily much too small to be rat, she thought. Probably a mouse. Inevitable really in a place like this.

She retreated, switching off the torch, and sent the ladder swinging up and out of the way, before pulling the trapdoor closed after it. Her hands were filthy now, and probably the rest of her as well, but she couldn't face another shower after today's two interruptions.

Once she'd washed at the kitchen sink, she made a mug of tea and took it to bed. Tonight the various academic journals seemed wrong. She wanted comfort. A phone call to Will or Aidan would have done the trick, but she'd have to go out again for that and she was tired.

She fell back on Kipling, reading the familiar adventures of Toomai of the elephants and then the story about the white seal. Soothed by the familiar language and rhythms, she read more slowly, occasionally letting her eyelids close, feeling as though she too was riding the gently swelling ocean.

A gun blasted in the distance and she sat up in shock, one hand clamped over her hard-beating heart, until she remembered

Roderick and his rabbits. Sinking back against the pillows, she relaxed. Somehow the idea of shot rabbits was no longer disgusting. If he dumped corpses on her in the morning she'd know they were kindly meant.

A vague memory disturbed her. Someone talking about how they hated kindness. Who had it been?

She frowned, ideas trickling into her mind and being rejected. Max Pitton? It was his sort of thing. But no. No! It was Charlie Trench, that first day at the Goose Inn. Someone had phoned him, clearly warning him against Karen. Memories sharpened. He'd addressed her as Eve. Eve Clarke? Had she had it in for Karen even then?

Karen's mind didn't turn up any answers, so she let it drift back to the rabbits. This time she might cook them instead of waiting until they were inedible and getting rid of them in an inconspicuous rubbish bin, as she'd done with the last lot. Stewed with onions and wild thyme. It sounded like something Titania might have said. Or Bottom or someone. Onions and wild thyme. And wild garlic too.

With her mind shifting and drifting, Karen reached out a hand to switch off the bedside light, then rolled over, pulling the checked blanket higher up under her chin.

Something was scratching near her head. Scratching and swishing. Instantly alert, her body flooding with adrenaline, Karen lay and listened. Someone was outside the bedroom window, trying to get in.

Footsteps, heavy but careful, sounded from outside. Her eyes swivelled, following the direction of the steps. Whoever he was, he was circling the chalet, feeling for any weakness he could use to get to her.

Karen reached for her phone. Her brain was working far too smoothly for her to forget the lack of service here. Somehow she was going to have to get the phone out of the chalet and up the twisty road to the point in the woods where it would operate again.

The intruder was at the front now, and it sounded as though he was working at the lock in the main door. Even if he managed to open that, there would be the top and bottom bolts to deal with. Had she tucked their stubby handles down, holding them firmly in place? Or had she left them standing proud, so that a determined person with some kind of angled tool stuck through the letterbox could push the barrels through their staples?

Would it matter anyway? What if he lost patience and simply kicked in the door panels? It wouldn't be hard, but it would be loud. And so far he seemed to be trying to avoid too much noise.

Was this the man who'd stolen her knife? Or was it Roderick, frustrated in his rabbit hunt, wanting . . .

As her brain whirred through the possibilities, Karen remembered the police. Could it be one of them, as suspicious of her as Trench had been? She listened more carefully, trying to assess the quality of the noises he was making.

No, it couldn't be the police. Too surreptitious. Any of them would have come in with all the legitimate noise of a man doing his duty.

Silently sliding out of bed, she zipped on her jeans and pulled a sweatshirt over her head and bent to stuff her feet into trainers.

She looked up towards the trapdoor. Granny had had the hearing of a bushbaby or a bat, but even so Aidan had learned to open the trap and let down the ladder without waking her. The two of them had made a private nest up in the roof space, only later working out how to lift the felt that lined the roof, then the weakly attached shingles, so they could let themselves down over the side of the chalet.

Karen had the trapdoor open moments later and winced as the old ladder squeaked as it swung down. She paused, one foot on the bottom rung and her hand on the rail. In her own silence, she could hear him still patiently working on the front-door lock. He was definitely no police officer.

Climbing the ladder took moments and she paused again when

she'd swung it up behind her. The safest course was probably to stay here in the old nest and simply wait him out. But she was too wired for that.

She secured the trap behind her, then eeled her way along the rough joists, taking care never to let her weight settle between them, to the corner of the roof, where the felt and the shingles had once been loosened.

Conveniently the corner was on the opposite side of the chalet from the front door. She pressed her fingers upwards and was flooded with triumph when the felt lifted.

The shingles creaked. When she paused for safety, she could hear that the intruder had paused too. Then a woodpecker began hammering at a tree trunk and she blessed it. Hearing more scraping sounds, she knew the intruder was back at work. She pushed on, shoving the loosened shingle right away.

She was bigger now by a good six stone and three foot six than she'd been when Aidan had first brought her up here, but the old technique came back to her. Placing her palms either side of her body as she stood on the joist, she pulled herself upwards. Her upper-body strength, fired by the danger, met the challenge and her head was out and into the fresh darkness, when a cry made her flinch.

Had he seen her head, silhouetted against the stars? Then the cry came again, too animal, too frightened and too small to come from a grown man. She pulled on, trying to get her shoulders through the gap.

The space was too small, too tight. This was like a dream she'd had throughout her childhood of climbing through suffocatingly small passages to a chamber only just big enough to curl into. Her arms were tight and the effort was turning to pain. Her muscles burned.

The force had to change now from pulling to pushing. She drove the muscles on, twisting so that her shoulders were diagonally across the gap. They emerged. This was getting easier. She had one knee on the edge, then the other.

Splintering sounds came from below her. He must have lost patience and be kicking his way in. Less worried about her own noise, she swivelled in the old way so that she was lying face down, her sore hands clinging to the edge of the next shingle. She let her legs slide down until she was spreadeagled against the roof.

The crashing at ground level was getting louder. He'd definitely lost his temper. Triumph at her escape turned back into fear. Real fear this time. If he was this angry now, he could do anything. She let her hands unclench and slithered down the roof slope and over the edge to fall on the soft weedy earth in what had once been a flower bed.

Now she ran, straight into the woods. She'd skirt round in a while to get back to the road, when she was sure he couldn't see her.

Trees clustered all round. She should have brought a torch and a compass. The stars weren't enough to show her anything but grey trunks in all directions. Whirling, she tried to make herself stop, to be still enough to work out which way she was facing.

It's only two minutes since you left the chalet, she told herself. You can't get lost in two minutes.

She heard running steps and panting from behind her and forced her feet to stay still, shoving her right hand under her sweatshirt so she could bring a bunch of the soft cotton material up to her face to muffle her own breathing.

He didn't say anything. Even if he'd yelled threats at her he would have seemed less menacing.

The steps began again, coming closer, rustling as his feet pushed aside the nettles, brambles and ivy that made up the undergrowth. Karen had the phone in her right hand as well as the bunch of fabric so she could use her left to feel ahead of her in the murk. Her skin met the hard roughness of tree bark and she clung on, still breathing through her sweatshirt. The cold on her bare, sweating midriff was weirdly comforting. If she kept absolutely still and soundless he might go, just as the debt-collectors had once been tricked into abandoning their hunt.

And then steps sounded ahead of her as well and her small hope died. The man behind her moved in the undergrowth, but he didn't retreat. No one spoke. Then a light blasted out from the trees and Roderick's voice called:

'Doctor Taylor? Is that you? I can't see your face. Is it you? Doctor Taylor?'

The man behind her moved on towards the beam, as though it was encouraging him. Karen couldn't see Roderick because of the brightness of the light he was shining directly into her eyes. She knew she must be clearly obvious to the man behind her, so she swung round to face him.

Spike was coming nearer and nearer, directly in the path of the light. Brightness glittered on his golden hair and made his eyes shine. His lips were drawn right back into the worst of his smiles, baring his teeth. And his hands were raised and curved, like claws, at chest height.

Sandwiched between the two of them, visible now to both, Karen let her sweatshirt drop. She was still a long way from any possible phone reception and trapped too far from the chalet to find any kind of refuge – or weapon – there.

Spike speeded up. Only feet away from her now, he was muttering in a low vicious susurrus. He seemed to want to drive her towards the light.

Were they partners in this? Had it been Roderick who'd stolen the sushi knife and got it to Spike? Was this all part of a long-planned plot? Karen's mind churned as fast and sickeningly as the undigested sandwich in her gut.

'Don't . . .' she started and, stepping back, tripped over a bramble cable and crashed down on the ground just as someone's shotgun exploded.

Chapter 16

'Doctor Taylor. Doctor Taylor.' Roderick's deep voice sounded terrified, breathless. Someone was groaning. 'Doctor Taylor. Are you all right?'

Karen levered herself up on one elbow, feeling a sharp pain in her shoulder muscles and pins and needles in her crushed hand.

'I'm OK,' she called back, grimacing. 'See to the man. I think you must have got him.'

'Good. I only had one cartridge left, and I could see he was coming for you.' Roderick was standing over her now, holding out one hand to help her up. The other was encumbered with his shotgun. A powerful smell of dead animal hung about him, and cordite wafted out from the twin barrels. 'When you fell I thought he'd hurt you.'

Karen ignored his offered hand and pushed herself off the ground. 'We must see how bad he is.'

Roderick swung his light so it split the murky darkness, picking up bright pinpoints of reflection that must be the eyes of small cowering animals. At last the beam revealed Spike, clutching his gut and writhing on the ground. Karen saw blood, bright and thin, leaking between his dirty fingers, and grabbed her phone.

'We must get an ambulance. Stay with him while I run up the road to where I can phone. If I can ever find the fucking road.'

'Take my light,' Roderick said calmly from a kneeling position by Spike. 'He's not badly hurt. I only caught him in the side. Peppered him. But he is bleeding.'

'I know. Stay with him. Don't let him move.'

The torch helped her find the road easily, only about fifteen feet away from the spindly tree she'd clung to, and she ran up it towards Reception Point. Soon her lungs were burning and her eyes smarting and she knew she should have retreated to the chalet for her car keys and driven here.

At last she reached the right bend in the road, pumped 999 into the phone, and reported the existence of a man peppered with shotgun pellets, lying bleeding in the woods.

The despatcher promised an ambulance within ten minutes, so Karen waited to guide them to the place where Spike lay and took the opportunity to phone the number DCI Trench had given her the first time they'd met, when she'd been a respected professional and not a suspect. The idea of dragging him out of sleep gave her intense satisfaction after the day's punishment.

His voice was gratifyingly fogged.

'DCI Trench? It's Doctor Taylor here. Spike Falconer is lying about quarter of a mile away from me in the woods near my chalet, incapacitated by a shotgun wound. I thought you should know.'

'What? You . . . How . . .?'

'I've called an ambulance,' she said calmly, 'and they'll be here in minutes. Actually, I can hear them now. I thought you might want to talk to him while you can.'

'Is he dying?' Trench's voice was crisping up as he came to full wakefulness. 'Who's with him?'

'Roderick, my neighbour, who you may know as the Elephant Man. He shot Spike in defence of me. At least I think so. And, no, I don't think the wounds are serious.'

The idea that the two men could have been working together, with Spike herding her nearer the shotgun barrels, made her throat constrict all over again. If she hadn't tripped would she have taken the pellets rather than Spike? Memories of their antiphonal advice to stew rabbit with onions and wild garlic tightened her larynx even more.

Then she remembered Roderick's dismissal of Spike's sufferings, and the gentleness with which he'd tried to help her up, the generosity of giving her his only light – unless that was all part of some double game. If so, what were they planning next?

'Here's the ambulance. I've got to go,' she said, pressing down the fear with her usual practicality.

As she clicked off the call and waved at the man who dropped down from the ambulance and walked towards her, she felt the phone vibrate in her hand. This wasn't a new call, but the voicemail service warning of a message. It would have to wait while she explained to the paramedic who Spike was and what had happened.

Standing over Spike as the two paramedics strapped him into a stretcher, Karen felt him grasp her wrist so tightly it hurt. She pulled away but couldn't get free.

'You knew I wasn't going to do anything to you, didn't you?' he said, his voice squeaking in excitement. 'When you fell and screamed, you knew it wasn't me you had to be afraid of. Didn't you, Doctor Taylor? You knew I wouldn't hurt you, Doctor Taylor.'

'I wasn't sure,' she said truthfully.

'But I was coming for help. I didn't want to be out here all on my own. I *trusted* you. There's no one else.'

Manipulation, she reminded herself. Spike's an expert in manipulation.

'How did you know where I lived?' she asked.

He looked disconcerted for a second, then said with all the straightforward innocence of a child:

'Jim told me. He told me to come here and wait near your chalet for him to fetch me and take me off the Island. But he didn't come. So you were the only one left to help me get away.'

'What about your cousin?' Karen said, disturbed by the idea that Jim Blake could have betrayed her whereabouts to anyone as dangerous as Spike. 'Peg, isn't it, who lives at the Goose Inn, and who visits you regularly? Don't you trust her?'

He shrugged, his gym-broadened shoulders filling the whole of the narrow stretcher. '*She*'d never do anything to get me away from the Island. Wouldn't know how. She visits me sometimes but that's only because she hates my parents as much as I do. I knew *you* would get me away.'

'Ready now?' said one of the paramedics in the gentlest voice Spike could have heard for years.

Spike lay back, visibly relaxing, and let go of Karen's wrist at last. She hoped he wasn't going to tell the police he'd 'known' she would get him off the Island. But even if he didn't, the paramedics might. After all, she wasn't the patient. Confidentiality rules might not operate here.

'OK,' Spike said to the first of them. 'Are you taking me back to Parkhurst?'

'We'll get you checked over in Casualty first, but officers will meet us there,' said the paramedic, apparently quite unfazed by the idea that he had a notorious killer on his hands, restrained only by everyday webbing straps. 'Doctor Taylor, are you coming with us?'

Karen thought of the empty chalet, with its front door panels kicked in and the gap she'd made in the roof. And Jim Blake's assignation there with Spike. And the prowler or prowlers she was sure she'd heard in the past. Heavy drops of rain fell on her head and decided her.

'I can't. I must secure my house. But I'll come in the morning.'

The paramedic drew her a little way from the stretcher. 'He'll be back inside by then, unless he needs an operation and it doesn't look like that to me.'

'Fine,' she said, relieved that he'd either not heard or not believed Spike's suggestion that she would have got him off the

Island if he hadn't been shot. 'I'll see him there then. It's where we've had all our other encounters.'

'OK.'

When they'd gone, she turned to look for Roderick, but he'd retreated, as though the thought of too much human contact repelled him. She still had his lamp in her hand. And she had a message on her voicemail. She walked back to Reception Point and pressed the buttons to retrieve it.

'Karen? Hi, it's Will here. Call me back as soon as you can, whatever the time. I'm not operating first thing tomorrow, so you won't be disturbing me. And we need to talk.'

She phoned him back. He sounded wide awake, as though he'd been waiting for her call.

'What's been happening?' he said, sounding sharp with anxiety. 'I've had the police on the phone several times. Are you OK?'

'I'm fine now. It's a long story. They don't want me to leave the Island, so it might . . .'

'I'll come back to you. It's easy. That way I'll be on hand if they want to ask me more questions. But what has happened?'

She told him. At the end, he said: 'So that's why they kept asking me about the knife and whether you'd asked me to bring it. I thought . . .' His voice choked. Then he coughed. 'When I asked if you were hurt, they brushed off my question. I . . . I phoned the hospitals to make sure you weren't . . .'

He'd never sounded so tentative. For a while she couldn't understand it, then she made a guess.

'You didn't think I'd used it myself, did you? On my wrists or something?'

There was a pause, filled only with careful breathing. 'Something like that,' he said eventually.

'Nothing so dramatic. In case they still haven't told you the truth, it was stolen from the chalet and possibly smuggled into the prison for use in Spike's escape. But don't worry, my weird champion of the woods has just shot him, so he's on his way to hospital and I'm safe. Although I will have to patch up the chalet now, where he kicked down the door.'

'Don't try to be superwoman and do it yourself. Collect your valuables and go to a hotel for the night. Get a workman in the morning.'

She shone Roderick's lamp on her watch. 'It's three-thirty. No hotel's going to take me in now. And what a waste of money anyway. Spike's in hospital. He can't do anything to me.'

Pausing, she thought of Max Pitton driving her on, telling her to ignore all her instincts to make herself safe and hide.

Take this as a test, she thought, almost hearing his deep voice saying it all over again. If she passed this time, she could wave her triumph at him whenever he chose to goad her in the future.

'I'll be fine,' she said aloud down the phone to Will. 'I'm going to bed. If you can come at the weekend, it would be wonderful.'

'What about Spike's accomplices? I think you ought to get the police to give you protection, and . . .'

'Don't make me laugh, Will. They haven't got the budget to go searching for corpses they're sure are buried around the Island. They're certainly not going to pay officers to keep watch over someone they still suspect of being in league with a major criminal, i.e. me. Anyway, I don't need protection.'

She thought again of Jim and what he'd been planning when he instructed Spike to hang around her chalet, and what Jim might do if he got to hear that Spike had now been safely removed to hospital without hurting her. Her knees shook with the effort of keeping upright. But her voice worked fine, sounding amazingly confident.

'I'm too tired to do anything but go back to bed, Will,' she said. 'I'll be OK.'

The last of her strength was just enough to push the saggy old sofa across the broken door that Spike had kicked in. Then, she fetched one of the least pathetic kitchen knives and put it under her pillow, where she could easily get at it, and wrapped herself in both squared blankets. Reminding herself that this was a test, a kind of quest that would lead her eventually to some kind of freedom from the weight of fear that Peter's death had loaded onto her, she let go and waited for sleep.

The sun was blazing in through the windows. Already it felt hot on Karen's face. Squinting at the clock told her it was nearly noon and that her powers of mental self-discipline were working a great deal better than they ever had in the old days. If she could sleep after last night's excitements and in a house as insecure as this one, she'd won something important.

No one interrupted today's shower and she let herself stay under the hot jets until she'd emptied the immersion heater completely. Then, clean, soothed and dripping, she found a towel and squelched out to make tea and bacon sandwiches.

The sofa seemed a lot less heavy than it had last night. She pushed it back into its normal position, and went to dress while the bacon cooked, trying to think how she could find a trustworthy workman to secure the house. What she needed was a recommendation from someone influential enough . . .

The acrid smell of burning forced her to the cooker only just in time to rescue the bacon before all four rashers were spoiled. If she cut off the fat, these would still be edible, especially if she sandwiched them between slices from the last of the wholemeal loaf. The bread was crisping at the edges with staleness, but that didn't matter.

She was still chewing as she got into the car to drive to Reception Point. There, swallowing her latest mouthful, she tapped in the number of the White House.

As she'd hoped, it was Sylvia Falconer who answered and not her husband. Karen explained what she needed, and why.

'I'm so sorry, Doctor Taylor,' she said in the most formal tone. 'Naturally I had no idea Spike would . . . If I'd guessed he might come after you, I'd . . .'

'The police did tell you, didn't they? That Spike had escaped, I mean.'

'Oh, yes, of course. They telephoned from the prison first thing, to warn us. Spike had apparently been talking quite wildly about . . .' She coughed. 'About how much he hates . . . well, us, and what he'd like to do now. The police were afraid he might be coming for some kind of revenge. I don't think anyone had any idea he could attack *you*.'

'He *said* he was coming here for help,' Karen said, making it clear she didn't believe the claim. 'Even so, he was angry enough to smash down my front door, which is why I need to get it patched up.'

'Of course,' Sylvia Falconer said again, in a voice of gentle, restrained apology. 'I'll telephone our most trusted carpenter now, and tell him to call on you right away. It's the least I can do. Will you be there for the rest of the day?'

'Unless the police summon me.'

'If they want to talk to you, they'll simply have to come to your house.'

Fine, Karen thought. How nice to be in a position to expect officialdom to mess you about only at convenient moments.

'And if there's anything else I can do to help, I do hope you'll tell me, Doctor Taylor.'

'Well, if you mean it . . .'

'Of course I do. Spike is my son. I may not have any control over what he does, but there's a responsibility, still.' She paused, then added: 'And always.'

'In that case, I should very much like to come and ask you some more questions, to help me understand him. I know your husband said I mustn't bother you, but it would help my work.'

A pause was broken by a few clicks, almost as though someone was tapping the line.

'I would do anything to help anyone understand Spike,' Sylvia said at last in a voice that was strained enough to explain any amount of clicking. 'My husband needn't be bothered. I think in many ways he finds talking about it all harder than I do. He'll be busy at a meeting on Tuesday morning next week, from about ten until just after lunch. If you wanted to get here at, say, half-past ten, we could have some coffee and talk. But please don't bring a tape recorder. It must all be off the record.'

Ah, thought Karen, so you are going to tell me something that matters. Good. Aloud, she said:

'Thank you. I'll be there. And I'll go back now and wait for your carpenter. That's really kind, Mrs Falconer.'

The chippy was a stalwart man in his thirties, who accepted a mug of tea but didn't want to talk about anything except the work in hand, which suited Karen. He inspected the damage to the door, then climbed into the roof space, and came back, dusting his palms on the seat of his jeans.

'D'you want me to fix the leaks while I'm about it?' he said.

'Why not?' Even if she were here only for the summer, there was no point letting in more rain than necessary. 'If it's not too expensive.'

'It's all paid for,' he said.

'But . . .'

'Mrs Falconer's settling the bill. She told me to do anything you needed. I've worked for her and the colonel for years. They both know I don't rip people off. And I don't gossip.'

Wow, Karen thought. She really does feel responsible.

'I'll do the door first,' he went on, 'then start on the roof. That way at least you'll be secure for tonight, even if I can't finish the roof shingles today.'

She watched for a few minutes, enjoying the sight of his neat skill as he took the front door off its hinges and carted it out to his van. He'd just slammed the van doors shut on the wreck of the old door when she heard another car coming down the road.

DCI Trench was driving, but, this time, there was no one in the passenger seat.

So I'm not to be arrested after all, Karen thought, as she waited on the little porch, preparing herself for whatever he was going to throw at her this time.

He raised a hand as soon as he got out of the car. A sign of peace, perhaps, or a way of warding off attack.

She leaned sideways to tell the carpenter she wouldn't be long, and stepped out to meet Trench.

'In this weather we can talk out here,' she said. 'That way we won't interrupt the work or worry him. Is there any news of Jim Blake?'

'Not yet. But Spike's back at Parkhurst, not even in the hospital wing. The pellets did no real damage. He was luckier than any of his victims.'

'Something's been bothering me,' Karen said.

'Like what?'

'Why did Spike make such a fuss about an insignificant glancing wound last night, when he simply laughed as the tines of a fork were dragged through the flesh of his cheek? That must have been agony. Much much worse.'

Trench stopped in his tracks. 'What fork?'

'Didn't your scout at the prison tell you? Huh! What was he thinking of? It happened after I missed the visit. Jim told me about how Spike laughed as the blood ran down his face. But last night he was on the ground in a foetal curl, whimpering.' She gave him the only details she knew of the attack in Parkhurst.

'Maybe the shotgun reminded him of the picnic massacre,' Trench said. 'But you're the shrink, Karen. You explain it.'

'You could be right,' she said. 'Or it could be something quite different: he was still in charge when the other con shoved the fork in his face. Jim was sure Spike had deliberately wound him up to make him attack. Roderick and his shotgun came out of the blue. That could have made Spike feel vulnerable enough to retreat to babyhood – or what he remembers of it.'

'He talked to you? What did he say?'

'Nothing about the escape. But he did say that Jim had ordered him to come here to the chalet and wait for him. And like I said when you stormed round here yesterday: Roderick told me a big red-headed bloke came by here asking for me.'

'Doesn't make sense. Why was Jim telling Spike what to do?'

'No idea,' Karen said, pointing to a substantial fallen tree. 'I need to sit. Yesterday's events took it out of me. And my right foot's a nightmare of blisters. Agony.'

'It'll make our arses go green,' said Trench, looking at the mossy, lichened log with disfavour.

'Who cares? I need rest and support. Tell me something.'

'If I can.'

'Why aren't you haranguing me and treating me like a suspect today?'

Trench laughed, but his self-consciousness made the sound tinny, artificial.

'One: you phoned last night to say you'd got Spike; two, your boyfriend confirmed your story about the sushi knife; three, he volunteered information about prowlers, said he'd been worried by some near your house and heard one during a night he spent here.'

'So you've decided my story checks out. That's still not enough to bring about such a change in you. You were brutal yesterday, when you bloody well owed me. You should have been on your knees thanking me for saving your career by rescuing that child.'

Karen watched Trench's face and thought she'd rarely seen anyone look much more shifty.

'Out with it,' she said when she thought he'd had nearly enough punishment.

He didn't say anything, but he still looked guilty enough to confirm her suspicion that there was more to come. Eventually he offered it.

'We found keys hidden in Jim's flat,' he said. 'Newly cut. I came to try them in your locks. If they check out . . .'

'They'll explain how the sushi knife could've been stolen without my knowing there'd ever been a burglar,' Karen said, remembering the day Jim had been on reception duty at the prison when she'd had to hand in her keys.

Could he have had a spare set cut then? But if *he* had stolen the sushi knife, whose was the blood on it? Who had he needed to threaten – and cut – to get Spike out of Parkhurst?

Was it Spike himself?

He'd certainly seemed lost and scared yesterday night, as well as angry. And he'd responded well to prison existence, clearly finding it less frightening and – usually – more comfortable than living rough outside.

'I was right about this log,' Trench said, interrupting her speculation. 'I can feel damp through my jeans. Let's go back. I need to check the keys.'

'God yes. And before the chippy chucks the old locks and ruins my chance of establishing my innocence.'

'Sure. And I'm sorry, you know, Karen, for . . .'

'That's way too submissive, Charlie. I can't believe you're a submissive man. What else have you got to confess?'

Trench exhaled so deeply it sounded like a sigh, but with anger rather than resignation.

'We checked up on you. You said you came from North Yorkshire. I've got a mate up that way. In traffic. He . . . he was there the night your old man died.'

Karen felt her hands clench, with the nails digging deep into suddenly sweaty palms.

'And that makes you submissive because . . .?'

'Because,' he said, swaying towards her as they walked slowly back towards the chalet, 'it makes me see why you couldn't wait to save the kid yesterday.'

'I don't see why.' She didn't see his face either, because she couldn't bear to look. She speeded up and was appalled when he reached out to grab her left hand, which was still clumped into a damp ball of tension.

'Karen, wait. Stop.' He was trying to force her fingers away from her palm. 'Let go. Let it go. Relax.'

'Please don't touch me,' she said, pulling against his strength.

'Karen, I know I screwed up yesterday. Don't make this harder than it's got to be.'

'I don't need an apology. I just need to be let alone.'

'In a minute. Listen first: you clearly couldn't stand by and risk having to watch the kid die in front of you. Didn't make sense then, but, like I say, I understand now.'

'I don't see why.' She did not want this conversation. She so did not want it. But nothing could stop him now.

'My mate in Yorkshire told me how you had to hold your husband's hand as he bled to death waiting for lifting gear. That can't have been one to cut out and keep.'

A second's incomprehension was followed by a nod as Karen worked out what he'd meant.

'So,' he went on, 'yesterday makes sense now. You couldn't watch anyone else die. Call me if you need me.'

At last he let her go and strode off towards the carpenter, rattling a bunch of keys in his hand.

Karen turned away and headed off down the road in the direction of the sea. She wanted to close her eyes but knew that if she did all the old pictures would unreel as though her brain were a screen taking film from only one projector.

Peter's chest and abdomen bashed in where he had hit the steering wheel when he'd been thrown upwards from the seat during the impact. No air bag in the vintage Ferrari, of course. And, as they later discovered, a great swelling bruise on the back of his head when he'd hit it on something during the rebound. And his eyes focusing on hers, and his voice almost normal at first, talking to her, his voice reaching out to her like his bloodied hand. And the kindly, horrified police officers, who had been chasing him as he roared along at speeds far, far too great for the narrow country lanes, urging her to go on holding him, talking to him, keeping him alive until the rescue services could reach them.

Peter's eyes glistened in the oncoming headlights. Small animals screamed in the undergrowth just as Karen was screaming in her mind, screaming about how she'd never really wanted him to die, never meant any of the fantasies about putting a pillow over his snoring face and holding it there until he suffocated. Never thought, on the night when he'd fallen into a drunken sleep, prone on the hearthrug, that she could put one knee in the small of his back and put her hands on either side of his head and jerk it round so that she broke his neck.

'Kay,' he said, sobbing a little as he bled into the ludicrous Ferrari. 'Kay. Kay. Make it stop. Make it stop. It hurts. Get me out. Get me out. Let me see. Pull down the mirror. I need to see. Make it stop. Kay. Kay. Save me. Save me.'

And then the words slurred and slowed and turned into a meaningless soup of sound as his ability to speak dwindled. His face changed too, or as much as she could see through the blood.

Bleeding into the brain, the doctors had said later. The wounds in his chest and abdomen would have killed him on their own, but there was blood oozing and seeping into his brain, piling on pressure until the whole thing shut down. I'm sorry. You couldn't know. And you couldn't have done anything even if you had known. Everyone got there as quickly as they could. No one could have done more. And he died holding your hand. That's the most important thing. Touch helps the dying, really it does. The last thing he'd have known as he lost the ability to think at all would have been that you loved him.

Karen wanted to be sick.

*

Later, when she'd pushed some of the unbearable memories back into the mental box where she kept them, Karen trudged back to the house, to be greeted by the carpenter's voice:

'Doctor Taylor, I've brought some extra locks. If I put a Yale a third of the way from the top and the deadlock a third of the way up from the bottom, is that OK?'

'Fine,' she said, swallowing and trying to forget the past, and failing.

In an instant she was back in the nightmare, feeling her bare feet on the tarmac of the damp road and the thin stuff of her nightdress rubbing against her skin. She knew the fabric must be transparent in the moonlight. No one said anything but she was horribly conscious of it as she stood, surrounded by strong sympathetic cops in uniform, who knew nothing of her most private thoughts about Peter's death.

The memory of feeling absolutely lost rushed back and with it the sensation of being unfairly alive in a cold, empty world. In that moment she had recognized that what she'd felt for Peter in the beginning, before they'd gone to war with each other – the overwhelming urge to be with him and make good everything that had ever happened to him in his life, from his failures in exams to the overpowering demands of his mad Biblically obsessed mother – had never gone completely.

Everything else Karen had felt as they'd shouted and fought and hurt each other had disguised it. His behaviour, her fury, her *loss*, had overlain everything else until she'd forgotten all sense of ever having cared about him at all. The crash had brought it all back.

Forcing herself now, she remembered the next bit, her life-saving absolute determination to find out how the human mind worked so that she could understand everything they'd both done and find a place in the world where she could do something useful and not hurt anyone else, or be hurt, or be dogged by guilt for ever.

She'd saved a child's life yesterday. Was that going to be enough to stop the guilt?

Chapter 17

'You look atrocious,' Will said as he opened the door of his duplex penthouse in Lewes.

He, of course, looked as though he'd just stepped out of the shower and been dressed by a wardrobe specialist. His faded denim jeans were pristine and the superfine cotton shirt tucked into them could have been new. Today's was pale-blue rather than pink, almost the same colour as the jeans. He'd rolled up the sleeves to show his wiry forearms with the fine golden down all over them. Every fold of the shirtsleeves could have been measured with a ruler.

The weight of his hands on her shoulders helped to anchor her.

'Not that I'm surprised,' he said. 'From everything Trench told me, you've had a hell of a time even without being on your own in the dark, facing your psychopath. Have you been sleeping? Or eating?'

'Not a lot. But, you know, it's not so much Spike coming after me that's thrown me like this; it was something Trench said later.' She hesitated and ran her right hand through her thick blonde hair. At least she'd remembered to wash that.

'Are you going to tell me? You don't have to.'

Will was pulling her towards him, wrapping his arms around her back, stroking her hair with his cheek. Unlike Charlie Trench, he'd shaved so carefully his skin felt like silk. She liked the sensation of it against her hair.

'Yes,' she said, after a moment, pushing herself closer into him. 'He forgave me for screwing up his crime scene, when the child was taken hostage, because he'd been talking to a mate in the Yorkshire force, who was there when my husband was dying in his Ferrari . . . and that unsealed some very old, very deep, and very scary wells of undigested feeling.'

'Why?'

She would never have chosen to tell her detached elegant lover what she'd done and been and felt and seen. In fact she'd resolved not to reveal anything. But she needed to get rid of it now. If she'd been treating Spike, she'd have been having supervision, which would have helped. But she wasn't treating him, so she hadn't had any counselling over any of this. And Max Pitton was too Machiavellian to be given clues to this part of her interior life.

'Tell me.' Will sounded gentle, almost soft, which wasn't like him at all.

She had loved the hardness of his muscles and his air of untouchability, invulnerability. But now it was his cosiness that tempted her into indiscretion.

And so she did tell him. Some of it anyway. She pulled herself away from his arms, sat on the bottom of his stairs and talked.

'But why did you want to kill him?' Will said half an hour later. He spoke so calmly that she answered without thinking.

'Because he wasn't available to me.'

Then she heard the bizarre words banging about in her head and shook it hard.

'No. That's not right,' she said. 'I wanted to kill him because he was always pretending. He pretended to be rich and bought our lifestyle on money he didn't have. And the closer he got to being found out by the bank, the more determined he was to make himself look rich. And when he was at home he drank himself insensible whenever he could so that he didn't have to answer any of my questions. The only times he ever said anything real were when we were fighting.'

Karen looked bleakly back at the past and saw one truth for the first time.

'Which must be why we fought so much. I'd never lost my temper before I met him. And the things I said, the things I did, scare me still.'

'Oh, come on, Karen. Nothing you could do would justify a comment like that. You're a careful, thoughtful, gentle woman. He must've provoked you.'

'That's true enough. But he wasn't the only one who went in for provocation. One thing that could always get him going was me saying I'd get a job to bring in some money to pay a few of our debts. He always yelled at me then so I was more than justified in yelling back. I think his theory was that it would send out all the wrong messages. He wanted me to dress up and smile and be arm candy and pretend to be as confidently extravagant as he always was. One night he weakened enough to admit it was only if the two of us played rich well enough that he'd be able to keep the bank quiet.'

Dizzy, she paused to fill her lungs, having poured out the words without taking many breaths. Then she went on again:

'The night he said that was the one when I threatened him myself. I said – more or less – if he didn't clean up his act and sell that effing great palace we lived in, and the jewels and the clothes he'd bought me, and pay off all his debts, I'd . . . I'd take steps to make him do it.'

Will didn't speak for so long she began to worry. At last, he said: 'How did he deal with a threat like that?'

'He didn't. He took the Ferrari out, was picked up rampaging along the tiny roads at some ludicrous speed, and followed by the police until he smacked the car into a tree at the bottom of the garden.'

'I expect,' Will said with the care of someone treading on

slippery stepping stones in a raging torrent, 'your first answer about his unavailability was the real one.'

Karen turned away in instinctive rage, the kind she'd learned was the most illuminating confirmation of anything anyone ever said to her.

He was right, of course. She'd longed for a warm family existence all her life. Marrying Peter, she'd found even worse loneliness than before.

'Karen?'

At the sound of Will's voice, she looked up and saw how worried he was.

'I was back in the past,' she said, licking her flaky lips. 'Not a good place to be.'

'No,' he agreed. 'So let's go out and eat. I've booked a table at a Spanish tapas place I like in Brighton. No raw food, of course. Can you bear good hot *patatas bravas* and things like that?'

'Sounds great,' she said, leaning against him, realizing he knew her well enough to avoid making her tell him anything else.

'OK, let's go. And pray for a parking space.'

Walking beside him through the Brighton Lanes, among crowds of excited teenagers and tatty tourist shops, she felt suddenly younger, as though she might start out on adult life all over again. Clean slate. New opportunities. New man. No guilt.

No guilt of any kind.

Will slung an arm around her shoulders and pulled her close enough to kiss her hair.

Waking in the night, with a mind as clear as fresh water and no fear to muddy it, Karen thought: Was that why Spike shot the family? Did he see in their jolly picnicking everything he'd never had, either with his natural parents or with the Falconers? Did the anger take him over and make him blast them into nothingness because they had everything he'd always been denied?

That could explain the puzzling vulnerability he'd shown when Roderick shot him, she thought, sitting up and letting the light summer duvet fall away from her body.

It could also help persuade Charlie Trench that Spike was not the man who'd killed and sliced the woman at Alum Bay. If dispossessed rage was his reason for shooting the Sanders family, then he'd have had no reason to attack a solitary swimmer.

Maybe Spike's vulnerability *is* real, she thought. Maybe he was faking the faking of fragility in his story about scaring tourists.

She knew all about the false self people assumed in order to hide everything about their real characters that shocked or distressed them. But in most cases, the false self presented to the world was one of strength and ability, used to cover up inadequacy and messiness. She hadn't come across many who pretended to be more chaotic and violent than they actually were. Or, in the language of the tabloids, more 'evil'. What unbearable truth was Spike hiding behind his false self?

Will moved beside her, as though her racing brain had disturbed him. She guiltily eased herself down again so that she was lying flat, but she didn't pull up the duvet. That much movement could tip him over into full wakefulness, and he needed his sleep. The responsibility she'd feel if he were too tired to operate safely would be more than she could cope with right now.

Lying, listening for his breathing to slow and deepen again, she thought that she'd never heard him snore. He must, of course. Everyone did, male or female. But perhaps he did it, as he did everything else, neatly, soberly, moderately. Safely.

'What's up?' he said, without moving his head. At least that's what she thought he'd said: the words were slurred with sleep.

She looked sideways and saw the gleam of his open eyes in the grey dawn light.

'Nightmares?' he said, running his tongue around the inside of his mouth.

'No. Sorry to disturb you. I woke with a thought, that's all.'

'We're all afraid and guilty at heart,' he said, pulling his mind into gear with an almost visible jerk. His words were now delivered with his usual hard-edged pefection. 'You don't have to pretend with me.'

'You're not afraid or guilty. I've never seen you show the slightest anxiety about anything.'

He laughed and pulled her towards him, brushing her bare shoulder with his lips.

'Doesn't mean I don't feel it. I never make a single cut in any patient without having to discipline myself. The first time I operated, I was sick before I went into theatre. And I cherish the memory of that display because if you're not afraid, you're not careful enough.'

'That's different. That's a rational fear.'

'I have the other kind, too. If you must know, I'm absolutely terrified of potatoes.'

She laughed politely. 'You don't have to make jokes to calm me down. I meant what I said. There was no nightmare. I woke with an interesting idea. Go back to sleep.'

Rolling over, away from him, to signal that she meant business, she felt his hand on her back.

'I mean it. I have this mad terror of raw potatoes. Once had a bagful that went rotten, positively liquified and spread all over the kitchen of the flat I shared at medical school. The stench was indescribable. Decomposing bodies. Filth. You name it, it doesn't come anywhere near those potatoes. I've never had them in the house since. It's why I have to eat out whenever I want spuds.'

And then his hand moved and he pushed her gently onto her back. Looking up at his face, she thought she'd never seen eyes that expressed such a powerful mixture of excitement, laughter and determination.

Later, her last thought before her whole body seized in orgasm was, 'Stop analysing. You can let it rip this time. You can't hurt this man. He's impregnable.'

Chapter 18

'So will you come?' Trench's voice sounded so warm, so immediate, that Karen felt as though he were only inches away from her, instead of phoning from the other side of the Island. 'You'll like it.'

She was leaning on the rail of the ferry, enjoying the wind in her face too much to think clearly.

'Why? Powerboats aren't really my kind of thing.'

'How can you say that? Power, skill, thrust. Amazing engines. Real speed. What more could anyone want? This race is a one-off. The speed limit's been lifted. The best in the world'll be there. You *can't* miss it. I'll feed you first.'

'At the Goose Inn?' she suggested with tartness in her voice. 'You'll have to brief me a bit more clearly if you want me to get anything out of your source there.'

'Don't be like that. This isn't work.' His voice had cooled a little. 'I owe you after last week. Wanted to make it up. But if you . . .'

'OK. Thanks,' she said. Then she remembered her appointment to see Sylvia Falconer. 'At least, it depends on the time. I'm busy in the morning on Tuesday.'

'No problem. Pick you up at the chalet at one-forty.'

Karen clicked off the phone and stuffed it back in the pocket of her fleece, planning to go carefully through her notes and tapes so that she could make the best use of her time with Sylvia on Tuesday. It would be a rare opportunity and probably not repeatable. She mustn't waste a moment on anything that didn't matter.

Sylvia's shirt-waister was made from the palest apricot linen, which gave a little more colour to her face than the grey one had. The sun was pouring into her drawing room through the long Georgian windows, picking out pinks and crimsons in the faded rug and glistening on well-polished brass handles and bits of golden inlay in the furniture. The whole effect was of amazing warmth. And Sylvia's welcoming smile looked a lot easier than anything she'd shown during their first encounter. She moved more freely too.

'Would you like some coffee, Doctor Taylor?'

'Let's not bother with that, unless you want it,' Karen said. 'I had breakfast late this morning and we've got lots to talk about.'

'Then do sit down.' Sylvia waited politely until Karen had wedged herself into a corner of the vast sofa, before sitting in what was obviously her usual chair on the left of the white marble fireplace. 'And let's get started.'

'Fine. I wondered if you could tell me a bit about your other son, Silas.'

The fine lines on Sylvia's face deepened and the new light in her eyes dimmed. 'Why? I thought you wanted to know about Spike.'

'I do.' Karen leaned forwards, over the pad she'd laid on her knee. 'But I have a feeling that the key to what he did as a child must lie in his relationship with Silas.'

Sylvia's beringed left hand fluttered to her chest, and she repeatedly stroked the ridge of her collarbone. The tip of her tongue flickered across her lower lip, once, and then again.

'I don't think so,' Sylvia said.

'Why not? What's Silas like?'

'As my husband said, making a great success in his City job.'

Sylvia withdrew her hand from her collar bone, and her voice was firm.

'You know that's not what I meant.' Karen tried a smile, but it evoked no response. 'Is he strong, weak, dogged, frightened, angry, grounded? Does he have friends? Is he easy to be with? Does he have a relationship that works?'

'Probably all of those, at one time or another.' This time Sylvia did smile, but as though to a stranger. All the old chilliness was back in her expression. 'He had a charming girlfriend, a doctor called Margaret Spack, but she broke it off a while ago. I don't know if she has a successor yet.'

'Did he ever talk to you about Spike?'

'Only to say that he didn't want any of his friends in the house if Spike was here. My husband told you that last time you were here.'

'Were they rivals?'

'Of course. All boys are, don't you find, Doctor Taylor? Men, too.'

'How did Spike and Silas's rivalry manifest itself?'

'The usual ways. Each wanted the other's toys, each wanted more of whatever the other had. There was nothing strange in it. I always knew it would be even harder for Spike to deal with his memories of his own mother once Silas was born and so I did everything I could, leaned over backwards really, to make sure he could see I wasn't favouring Silas over him.' She licked her lips again. 'Just occasionally I have wondered whether I might have overdone it. You know, telling Spike he was chosen, special. I have wondered whether . . . people might have misconstrued it.'

Karen suppressed the urge to lick her own lips, then spoke with care as she approached the real things she needed to know. 'Spike's told me he fought Silas's battles at school, and he hinted that he might have done the same here.'

Sylvia lowered her eyelids, as though determined to hide anything that might show in her eyes.

'D'you think that's true?' Karen said, pushing for an answer.

'Possibly. At school.' Something in the way Sylvia's skirt was arranged across her knees didn't please her. She fiddled with the central pleat, straightening the edges then collecting a small bunch of material between her fingers so that she could shake the skirt to make the hem fall more cleanly.

'Only possibly?'

Sylvia looked straight at Karen. 'Spike has always found it hard to tell the truth,' she said. 'At first I thought it was wilful, then I came to see that he didn't always know what was real and what was something his poor damaged mind had invented for itself. I tried never to blame him for the lies, and I certainly never punished him for them.'

'Talking of his way with the truth,' Karen said, sharing Sylvia's view that Spike didn't always know when he was lying, 'did you ever wonder whether he might *not* have been lying when he claimed he hadn't touched the dog? Lara, I mean.'

Sylvia coughed, as though she had a fishbone stuck across her throat. 'I *longed* to believe he was innocent. But who else could have done it?'

Once again her left hand rose, as though without her even being aware of it. This time it cradled her throat. Her thumb moved slowly up and down, stroking the soft, wrinkled skin of her neck.

God, she needs kindness! Karen thought. I wonder how much she gets in this house.

A clock chimed, with a tinkling faraway sound that suggested it was very small, very old and probably immensely valuable. Sylvia withdrew her hand from her neck and peered at the tiny gold Rolex that hung loosely from her wrist.

'We'll be running out of time soon,' she said, looking anxious. 'So if there's anything important you need to ask, Doctor Taylor, can you be quite quick?'

'Are you afraid of your husband?' Karen said, before she could stop herself.

Sylvia's face paled: 'Don't be absurd. But he asked you not to come here again. I would hate you to be the victim of an angry outburst. He doesn't like his ord . . . his requests to be ignored.'

'Of course. I'm sorry.' Karen tried a sympathetic smile and thought she saw a hint of movement in Sylvia's perfectly coloured lips. 'I can't help believing you still have real feeling for Spike, in spite of everything he's done.'

Something glistened in Sylvia's eyes. This time it was her right hand that moved, so that she could wipe one finger under each eye, clearly to make sure the tears hadn't fallen. She recrossed her legs, wincing, as though her joints were arthritic.

'He's my son,' she said very quietly when she'd recovered. 'And always will be, even if I didn't carry him inside me. I love him.'

'And yet you banished him from the family, and this house, didn't you?'

This time Sylvia did look directly at Karen, challenging her. 'One of the doctors, one of the many doctors to whom we took him, said that the only way we could ever help him free himself from the smack, and the skunk, and whatever else he was taking, was to cut off all material support. We *had* to do it. They were making his personality disorder even worse. We had to do it.'

'That must have been hard when you felt so protective of him.'

'It was very hard, Doctor Taylor.' Her voice sounded forced. 'I doubt if you can imagine what it cost me.'

'Did you ever see him after that?' Karen asked, still trying to separate the different realities that made up this woman's complicated relationship with her adopted child.

'That was my weakness. Whenever he came here hungry, dirty, desperate, I couldn't bring myself to refuse him help. I'd give him clothes. He was always so cold, you see, and his skin was awful. No vitamins, and not nearly enough washing. Even without the drugs his skin would've been poor. As it was . . .'

She covered her mouth with both hands, obviously fighting for control. When she had it, she went on again:

'If I was alone,' she said, 'I'd let him into the house and feed him up and give him food to take away in Tupperware boxes, along with sleeping bag, blankets; that kind of thing.'

'And money?'

Sylvia shook her head. 'I managed to hold on to that much discipline. I knew he'd only buy more drugs with any cash I handed over, and I longed for him to be free of them.'

'When was the last time he came?' Karen tried not to let her note-taking interfere with her perception of everything Sylvia didn't say. She wished she'd broken the rules and brought her tape recorder, hidden in the linen bag, but she hadn't. And now it was too late.

'The day before the shooting, the Sunday,' Sylvia said in a voice that dragged with reluctance and pain. 'My husband and Silas were out somewhere together, so I let Spike in. His clothes were awful, matted with dirt and thin with wear. His skin was worse than ever, with sores and spots and cuts. He looked as though he'd been pulled face down through a bramble patch.'

'I can see why you needed to help him. But did you just say Silas was here that weekend?'

'That's right. He comes back every so often. He'd gone for a walk with his father.'

'And Spike came, conveniently when they were out. D'you think he'd been watching, waiting until the coast was clear?'

'Probably,' Sylvia said with her eyes closed. 'He was in a terrible state. Nothing I could give him was enough that day. Not the clothes or the food. He started ranting. I think now that he must have smoked some crack or something like that because he was aggressive in a way he'd never been before. He shouted that I *owed* him money, that he *needed* money, that he wouldn't leave until I'd given him money. I knew my husband and Silas would be back soon, and I had to get Spike away before they saw him.' Her voice faltered.

Karen had the feeling Sylvia had been needing a reason to tell this story for a long time, to account for what she had done and, perhaps, get some kind of absolution. Karen waited in silence until Sylvia was ready to carry on.

'And I was so scared,' she said, 'because I knew what might happen when they found him here, that I lost my temper. I shouted back, that Spike had ruined my life, that I'd wanted him out of it for years, that it was only guilt that forced me to give him anything, that I would never give him any more money, that I wanted him gone now and for ever.' Her voice broke, and the sticky-looking tears glided down her cheeks at last, sliding over the top of the delicate powder. 'That I wished I'd never adopted him.'

Both hands flew up to cover her face. From behind them, she completed her confession:

'The next day he went and shot those four people. It was my fault they died. I can't . . .'

A phone rang in another room. Sylvia jumped, then pulled a fine lawn handkerchief out of her sleeve and set about tidying herself up. She checked her watch again too. Her face looked as though some vacuum pump had sucked away the tears and all sign of emotion.

'You *have* to go. He might come home early and he mustn't find you here. Please, Doctor Taylor. Go.'

Karen stood up at once. She reached towards Sylvia, wanting to lay a comforting hand on her shoulder and express some of the vast sympathy she felt.

But Sylvia wasn't having any of it. She took Karen's hand firmly and shook it, then let it go. Sylvia's palm was quite dry, as though her body no longer produced the normal physical responses to strong emotion.

Karen had never encountered anything like it in her professional life and she found it almost as disturbing as some of Spike's contradictory behaviour. She opened her mouth to ask a question.

'Thank you for coming,' Sylvia said, as though seeing off a lunching friend. 'Goodbye, Doctor Taylor.'

Karen left, her mind buzzing with conflicting ideas. You could analyse that confession and all the unspoken stories of life with Colonel Falconer and the two ill-assorted boys in dozens of different ways, she thought.

As she turned out of the drive, she checked her rear-view mirror and saw a low-slung gleaming black car bearing down on her, much faster than it should be driven along roads like these. She put her foot harder on the accelerator to increase her own speed and the space between them. The black car slowed dramatically, before whipping round into the drive, with a neat manoeuvre that reminded her of an arrogant skier's turn, the kind that has the ski's edges crunching into the snow and sending up a spurting spray behind.

Maybe I didn't leave soon enough, Karen thought. That poor woman. I hope he didn't recognize my car.

She glanced at the clock on the dashboard. Twelve fifteen. I'll have to hurry, she told herself, if I'm to transcribe those scrawly notes before Trench comes to pick me up. Do I really want to watch powerboats racing up and down the Solent?

The answer was obvious. No, she didn't. But she did want to rummage around in Trench's mind for everything he hadn't yet told her about the Falconer family.

With that thought came a clear memory of the cars parked outside the White House the first time she'd been there, when she'd specifically gone to talk to Colonel Falconer. None of them had been a black Porsche. And Sylvia had distinctly said her husband wouldn't be back until after lunch.

Who had been driving just now, taking that turn as though he knew it well enough to judge precisely the speed and angle he'd need?

Karen saw a lay-by ahead and switched on her left indicator. Pulling off the road, she sat with the engine idling for a full minute, before setting off again, turning right out of the lay-by to return the way she'd come.

Back in the drive up to the White House, she saw the Porsche parked right outside the front door, rather than tucked away by the greenhouses. She drew up behind it and was just getting out when the grand front door of the house opened and a stocky young man emerged.

Dressed in dark-green cords and Tattersall-checked shirt, with well-polished brown shoes, he looked very much at home under the elegant white portico. He didn't bother to descend the four shallow steps to her level but waited for her, standing at the top. If he'd been dressed for riding and had a whip in his hand, she thought he'd be thwacking his boot with it. He looked the epitome of arrogance.

She smiled up at him and put her foot on the bottom step.

'That's far enough,' he snapped, staring down at her as though she were a beetle he was about to crush under his shoe. 'You are Doctor Taylor, I presume?'

'That's right.' She thought of making a Stanley-and-Livingstone kind of joke but decided he wouldn't appreciate it. 'And you are?'

'Silas Falconer. I thought my father had made it abundantly clear that this family does not wish to talk to you any more. You should've known better than to take advantage of his absence today to harass my mother.'

Karen climbed up to the step below his, moving as easily as she could, and smiling with all the confidence of an equal. 'I thought of something I needed to ask her.'

'I don't know how you found out about my father's regular Tuesday meeting, but if you think she's ever going to be left alone again for the amusement of people like you, you're . . .' Silas breathed deeply, as though to control his temper, then said in a slightly more moderate voice: 'You'll find you're wrong.'

'But . . .'

'Don't push me, Doctor Taylor. And don't think you can lie in wait for my mother anywhere else on the Island. The food is ordered over the Internet and her hairdresser visits.'

'You sound like her gaoler,' Karen said, riveted by what he was revealing about the Falconers' lives.

'Don't be ridiculous. She has suffered terribly from what my adopted brother did. My father and I will always take steps to prevent any more intrusion from prurient sensation-seekers like you. Now, will you please leave the property? Or do I have to call the police?'

Karen looked to the side, where she could see Sylvia sitting in her chair, clinging to its arms, absolutely rigid. Was it terror or anger seizing her like that?

And which of them had made her feel it?

A dark-blue rucksack with a rolled rug strapped to it dangled from Trench's hand when he locked his car outside the chalet at precisely twenty to two. Karen opened the front door and called out:

'Aren't we driving? It's a hell of a walk to Cowes and I've already got blisters.'

'Not Cowes!' he shouted back. 'Better view from the beach near here.'

He walked towards her, moderating his voice as he came closer. 'Not much more than a mile. Can't you do that?'

Karen looked down at her long tanned legs in their cropped white linen trousers, then at the thin-soled jewelled sandals on her feet, which showed off the pristine newly applied varnish. 'I can manage a lot more than a mile, but this beach is made of wicked shingle – unless you know a secret path above it.'

'Exercising on shingle's good for the leg muscles, and the glutes,' he said, with no pity at all. He gestured to his own trainers and well-washed black jeans, adding: 'Get into something meant for walking and you'll be OK. Come on. No time to waste.'

'You'd better come in and sit down, while I change my shoes,' she said. 'You should've warned me we'd be roughing it.'

'Cowes is boring. And crowded. Watching the race from a spot I know on the beach down here, you get to see the turn. That's the best.' His voice speeded up at the very thought of the excitement to come in a way Karen found endearing. 'It's split-second timing then or you screw up.'

She left her bedroom door open. Shoe-changing didn't need privacy. She reached for some red-and-white-striped socks, then thought of the gap between them and her cropped white trousers, and realized she'd have to change into jeans, too. She pushed the door shut after all, and, in order to avoid seeming unfriendly, shouted through it:

'D'you race yourself?'

'I wish,' he said, making his voice throb with exaggerated regret. 'You need millions – or a sponsor – for that.'

'And you're probably far too old now,' she said, refusing sympathy. She wriggled into a pair of clean jeans, made tighter than usual by their recent laundering. She tugged the zip upwards, shaking her fingers to get rid of an ache in the overworked muscles. 'You won't have the reactions or the sight to make that kind of precise judgement any longer.'

'I always knew you were a hard woman. I shall enjoy watching you suffer on the shingle. Come on. Hurry up.'

Safely into her indigo jeans at last, with a floppy cotton hat dangling from one back pocket like a golfer's glove, in case the sun became as unbearable as it had on Chillerton Down, and a tube of suncream stuffed into the other, she emerged to find him still waiting but jiggling with impatience.

'Carry on while I get my keys,' she said. 'I'll follow you out.'

He obeyed. She locked the house, then hurried after him down the track towards the beach. Now they'd had nearly a week without rain the mud had dried completely, but it had left hard ridges and craters, which made walking uncomfortable, even in trainers.

Five hundred yards to the beach, she thought, and then a mile over the stones. My muscles *are* going to get a good workout. And this is supposed to be a treat-by-way-of-apology. I'm glad I'm not on the wrong side of him any longer.

The walk took them nearly forty minutes, as they slipped and slid on the smooth round grey pebbles. But it was worth it. The place he'd been aiming for was wider than the rest of this apology for a foreshore, with a smooth unpebbled patch for sitting on and a steep cliff of the wickedly soft, friable, clay-ey earth to lean against. A twisted tree grew out of it to provide shade, and gulls swooped and wheeled low over the lapping waves. Their screams had always spelt holidays to her. She smiled to hear them now.

Leaning back to rest against the low cliff, becoming aware of how hot she was, she hoped her face wasn't as red and damp as it felt. His skin was irritatingly dry and he wasn't even short of breath. Now she looked properly at him, she realized he must be easily as fit as Will.

But not as sinewy, she thought in satisfaction.

At the sound of a mechanical roar to the right, the gulls rose with even sharper screams, powering high into the blinding blue sky before they fled.

'We're late,' Trench said, as he unrolled a waterproof-backed rug and spread it over the smooth patch of ground above the pebbles. 'Should've got lunch out of the way before the first heat. Here, take these.'

He'd unzipped the bag and was holding out two plastic stemmed wineglasses.

'Sauvignon Blanc OK? I know you're not a beer-drinker.'

'Sauvignon Blanc sounds great,' she said. 'I didn't realize you were bringing food and stuff. I'd have contributed something if you'd told me.'

'Have you eaten?'

'No.'

'Great.' He poured the wine with a satisfying glugging sound, then ground the bottle into the soft earth. 'Nothing fancy, just ham-and-cheese butties and strawberries.'

'Perfect. Now, tell me about this race.' She could see a line of brightly coloured buoys directly ahead of them. 'Presumably this is where they turn.'

'Yeah. They'll be along any minute. There's usually a serious speed limit, but like I said, it's been lifted for this one race.'

'I wondered about that. It's only something like six knots, isn't it?'

'That's inside the harbour at Cowes. Bit more in the rest of the Solent, but not enough for serious racing.'

'You know, I'm beginning to think I should feel honoured that you wanted me to come with you today.'

'Too right,' he said, pouring more wine into her glass. 'Now concentrate: what you're going to see is power mixed with skill like you've never seen it before, except maybe in heavyweight boxing.'

'I can't say I see a lot of that,' she said, laughing and thinking of all the times Peter had lectured her about his latest sports enthusiasm. Like Trench he'd assumed she'd be interested enough to want to know all its rules and records.

'Tell me about your bloke,' he said suddenly, holding a sandwich in the air. 'He seems a bit of a . . .' he hesitated, then added, 'a bit of a neat-freak for a woman like you.'

'And what – in your opinion – would be my kind of man?'

He took a huge bite of sandwich, watching her over the bread. When he'd swallowed, he said: 'No idea, except not that. What's he got that turns you on?'

Karen was interested in his directness, and in the hints of hostility. 'A long sinewy torso,' she said, with truth but not the whole truth.

A more accurate answer would have been: he never fights, never even argues. I know where I am with him. I think I could be safe with him. And he with me.

What would Max Pitton say to that?

Trench was holding the sandwich out wide so that he could look down at his own chunky powerful body. He shrugged.

'I think they've started,' Karen said, glad of the distraction. She wasn't going to tell him that in spite of his muscles he looked far too like Peter for her to fancy him in a million years.

A second later, four long slim boats surged forward, rearing up out of the sea, bouncing on their tails. She had a confused vision of powerful young men in brightly coloured Lycra suits as the boats slowed almost to a halt and swung round, scattering spray in a perfect arc, before zooming and bouncing back the way they'd come.

Rather like Silas and his Porsche, she thought as she, too, took a bite of sandwich. It was very good, with thick juicy slices of ham, sharp Cheddar and a hint of mustard between slices of soft brown bread.

Trench was on his feet now, walking down to the water's edge for a better view of the next heat. It would be only fair to join him, she thought, taking a swig of her wine, before grinding the base of the glass into the clay. Picking up another sandwich, she followed him.

He turned at the sound of her footsteps. 'Wasn't it great? Think how it feels, slinging one of those things round. Split-second placing and timing. One micro-instant of bad judgement and you'd stall – or catch the other bloke's tail. Then boomph! You're history.'

Are all men small boys at heart? she wondered, yet again thinking of Peter and his delight in his stupid, dangerous, explosive car. Playing with it, just as Aidan had played with his toy trucks at the age of three, crashing them together, adding the sound-effects.

The next heat was gearing up. She could hear the engines and smell them, too. Or maybe the pungent, oily, evocative scent of unburned fuel was only the last lot's petrol vapour hanging in the air.

The roar of acceleration battered at her ears. Trench grabbed her wrist and tightened his hand so much she nearly screamed. He was practically dancing on the stones, shouting.

Something bobbed up in the sea directly ahead of her, something cylindrical and about two yards long, with dark-red seaweed wrapped round one end. No, not weed: hair. Thoughts flashed through her brain far faster than her mind could find words for them. Everything else slowed down, even the powerboats and the gulls, which coasted on the air currents,while she groped for words.

She shouted at Trench, but he couldn't hear over the engines' roar. She punched his arm with her free hand. He didn't respond. She punched him harder. He turned his head. His face was full of fury.

'What?' he mouthed over the crashing noise.

She stuck out her free hand, pointing as the boats ripped through the water, sending up fountains of it either side of their hulls like the toughest feathers on a vast bird of prey.

'A body,' she said, far, far too late.

The leading boat, ahead by only one of Trench's micro-instants, swerved, as though to avoid the body, and was thrown right off its line, crashing into the next one. A wall of fire hid everything as a tremendous force thudded into her, felling her. Her eyes boiled. Her ears rang.

Burning. Hurting. Lungs pounding. Nose, mouth and teeth, pressed into ferocious hardness.

Time passed.

She was lying face down with her teeth clamped around a pebble, her tongue jammed back in her mouth, almost choking her, and a heavy weight on top of her. Bending her head right round, feeling the tendons in her neck cracking, she realized the weight was Trench.

Was it the blast that had flung him here? Or had he seen what was going to happen in time to push her to the ground? Was he still alive? Or had he died for both of them?

She could feel liquid running down one of her cheeks. Blood? Sweat? Tears? The ooze reached her mouth. She stuck out her tongue to taste it.

Not tears. Too salty and metallic for that. Blood.

She forced herself to turn her head sideways again and said his name, feeling more blood running into her mouth.

No answer came.

With a supreme effort, afraid half her muscles would tear, she heaved him up and pulled her body sideways over the agonizing shingle so she could scramble out from underneath his weight.

She listened for his breathing, but her ears were ringing too loudly to catch anything. Her scraped cheek could still feel. She held it over his mouth and felt his breath on it.

He was still alive. She sat back on her heels, letting herself breathe and calm down. Then she caught the smell of burning cloth and skin, and she reared forward to see that a piece of flaming debris had landed in the middle of his back. Already it had eaten right through his clothes. Where it had been his body was raw and blistered.

Grabbing her shoe to protect her fingers, she flicked the red-hot metal away from his back and turned him onto his side in the recovery position. As soon as she'd made sure his airway was clear, she looked up, beginning at last to recognize other sensations.

The smell was worse, not only burning fuel and plastic and skin, but flesh, too. Like a barbecue. She blinked to clear her dried-out scorched eyes and looked out to sea.

Two boats had cut their engines and were wallowing outside the danger zone. Within it, the pool of flame was slowly widening. The sea itself looked as though it was on fire as floating fuel lit on the surface of the water.

One of the untouched boats backed further into safety, bucking and rocking on the remains of the wash.

For one mad moment, Karen could see only the superb colours, the red, yellow and flaring orange of the fire and the bright-blue sky and green water. Then she saw what was floating towards her on the waves.

A hand, snapped off at the wrist, presumably by one of the propellers, unidentified charred lumps, and – oh, God! – a head.

She turned away, fighting the urge to vomit, and dimly, through the ringing in her ears, heard a voice shouting at her with a heavy Italian accent. The voice wasn't loud enough for her to make sense of the clash of sounds. She looked back at the boats, raising her hand to cup her ear. The man shouted more loudly and she fought her brain to make it distinguish words in the cacophony.

'We have radio'd. Help coming.'

That's something, she thought, reaching down through the horror in her mind for sense and sanity, because our phones probably won't work down here.

She turned to face the nearest of the safe boats and saw a young blond-haired creature in bright-red Lycra, with his hands making a megaphone around his mouth.

'Ambulance and police is coming. Racing is stopped. He living, yes?'

'Yes,' she shouted back, turning to check that Trench was still breathing.

His back looked terrible. The longer he stayed unconscious, the better. She didn't want him coming round until he was in hospital with the strongest analgesics available.

'Yes, he's still alive,' she called across the still-smouldering waves. 'You OK?'

'We, yes. Is good. Help coming. Not long.'

Not for the now headless man in the water, she thought, keeping her eyes directed well away from the round, dark-red-topped object that rolled and lolled in the slow surf.

How many of the others from the powerboats were dead? Presumably the drivers and navigators of both exploded boats.

Even if the blast hadn't killed them, the fire must have. Or the sea itself.

But the first man must have been dead before he'd been hit, she thought, grasping for anything to stop her thinking about the head that kept catching her peripheral vision, however hard she tried to avoid it.

His body had bobbed up from nowhere, just as the boats zoomed across from Cowes. No one ever swam here off this dingy beach, even when there wasn't a powerboat race. And no one would have been mad enough to ignore the buoys, let alone the noise of those growling engines. And no one's head could have been ripped off even in that explosion unless there had been damage first.

Damage like a garrotte? Like a wire snare snapping too tightly around a rabbit's head and ripping it off the body?

A grunting, snuffling sound from Trench made her drop to her knees beside him. His eyes opened as adrenaline powered him upwards into consciousness and a recognition of pain.

'Stay still. Shh. Shh,' she said, as though to a child waking from a nightmare. She leaned heavily on his uninjured shoulder, determined not to let him roll his burned back on the mucky ground. 'You're alive. I'm alive. We're OK. And help's coming. But you need to stay still and not lie on your back.'

'The boats,' he said, in a thick painful voice, running his tongue around his lips. 'More coming. Must be stopped.'

'The others have radio'd. We just have to wait.'

'Can't do that,' he said, pulling his knees up towards his chest as though getting ready to roll himself into a kneeling position. He gasped, with a muffled roar, then fought for control. Sweat poured over his face and his upper teeth made great dents in his lower lip. His breaths sounded like fabric tearing. At last he won.

'You hurt?' he said.

She shook her head. 'Thanks to you, I'm fine. You took the whole blast. The skin on your back is damaged. Try not to move. You need expert help.'

'And buckets of morphine,' he said with grim humour even as he groaned again. The sound of sirens came unmistakably towards them on the wind. 'Thank God!'

His eyes closed as he stopped fighting.

Chapter 19

'And the body is almost certainly Jim Blake, the prison officer,' Karen said into the phone as she leaned against her car at Reception Point. 'Apparently he had some tattoos a colleague could identify. Obviously they'll check DNA for absolute certainty, but there doesn't seem much doubt.'

She tried to suppress all the memories of the water-darkened red fronds she'd originally thought were seaweed.

'Murder or suicide?' said Max Pitton, his bucket-of-gravel voice untempered by any kind of sympathy.

Didn't he understand what she and Trench had been through? Bastard!

'They don't know,' she said coolly, determined not to give him the satisfaction of sounding weak. 'The general assumption is that Spike forced Jim to get him out of the prison, tortured my address out of him, then lost his temper for some reason, dragged Jim to the beach, killed him, probably with some form of strangulation, perhaps a cheese-wire garrotte, and threw him in the sea.'

'It doesn't make sense.'

Karen was about to agree and say she thought it had been Jim who had stolen her sushi knife, and Jim who had taken the lead in telling Spike where to go and what to do after the escape, but Max wasn't waiting for any comment from her.

'In all my years living here, overlooking the Solent,' he said,

'I've never seen a powerboat explode, even when they've crashed. I don't understand the fiery aftermath either. With all that cold seawater to put out the flames, it shouldn't have been nearly as dramatic.'

'I didn't make it up.' Karen could feel herself weakening. 'It's what happened and there's nothing I can do to change it. I've got to go. My head's still agony from the blast; my hearing isn't right yet; I'm waiting for news of Trench, the cop, who risked his life to save me. They won't tell me how bad his injuries are. Which means . . .' She couldn't go on.

The thought that a man of his physicality could be turned into an invalid was unspeakable.

'What does Spike say about it all?' Max had always been ruthless, but this lack of any human feeling seemed over the top, even for him.

'I haven't had the time or the energy to go back to the prison to find out,' Karen said, hearing sharp dislike in her voice and not caring. At least it was better than sounding pathetic.

'But you'll go first thing tomorrow, won't you? You mustn't ignore an opportunity like this. The discovery of Blake's body could be the chisel you need to crack open Spike's defences.'

Karen took the phone from her ear and just looked at it. How had she ever admired this man, thought his favour her only safe route to power and success?

His voice quacked on, louder and louder, yelling out her name. He must be shouting now. She put the phone back to her ear.

'Bad reception even here. I must go. I'll report in due course.'

'Will you promise me that you'll go to the prison tomorrow? You mustn't slack off, or you'll be throwing away everything you've got so far, everything that's happened. And if you don't get this paper out soon, all my work schmoozing the lawyers to get you in as an expert witness next year will have been for nothing.' Max paused. Karen didn't say anything. At last he went on: 'I don't forgive people who waste my time. Karen? Karen?'

She wasn't going to promise anything.

'Karen!'

'What?'

'I thought you'd gone. How's the child, by the way?' His voice was less aggressive now. Maybe he'd picked up something of her resistance.

'On her way back home to the mainland with her parents, according to DCI Trench,' Karen said. 'The hospital discharged her as soon as they were sure there were no internal injuries. And the police don't seem to believe she could tell them anything useful.'

'Had she been sexually assaulted?'

'No, thank God.'

'Makes sense. You know most hostage-takers have severe personality disorders, don't you? This will make an interesting footnote in your paper. You're lucky to have been so close to it all.'

This last demonstration of callousness was too much.

'Prof, I have to go. As I say, I'll report tomorrow. And you needn't worry: I haven't forgotten why I'm here.'

Karen clicked off the phone and went on leaning against the wing of her old car, too battered to move. Who did he think he was, talking about that child's suffering as though it had been laid on by fate to prevent her wasting his time?

A soft footfall in the undergrowth made her turn her head.

'Doctor Taylor?' said Roderick as he emerged from the trees. 'Are you all right? When I didn't see a light in your chalet, I wondered if you'd been involved in that explosion.'

'I'm fine, thank you, Roderick. Fine but very tired. I must go back now.'

'That's a relief. I was very worried when I thought *you* might be hurt. I never thought you'd go anywhere near a race like that. Go home and get an early bed. You don't look well, you know. I'll leave you some more rabbits in the morning. I've had them hanging since the night I shot that man for you. I didn't give them to you then because they wouldn't have made good eating but I've kept them specially for you hanging in my larder. They're about right now; the meat should be nice and soft. I'll skin them. Gut them too. And take the heads off. I know you don't like the heads left on.'

The mention of the heads was too much. Karen wondered if she'd ever forget the sight of Jim's rolling towards her through the waves.

Roderick came closer. She could smell him, not as pungent as he'd been on the night Spike had crashed into the chalet, but still acrid, strange and feral. He touched her and she flinched, then had to apologize, adding:

'It's been a bad day. I must get home. Thank you. Goodbye.'

She pushed past him to get into the driving seat and couldn't stop herself pulling the door shut with a bang and pressing down the locks.

A hurt expression lengthened his red face. She leaned forwards until her forehead rested on the steering wheel. She could *not* take responsibility for the Elephant Man's feelings.

'What happened to your face?' Spike said as Karen sat down opposite him in the familiar interview cell at Parkhurst two days later.

Today the sun was shining through the small high window directly into her eyes. She shifted her chair sideways, further from the panic button.

'I fell on the beach,' she said.

'You look as though someone held you down and rubbed your face in broken glass.' His voice was analytical, almost as though he was making a report to a disinterested third party.

Didn't he know what had happened? Everyone else on the Island seemed to. Wherever she'd been since the explosion some-one had stopped her in the street or the shops to express sympathy and admiration for the way she was 'up and about again so soon, dear'.

'There was an explosion when two powerboats collided during a race,' she said. 'Hadn't you heard?'

'Of course. One swerved when the driver saw Jim's body and crashed. I didn't know you were there.'

'Only by chance. Who told you it was Jim's body? I didn't realize anyone knew for certain yet.'

His beautiful face creased as he giggled. 'Surely you've seen how news flies round this place, Doctor Taylor? You couldn't keep anything secret. It's Jim's body. His head was ripped right off you know. Right off, Doctor Taylor. But it'll be all right now.'

'Don't you mind about Jim's death?' she said, ignoring his rising hysteria. 'I thought you liked him.'

The laughter lines smoothed out, and he shrugged. 'He was useful. Better than some of the other screws. But why would I like him? He kept me locked in here. And he spied on me for Pa.'

'Except that he didn't keep you in here, did he? He unlocked the gates for you the other day. It was him who got you out, wasn't it?'

He shrugged again. His eyes looked flinty, and his mouth gave nothing away.

'And then what?' Karen said, feeling for the verbal chisel the prof had recommended. 'Didn't you say he'd told you to go to the woods that night?'

'The woods where your chalet is? Where your mate shot me?'

'Yes.'

'Yeah. Told me to lie up there, out of sight, and he'd bring me food and money and new clothes and get me to the mainland.'

'But why?'

Spike shrugged again.

'I mean, why was he telling you to do anything?'

'What d'you mean?'

'You forced him to get you out of here. Why would he be giving you orders?'

'Me? No, I didn't.' Spike's puzzled frown looked real. But then the sun was behind him, making it hard to see subtleties in his expression. And everything he'd already told her had shown what a good actor he could be. 'He came to my cell in the night and said, "Come with me. Now."'

'And you just went?'

'Yeah.' A small smile, not particularly attractive, pulled Spike's face out of shape. It was a while before she realized he felt ashamed. 'You do in a place like this. They take your courage and your drive and make you a passenger, so you do what you're told. I went with him. Didn't know why. And found myself getting dressed up in a screw's uniform, then outside the gates and on the back of his Yamaha.'

'So where did the sushi knife come in?' Karen asked, leaning sideways to avoid the sun's glare and watching his face with extra care.

She'd noticed he was having no difficulty telling this particular story. Was that because the events it dealt with were so recent? Or because they had nothing to do with his family?

'What knife?' he said.

'The white ceramic sushi knife they said you used on Jim.'

'Ceramic knife? Like china, you mean? Why're you looking at me like that, Doctor Taylor? I'm not mad, you know, Doctor Taylor. Why're you talking about knives again, Doctor Taylor? You're obsessed with them, aren't you, Doctor Taylor?'

She was surprised at how quickly his speech could change from that of an intelligent man in control to this kind of gibber.

'What are you up to, Spike?'

'What d'you mean?'

'This isn't you, this hysteria. You put it on whenever you don't like the way our conversation's going. What's bothering you so much now?'

'Nothing. Must be because of me wounds,' he said, switching persona again and letting his head roll a little, while his tongue edged out of the side of his mouth. 'Shot I was, like a rabbit, by your mate in the woods. It fucking hurts, too. Could explain anything.'

Oh, stop it! she thought. Clearly she wasn't going to get anything useful out of him today. Nothing to placate Max. Nothing to put in her paper either. Nothing to help Spike himself, even if she'd wanted to help him.

'I've met your brother at last,' she said. 'I didn't know he still came here.'

'Silas?' His face flushed and a quite different smile made him look suddenly younger, almost eager, and absolutely normal. 'Here, in the prison? Is he coming in to see me? Is that why . . .' His voice stopped.

'Why what?' Karen said.

'I don't know what you mean.'

'You were asking me whether Silas was coming here to the prison and whether that was why . . . and then you stopped talking.'

'I don't know what you mean,' Spike said again. 'Did you see him here?'

'No,' Karen said, giving up. 'I met him at the White House.'

The eagerness drained out of Spike's face.

'What's the matter?' Karen said.

Spike hunched his shoulders and looked down at the floor.

'Did you expect Silas to come here?'

Spike didn't move. Karen had a sudden image of his face when he'd denied ever phoning the White House after he'd been arrested, when she could see from the pristine police records that he had. He'd clammed up on her when she'd asked questions about that, too. Had it been *Silas* he'd spoken to that day and not his father at all? Had he waited fruitlessly for Silas to come to his rescue?

'Spike?' she said, making her voice gentle. 'Will you tell me about Silas?'

Spike looked up at her at last, and his expression was dead. There was no light in his eyes and no movement in his lips. He looked in control and impregnable. She knew she'd get nothing more from him today.

Visiting at the hospital was forbidden until after the 'quiet hour' between one and two-thirty, so Karen drove to the Goose Inn. She had an important question to put to Peg, and getting there and back would take up the time nicely.

Peg was looking better. Karen smiled at her, thinking once more: who on earth is called anything so dated in the twenty-first century?

'Hi!' Karen said. 'How was last week? Did you make as much from the yachties as you'd hoped?'

'More or less,' Peg said, smiling back. 'Good to see you, Doctor Taylor. What'll it be? Tomato juice and Worcester sauce, or bitter for once?'

'Better make it juice and sauce,' Karen said. 'I'm on my way to the hospital to see DCI Trench this afternoon. I don't want the nurses thinking I'm an alkie who drinks at lunchtime.'

'Yeah. I heard about that. He saved your life at the powerboat races, didn't he?'

'More or less.'

'You *have* been in the wars, haven't you?'

'You mean with your cousin coming for me once he'd got through the wire?'

Peg turned away, using the excuse of finding a less-than-usually dusty bottle of tomato juice to avoid having to answer.

'When did you last see him?' Karen said.

'Nearly a month ago now. I should've gone this week, but I've been too busy.' Peg's face was red with the blood that must have run down into it as she hung over the juice bottles. 'He didn't give me any idea he was planning an escape or anything like that when I last went to the prison, honest.'

'I never thought he would have. What I wanted to ask, though, was whether you've ever taken him things from your aunt. Money or phone cards or anything like that.'

Or loops of wire for home-made garrottes, Karen thought, but she kept it to herself.

Peg's expression was so unguarded that it wasn't hard to read the answer.

'Is that why you went to Parkhurst so regularly?' Karen went on. 'Rather than because of your own affection for Spike, I mean?'

'I feel sorry for her, you know, and the colonel doesn't let her go anywhere near the prison. Thinks it sends out all the wrong messages about Spike.' Peg had finished pouring Karen's drink and was diligently wiping down the bar, staring down at unnoticeable marks 'I wouldn't go anywhere near him myself if she hadn't begged me. I hate him for what he did to those picnickers. And to all of us, too. Nothing's been the same since he killed them. Never will be now. People talk about us all the time because of him. And come here asking questions, too.'

Karen thought of how Spike had told her that Peg visited him because she shared his hatred for his parents. Was anything he'd told her true? Or was his mother right when she said he was simply unable to tell the difference between his fantasies and reality?

'Is that why your aunt's so frightened to let anyone know she still tries to help him?' Karen said aloud.

'She feels guilty.' Sadness roughened Peg's voice. 'She thinks it's all her fault. First she couldn't have kids, so they had to adopt, and they got Spike, poor devils. He's like a dark germ in their lives, you know. Always has been. Once they had him they were ruined. Spoiled. For ever. Then, nearly as soon as they'd brought him home, she did fall pregnant, and Silas being born so soon was what sent Spike mad. She thinks he and Silas . . .' Peg broke off as another customer came through the pub's door.

Karen mentally cursed his arrival, then ordered herself a helping of chicken-and-olive pie and took her tomato juice to the familiar table under the window. With luck the newly arrived man would down a drink and disappear.

He didn't. He settled on a stool beside the bar, opened a packet of crisps, and took his pint with the slow appreciation of a man with all afternoon to waste. Only when the microwave's bell pinged and Peg pulled out the pie to bring across to Karen was there the slightest opportunity to finish the conversation.

'I'd better pay you now,' she said, as a way of holding Peg at her side. While she fumbled for change in her bag, she added: 'You were just going to tell me what your aunt thinks about her two sons.'

'No, I wasn't,' Peg said without expression, looking blank. 'Five ninety-five, please. Great. Thanks.'

'Before you go,' Karen said, 'did Spike ever hurt you when you were a child? Or try to hurt you?'

Peg took several steps backwards, shaking her head. Her skin paled and she laid a hand protectively over her bump.

'Sylvia wouldn't have let anyone touch me. She was always there whenever I went to the White House. She never left me alone with any of them: not the colonel, nor Spike, nor Silas. She wouldn't. I've got to go.'

For the rest of the twenty minutes during which Karen spun out the eating of her pie, other customers came and went, and Peg served them all with a cheerful smile, chatting, teasing, thanking them. Never once did she look in Karen's direction.

Just as Karen was getting her things together to leave, Peg took the pins out of her brown hair and let it fall around her face, long enough to hang just below her shoulders. She rubbed her hands through it, then collected it into a bunch at the back of her neck and twisted it up again, pushing in the pins without needing a mirror.

In that one unguarded moment when it had been loose, she had looked remarkably like Isabelle Sanders and the murdered swimmer, whose photographs Trench had showed Karen here when they'd first met.

Karen looked at a stall selling flowers near the hospital, then decided the bunches were all too girlie for Trench and abandoned the idea of getting him anything. At the reception desk in the main foyer, she found a short queue. Eventually she reached the head of it and asked where she could find him.

'Don't bother,' said a harsh voice behind her.

Karen turned and saw DS Eve Clarke, with a more than usually aggressive expression on her gaunt face.

'You can hardly stop me visiting the man who saved me from a severe burning,' Karen said, thinking DS Clarke looked ill enough to be an inmate here. Why didn't she exfoliate her grey skin? Or even use a bit of straightforward soap?

'I could if I wanted,' she said with a kind of pettishness that seemed at odds with her usual acerbity. 'But that's not what I meant. He's out cold. They've got him under incredibly strong painkillers. You wouldn't get anything out of him, even if they let you see him.'

'Did they let *you*?' Karen asked, wondering what she'd ever done to make the woman quite so hostile. It couldn't be just because DCI Trench had boasted of how she was going to help him clear up all the unsolved killings on the Island.

'Of course,' DS Clarke said. 'We're . . . colleagues. I'm official.'

'Fine,' Karen said aloud, thinking: you can't guard him 24/7. I can always come back later. 'See you.'

'Wait.'

'What now?'

DS Clarke pushed her face so close to Karen's that she could see the open pores on the other woman's nose, and two minute but hard-looking black bristles growing at one side of her chin. Perhaps she hated herself as much as she hated Karen. Only a woman who despised herself could take so little care of her appearance. The grime and bristles weren't like Trench's scruffy clothes and stubble; those, Karen was certain, had been carefully planned for maximum impact.

'Just because he's changed his mind again and decided you're clean after all,' said DS Clarke with spite in every word, 'that doesn't mean the rest of us agree. We *know* you had a part in Spike's escape *and* in setting up that hostage scene. No one would have taken the risks you did unless they knew they were safe.'

'Good luck with finding evidence to prove that bit of nonsense,' Karen said, not bothered by the repetition of these absurd accusations.

'I don't need luck. You'll have left traces somewhere, Doctor Taylor. People always do, however knowledgeable they are; however careful. We'll find them. And when the new temporary SIO arrives to fill in while DCI Trench is stuck in here, he'll know how to deal with you.'

DS Clarke didn't wait to allow Karen the last word, swinging round on her heel and striding out of the hospital. If her short skirt hadn't been quite so tight, the striding would have been a lot more effective.

'He's in Ward 14,' said the receptionist, smiling as though he'd enjoyed the spat.

'Thanks.' Karen waved and headed for the lifts, in spite of the suggestion that Trench was out of it and unable to communicate. She wouldn't trust any information given with the kind of venom DS Clarke had shown.

He was sitting up in bed, wide awake and eating grapes, when Karen reached Ward 14.

'Hi,' she said and saw the old wicked smile creasing up his face. As usual he hadn't shaved, but there was more excuse this time. 'This is a surprise. I was told you'd be comatose. How are you doing?'

'Hurts like fuck, but there's no serious damage. Could've been a lot worse. There are the burns, but they're not as bad as they felt, and I've got a couple of broken ribs. Otherwise no more than bumps and bruises and a sprained ankle. You?'

'I'm fine. We were amazingly lucky, you know. My ears stopped ringing fairly soon, and the headache's gone now, too. I wanted to thank you.'

'You already did, Karen.'

'And I wanted to ask you something about Spike and his family.'

Trench's smile widened. 'You had me worried for a minute. I thought you'd gone soft.'

'Soft? Me?'

'Surprised me, I must say. So what d'you need to know?'

'Silas.'

'What about him?'

'I met him for the first time just before you and I went for our walk along the beach, and I didn't like him at all. I wondered . . .'

'Come on. Out with it.'

Was she mad to have picked up tiny oddities and hesitations in what Peg had just said to her, added them to her own dislike of the way Silas had talked about 'protecting' his mother, and come up with the idea that he would do more or less anything to silence her? After all, Sylvia must have known the truth of what had happened within her family, whether she admitted it or not. Mad or not, Karen was going to have to find out.

'Given that I was set up for Spike's escape – with the theft and then artful semi-concealment of my sushi knife – I've been wondering whether Spike himself might have been set up for the killing at Chillerton Down,' she said, letting the words come out so fast they might sound accidental. She toughened her delivery and added, 'And whether the setter-up was Silas.'

Trench's smile faded and he leaned back against the pillows, looking exhausted.

'You're mad. Why would Silas arrange for his brother's escape from prison in the first place? And why try to pin the blame on you?'

'Because I was seen to be – or thought to be – getting a response from Spike,' Karen said patiently. 'What if Silas . . .? Well, if you don't like my identification let's make it a nameless person. What if *someone* heard that Spike and I were getting on so well they were afraid Spike might give me facts that would lay bare the whole deception, identify the mind behind the crimes? Someone who went on to kill Jim Blake because after the escape he, too, would have been in a position to betray the real perpetrator?'

'Barmy.' Trench now had his eyes closed.

'It may sound unlikely, but look at it without everything you think you know about them all. You've got two boys, one older and rougher than the other, possibly bullying him in the way older siblings can. They're in competition for everything, including their mother's attention – and affection.'

'I'm looking but I'm not buying,' he said. Charlie's eyes were open again, which gave her a small sense of encouragement.

'She told me she leaned over backwards to show Spike she didn't love him any the less because he was adopted,' Karen went on. 'She told him other children were merely born to their parents but he was chosen. He was *special*. What if Silas overheard and resented it? There he was, hearing over and over again that, unlike Spike, he was not special. He was younger and less effective, physically weaker too, probably more scared. Less loved. Less important. Less everything.'

'So?'

'Don't you think he might have taken action to make his mother see the adored elder boy was actually a murderous freak and not the perfect, chosen angel she kept telling him he was?'

'Are you telling me you think Silas slashed the Labrador? At age five? You cannot be serious.'

'OK, maybe that one doesn't work. But five isn't much younger than seven, and no one seems surprised that seven-year-old Spike did it.'

'He had form. Silas didn't.'

'Maybe. Anyway, I was thinking of the shooting of the pic-nickers. And maybe the deaths of your other dark-haired women, like the swimmer. I told you before that the two types of killing are so different they're more likely to have been committed by two separate people.'

'I didn't buy that either,' Trench said with a grimness she hardly noticed because she was concentrating on making him see it all her way.

'If the family were shot as a way of getting Spike into trouble,' she said, 'then I think the not-fitting would fit with the rest in itself, if you see what I mean.'

'Stop thinking and save us all a lot of bother. Silas had an alibi.'

Karen stood at the foot of Trench's bed, watching his expressive stubbly face. The round dark eyes showed a lot of pain held under control, impatience, and something else.

'You mean you *did* suspect him?' she said after a while. 'You got him to account for his whereabouts that day the family were shot? Why?'

'Me? No. I wasn't on the Island then. Concentrate, Doctor Taylor.'

She noticed the way he used her offical title again. A few minutes ago, she had been Karen.

'Someone, belt-and-braces kind of officer, took statements from everyone in any way connected,' he went on. 'I checked them as soon as I saw Spike must've been responsible for our unsolveds.'

'And what *was* Silas's alibi?'

'Hospital in London.' Trench sounded almost as dry and precise as Will would have been in the circumstances. 'Collapsed on his way to work and hung around A & E nearly all day, waiting for scans and such. It was a particularly busy day with a multiple RTA, so there were queues for every kind of scanner and special-ist. Took hours to process them all.'

'Sod it! Well, he could still have killed the swimmer and your other lost dark-haired beauties.'

'Give me a break, woman. OK, Silas could've done those. But it's not likely. I heard you'd got the hots for Spike, but I didn't believe it. Now I'm not so sure.'

Someone brushed past Karen, ignoring her completely.

'What the hell have you been doing to yourself, Charlie?' the newcomer said in a voice quite at odds with the aggressive words. She sounded warm and most desperately anxious. 'And why wasn't that hard-faced girlfriend of yours looking after you like she should've?'

He grinned. 'Mum. As I've told you before she's *not* my girlfriend. Why the hell have you come all this way?'

As she bent down to kiss him, he looked at Karen across her shoulder and mouthed 'Sorry'.

'You may not think she's your girlfriend,' his mother said crossly as she stood up straight again. 'But she does. Now tell me, son, how bad is it? Truly now.'

He looked around her to jerk his head at Karen in an unmistakable order to go and leave them alone. She nodded and walked out of the ward.

How convenient for Silas to have such an extraordinarily helpful alibi for the day when his brother went berserk and killed four people, she thought. It was enough to make you think he'd had advance warning that there was going to be trouble.

Silas did not look like the kind of man who'd collapse on his way to work either. Unless that hair-trigger temper was a sign of the kind of Type A aggression that can lead to heart attacks. Maybe. It could fit.

Karen drove to her favourite Internet cafe and logged on to her email. She found a message from Aidan:

How's it going? I don't mean finding the key to Dangerous Severe Personality Disorder. I mean things with Will Hawkins. I've been looking him up, you know, and asking around. Sounds like a good man. Very successful anyway for a surgeon of his

age. More important: never been married, but a string of beautiful girlfriends, although luckily none for the past three
months, so he's not trying to run two of you at once. His colleagues agog to know more about you, but I'm keeping mum.
Take care. A.

Karen smiled at the screen, as though there were a webcam so
that Aidan could see her. How typical that he'd been checking up
on Will, making sure she wasn't getting herself locked in to
another destructive relationship.

The oddity of his being able to do it from the other side of the
Atlantic struck her. Of course he had lots of friends in both
the legal and medical professions, but most of them were in the
States, where he'd qualified. Was the professional world really
small enough for him to ask these sort of questions about a British
neurosurgeon?

And how would Will feel if he heard that an American lawyer
had been asking about his love life? For a man who gave away as
little as Will, and who clearly liked his privacy, it could be tricky.
Karen realized he'd never mentioned his friends, or introduced
her to any of them.

They'd been together for less than four months, of course, but
wasn't it odd that he hadn't mentioned a single other person?
Even when he'd been confessing his fear – or the fear he'd made
up to comfort her – he hadn't said a word about his family or the
other people he saw when he wasn't working.

She quickly typed an email to Aidan.

Good to know my bloke's not running a harem, but I hope your
researches were discreet. Wouldn't want him to think I didn't
trust him.

Btw, since you're so good at finding out about people, could
you turn your detective skills to a City whizz-kid called Silas
Falconer? I don't even know what he does in London but he's

said to be successful. Any info your amazing net of contacts can fish up wd be most gratefully received.

Hpe all well. Love, K.

There were other emails in her in-box, mostly from Max, all variants on the first, which said:

You promised to go to the prison to talk to Spike. What have you got? You're halfway through your stint on the Island. You mustn't slack off now. You need some conclusions if you're to make your paper work. Call me.

Shan't, she thought crossly, then reached for her phone.

Chapter 20

Max Pitton was sitting at his favourite table in the Southampton restaurant where they'd taken Will on that first evening after his lecture. A glass of red wine was half-empty in front of him, and there were the crumpled wrappings of three packets of bread-sticks on the cloth.

His heavy face looked even more jowly than usual, as though he'd been forgetting his anti-cholesterol diet more often than usual. The silver lines that ran all through his mop of dark hair were broader, too. Altogether he looked older to Karen, even though it was only a few weeks since she'd seen him every day.

Karen remembered with a sharp burst of pleasure how much she liked him. Which was, of course, why it hurt so much when-ever he set about goading her into risking all her hard-won security. With luck he'd be in one of his gentler moods tonight. She could do with a bit of gentleness.

'Am I late?' she said, slinging her sloppy brown-leather shoulder bag on the banquette and sliding her long body into the gap after it.

'Only a few minutes. I got here early.' Max leaned across the unnecessary candle flame to peer into her face, and she had the usual impression of a laser-like mind behind the heavy face.

She wondered what hers showed and knew there was no point asking. He would only turn her question back into something else and sound like the worst kind of interrogator if she tried. And after everything that had happened in the last ten days, she wouldn't be surprised if she were betraying all sorts of stuff she'd rather keep private. The last time she'd let herself look closely at her reflection, she'd seen startled eyes and bitten lips and a general disintegration of the impregnable facade she liked to present to the world.

'So, revisiting Paradise Lost hasn't brought you peace of mind,' Max said, relaxing against the chair back again. 'Have you ever read *Le Grand Meaulnes* by the way?'

What was the point of pretending not to understand? He'd know if she lied. And he was being fairly kind – so far.

'Not yet,' she said, finding a formula that would answer both questions and preserve her self-respect – and her privacy.

'What's the chief impediment to mental comfort?'

'That I can't get any kind of handle on Spike. I don't understand the triggers that make him react, and nothing I've seen of him, or heard from him, fits.'

'Fits what: your assumptions about DSPD?'

'Those definitely. But he doesn't fit the crimes either. And I don't know whether he's deliberately muddling me, or whether his mind is so disorganized there *is* no handle for me to get. Or whether . . .' She hated to think of the lacerating contempt that would follow any half-digested account of her suspicions of Silas, so she stopped herself offering it up to him.

Max swallowed a big slug of wine, then signalled to the waiter for menus, even though they both chose the same dishes every time they came here and barely looked at the others on offer.

'But that's the difficulty with DSPD. There are no immutable patterns,' he said, as though to an anxious first year undergraduate.

It was time for Karen to show her teeth.

'Although we know there are two distinct types of violence,' she said. 'There's the disorganized sort, as shown in the picnic massacre. A family with no connection to the gunman, happening to

be in his line of sight on a day when he was armed and feeling . . . what? Sudden jealousy of their safe and satisfactory lives?
Afraid of them?'

'More likely the former. Or they could have impinged on something he was doing. Thinking, even. Get him to tell you what that
was and you may find the key.'

'It's hard to get him to tell me anything that matters. Whenever
we come anywhere near it, he retreats into manic giggling and
repetition. It's almost like hysteria.'

'Karen,' Max began, his voice was softening and his eyes looking kinder, less penetrating over the candle flame. This kind of
gentleness was usually the prelude to a particularly swingeing
piece of criticism.

She braced herself.

'How well do you remember your Winnicott?'

She thought for a moment about one of the most humane and
believable analysts of the middle part of the last century, who had
written so much that she couldn't instantly work out what Max
wanted. Then she saw it.

'You're talking about "manic defence", aren't you? But that
was really Melanie Klein's idea. Winnicott just added his own
gloss to her theories.'

Max's bizarrely jolly smile warmed his dark face.

'You've a good memory for the history of analysis. I'll say that
for you.'

'I've been specifically researching the roots of aggression for
this paper. Of course I remember which of them came up with
which theories.'

'Then don't you see how "manic defence" fits Spike's case?'

Karen dredged up one of the quotations she'd used in the notes
for the first draft of her as yet unwritten paper.

'It's used to hide the unbearable inner reality, usually in connection with depression. Didn't Winnicott write something like:
"As the depressive anxieties become less . . . and the belief in

good internal objects increases, manic defence becomes less intense and less necessary."'

'That's right. But there are those for whom belief in good internal objects never happens. Like Spike. Think of how that paper of Winnicott's went on. Have you got it in your head?'

Karen shook her head. 'Not to quote, no.'

Max's smile was tighter now, as though he felt uncomfortable. She wondered why.

'First of all he talks about what you see in a music hall, which isn't relevant any more, and which I couldn't begin to get right. But his description of the manic defence *is* still relevant, and it goes like this: "Here is exhibitionism, here is anal control, here is masochistic submission to discipline, here is a defiance of the super-ego." Doesn't that remind you of everything you know about Spike?'

'Exhibitionism, control, submission to discipline,' she repeated. 'Of course. Although he didn't do much submitting to discipline until he found himself in prison.'

She remembered how Jim had told her of his discovery that prison suited Spike because the rules and sameness made him feel safe.

'But it doesn't help me with my paper now. I can add my particular take on everything everyone else has written about his case, synthesize that with all the new theories about physical development, particularly in the right brain, but I still haven't got enough to make a paper worth writing, let alone submitting for publication in the hope of making my name.'

As she spoke an idea sprouted in her mind, like a seedling just breaking through the tough outer casing of the testa. Although she was still aware of the dark, brooding presence of her mentor across the table, and the hovering waiter, and the clatter and colour of the restaurant behind him, she was completely focused on ideas about how Silas and Spike might have interracted as they grew up in fear of their father, and about the violence that at

least one of them had used as an outlet for his own unbearable
feelings.

'Are you feeling all right?'

Max's voice broke through her thoughts. She made herself
look outwards again.

'I had a thought,' she said, making it casual. 'Too new to lay out
for you yet, but worth exploring. I'll tell you when I'm a bit further on and have a chance of convincing you.'

'All right. But what are you going to eat?'

'*Spaghetti puttanesca*, of course.'

'He was just telling us about one of the specials. I didn't think
you were listening.'

'Is very nice,' said the waiter, standing with his order pad between
his hands and flapping it, which made the candle flame flicker
wildly. 'Very tender, cookin' with oil and mostarda and 'erbs.'

'Sounds great, but what is "it"?' Karen asked, seeing his puzzlement turn to the kind of patience reserved for the seriously
weird.

'*Coniglio*. Rabbit.'

She gagged and tried to cover the instinctive reaction with a
gulp of water.

'I'll stick to the *puttanesca*, please.'

'Fine. And I'll stay with *fegato*. Thank you, Mario.'

Karen thought about reminding Max that liver was heavy on
cholesterol, then caught his eye and knew she didn't have to tell
him anything. When the waiter had gone, Max poured more
water into her glass.

'Something is wrong, Karen. Are you sure you're not ill?'

'I was distracted and then he spooked me talking about rabbits.'
She laughed uncomfortably. 'Don't ask. It's not important and it's
far too long a story to tell over dinner. How was your trip to
Turkey?'

Her mind drifted as he talked of mountains and mosques and
people he'd met. The most revolutionary and career-building

paper she could possibly write would be the one that unravelled a kind of double-helix of violence and disorder in the Falconer household.

Could Silas be even more interested in display, anal control, and masochistic submission to discipline than Spike himself?

Or maybe it was still more complicated and interesting. Maybe Spike hadn't simply been framed by Silas. Maybe they'd been partners in a folie à deux, with Silas providing the controlled intelligence behind the crimes and Spike the disordered excitement needed to carry them out – and the muddled devotion to take all the blame. Maybe the first discipline to which Spike had submitted had been Silas's. Was that possible?

Spike had definitely tried to protect Silas from the bullies at school. And he'd looked pink and excited and pleased when he'd thought Karen had told him that Silas was in the prison. Was that enough to . . .?

'Karen!'

Max had noticed her glazed eyes and lack of attention.

'Sorry. Living in the chalet has shut down all my normal social graces. I missed the last bit. Tell me again.'

This time his smile was even more Machiavellian than usual. 'And bore us both? No. Why don't *you* tell me how you're getting on with Will Hawkins.'

She felt her face heating up and hoped the light was dim enough to hide her colour. Her dealings with Will were far too private to be offered up to amuse Max.

'Broken through the ice cap yet?' he said, challenging her as so often before. 'I think he's the chilliest, most defended man I've ever met.'

Karen drank some wine and worked for a detached academic kind of delivery as she said: 'He told me you'd informed him that I had the hardest shell of any woman you've ever met. Have you been setting us up for a battle, like fighting dogs or something, Prof?'

He didn't answer, which was a confession in itself.

'You bugger,' she said, forgetting all about sounding detached and academic. 'You're working on something to do with mature relationships in dysfunctional people, aren't you? And you're using us as experimental subjects . . . Oh, you utter *shit*!'

She thought about leaving him in the restaurant, to eat humiliation with her food as well as his own, and pay the whole bill to boot. Then that seemed childish. And the glint in his narrowed eyes suggested he'd enjoy it, and would use it as evidence for whatever florid theory he was drawing up about her. Thank God she'd never given him any details about the night Peter died.

'Actually,' Max said, raising his wine glass and watching her over the rim, 'you're two of the people I most admire and care about, so I thought you might find something in each other to assuage your solitude.'

His voice was serious enough to make her want to believe him, and in a way that was worse. As was the suggestion that he'd known Will well before he'd introduced them over the lecture about the prefrontal cortex. What was he up to now?

Later Max walked back to the Red Jets' terminal with Karen and said: 'If you want to crack him, you're going to have to use shock tactics.'

She paused, one foot on the jetty, and turned. Max was standing directly under a street light, with its yellow glare making him look positively devilish, if any devil ever had such a stocky body and generously doubled chin.

'Are we talking Spike here, or Will?'

'Spike, of course.' Max looked hurt, which was absurd and so instantly put her on guard. 'I wouldn't presume to advise you on your dealings with a boyfriend. Don't forget Spike's not your patient, so you're not constrained as you would be if you were treating him.'

'Except by ethics and decency. He's a deeply damaged man.'

'Who has killed at least four people. Remember to save some sympathy for the victims.'

She kept her thoughts to herself, waved goodbye and went to a seat at the front of the craft. Ready to enjoy the sight of the water cloven by the bows for the twenty-three-minute crossing as the Red Jet zoomed across to the Island, she was suddenly reminded of the last time she'd looked at speeding boats and the spray they sent upwards. Just before an explosion and a head rolling towards her in the shallows.

'Have you ever had a head injury?' Karen asked Spike the next morning.

The sun was blazing in again, lightening his hair and casting a kind of whole-body halo around him. He didn't look as though he was suffering as a result of Jim's death, or missing the privileges he'd lost in punishment after the escape. In fact he looked almost smug.

'What're you after now?' he said, grinning. 'You want to claim I was kicked in the skull so I lost it and it's not my fault I killed that family? That's not going to help me at my appeal. They'd shove me in Broadmoor and that'd be worse than here. At least I've a chance of getting out of *this* place.'

I wouldn't count on it, she thought, then said: 'No, but have you? Most people have fallen off their bikes or something like that by the time they get to your age.'

He tipped his chair back. 'Yeah. Well, I was doing this once. It always wound up Pa and he said I'd end up with another crack in my skull.'

Karen remembered her own discomfort at the danger in which he was putting himself whenever he tilted his chair so far.

'And one day Silas came along behind me and thought it'd be funny to kick the back legs away. Would've been OK in the dining room because we had a thick carpet there. But it was on the terrace. I went arse over tit, but backwards, and cracked my head open on the edge of the stone.'

'Right,' she said, thinking: here's yet another effective story. He *can* tell them whenever he forgets to pretend to be out of control. 'How old were you?'

He shrugged. 'Fourteen maybe? Can't remember. Does it matter?'

'I doubt it.' She smiled. 'Did you need stitches?'

'Yeah. They took me to the hospital in Newport and I was there all day while they fiddled about with tests for this and that.' He laughed and let the chair clang forwards onto all four legs. He looked more straightforwardly amused than she'd ever known him. 'I've never seen Silas so scared. Everyone knew he'd done it, see, because my mum just came out onto the terrace in time to see him kick my chair. And he was afraid he'd be the one who got the punishment *this time*.'

Karen was glad she had her tape running and didn't have to concentrate on writing this down. There were odd emphases here and there, and a lot Spike wasn't telling her that might suggest itself on second or third hearings.

'So you were X-rayed, were you?'

'Scanned,' he said, making her feel so triumphant she had a hard time keeping her face calm.

'Would you be prepared to let me ask to see the scans?' she said. 'I'd have to get your permission.'

All the liveliness in his face closed down. He stared across the table, his eyes narrowed and his beautiful mouth pinched.

'Why?'

She thought about lying, about providing a comfortable excuse, then decided she owed him the truth; some of it anyway.

'Because I have a theory that being afraid makes physical changes in bits of the brain, and I'd like to see a scan taken at precisely the moment when you had things to fear.'

He laughed. The sound made her feel as though her blood temperature had dropped by at least ten degrees.

'I wasn't afraid, Doctor Taylor. I thought it was funny.'

'You must have been scared. Pain. Blood. Going through one of those huge old-fashioned scanners. Claustrophobia. Wondering how much damage had been done to your head.'

He'd stopped laughing, but the smile that curled his lips was even more disturbing. He licked them too, letting his tongue linger in the centre of his upper lip.

'But I like pain and blood,' he said. 'You know that, Doctor Taylor.'

One finger stroked the four parallel scars in his cheek, but his gaze never shifted. Knowing how much he wanted a reaction, she kept a small patient smile on her own lips and waited, saying nothing.

'That's what it's all been about,' he said, his voice rising in timbre and tension, heading towards the hysteria that came upon him whenever he was on the brink of saying something really useful. 'Pain and blood. Blood and pain. Pain and blood, Doctor Taylor.'

You'll need to shock him if you're to crack him, Max had said.

'I don't think it's been about pain and blood at all,' she said, holding his gaze and breathing with enough care to keep her voice as steady as her eyes. 'I think it's all been about Silas. He's the one who likes the pain and the blood, isn't he? But he's never taken the responsibility. You were always his fall guy. Not just when you physically fell off the chair, but . . .'

Spike was on his feet now, leaning towards her across the table. She had never seen such pure, concentrated fury in anyone. Forcing her gaze away from his for a second, she made herself look at his hands, splayed now on the tabletop. The knuckles were scraped and swollen, as though he'd been in a fight – or perhaps been banging his hands against the walls in frustration.

She raised her eyes and stared at him.

'Say that again,' he said, and he sounded calm and cold and utterly in control.

Her finger strayed towards the panic button. While Spike was on the far side of the table, even leaning so close that she could smell the cornflakes he'd had for breakfast, she was safe, but with such violent and unpredictable changes in his mood she wasn't taking any chances.

She said nothing.

His nostrils flexed and when his lips parted in a gesture that was nothing like a smile, she saw his teeth were clamped together, across the tip of his tongue. It must hurt, but he showed no sign.

'You come in here, playing games with me,' he said so quietly she had to strain to hear him, 'trying to trap me. You insist on being alone with me so you won't have any witnesses to what you're trying to trick me into saying. But that means you haven't got anyone to protect you now. And you can take your finger off that button. They couldn't get here soon enough to save you. Bitch.'

'Sit down, Spike,' she said, keeping her finger where it was.

He let his teeth part and licked his lips again. 'Did they tell you how Jim Blake died?'

Oh God, no! she thought, seeing it all over again: his head rolling towards her through the surf.

Was this what happened with Jim? Was the escape real after all? Did Jim somehow fail you or arouse this kind of mental aggression and then find it turning physical?

'He drowned,' she said, speaking as coldly as Spike, and with even more calm. The one thing she knew for certain was that she must not allow herself to show any fear that could ratchet up his excitement and therefore the danger he represented to her.

'No.' His beautiful face was wiped of all expression, but he giggled.

She felt as though insects were crawling under her clothes, covering her whole skin.

'If you ask the right people, Doctor Taylor, you'll find he was strangled first and then thrown in. Strangled with the wire from a bike's padlock. Cut right into the flesh of his neck, you know, Doctor Taylor. Cut it right to the bone. Like I told you, wire sometimes does that, like with rabbits when you snare them. Right in, through the skin and lots further too, Doctor Taylor. Right as far as the big bones of the spine. They go right up inside the skull, you know, Doctor Taylor. Right up.'

Karen kept her face blank, proud to feel the solidity of her control. In spite of the crawling, itching sensation in her skin, she could still feel calm. Even her dodgy gut was behaving itself and the saliva in her mouth, always responsive to any fear she felt, was normal.

Spike straightened up so he could lift his hands from the table. He looked away from her so he could concentrate on them, turning them one way then the other. The sunlight fell across his reddened, swollen knuckles and picked up the clean white half-moons at the base of the nails.

'D'you know how easy it is to strangle someone, Karen? Particularly a woman. You don't need wire with women.' The teetering excitement in his voice had gone. He sounded serious and in charge again.

'Like the swimmer?' she said. You need shock to crack him. 'The woman swimmer you strangled at Alum Bay and then sliced up?'

Surprise chased the tension out of his expression, and the surprise looked genuine.

'What swimmer?' he said, distracted from the threats as well as the fantasy that had been exciting him so much. 'What slicing?'

'We'll leave that till next time,' she said. 'You'd better sit down again, while I ring to be let out.'

The inward expression in his eyes suggested he was worrying away at what she'd said, trying to make sense of it. But he did sit down.

Deeply grateful, still controlling her breathing and reactions, Karen collected her papers and her tape recorder and stuffed

them into her canvas bag. She wouldn't look at him as she rang
the bell, trying to keep her conscious mind absolutely blank. At
the door, she greeted the officer, who'd unlocked it, then half-
turned to say casually:

'See you tomorrow, Spike.'

He held up his hands in a cup shape before ramming the fingers
together, just as he'd done once before to show her how he strangled animals. And then he giggled.

Chapter 21

Outside, she waited for the main gate to clang shut, then turned, as though to unlock her car and found her hand clamped to the key, unable to move. Her other hand flew up to cover her mouth as the saliva poured into it.

You're not going to be sick, she ordered herself. You're not going to be sick. There was some cause to be frightened in there and you held on. There's no cause now. You're out. You're safe. You are *not* going to be sick.

And then a different part of her brain lit up as she thought: He didn't know anything about the swimmer. He really didn't.

Saliva could be swallowed, she discovered, without conscious thought or any difficulty.

There *had* been two quite different minds involved in the violent killings on the Island, just as she'd always thought. She wondered yet again where Silas had been when the swimmer was strangled and slashed.

But she had enough to do finding out about his suspiciously perfect alibi for the death of the Sanders family on Chillerton Down.

'Are you all right?'

At the sound of a vaguely familiar voice, she turned and recognized the slight man in a rumpled grey suit as the prison governor, whom she'd met during a brief interview when she'd first applied to study Spike. The governor had told her then that he'd do anything he could to further her research: the more she could tell him about DSPD and the best way of dealing with it in a prison setting the better.

'It's Doctor Taylor, isn't it?' he said, coming closer, with a smile on his pleasant ordinary face. 'Good to see you. How are you getting on with Spike?'

'Not at all well,' she said, determined to protect her new ideas until she had some evidence to support them. 'Each time I talk to him, I think I've got a better idea of how his mind and emotions work and then, the next time, I realize I know nothing.'

He smiled, looking more like the exhausted kindly father of ten small children than the governor of a tough prison.

'I've often thought it was like trying to hold a fistful of water and carry it without spilling any,' he said. 'Talking to Spike, I mean. I've given up, except when he asks to see me. Anything I can do to help you with him?'

'He's just told me that Jim Blake was strangled before being drowned.'

'I gather that's true,' said the governor. 'What's the problem?'

'It hasn't been reported in any of the media.'

The governor looked at her with pity. 'Haven't you discovered yet that nothing can be kept confidential here? Some of my officers have friends in the police. Families of some of my inmates have friends in the police. Someone in the force, or perhaps the coroner's office or the lab talked, and whoever heard passed it on. And probably at about fifth hand, it reached one of my inmates and then it would have been all over the wings. I don't know whether Spike's guilty of killing Jim. We'll just have to wait for the investigation to be completed. But you can rest assured that he could have got any amount of sensitive information without having been involved.'

He checked his watch, then started walking towards the parked cars. 'Sorry to rush, but I'm in danger of being late. Anything else I can do for you?'

'Not at the moment. Thank you. And thank you for easing my path with Spike. It's a real help.'

'Have you found anything useful for your research?' he asked, as they reached his car.

'Not yet.' Karen remembered to smile. 'Goodbye.'

In Cowes she logged on to her email and nearly cheered when she saw she had a message from Aidan in the in-box, labelled 'Silas'.

Can't help on your Silas Falconer fellow. Only info from any of my mates in the UK medical world (the ones who are so curious about you and Will Hawkins) is that someone called Silas Falconer used to go out with an A & E house officer called Margaret Spack. Don't suppose that's much help. If I knew anyone in banking I could probably do better, but I don't.

'You'd be surprised,' Karen muttered, remembering what Sylvia Falconer had said about one of Silas's girlfriends.

Karen clicked out of email and on to the most used social networking sites, but she found no useful leads there. Back to Google, she typed in 'Margaret Spack' and again found nothing. After a moment, she changed the first name to Maggie, planning to go on to Mags, Meg, and any other variant she could imagine.

None was necessary. Maggie Spack was a director of a medical press agency. Clicking through the site to the directors' biographies, Karen discovered that her quarry *had* been a doctor, 'specializing in emergency medicine', but had stopped practising four years earlier.

The coincidences were piling up. And the elaborately unbreakable alibi was looking dodgier by the minute.

Karen saved Maggie Spack's contact details on the memory stick she always carried with her, then flicked back to her own email in-box. Amid the offers of ever-more bizarre pharmaceuticals and penis extensions was a message from an unfamiliar name.

She opened it to see something as formally presented as an old-fashioned letter:

Dear Doctor Taylor,

The police refused to give us your contact details, which is why we've Googled you to get your email address. We just wanted to thank you for everything you did for our daughter, Ellie. Without your courageous intervention anything could have happened. We can't bear to think about it.

We understand that you are a psychiatrist and would very much like to consult you about the most appropriate help we should seek for Ellie now. She won't speak about the experience of being taken hostage and we are sure that bottling it up must be deleterious.

If there is any help or advice you can give us, we should be so very grateful.

Yours sincerely,

Thomas and Mary Bridger

They had trustingly typed in their full address, including the post code, and their landline and two mobile numbers. They lived at the other end of Hampshire, not at all far from London and the press agency where Maggie Spack worked.

Karen transferred their details to the memory stick, too, then reached for her phone to arrange to meet them and explain the difference between the psychiatrist of their assumptions and the psychologist she actually was.

Maggie Spack, she thought, had better be taken by surprise. Karen wanted every possible advantage on her side. Shock was the greatest, as the prof kept reminding her.

Before she'd pressed the first digit on the phone, it rang.

'Karen Taylor,' she said.

'Doctor Taylor, it's DS Clarke here. We're at your chalet and would like to talk urgently.'

'About what?'

'As I said when we met at the hospital, we've a new temporary SIO from the mainland dealing with the Jim Blake murder, now that DCI Trench is in hospital, and he needs to talk to you. Today.'

'Unfortunately, I'm not on the Island at the moment,' Karen said, clicking out of her email and closing down her session on the cafe's computer. She tried to keep her voice calmer than her manic fingers. 'I'll phone and fix a time with you as soon as I get back, probably tomorrow evening.'

'That's too vague. I need a time now.'

'OK,' Karen said. 'I could be with you around seven o'clock.'

'In the evening?'

'Yes.'

'That'll have to do. We'll be waiting. And this time bring a lawyer with you.' DS Clarke cut the connection before Karen could comment, leaving her to stare at the phone.

Bring a lawyer with me, she thought. Why? Are they planning to *arrest* me?

They had to be. There was no other explanation. Remembering how much she had to do and find out, she abandoned the Internet cafe and ran for Fountain Quay, where the Red Jets had their terminal. One should be leaving within the next seven minutes.

If DS Clarke bothered – and had the budget for it – she could pinpoint the precise spot where Karen had been when she answered her phone, which would not help her reputation in any subsequent enquiry. But it didn't seem likely. And it was too late to correct in any case.

Chapter 22

Karen had a stitch by the time she saw the entry to Fountain Quay. The pain was making her even more breathless than the race. She drove her fingernails into her palms for distraction and ran on, shoving exactly the right money for a one-way ticket through the gap in the glass window of the office.

'Southampton,' she gasped. There were half-moon-shaped dents in her palm, dark red in the glistening skin, from where her nails had pressed down so hard. One had even broken the skin and was oozing much brighter blood.

The man in the booth took far more time than he needed, counting out her money and pressing the buttons. But the machine spat out the ticket in the end. She grabbed it and ran again, just leaping aboard the catamaran as the ticket collector was closing the gate.

She collapsed onto a seat, both hands now pressing into the pain in her side.

'Tickets, please!'

Karen dragged one hand away to hold up her ticket.

'You were lucky,' he said, with an intimidating edge to the comment. 'We're not supposed to wait.'

She nodded her thanks and waited until the pain had more or less gone before fishing her phone out of her bag. It was a bore to be without clothes or notes, but she wasn't going to risk being picked up by DS Eve Clarke before she'd got more ammunition of her own.

Had Clarke been winding up the new SIO's suspicions for fun? Or had the team actually found more evidence that had been designed to point in Karen's direction? They had to have some reason to pull her in. Senior officers in murder enquiries always had too much to do to waste time on games-playing or private battles.

Max Pitton answered her call after two rings.

'I need your car,' Karen said.

'Why?'

She laughed. 'Because I'm on the run.'

'So I hear.'

'Don't be ridiculous. It was a joke. I had to leave urgently, and there are people I need to talk to. I have to have a car to get to them, and mine's stuck outside the chalet.'

'The police have been on to me. A Sergeant Clarke. She wanted to know if I'd heard from you, or knew where you were. I said as far as I knew you were safely on the Island, doing the work you were supposed to be doing. Now, I hear you've . . .'

'Oh, stop it!' she said, recognizing the long-winded preamble he occasionally used for jokes and teases. In a way, she thought, their relationship was more like something between siblings than mentor and junior member of a university department. Maybe she put up with such a lot from him because he fitted into the gap left by Aidan.

'Come on, Prof, *can* I have the car?'

'I don't suppose I can stop you taking it. I get so careless these days, I tend to leave the spare key in the glove compartment and often forget to lock the doors. When are you likely to get to it? I wouldn't want anyone else taking advantage of my carelessness.'

'You're a jewel among men,' she said, forgiving him all the bad times he'd given her. 'I'm on the Jet. I'll be outside your house in about twenty-two minutes.'

'Don't ring my bell. I'll see you when you're done with all this.'

'Absolutely.'

'And, Karen?'

'Yup?'

'Don't do anything really stupid, will you? You need a pristine reputation if you're ever to become the expert witness I want you to be, and you do seem a trifle accident-prone just now.'

'Point taken. Bye.'

That done, she phoned the direct line of Spike's solicitor, who had made all the arrangements for her visits to him in the prison.

'You have reached the voicemail of Sam Potter. I'm either on another call or away from my desk. Leave a message and I'll get back to you as soon as I can.'

'Hi, Sam. It's Karen Taylor here. Your client Spike Falconer had a brain scan on the Island when he was about fourteen, following an accident at the White House. I am very keen to see this. He seems happy enough for me to have a look. Could you get hold of it for me? You have my email address, so if you could send it that way I'd be really grateful. Otherwise to my postal address at the university would be fine. Many thanks.'

Then she called the prison to leave a message, warning Spike she wouldn't be able to keep her appointment to see him tomorrow. Remembering the scars on his cheek, she hoped this time the prison officer would pass the message on.

The next call was to the Bridgers and it lasted her for the rest of the voyage.

When she saw Max's car neatly parked outside his house, she had a moment's angst that he might have been stringing her along and be ready to leap out of the building with a phalanx of arresting officers. Several people were walking along the street, all of them strangers and none of them interested in anything she was doing.

Her hand on the door, wondering whether the alarm was about to shriek out and make them curious, she pressed down. The handle yielded, the key was in the glove compartment as Max had promised, and she was in the driving seat and away without anyone stopping to question her.

He didn't have satnav, but the Bridgers lived near Farnham, so it was an easy journey with plenty of signposts. Once she was free of Southampton, all she had to do was head on up to Winchester, then along the A31: only about forty miles in all. She was at least an hour ahead of the post-work rush, so she should be there by 'tea time', as they'd asked.

'Tea' for the Bridgers turned out to be the old-fashioned kind with sandwiches, scones and two sorts of cake, and a fine Darjeeling poured from a white porcelain pot. Ellie drank milk with great neatness from a bone-china mug with her name painted between sprigs of pink roses tied with pale-blue ribbons.

Karen was relieved to see she was dressed with much more modern practicality in a pair of blue shorts and a skimpy striped top. Her fine blonde hair was tied back in a matching blue scrunchie. She didn't smile or speak or eat, but she drank her milk. Her parents chatted to each other and to Karen in a stilted way about the weather and the state of the traffic on the A31 and the charms of the small villages around Farnham.

'And what's your work, Mr Bridger?' she asked during an uncomfortable pause.

'I'm in the City,' he said.

'Specifically?'

He looked shifty and suspicious at the same time. She knew enough to understand that meant he was in the middle of some big deal and not that he was awaiting a summons for a criminal offence.

'I only ask,' she said, 'because the man involved in what happened has a brother in the City. I wondered if you'd ever come across him. Silas Falconer.'

He shook his head.

'And what about Dan Sanders, the man who . . .?' Karen

glanced at Ellie and knew she couldn't explain that Dan was the man who had been shot with his wife and children on Chillerton Down.

'I did know him, yes. We never had any close dealings, but I used to see him around, poor b . . . poor man.' Bridger's face seized up in a frown. 'You don't think there's a connection?'

'I can't see how there could be,' Karen said, 'but it *is* a coincidence that all three of you were once working in the same square mile of London.'

A faint smile lit his haggard face for an instant. 'Along with thousands of other people. Don't read anything in to that. Please.'

He let his eyes slide sideways, directing her to his daughter, still sitting tidily at the table holding her pretty mug.

'Would it be all right for me and Ellie to do some drawing?' Karen said obediently. She turned to the silent child. 'Would you like that, Ellie?'

Both parents held their breath. Karen could hear the tension in their silence and feel them willing their daughter to answer. She didn't speak, but she did eventually nod.

'Great,' Karen said in her easiest voice. 'I've brought some paper and the kind of waxy crayons that have really bright colours. Where shall we go?'

She directed the question to Mrs Bridger, but Ellie slipped from her chair and inserted her hand into Karen's and pulled.

Mrs Bridger started to breathe more easily again and her husband gave Karen a tiny thumbs-up gesture. She allowed Ellie to tow her into an elegant conservatory that had been built along the side wall of the house. The floor was of grey-green matt tiles, and the walls a lighter version of the same colour, which prevented the unbearable white glare of most conservatories she'd seen.

Pink, lilac and white flowering plants spilled over the edges of great celadon tubs and tumbled down from two tall stone columns. Karen couldn't identify the plants, but their mingled scents filled the whole warm room with a sweetness so fresh it didn't seem cloying.

A metal table covered in verdigris stood in the centre, with four cushioned chairs around it. Ellie tugged at one, but it was too heavy for her, so Karen pulled it out, watched her scramble into it, and then pushed it towards the table as though she were launching a small boat.

'D'you know what you want to draw?' Karen said, spreading a large plain pad in front of Ellie and opening the box of crayons.

The child nodded and selected the dark-blue crayon to draw a short stick figure with another, much bigger, looming over her. They had empty circles for heads and no hands at the ends of the arms. Nothing suggested ropes or guns or even minor explosions. Karen waited.

Ellie's small hand reached out and took the yellow crayon. She used it to draw a huge house behind the two stick figures, with many windows and a big pedimented door.

So far so good, Karen thought. But it was as far as Ellie wanted to go. She put the crayons back and waited.

'You haven't coloured in the people's heads,' Karen said cheerfully. 'I don't know what kind of hair they've got, for instance, or what colour their faces are. Have they got suntans?'

Ellie reached for the yellow crayon again and Karen held her breath. The child stick figure was given a scrawly yellow mop. Then Ellie hesitated, before reaching forwards again with the same wax crayon.

That's one theory gone, Karen thought, as she waited for the yellow point to land on the adult's head.

Ellie ignored him and pushed the point of the crayon down in the middle of the house and scrubbed it to and fro across the paper until the whole house had been coloured yellow, except for the windows. She filled those in with a black crayon, as though she could not bear the thought of what they might reveal.

Then she put the yellow crayon back and hesitated. At last she picked up the orange one, and gave the looming adult figure a good flaming mop. And, without any more prompting, she dabbed the now-blunt point on the figure's face, giving him vast freckles.

'Thank you,' Karen said, knowing that the drawing could never be used in court evidence because it had been collected so informally and without witnesses who'd be able to testify to Ellie's independence in picking not only the subject of the drawing but the revealing colours she'd used.

Karen wished she knew what Ellie had managed to tell the police, either in words or in some non-verbal way like this. They should have asked her to give her story, even if they were convinced that Spike had taken her.

Still, evidence-gathering was not the only thing that had brought Karen here.

'The red-headed man is dead now,' she said quietly. 'You won't ever see him again, Ellie. And he can never hurt anyone else.'

Ellie looked at her with wide eyes, sucking her lower lip. Then she rootled in the crayon box again and took out the pink one. Having turned the page in the big sketch book, she started another drawing, full of flowers. She was concentrating hard now, with her tongue clenched between her teeth, and her hand movements speeded up. One crayon was chucked back in the box and another picked up, and then another, to create a multicoloured flower bed.

Then came a seated stick-figure with long yellow hair hanging either side of a round button of a face, and a smaller stick-figure in its lap.

There was soon a huge yellow sun in the sky above them, sending out perfectly straight rays, and last, in bright turquoise, the simplified wing shapes that have always signified birds in children's pictures. Nothing could have said 'safety' more clearly.

'Was that how it felt when we were in the garden?' Karen asked, almost winded by the size of the compliment, and Ellie nodded. Then she smiled, a tiny fugitive smile. But still she didn't speak.

'Thank you, Ellie.' Karen got up. 'I need to talk to your mummy now. Will you be all right here?'

Ellie nodded, then hesitantly tore the two pictures from the pad and offered them to Karen.

'They're lovely. Thank you.'

Karen hurried back to the living room, where the Bridgers were waiting in silence.

She spread out the drawings for them, saying: 'I don't think you need worry too much. Ellie's guarding her privacy because what happened is still too difficult to talk about, but she's not in denial about any of it. And even if it's difficult to express, the fear isn't paralysing her. She'll be OK. Just give her time.'

'Thank God.' Mrs Bridger took her husband's hand and tightened her fingers round it. 'How can we help her?'

'She would almost certainly benefit from psychotherapy – to help her deal with what happened. There are some very good practitioners round here. I put together a list in case you wanted it.'

'May we say you recommended them?'

'Of course. They won't all know who I am, but they have all been highly recommended to me.' Karen hesitated, then, remembering all her rage at some earlier psychoanalysts, added: 'And none of them would do her any harm.'

'That's the most important thing,' said Tom Bridger. 'We can't thank you enough, Doctor Taylor, not just for this. Today, I mean. But for saving her at such risk to yourself.'

'I was fairly sure there was no one in the house with her by the time I got there,' Karen said. 'And if I hadn't been around, the police would have got her out soon enough. They're good at this kind of thing.'

'Not according to the press,' said Bridger with the kind of force Karen imagined he must use in the City.

'Every job has some people who are less good than the best. Why should the police be any different?' she said, thinking of DS Clarke and her unnecessary and counter-productive aggression. 'I must go. Thank you for letting me see Ellie. I hope it all goes well.'

They shook hands, and Bridger escorted her to Max's car.

Chapter 23

As Karen drove on towards London through the thickening traffic, she planned her approach to Maggie Spack. She would already have left the office by now, but Karen could think of at least four different ways of getting access in the morning. In the meantime, she ought to warn her mother of her plan to stay the night. A lay-by was signalled, so she flicked on her indicator and swung the old but powerful Audi off the road.

Both her parents were out, which made life very easy.

'Hi, it's me,' Karen said into the answering machine, 'on my way to London. OK if I stay tonight? I've got my keys so won't need to bother you, and I'll pick up some food. Hope to see you later.'

More and more vehicles joined the traffic from every side road as she slogged up the A3. The queue slowed almost to a standstill once they reached Kingston. Karen couldn't think why so many people were pouring *in* to London during the rush hour. Eventually she picked her way through the back streets of Earlsfield and Wandsworth, stopping at a handy supermarket to load up with cheese, wine, decent bread and fruit, to reach her parents' flat soon after seven.

Taking up half the top storey of an old school, its windows offered a magnificent panorama of London north of the Thames. On a clear day you could see all the landmarks from St Paul's and the Gherkin to the Post Office Tower. Tonight, in a kind of murky pink-grey haze, there wasn't much of a view.

They had bought the place as a shell nineteen years ago, during an unexpectedly flush moment and, having no mortgage, had hung on to it through all the ensuing crises. Their rationale for never using the flat as collateral for a business loan was that if everything else failed, they would still have somewhere to live that didn't entail moving to the Isle of Wight.

The red light on the answering machine was winking, which suggested they hadn't been back to pick up their messages since she'd phoned. That suited Karen. She wrote a note to leave on the table in the huge main room, which served for eating, sitting, working and watching the huge flat-screen television. Her father's old table football set was still in pride of place to the left of the enormous unused hearth.

Having left her note, she put the food in the kitchen, opened the wine to let it breathe, and took herself off to the guest end of the flat for a long hot shower. As she was towelling herself dry, she heard someone coming in.

'Hi!' she called, as she opened the bathroom door.

'Karen? That sounds like you,' said her mother, Dillie, in a voice that held nothing but exhaustion.

The business must be heading down again, Karen thought. At other times nothing could fatigue Dillie, not twenty-four-hour stints in the office or even the worst of bad-tempered clients giving her grief.

'Yes, it's me. You on your own?'

'For the moment.'

Karen dragged the dressing gown off its hook, wrapped it round herself and padded out, leaving damp footmarks all over the polished wooden boards. Dillie looked as played out as she'd sounded, so Karen kissed her.

'D'you mind if I stay tonight?'

'Frankly, I'd love it. But I haven't got anything to feed you on.'

Karen pointed towards the kitchen. 'I loaded up on the way. It's not much, but it'll keep us from starving.'

'Something needs to.'

Karen slung a damp arm around Dillie's shoulders. 'Things will pick up soon. They always do.'

'Maybe, but it's hard to remember that when you have to keep switching your credit cards around to catch the next zero-interest rate deal.' Dillie rubbed her forehead with both hands and blew out a tremendous sigh.

Karen saw that her scarlet nail varnish was chipped and the nails beneath grimy.

'It was fun when we were in our twenties,' Dillie went on, 'but honestly, you know, once you're sixty-two you want a bit of payback and some peace, not the same old struggle on and on and bloody on!'

'I'm sure. I opened a bottle. D'you want some?'

For the first time in Karen's life, her mother put both hands on her face and pulled her forward to be kissed.

'Karen, darling, that's the best news I've heard in months.'

'You put your feet up, then. I'll get some clothes on, and I'll bring you a glass and some grub. OK?'

'Heaven.'

'Can I borrow some pants? I didn't have time to pack any clean clothes.'

'Sure. Help yourself.'

Her parents' bedroom was in its usual state during one of their more depressed periods, and Dillie had obviously sacked the cleaner again. Books teetered in heaps all around the walls. The dressing table was a mess of cotton-wool balls, make-up tubes, bottles with their lids off, torn envelopes, bills and flyers for exhibitions, new credit cards, Internet deals and more. Pale dust lay over it all, as though someone had held a giant sieve of flour just under the ceiling and shaken it hard.

Drawers were open, with tights and the sleeves of shirts and sweaters hanging out. One side of the great bed was neatly smoothed – her father's – the other was a muddle of crumpled sheet and lump of unshaken duvet, with three battered Georgette Heyer paperbacks muddled up in it all.

It's really bad then, Karen thought, helping herself to two pairs of clean cotton briefs, and a plain V-necked black T-shirt, which would do for tonight and tomorrow morning, so long as she didn't drip wine down it.

'I had your mother-in-law on the phone the other day,' Dillie said as they shared the last of the very ripe Brie.

'What did *she* want?' Karen said, remembering for the first time in days that she'd been supposed to tackle Helen and tell her to stop spraying dangerous accusations around.

'Donations for one of her charity auctions, and an introduction to my best clients for a really stonking lot. Didn't she ask you for anything? Bid now for a day with your tame shrink.' Dillie laughed. 'I can see them lining up. You could have earned her at least a fiver.'

The state of the business must be even worse than I thought, Karen decided.

Careless as her mother had always been, preoccupied and uninterested in her children, she had never mocked them like this until bankruptcy was a real possibility.

'She's stopped phoning me direct,' Karen said.

'Why? What happened?'

Karen shrugged. She could have done without this conversation right now.

'Oh, nothing much. She wanted to tell me all over again how it was my fault Peter drove into that tree. I told her she was lucky she didn't know the whole story, or have any idea what her beloved son was like, and if she didn't want me to enlighten her, she'd better stay off the phone.'

'She told me all that, too,' Dillie said casually, pouring the last of the bottle into Karen's glass, which was her way of offering comfort.

She planted both elbows on the thick glass top of the trestle table and smiled encouragingly.

'I shouldn't have done it,' Karen said.

'Probably not. But there's a lot we've all done we shouldn't have. Forget 'em all. Fuck 'em all.' Dillie's worried eyes sharpened as she focused on a new idea. 'Why're you in London? You're supposed to be in that miserable hut on the Pile of Shite.'

'I have to see someone tomorrow on what may be a wild-duck hunt.'

'Goose. Goose hunt.' Dillie's voice was slurred, too. 'No: chase. A wild-goose chase. That's right. I'm sure that's what's right. Nothing about ducks at all. What're you thinking of?'

Karen laughed, truly cheerful at last. 'I know, Dillie. The real phrase is just such a cliche, it's easier to turn it into a joke.'

'Nothing wrong with cliches. They're what we live on. Karen, you know how you once said that Peter . . .?'

'You know, I'm knackered. I'd better go to bed. Will you be OK?'

'Sure. Your father will be back in due course. And then we'll know whether we'll live to fight another day.'

'Who's he with?'

'The client we've been stalking for two years. The hunt's cost us millions, but if we get him we'll be worth *billions*. Well, more or less. His account'll see us through to retirement anyway. Off you go. Your eyes are disappearing with sleepiness. I'll see you in the morning.'

Karen woke to a scream, a long wild shriek that had her out of bed, tripping over her sheet, and grabbing the dressing gown before she could think. She'd got only one arm into a sleeve – and that was the wrong one – by the time she burst into the main room.

Her parents were dancing together, while her mother screamed out tension and triumph.

'Christ! You had me worried,' Karen said.

Her father looked round and laughed. 'Good to see you've still got an amazing figure,' he said, 'but aren't you going to get cold? You'd better get back to bed. We're certainly going. God! I could sleep for a week now. Come on, Dillie, darling. Bye, Karen.'

As they disappeared into their end of the flat, she thought how familiar the scene had been. Absorbed in each other and their business to the exclusion of everything and everyone else.

She went back to bed, composing a funny account of it all to email to Aidan in the morning. You had to laugh, she thought.

The alternative was unthinkable.

They were still asleep, both of them snoring loudly, when Karen slipped out of the flat next morning. She'd decided on her strategy and, buying a day parking ticket so she could leave Max's car outside their flat, she took the Tube into central London, where she gritted her teeth and spent a fortune on a magnificent tied bunch of mixed white scented flowers. Having written a message on the accompanying card, she walked in to the offices of First & Best Medical News Agency, and asked to speak to Maggie Spack.

'You can leave those with me,' said the receptionist. 'Save you time.'

Karen smiled. 'It's fine, thanks. I promised to deliver them personally.' She wrinkled her nose and made her voice childishly amused and naughty: 'It sounded quite important, actually.'

The receptionist gave her a conspiratorial smile in return, saying: 'OK. Take a seat then.' She rang an internal number, then looked up again to add: 'She won't be long.'

Karen waited, idly looking through the glossy brochures in a swivel stand, and learned that the agency offered worldwide coverage of all matters medical, nutritional and pharmaceutical.

'You wanted me?' said a pleasant unaccented voice.

Karen looked up to see a comfortably shaped woman, who appeared to be in her late thirties, dressed in khaki cargo pants, a yellow sweater with a hood trailing down her back and gold trainers.

'Are you Maggie Spack?' Of all the types of women who might have appealed to Silas Falconer, City whizz, this was the least likely. She must be ten years older, too. Karen's heart sank.

'That's me.'

'These are for you,' Karen said, offering her the exquisite flowers.

'Wow!' Maggie did all the right things: plunged her nose into the flowers and produced a gratified murmur to approve the scent; then held the bouquet further away, the better to see it. 'These are gorgeous. Who're they from?'

'There's a note.' Karen pointed to the small white envelope attached to one of the sturdier stems.

Maggie gave the flowers back to her to hold and opened the envelope. As her eyes moved from the first line to the second, she swayed, and all colour drained from her cheeks, leaving only a few dark-red threads of broken veins. She looked old. And frightened.

Chapter 24

'Who are you?' Maggie Spack said in a voice so strained it was painful to hear.

'Karen Taylor, forensic psychologist.'

'I knew it. What's he done? Who's he hurt?'

'We need to talk,' Karen said firmly. 'Is there somewhere we can go? A coffee shop, maybe?'

Maggie looked backwards, as though she thought crowds might be watching them. Only the receptionist was there and she was furiously typing at her keyboard, failing to hide her burning curiosity.

'I'm off for half an hour or so, Belle. Can you hold the fort?'

'Sure.'

'And put these in water? They can go in the boardroom.' Maggie shivered, but her voice was almost steady. 'Great. Thanks. Now, Ms Taylor, come on. And talk.'

Karen waited until they were sitting on soft chairs in the window of the nearest Starbucks. Only three quarters of an hour after the start of most people's working day, the place was more or less empty. The two baristas were uninterested in anything except their own conversation, and the only other customers were reading at the back of the shop.

'I need to know about Silas's collapse and the day he spent in your care in A & E.'

Maggie stared at her untouched latte and turned the long packet of sugar round and round between her fingers.

Karen liked her. The reaction wasn't trustworthy. She'd often liked – once even loved – people who turned out to be utterly devious, or at best careless of everyone around them. But there was something appealing about the contrast between Maggie's age and ordinariness and the bizarre clothes she'd chosen. Her voice was good, too: round and unselfconscious, even when she was in shock.

'Why?'

'Because it was too convenient an alibi,' Karen answered. 'Because of the violence of your reaction to the flowers. And because, good and dedicated doctor though you were, you've left medicine. What happened?'

A tear welled in Maggie's right eye, and she dashed it away with a knuckle, before licking her lips.

'I thought of changing my name,' she said steadily, 'but I needed my medical experience to get the job at First & Best, so I couldn't. And it's been four years. I thought . . . His brother went down, didn't he? I thought it was all over when that happened. I've just begun to get my real life back, to get some confidence in the future. I . . . Oh, shit!'

She looked at Karen, with a mixture of despair and anger making her damp eyes look like weapons.

'How did *you* get involved?' Maggie said.

'I'm researching his brother's case.'

'Why?'

'For a paper on DSPD.'

'And . . .?'

'Chatham House Rule?' Karen said, referring to the principle established in 1927 that information could be shared and used but never publicly ascribed to the speaker.

'Both ways?' said Maggie, with a beady look in her eyes.

'Absolutely.'

'OK then.'

'Great,' Karen said. 'I think there was a seriously dysfunctional sibling relationship between the brothers. I've been thinking that it was possible Silas set up various crimes and Spike, abnormally compliant for all sorts of reasons we haven't time for now, carried them out and took the rap. But now I'm not so sure. I think Silas could have done them all, without any input from Spike.'

She paused and Maggie said baldly: 'Why?'

'It'd take too long to give you the whole convoluted trail through my mental processes, but the gist goes like this . . . 1) I don't think Spike has a dangerous severe personality disorder at all. 2) An attempt was made, neatly and intelligently, to implicate me in springing him from gaol just before the murder of the only officer who ever took an interest in him. 3) I think whoever planned that once used the same manipulative skills to make Spike look guilty of all the crimes he's supposed to have committed, including the picnic massacre on Chillerton Down. 4) Silas has an exaggeratedly strong alibi, in which I simply do not believe, for the date and time of the shooting. Ergo, it must be him.'

Maggie stared. 'You've some imagination, haven't you?'

'If I'm right,' Karen went on, 'then Silas is a serious danger to the public. I have to find something that will persuade the police to stop him before anyone else dies.'

'Why don't you just tell the police all that?'

'They aren't feeling very cooperative with me right now,' Karen said, thinking of Eve Clarke's determination to get her for something. 'Which is why I need some . . .'

'Ammunition?' suggested Maggie while Karen searched for the right word.

'Evidence,' Karen said. 'But it needs to be strong enough to overcome all the official prejudice against me. At the moment it doesn't look as though they'll believe anything I say.'

'Of course not. The Falconer family practically owns the Island, and the old man is on the Police Authority. He has the power to hire whoever he wants, so he'll always be in control in any criminal matter.'

'He can't be the only member of the authority.'

'No, but he's immensely influential. And he's a bully. In fact, he can be seriously frightening.'

'How d'you know all this?' Karen said. 'I mean, I'd heard that you went out with Silas for a while, but I didn't realize you'd become a member of the family.'

'God forbid! I'd have hated that. But I was treated to a few of their war stories. Not a happy bunch, I have to say.'

A gaggle of noisy shoppers burst into the coffee shop then, and chattered loudly about precisely what kind of sweet gloopy drinks they wanted. Karen waited until the noise levels dropped. She didn't mind the pause. When at last quiet resumed, she leaned forwards over her knees, looking up into Maggie's face.

'So will you tell me what really happened that day? Under the Chatham House Rule, again.'

'What good will that do you? If you don't have a signed statement or equivalent, the police will just dismiss it, along with every other whisper and suggestion about the family that they've ignored for so long.'

'Not necessarily. If I can give them enough information, then they'll have to investigate.' Karen thought of Max Pitton, who would surely back her on this. 'And I have some quite big guns behind me too.'

Maggie finished her latte, then wiped the milk moustache off her face with a paper napkin.

'Silas and I had been going out for a few weeks. I liked him. Looking back, I can't think why, but he could be charming. And he was so interested in my work. He'd hang around for me if I was late off shift and never make a fuss. Which was endearing in a man who could be so aggressive to everyone else who kept him waiting or pissed him off. My apparently unique ability to keep him calm stopped me seeing him straight, if you see what I mean.'

Charming, manipulative, conscience-less, Karen thought. It fits.

'And then one evening,' Maggie went on, 'he asked me if I would help him out. We'd just made love and it was the first time it had worked for me – with him, I mean – and I was feeling dependent and trusting.'

Maggie stalled, and Karen supplied the necessary prompt. 'Did he say why he wanted help?'

'I need more coffee,' Maggie said. 'What about you?'

'I'll get them in a minute, but let's do this now. Did Silas tell you why he needed help?'

Maggie surrendered. Karen could see it all over her body, in the way her shoulders sank and her chin softened, and hear it in her voice. Everything would come out now.

'He said it was to do with work. There was some ghastly deal that stood to make his bank millions and put him in line for an even bigger than usual bonus, but he had to be seen to be utterly uncontactable for nine hours. He told me he was going to retain an out-of-work actor to pretend to be him, give his name, d.o.b., etc., and fake the symptoms of a mysterious collapse that would need a day's worth of testing.'

Maggie rubbed her eyes, smearing mascara all around. She must have forgotten she'd used make-up this morning. Then she caught sight of the waxy black colour on her fingers and said she must wash. Once again Karen stopped her leaving. Any break in the confession could give her back enough independence to throttle it. Somehow she had to be kept talking.

'OK, then,' Maggie said. 'I gave him all the information he needed to brief his actor and waited for the call. One Sunday evening Silas phoned and said, "It's for tomorrow, Monday; he'll be with you by eight-thirty in the morning." I did nearly everything we'd agreed, avoiding only one highly intrusive test that could have caused damage to his stand-in, signed everything that was needed and addressed the man as Silas all day.'

'Then what?' Karen said, wishing she'd never suggested the Chatham House Rule. Without that, she could have taped this story and presented it unedited to the police who were waiting for her on the Island.

'Then we went on as before. Although Silas soon began to get much less friendly and cooperative. Quite spooked me in fact. And one night he lost his temper when I spilled some wine on his shoe and I thought I was in for it. That time he pulled back, but later, after I'd heard about his brother and asked one too many questions about him, Silas . . .' Maggie hesitated, twisting her fingers in and out of each other. At last she added: 'Well, he really lost it.'

'Lost it how? Physically?'

Maggie shook her head and shuddered. 'No. I used to think that would have been easier, but then no one had told me he could be a killer. Christ! I hope you're wrong.'

Karen had no comfort to offer, so she kept quiet.

'He just ripped me apart with words. Everything about me disgusted him, it seems. He'd loathed . . .' Maggie grabbed the paper napkin and scrubbed her eyes with it. 'You don't need to know. Then he ended up by saying that if I ever so much as mentioned him or his brother or the day the actor had spent in hospital, he – Silas, I mean – would report me to the GMC and that would be the end of my career. I don't suppose he was right about the GMC, but it wouldn't have helped.'

'So you pre-empted him and left, did you?' Karen said, committing one of the cardinal sins of her profession by asking a leading question and interrupting a willing speaker.

'No. God no! I was more than happy to keep quiet about them all. The whole memory sickened me. Literally. No, I . . . He . . . He'd destroyed my confidence. Every time I had to make a decision after he'd delivered his diatribe, I froze. I knew I'd make a mistake and could kill someone with a misplaced syringe or a wrong dosage. Anything. For a while I battled on, then I realized that if I didn't cause someone else's death I'd die myself from the stress of it all. I left.'

This time Karen waited for more. Nothing came.

'And have you had any contact from him since?'

'Not till those flowers you brought.' Maggie frowned, obviously remembering them for the first time. 'How did you . . .? I mean, what are they about? Why have you . . .?'

'I'm sorry about those.' Karen meant it. If she'd known what Maggie had been through, she might have found another way of approaching her. As it was, she had to be glad she hadn't known. 'He didn't send them. I bought them and wrote the card myself.'

Maggie looked revolted. Karen thought she'd better provide some kind of apology.

'Unethical, maybe,' she admitted, 'but I had to hear this, and there wasn't time to reach you in any other way. I am sorry, though.'

Karen wondered whether she was going to be threatened with exposure and professional disaster herself, but after a while Maggie said: 'Weren't you going to get more coffee?'

'Sure. Same again?'

'No, I don't need any more. I'm going back to work so I'll leave you here.'

Maggie was on her feet, so Karen joined her.

'You won't warn anyone, will you?' Karen said. 'Not Silas or his parents or anyone else.'

'Why would I do that? If you're right about Silas – and I would not be unbearably surprised – I'm lucky I got away with a lost career.' Maggie paused and looked at Karen with more sadness than rage. 'That's true, isn't it?'

'I think it could be. Thank you for what you've done. It took guts.'

'I don't want to go into court. But I can see you might need to tell the police what I've told you. If so, please wait until Silas is in custody before you mention my name. Please.'

'He really frightened you, didn't he?'

Maggie was halfway to the door. At Karen's last, quiet question, she turned back, astonished.

'*Frightened* me? That's a weaselly inadequate word for what he did.'

She pushed open the door and strode past the big plate-glass window, back to the safety of her work. Karen was left wishing she were a devout Catholic and could go to her priest for confession and absolution.

Her nearest equivalent was Max, who would need his car. She looked at her watch. There would be time to get back to Wandsworth, pick up the car, drive to Southampton, have an hour with him, and still catch the Red Jet that would allow her to present herself at the police station for DS Eve Clarke's interrogation at seven.

Karen hadn't time to organize a lawyer now, but that was just too bad. She'd offer the police her theories and then merely say 'No comment' to anything else they asked. That way, no one could touch her. Lawyers could come later if they refused to see reason.

As she sat on the Tube, Karen ran through everything the police would have to find out now, starting with Jim Blake's financial affairs. Ellie's picture had confirmed Karen's own view that he had been the hostage-taker, and there was no way he'd have done anything like it on his own behalf. Someone must have paid him. It could have been Spike with the money his mother sent by means of Peg's visits. But Karen much preferred Silas for chief suspect.

Spike's puzzlement had been absolutely convincing when Karen had asked him about why Jim had been giving him orders after the escape. Manipulative Spike might be, but his lack of comprehension had seemed too convincing to be part of one of his games. And with the evidence of Silas's extraordinarily complicated false alibi, he had to have been involved.

In which case, presumably he was also the person who had killed Jim, before throwing his body in the sea.

Could he also have sabotaged one of the powerboats?

As Max had said, they shouldn't have exploded so violently, nor should the leaking fuel have burned like that on the surface of the sea. The tanks in those boats weren't big enough to hold so much fuel that it wasn't immediately diluted by the water. Maybe Jim's clothes had been soaked in oil, or there'd been oil-filled bags under them, ready to explode when the boats hit them. Or one of the boats had been carrying more fuel than it should have.

But all that was for the police. Karen had done enough already.

The Tube shuddered to a squealing halt, midway between Stockwell Station and Clapham North. Karen looked at her watch again. So long as they got going soon, she'd still have time to see Max before she had to cross to the Island.

Chapter 25

The road through Wandsworth, Putney and Sheen seemed to be all bottlenecks and illegally parked cars and dithering shoppers. Karen cursed and swore and hated the cars ahead of her, and the ones behind her. One in particular irritated her; she could barely see it in the clouds of exhaust from a rickety van, but it had a long low black bonnet and it nosed out of the clogged mass of vehicles at every possible opportunity, only to slink back when its driver realized there was no chance of overtaking.

At last, Karen saw the start of the M3 and relative freedom. She put her foot down at the first legal moment, pushing Max's car up to seventy and enjoying the thrust. The speedometer suggested she could get way past 150 mph and she was tempted to find out what the car could do and how her reactions would cope with the danger.

Memories of Peter's injuries forced her back into sanity, even before she remembered the speed cameras.

Driving often helped iron out the tangles in her mind to let her think more clearly. This afternoon, with the bright-yellow sun still high, she felt ideas begin to quicken. The dark trees of the Surrey countryside zoomed past her windows, causing no more trouble to her peripheral vision than the sun and the sky. She'd escaped the rush hour and was free.

Big blue signs offering routes and information loomed up, and she shifted in and out of the slow lane whenever she had to, barely concentrating on the coordination of brain, eye, hand and foot. The only repetitive thought that kept disturbing the even flow of ideas and suggestions and suspicions was that Maggie Spack hadn't told her everything.

According to the latest blue and white sign, Fleet Services would be available in only a mile. Karen pulled her foot back from the accelerator and watched the speedometer's needle swing back from 70 mph to 60, then 40. She turned on her indicator and joined the short line of cars sweeping off to the left.

None of the delights of service-station food or fuel could tempt her. All she wanted was to pull into the first parking space and dig in her bag for her phone. She still had Maggie's number and pressed it in.

'Maggie?' she said as soon as the phone was answered. 'It's Karen Taylor here. You're too sensible and too self-protective to have done all that without making a record.'

'Done what?' The warm voice was a little cracked now, as though with strain – or fear.

'Rigged Silas's alibi. You didn't leave medicine because of his threats, and you didn't change your name. If you were afraid he could really rubbish your reputation, you'd have done both. So you've got something on him, too. What is it? Forms signed by his actor stooge, with his fingerprints on them? Or a photograph? Did you have your phone with you and take a few shots for insurance? Is that it?'

Maggie said nothing, which was all the confession Karen needed. But it would never be enough for the police.

'I need one of them,' Karen said. 'Only one. And I promise I won't say where I got it until Silas is in custody, but I need it to make the police listen.'

Her mind speeded up, almost as though the silent Maggie were sending ideas through the ether.

'You looked him up, too, didn't you?' Karen said, as though in answer to an actual voice. 'The actor, I mean. You used the photographs you'd taken and you looked him up in, what is it? *The Stage*. Something like that?'

There were still no words, although the sound of Maggie's breathing told Karen she hadn't dropped the phone.

'So you know his name? Great. I won't make you tell me, because the police can perfectly well look him up for themselves, but I do need one of the pictures. Will you email it to me?'

This time a sigh sounded faintly down the phone, followed by a mumbled 'OK'.

'Great. My email address is on the card I gave you. I'll check my in-box as soon as I get back. Should be another couple of hours. Thank you, Maggie.'

Another sigh. Then nothing but the dead click of the connection closing down. Even so, Karen was satisfied. She put the phone in the glove compartment so she wouldn't be tempted to answer it if it rang, then checked her mirrors and turned on the ignition.

Out of the corner of her eye she saw a black Porsche quivering in wait.

'Coincidence,' she told herself as she put Max's car in gear.

And then it began. Every time she looked in her mirror the Porsche was visible, sometimes right behind her, sometimes three or four cars back. She would dawdle in the slow lane, letting her speed drop dangerously near thirty. He would loiter too.

She speeded up and it was as though there were a string between them. He matched her speed at every point. He swung in and out of lanes as she did. At one moment she took a suicidal risk, cutting right across three fast lanes of traffic to leave the motorway, and found him on the sliproad behind her only seconds later. When she drove three times round the first roundabout he followed and returned to the M3 with her.

Once, years ago, she and Peter had watched Spielberg's *Duel* together and Peter had talked dismissively about the weediness and suggestibility of the driver, who should have been able to withstand the emotional pressure of the faceless truck driver harassing him over miles and miles of empty desert road.

This is nothing like that, Karen told herself.

This was merely a black Porsche following her towards Southampton and the Red Jet catamaran that would take her back to the Island. She didn't know for sure that it belonged to Silas, but it seemed likely. Just as it seemed likely to have been the same car that had teased her all through Wandsworth and Putney and Sheen on her way to the motorway.

Had he been following her all day? Should she warn Maggie he might have followed them and – maybe – worked out what was going on?

Or was it just coincidence? Had he been in London in any case and caught sight of Karen on the Tube?

Unlikely. Especially if he was the kind of highly organized psychopathic killer she now believed.

The sooner she got back to the safety of the police station, the better.

But without Maggie's photograph, she was never going to persuade them of any of it. Silas would be left at large to terrorize and kill. Even if he couldn't get Spike out of prison to be his mask and fall-guy, he would find a way. Psychopathically disordered men always did.

Why had she been so stupidly law-abiding as to stash her phone in the glove compartment? Leaning across the car to get it now, at this speed, would be far more dangerous than merely putting in a number with the phone balanced on her knee.

Already they'd passed Basingstoke, and the Winchester exit wasn't far. There'd be lay-bys after that, once she was on the A33. She could stop then and phone Max and get him to meet her at the Red Jet terminal and take back possession of his car. He could do other useful things, too.

Could she trust him with her email password?

Passwords were easy to change, and she needed him to download and print off the photograph she hoped Maggie Spack had sent her. The trouble was everything else still loitered in her in-box.

All those emails from Aidan, and all the ones she'd written to Will and his to her were there for anyone who had the password. What a feast for Max if he really was writing a paper on mature relationships in dysfunctional people.

Could she trust him?

Max was waiting for her three quarters of an hour later, dressed in loose jeans, the usual linen jacket, and a dark-blue shirt that was strained across his gut. He was standing with one foot on a bollard and gazing out to sea in a pose that made it look as though he were particularly pleased with his new Italian loafers. But that kind of vanity was foreign to him, although not many of the other kinds. He was up to something.

'Hi,' she said.

'Is he still with you?'

'I think so, but I'm buggered if I'll look back and give him the satisfaction of seeing he's spooked me. Did she send the photograph?'

'Yes.' Max handed her an envelope, which she immediately slid up under her T-shirt. 'There are a couple of brain scans in there, too, which you might find interesting. I took the liberty of printing one off your email attachment. The other I . . . I already had. Take your time with them.'

The email attachment scan must have come from Spike's lawyer, which was helpful. And amazingly quick. She'd never known a solicitor respond so fast to any question. Spike must have given her a good reference.

But all this meant that Max had read the rest of her emails.

Bastard! Karen thought. I hope he didn't go far back.

'Silas will have seen us, you know,' she said aloud, patting her front to make sure the envelope was still safely there.

Then she thought of what she might face when she met Eve

Clarke on the Island. Pulling out the envelope so that she could remove the printed scans, Karen folded them and slipped them into the pages of the *Evening Standard* she'd been reading on the Tube. The photograph of the actor who had impersonated him went into her bag.

Max was looking quizzically at her.

'Silas will know you've given me something,' she said, 'and if he tries to get it, I'd rather he didn't grab the lot. I could probably satisfy him with the scans and you could print them out for me again, after all.'

'I think maybe I should come across to the Island with you,' Max said, as his thick black eyebrows met across the top of his nose.

'And leave your car at the mercy of parking tickets? Surely not.'

His face crunched into the most ferocious frown she'd ever seen.

'I'd rather have thirty tickets and know I could defend you,' he said, 'than watch you skitter off across the Solent with a killer on your tail.'

She laughed to hide everything she felt. 'It's rush hour now. The Jet will be packed. There's nothing he can do to me.'

'Except stick a knife in your side.' Max looked and sounded serious. 'Let me come with you, Karen.'

'No. I have to deal with this.' She had to reach up, tall though she was, to kiss his cheek. 'But it's sweet of you to be so fatherly, instead of urging me on to take risks like you usually do.'

'I don't feel fatherly.' He sounded revolted by the idea. 'But I do feel responsible.'

'For Silas Falconer stalking me?' she said, thinking: so he does have a conscience after all.

Max shook his head. The dark hair with its thick silver streaks flew about his face. 'For winding you up to go over there to Parkhurst, to dig around in Spike's subconscious.'

'When I asked you why you'd recommended him, you told me
he was the most accessible of the severely disordered killers in
prison. It made sense.'

Something in his darkening eyes and twisted lips told her that
hadn't been the whole story.

'What did you think I'd find when I saw him?'

Max's smile twisted even further.

'Come on, Prof. Out with it.'

He raised his hand as though he were about to pat her shoulder,
then let it slide back to his side again. He wouldn't look at her,
concentrating on the gulls that were arguing over scraps on the
edge of the jetty.

'I wanted you to see the difference between fantasies of killing
and the real thing. I wanted you to see the huge gap – the abyss –
between a man like Spike and you, and . . .'

Karen leaned closer so that their arms touched. 'And all I've
found is the similarities. I didn't know you'd picked up so much
about my . . . past.'

She could feel him shrug and then pull slightly away.

'How *did* you pick it up?' she asked.

'You let things drop occasionally,' he said, 'and gave me open-
ings to ask questions, so I always knew something was up.'

'That's not enough. Someone's talked. Not . . . not Will?'
Karen's voice had deepened traitorously. It was the only way she
had of keeping it from quivering.

'Will Hawkins? God, no. Does he know?'

'Not much. So, who was it?'

Max coughed, as though he had a crumb in his throat. It was a
harsh sound, as uncomfortable to hear as it must have been to make.

'So who? Come on, Prof.'

'No. Your boat's coming in. If you want a seat with some nice
protective strangers, you'd better get going. Good luck. And if
you decide you do need a lawyer, call me.' He smiled painfully.
'Maybe I'll alert one, have her on stand-by, just in case.'

The only lawyer I'd want is Aidan, Karen thought, even though he's on the far side of the Atlantic and practises the wrong kind of law.

'I'll be fine. Thanks for the loan of the car. And for downloading the photo. Bye now.'

She didn't wait for anything else from him, just ran onto the boat to find herself a seat with two elderly women laden with bags of shopping. Even though they were sitting in a row of three seats, it was obvious they wanted the middle one for their loot. And with spare seats all along both sides of the aisle, Karen did look cussed to be taking one of theirs. But they were all the protection she needed. And they were too polite to put their obvious outrage into words, merely shifting in their seats and exchanging glances of roll-eyed exasperation.

Silas Falconer strode past the end of the small row, then wheeled round to face her.

'Good choice, Doctor Taylor,' he said, all his teeth bared in a grimace that pretended to be a smile.

Chapter 26

Silas was sitting two rows ahead of Karen and her shopper-chaperones. As the catamaran cleared the Calshot Lifeboat Station, he very obviously pulled out his phone, hit a speed-dial key and raised the phone to his ear.

'Yes. Yes. That's right,' he said loudly into the phone. 'We're both on the Red Jet now. Should be landing in about fifteen minutes. Great. What? No. No, I won't hang around to chat.'

Which gave Karen fair warning. As she expected, she saw DS Clarke waiting for her on the quay, with two uniformed constables.

So, Karen thought, this is to be a truly public arrest. Which means Silas never meant me physical harm, only humiliation.

She knew how to deal with that and stepped on the quay with straight back and steady tread, arm outstretched to shake hands with Eve Clarke.

'You didn't need to come and meet me,' Karen said, using her most languid, confident voice. 'I could've caught a cab. But it was kind to think of saving me the trouble.'

Laughter bubbled up in her throat and she had to fight to keep it from emerging. DS Clarke looked outraged, as well as denied a treat.

'Shall we go?' Karen said, planning to keep the initiative as long as possible. She held out her hand to each of the uniformed constables as well.

'Hi. I'm Doctor Karen Taylor.'

One of them, younger and less experienced, took her hand and gave it a hearty shake, as well as smiling in a sloppy friendly kind of way. The other looked embarrassed and would neither meet her eyes nor touch her hand. He glanced towards DS Clarke, who shook her head.

Ah, Karen thought, he was wondering whether I was to be formally arrested and handcuffed, and has been told 'no' or 'not unless she resists', so the pantomime was worth it.

He had to touch her later, though, as he put his hand on her head to push her down into the back seat of the police car. He then took the front passenger seat, while his colleague got in on the far side of Karen, looking puzzled and embarrassed.

The drive to the police station took very little time and Karen was, at last, formally arrested, taken before the custody sergeant and required to hand over her possessions.

'I warned you to bring a lawyer,' DS Clarke said. There was a warm glow of satisfaction in her gooseberry eyes. 'We're going to have to leave you in a cell for a while, I'm afraid, until we're ready to interview you.'

She looked anything but afraid or even troubled. She looked as though she was having long-postponed fun at last.

'And I'm not sure how soon that'll be. The new SIO wants to be present and he's tied up at the moment. Are you sure you don't want us to call the duty solicitor?'

'Quite sure, thank you.' Karen watched as DS Clarke swished out of the custody suite, followed by her acolytes. Then she turned to smile at the custody sergeant and said politely: 'Do you think it would be possible for me to have my newspaper? If I'm to be here for some time, it would be good to have a chance to catch up on the news.'

He, too, looked in the direction where DS Clarke had disappeared, then smiled and said he didn't see why not.

So Karen was escorted to her cell and allowed possession of the *Evening Standard*.

Her cell was not a comforting space, walled in yellowish tiles, with a steel, lidless lavatory pan in the corner and a low upholstered bench-cum-bed under the window on the far wall. At least it doesn't smell of anything but Jeyes Fluid, she thought, taking off her shoes and sitting along the bench, with her feet up and her head leaning against the cold tiled wall.

She'd already read most of the paper on the Tube, but the crossword would give her some distraction. And nestling between the business pages were the two printouts of Spike's brain scans. She hadn't wanted to reveal their existence until she'd had a chance to examine them in private. Luckily, neither Eve Clarke nor the custody sergeant had thought of shaking out the paper, even though they had told her to empty her pockets and hand over her shoulder bag.

You've just got to wait it out, Karen thought. Don't give them the satisfaction of making a fuss. DS Clarke has probably not even told the SIO you're here yet.

Settling herself in for a long wait, she let the paper fall into her lap, closed her eyes, and began to construct the whole story of what she believed had happened so that she would be succinct and fluent when she eventually got her chance with the SIO. But the ideas kept drifting away from her like the seeds from a dandelion, and in their place came yet more memories of the night Peter had died.

Karen knew what her subconscious was up to. Guilty of wanting him dead for so long, she'd always felt at some level that she ought to be in a place like this, and so she had no real urge to fight it. Maybe that's why she hadn't been able to remember to phone her mother-in-law to remonstrate with her for all the accusations she'd been flinging in all directions. Maybe they'd seemed justified.

And maybe Spike had had a similar reaction. Charlie Trench had told Karen how odd it was that he'd been so relaxed about being locked up, how few questions he'd asked after his arrest, how few protestations of innocence he'd made. They'd all assumed that was because he wasn't as innocent as he'd later claimed, but maybe he'd also had a subconscious feeling of guilt and felt relieved of it by being in custody.

Had Silas's hatred so distorted Spike's developing mind that he'd learned to believe he deserved it? Coming on top of his natural mother's neglect and Colonel Falconer's obvious resentment of his existence, could that have been enough to make Spike believe he *should* carry all the guilt for Silas's crimes?

Two hours later, at nearly a quarter past nine, the door of her cell opened and the custody sergeant stood there, beckoning.

Karen shook herself down, straightening her jeans and the T-shirt she'd borrowed from her mother's drawer. She ran her fingers through her thick hair, feeling knots and flyaway ends but unable to do anything about them.

'Fine. Thanks,' she said. 'Let's go. Oh, is there any news of DCI Trench? He was looking better when I last saw him, but it was obviously still painful.'

The custody sergeant's affectionate smile told her a lot about his attitude to Charlie Trench, as well as explaining his relaxed attitude to her request for her newspaper. 'He's not too bad. Should be back at work within the week, they say.'

'Will he get this investigation back then?'

The friendly smile broadened. 'Should do, if all I've heard is right.'

'Great,' Karen said aloud, even as she thought: so that's why DS Clarke was so keen to arrest me now, while she still has some influence on the way the investigation goes.

The custody sergeant handed Karen over to a young uniformed woman officer, who took her to a clean impersonal interview room and waited with her until DS Clarke appeared with a much older man beside her. He introduced himself to her, and the tape, as DCI Perks, before DS Clarke spoke.

She was so tense Karen thought she might go ping if anyone touched her. She reminded Karen again that she had been advised to bring a lawyer with her.

'Yes,' Karen said with a patient smile designed to wind up Eve Clarke even more tightly.

Karen thought she saw an answering twitch of the lips from Perks. He looked so much older than Trench that Karen wondered whether he could have been brought back out of retirement to hold the fort until Trench recovered. No one mentioned the DI she'd met last time Eve had brought her in here, or explained what his role had been.

Perks wasn't nearly such an impressive figure, but there was a steadiness about the way he sat which suggested confidence, quite unlike the angry tension that was troubling DS Clarke.

'You see I don't need a lawyer,' Karen added, looking from one to the other. 'Now you're both here, I can tell you what I went to London to find out.'

'This isn't a free-for-all conversation, Doctor Taylor,' said the SIO. 'It's an interview because you are under arrest.'

'I know. But you haven't any evidence against me.' She glanced at DS Clarke and was surprised to see a smirk on her thin grey face. 'What? What is it you think you have?'

'That's not how we do things. We want to know where you went when you left the prison on Monday two weeks ago.'

Monday a fortnight ago, Karen thought, running through everything that had happened. *Was that the day I went up to Chillerton Down? I wanted to see where Spike had been found, off his head and lying in his thick tweed overcoat on a boiling hot day, and the place where the Sanders family were blasted to death. I think it was that day.*

Now why, she thought for the first time in all this, would Spike have needed skunk if he'd just had the supreme satisfaction of killing four people? Why didn't I think of that before? It doesn't fit.

'You met up with Jim Blake, didn't you?' DS Clarke said, dragging Karen back to the present. 'Come on. We have you talking confidentially to him on the CCTV from the prison reception area. You agree something with him, then leave, and ten minutes later he goes off duty and follows you, doesn't he? Where did you arrange to meet? You paid him then, didn't you? What was the deal?'

'This is nonsense,' Karen said. She felt entirely calm because the questions were so far from anything that could be relevant to Spike's escape or Jim Blake's death. 'I spoke to Jim Blake when he was on the reception desk in order to get my belongings back. My keys. That must be when he did it.'

'Did what?' said the SIO, glancing at DS Clarke, who was looking mulish.

'They've probably told you,' Karen began, 'at least I hope they have, that a distinctive knife was stolen from my chalet, although there was no sign of a break-in. Now, on that particular day – that Monday – Jim was on reception duty, instead of at his usual job on the wing. I handed my keys over to him, as I had to, and I assume he somehow had copies made, or pressed them into a mould or something so that he could get more cut to let himself into my house and take the knife without leaving any sign he'd been there. That must have been it. They weren't sophisticated keys at that stage.'

'What d'you mean "at that stage"?' Perks asked. 'Keys can't become more sophisticated.'

'They haven't briefed you properly, have they?' Karen allowed herself a small indulgent smile to show how unworried she was by all this. 'More recently, after Spike escaped from Parkhurst, he did break in so I had to have a new door. The carpenter installed much more modern locks.'

'So you are accusing a dead prison officer, with decades of experience and an excellent reputation, of stealing your keys, copying them, and letting himself into your house in order to steal the knife that was then used to force him to help an inmate escape. Is that it?'

'No, Chief Inspector, it isn't.' Karen allowed some of her irritation to roughen her voice; make it more intense, too. 'I am accusing him of stealing evidence to plant so that when *he* arranged the escape he could make it . . .'

'Hold on a moment.' Perks put up his hand as though he were stopping traffic. 'This is a man who ended up drowned in the Solent just near your house. Decapitated.'

'I know,' she said, ignoring the mental images of his head in the surf.

'Are you about to suggest that he arranged that, too?'

'This is getting surreal. Maybe I should have had a lawyer. She could've stopped you wasting time like this. Yours as well as mine.'

DS Clarke, who was sitting slumped and with her chin tucked into her neck, muttered something towards her own chest. Karen took a moment to work out what the words she'd used were: I wouldn't bet on it.

'Jim Blake has to have been paid to spring Spike,' Karen began, only to be interrupted by DS Clarke.

'We know that,' she said, her voice dripping with impatience and all the old contempt. 'We found the five hundred pounds you gave him under the floorboards in his flat.'

'I did not,' Karen said. 'And why would he have needed to lift my sushi knife if I had? I never gave Jim Blake any money at all.'

'None?' DS Clarke was looking suddenly alert.

Oh, shit! Karen thought and hoped her skin wasn't flushing. 'None, except for a tenner when he was collecting for a mental health charity.'

'That's a clever explanation for why we found your fingerprints on the note folded around the rest of the bundle of money in his flat, but I don't believe it,' Clarke said.

So that's your evidence, Karen thought. My fingerprints on

some of Jim's money. But it's not nearly enough. And it's far too neat. Someone *has* set all this up.

'What have you got to say to that, Doctor Taylor?'

'This, DS Clarke, and listen carefully because it's a bit convoluted.'

The sergeant twisted in her chair and looked as though she wanted to protest, but the SIO's authority was enough to keep her quiet.

'Yes, Doctor Taylor?' he said.

'As you must know, I have often explained that I have been deliberately set up here. Whoever did it went far enough to arrange for Jim to persuade me to give him money so that you'd find my prints on notes in his possession. But this is not the first set-up there has been in this case. And I don't think you can be aware of the earlier incident.'

'I'm listening,' said Perks, nodding towards the recording machines. 'And so is the tape.'

'I know. If you check the files for the shooting of the Sanders family, the so-called Picnic Massacre,' Karen said, speaking formally and at dictation speed, which she saw made DS Clarke so itchy she could barely keep still, 'you will see that Spike's brother, Silas Falconer, had a most comprehensive alibi.'

Perks glanced at DS Clarke. She nodded. 'He was in hospital in London, sir,' she said, 'having nine-hours' worth of tests and X-rays and such. It's all on file.'

'Except,' Karen said, enjoying herself now, 'that he was not the man in hospital being tested. This is what I've been trying to tell you. Silas Falconer paid an out-of-work actor to stand in for him on the very day his dangerously disordered adopted brother apparently massacred an innocent family. Now, don't you think that's interesting?'

Karen was out of the police station only twenty minutes later. She had all her belongings except the actor's photograph Max had printed for her, which the police had kept. Now, she was breathing the soft warm Island air, feeling the crackle of the *Evening Standard*, which still concealed the two brain scans.

Although the sun had sunk below the horizon, the sky was nowhere near dark yet. Its brilliant blue had changed into a clear grey with deep pinkish streaks across it. The sea was smelling purely salt for once and all the sticky meaty smells that had made the air so heavy during Cowes week had gone, as though someone had hoovered them away.

Karen went in search of her car. As she'd expected, there was a positive flowering of parking tickets stuck between the windscreen and the wipers.

'Worth it, though,' she said aloud, collecting them and stuffing them into the glove box.

The police now had all the information she'd gathered, except the scans. They could take it from here, find the actor, get a statement from him, interview Silas, and establish the truth at last.

Karen turned on the ignition, put the car in gear and set off, for once looking forward to being back in her dank, phone-less little chalet. Then she remembered Roderick's promise of more rabbits. If he'd been true to his word, they'd have been sweltering in the sun on her doorstep for thirty-six hours.

The smell was going to be revolting.

Chapter 27

'So, Prof, I'm nearly done here,' Karen said into her phone, as she sat in the driver's seat the next morning at Reception Point. 'Even though I haven't got what I came for.'

She had the door open, so she could sit with her legs out of the car and warm her upturned face in the sun that still sparkled through the trees.

'So what have you achieved?'

'Silas's arrest. He's being interviewed now. We should know more soon.'

'Are you suggesting that he's the one with a severe personality disorder?'

'I haven't enough data for that, Prof. But, like I said, I'm more or less sure Spike hasn't got one.'

Karen watched a small brown bird pick up a snail in its beak and bang it down hard on a flat stone. Several blows followed, then the bird delicately picked the still wriggling meat of the snail out of the smashed shell.

'Did you look at the brain scan from when he was a baby, Prof?' she went on. 'When he was taken into care after he fell off the changing table and cracked his skull?'

'Of course,' he said. 'I've had it in the file since I first encountered his case. Even at that stage it's clear his prefrontal cortex wasn't developing as it should.'

'And did you happen to glance at the one his lawyer sent me, taken when he was fourteen?'

'Naturally,' he said, a laugh lightening his gravelly voice. 'I wondered whether there could have been a mix-up in the hospital records, so I checked. There wasn't. It *is* Spike's scan. They took a whole series. All of them show the same thing.'

'An absolutely normal prefrontal cortex that could belong to you or me.'

'Interesting, isn't it?'

'Are you thinking what I'm thinking about super-mums?' Karen said, remembering the results of various experiments that had been done with laboratory rats.

The experiments showed that a neglected baby exhibiting all the behavioural problems consistent with a poorly developed prefrontal cortex could be transformed with exceptional care from a super-rat. Behavioural scientists and psychologists assumed the same must be true of human beings, although there was no ethical way of carrying out the experiments that would prove it.

'You can't escape it,' said Max. 'Something mitigated the damage, and that's the most obvious explanation.'

'It feeds into what I've been thinking for a while now,' Karen said. 'I believe Sylvia was always frightened of her husband and never much liked the son who is so similar to him. I think in the early years, before she was completely cowed, she and Spike developed a very close bond, and she got to him when he was just young enough for her to make good the early damage he'd suffered.'

Karen paused, recalling her two meetings with Sylvia Falconer and wishing they'd had more time together.

'I think Sylvia saw Spike as an outsider like herself,' Karen went on, 'and lavished the maximum possible care and love on him.'

'Are you suggesting Silas is guilty of *all* the crimes?' Max's tone made it clear he wasn't actually inviting an answer, more

expressing serious concern about Karen's sanity. 'All the misde-
meanours at school, and the slashed dog, as well as the killings
on Chillerton Down?'

'More or less,' she said.

'Then why are some so neat and planned and specific and
some – like the Picnic Massacre – so disorderly? It was you who
pointed out the discrepancy in the first place.'

'Because that's how Silas designed them.' Karen contained her
impatience. Max had never met any of these people. He'd had
only written evidence, and that, she was convinced, was never
anything like enough. She decided to lighten up a little, to give
him a flavour of the true story.

'Silas is clever, you know, Prof, and his flamboyant pursuit of
me from London to the Island shows what a theatrical imagination he has, just like so many people who use the manic defence
against their unbearable inner selves. On the day the Sanders
family was killed, I think he first made sure Spike had enough
drugs to put him out – presumably having given him the money
their mother had refused to hand over. Then, dressed in Spike's
old clothes, which Sylvia had just swapped for better ones from
the house, he took the sawn-off shotgun and rampaged around on
a killing spree. It must have done a lot to relieve his feelings.'

The Elephant Man emerged from the green murk of the trees,
with the familiar shotgun over his arm. Seeing her, he raised his
hand in greeting. She took the phone from her ear to waggle at
him so that he would understand why she wasn't going to talk to
him. He looked embarrassed and shuffled forward through the
dead leaves for a few more feet, then blushed and turned away.

'Why kill that particular family?' the prof was saying loudly
down the phone. 'Why on Chillerton Down? Why that precise
moment?'

Karen laughed. 'I love the way you always probe any account of
anything for every possible weakness.'

'No you don't,' said Max, sounding humanly sympathetic

again. 'You hate it and you bridle and you're sure I should believe you without testing you at all. I know exactly what you look like at this moment: pouting slightly and with more colour than usual in your face and a look of pure obstinacy in your eyes.'

'Maybe. At first I thought there could be something between him and Dan Sanders, both of them being in the City, but now I think it was a random chance. I think the whole thing was a set-up, designed by Silas as a way to get Spike publicly convicted of something serious enough to put him out of the way for ever.'

'But . . .'

'I think Silas had had enough of the games he'd been playing all along and wanted something different,' she went on quickly so that he couldn't break her train of thought. 'It was school holidays, so he could reasonably assume there'd be some tourists up there on the Down. It was the Sanders family's bad luck they were the ones he chose to kill.'

'You could be right, I suppose. So, what are you going to do next, Karen?'

'I'd love to interview Silas, but that can't happen yet, if ever. As I say, he's been arrested, but they've still got thirty-six hours in which to charge him or let him go. If they manage to keep him in on remand, I might get the chance to talk to him and find out more.'

'I doubt it. If he's the calculating kind you imagine, he won't cooperate. Spike will seem positively gabby in comparison. D'you think Spike knew what Silas was up to?'

'At some level, which I believe explains why he flithers about in interviews, sometimes sounding perfectly rational, sometimes maniacally giggling or producing fantasies of gross violence. I think that's his way of deflecting questions that could get too close to the truth.'

'Why wouldn't he give away his brother? Why take the guilt if he knew what really happened?'

'Whatever Spike's other problems,' Karen said, 'and there are plenty of those, he's had as his absolute bedrock that he's loved and protected Silas all along. You know how when people get drunk they hang on to one particular polite phrase because that's what their subconscious is telling them is the only absolutely safe thing to say?'

'I do.'

'Spike's devotion to Silas was like that, the one thing he knew was safe and real, whatever other turmoil he had going on in his mind at the time. Or, I suppose, however many drugs he'd been encouraged to ingest.'

Max said nothing for a moment, as though he was thinking through everything she'd said. Eventually he simply asked: 'We need to talk. Are you coming back to Southampton today?'

'Not yet, but soon.' Will was coming for one last weekend in the chalet, but she wasn't going to tell Max that.

By the time Will's ferry was due to dock, Karen had filled the chalet with flowers. Tall spires of pale-blue delphiniums mixed with pink and cream night-scented stocks brightened the dark corners and filled the whole shabby space with a smell almost as delicious as the ones that had permeated the Bridgers' conservatory. She'd changed the sheets and made sure there was plenty of hot water in the tank above the shower. The sushi knife was still in police possession, but its severely elegant box was in pride of place on the shelf over the sink.

The Elephant Man's latest rabbits were in the oven, simmering in a mixture of onions, white wine and French mustard, and she had chopped apples bathed in lemon juice waiting until the last twenty minutes of cooking time, along with a pot of thick crème fraiche to stir into the sauce at the last moment. The steam was already savoury, and she'd lost all her fear and disgust at the idea of eating rabbit. There was a tub of very good raspberry sorbet in the freezer, and a bottle of celebratory wine chilling in the fridge.

She lowered the temperature of the oven for safety, locked up and drove to Yarmouth to fetch Will.

Already there was a small crowd waiting to greet the incoming ferry. Gulls were shrieking their holiday message as they swirled on the warm air currents against a sky so clear and blue it looked as though someone had painted it in acrylic. And Will was standing by the rail of the ferry's upper deck, waving with a fervour quite unlike any of the icy, self-controlled behaviour he used to show.

He was dressed in sagging khaki chinos and a close-fitting black T-shirt, with his short fair hair sticking up on the top of his head, and he carried the familiar canvas and leather bag as though it weighed absolutely nothing.

'You look absurdly young,' she said, kissing his neck in greeting and breathing in great gulps of his familiar smell.

'And you look utterly transformed by your triumph over the cops. I must say I was ready to come and beat someone up when you told me they'd actually arrested you. What an outrage!'

'There was rather more to it,' Karen said, thinking of DS Clarke's attempts to keep her from visiting Charlie Trench. 'But as soon as the temporary SIO heard my evidence, or rather saw it, I was out of there.'

'How is Trench? Have you heard?' Will slung his bag into his other hand so he could put his right arm around her shoulders as they walked towards her car.

She'd never known someone who could match his step to hers so easily. Walking like this, or even just hand-in-hand, had usually been a matter of bumping into each other or tripping up. But with Will it was like having your own reflection walking with you.

'The last I heard he was out of hospital but still convalescing. Rabbit for supper. That OK?'

'Not the same ones?' Will's voice was thick with horror.

She laughed. 'Idiot! Of course not. Roderick delivered two fresh corpses. They should be good.'

*

Will was wiping a piece of baguette around his plate to catch the last drips of sauce, when they heard a car. He looked up, eyebrows raised.

'I'm not expecting anyone,' Karen said. 'They're probably heading for the big house down the lane.'

But the engine sound stopped and a car door crashed as though the driver had been angry enough to slam it shut.

'What the hell?' Will said, just as there was a heavy knocking at the door.

Karen opened it to see Charlie Trench. Her first impulse was to fling her arms around his neck to congratulate him on his recovery and thank him – again – for saving her from burns or worse. But his expression was too aggressive to allow either.

'You'd better come in,' she said. 'Will and I haven't quite finished the bottle, so . . .'

'I'm not drinking.' He was back to showing all the forbidding dislike of the day he'd suspected her of rigging the hostage scene.

'Then what can I do for you?' she said, taking a step backwards.

'You can stop fucking screwing me around and buggering up our investigation with your fantasies. Like this bollocks about how Silas Falconer faked an alibi so he could kill the Sanders family on Chillerton Down.'

'Hey! Steady on,' Will said. 'So she got it wrong. There's no need to . . .'

'I didn't see you there,' Trench said sharply, as though he had little more tolerance for Will than he had for Karen.

'Then why did Silas set up such an elaborate performance with a real-live actor to play him?' Karen felt all the pleasure of her evening with Will dying. 'Come in and sit down, Charlie. Whatever I've done, it's not going to help if you wear yourself out. You're only just out of hospital. I didn't think you'd be back at work for weeks yet.'

'We found a body,' he said, spitting out the words. 'Near Freshwater.'

'Claire something? The student who got a waitressing job there?' Karen said. 'Is it her?'

'Maybe. Looks at first sight like it could've been in the ground about eight years. Man walking a dog found it while I was in hospital. Female anyway; they can tell that at once. It's been post-mortemed and the bits and fluids are all at the lab. They'll know more soon.'

'That's great, Charlie. Really great. After all that scepticism, you must feel vindicated,' Karen said.

'Not any more.' His Geordie voice was harder than she'd ever heard it, and his dark eyes were hostile.

'I come out of hospital to hear the news and I'm flavour of the month.'

'I'll bet,' Will said, but he was frowning.

'Teams coming across from the mainland to scour the Island for all the other bodies I know are here. Everyone's falling in with me at last. And now, the woman they're calling *my* tame shrink makes them arrest Silas Falconer, and I'm blamed when it all goes pear-shaped. Christ! I'm never coming back from this one.'

'Pear-shaped, how?' Will said, standing even closer to Karen, as though ready to interpose his perfect body between her and Charlie's big fists, if it should come to that.

'His solicitor's handed over evidence proving Silas was flying to the States on the day of the Picnic Massacre.' Trench was talking now as though his words were pellets being shot one after the other into Karen's face.

'He was *in the air* when they were shot. So he's free and clear and we look like dickheads. And my career's up the spout. Again. Fuck it.'

'But if Silas was flying to the States, that means there's no doubt about him setting up a false alibi. He *lied* during the original investigation,' Karen said. 'How can you take that so lightly? There has to be a reason.'

'Stop it!' Trench shouted. 'Just for once keep your bloody mouth shut and listen.'

'Oi.' Will moved forward so that he was a bare foot away from Trench. 'You're in her house, sunshine. Drop the aggression.'

Trench thrust a hand at Will's shoulder, as though to push him out of the way. Karen saw Will grab Trench's wrist and tighten his fingers. Trench flinched.

'Stop it, both of you,' she said. 'Will, let him go. Charlie, come and sit down.'

She upended the wine bottle over a clean glass, half filling it, then pushed it towards an empty space on the table and unfolded the third camping chair.

'Sit.'

Trench didn't move.

'We can deal with the rest later, so concentrate on Silas,' Karen said, trying not to think about what he might do to her now he was out and running free. Thank God Will was here. 'So what was your reason for taking Silas's lies so lightly?'

Trench shrugged as though he knew at some level that he was being childish, then hooked his foot under the camping chair to pull it out from the table so he could sit down. Karen followed, but Will lounged across to the sink and leaned his back against it, crossing his arms, waiting.

'It was Mrs Falconer who gave us the false alibi originally; then when Silas was asked about it after the shooting, he backed her up,' Trench said. 'Says now he didn't want to humiliate her or get her into trouble by telling the truth.'

'Pretty thin,' Will said.

'Maybe. But there's nothing we can do to challenge it.'

'I don't care about that,' Karen said. 'What reason has he given for concocting an alibi he wasn't going to use? There has to be one. And I can't believe it's innocent.'

'He and some friends in the City, same vintage as him, had planned a nasty bit of insider trading that was going to net them millions,' Trench said through his teeth, with enough loathing to make her fear for her professional future. How could she have got this *so* wrong?

'The idea was,' he went on when neither of the others asked any questions, 'that if anyone found out what they'd done and traced the trade to Silas's computer, he'd be able to "prove" he was in hospital for nine hours. That way he could claim he was framed.'

Karen thought about it, added up the recklessness and the theatricality of the way he drove his expensive Porsche and had to admit it wasn't impossible.

'Then,' Trench was saying, 'his firm sent him to New York at no notice because someone else was ill, so he and his mates pulled the scam. Because he'd already paid the actor he let the alibi go ahead. Better waste money than make the actor doubt his motives, he said.'

'I still think it's pretty thin.' Will pushed himself away from the sink and came back to sit at the table. 'I was never convinced by the suggestion that Silas had wound up his brother to commit crimes on his behalf, but I'm definitely with Karen on this elaborate alibi. It's too much of a coincidence for Silas to have arranged it for the very day when he might have come under suspicion for the Picnic Massacre and then not used it.'

'Wait,' Karen said in sudden excitement before Trench could comment. 'The killing of the Sanders family wasn't in the original plan. Why didn't I see it before?'

The two men looked at each other. For the first time this evening they dropped their challenge and shared a moment of sympathy. Karen saw she was now the common enemy. But it didn't matter.

'Isn't that what I always said?' Trench said, setting up the challenge for both of them. 'Spike saw Isabelle Sanders, recognized her as the type he liked killing and was interrupted before he could get going on her.'

Karen pushed the idea away with the impatient gesture of someone shooing off a flock of predatory birds.

'You're wrong. *So* wrong. Listen: she was never the intended victim; nor was the rest of her family. It was Spike himself who was supposed to die that day. It must have been. And the poor Sanders family just got in the way.'

'*Now* what?' said Trench. This time he sounded tired rather than angry, as though he had been pushed through so many hoops he wasn't even going to bother to jump up to this one.

'Oh, Charlie, don't sound so dismissive,' Karen said. 'Human behaviour isn't rational in any absolute sense, but it always carries its own internal logic. The trick is to find that logic. And the only way of getting to it is to try one story after another until you find the one that works within its own terms and yet also fits all the externals.'

'Externals like facts? Or evidence?' he suggested in a voice heavy with irony.

'If there are any, yes,' she said, refusing to be cowed. 'Think about this one: Spike had been a problem for Silas all his life. Both their parents told me Silas was terrified of Spike, even though Spike still sees himself as Silas's champion. Silas is now becoming a big success, but he's known to have this brother who's a drug-addled layabout. An embarrassment. And an embarrassment of whom he was once fiercely jealous and probably still hates for the way their mother preferred him.'

'OK,' Charlie said. 'That much makes sense.'

'Then that last weekend, when Silas is staying at the White House but out somewhere with his father,' Karen went on, switching to the present tense as the pictures unreeled in her mind, 'Spike comes back on the Sunday, drugged up, ranting, smelly, hungry, demanding money with menaces. Sylvia, for the first and only time, loses her temper and tells Spike she wishes she'd never adopted him, that he's ruined her life.'

Karen could see the scene on the sweeping semicircular front-door steps. Sylvia shouting. Spike shouting.

'I think either Silas came back from the walk and overheard what was going on or Sylvia told him later that evening, and he decided that her volte-face gave him the permission he needed to get rid of Spike for ever.'

Karen paused as she tried on different aspects of the possible stories.

'I bet the plan was to shoot him with the sawn-off,' she went on at last, 'and make it look like suicide. Silas must have planned to disguise himself in Spike's old clothes, so that if anyone happened to catch sight of him on his way to the kill they'd assume they'd just seen Spike himself.'

'You want me to believe Silas set up that elaborate alibi within less than twenty-four hours?' Charlie said. 'Don't make me laugh.'

'No. Didn't I tell you? My source told me the alibi had been planned long in advance and Silas phoned up on the Sunday evening to say it would be needed the following morning, starting at eight-thirty a.m.'

'But when the killings actually happened Silas was in the air,' said Will, chiming in unnecessarily, Karen thought. 'He was on his way to the States when the family was shot. So, however ingenious your story, it *doesn't* work with the known facts.'

Karen glared at him. He was supposed to be on her side.

'Come on, guys,' she said. 'Don't be so negative. There must be an explanation for the alibi, and I don't believe in the insider-trading story.'

'Why not?' said Charlie.

'Because it's too similar to the story he told the person who helped him set up the alibi and I can't believe anyone as devious as he is would have taken such an unnecessary risk. It would've opened him to blackmail for ever.'

Karen thought she could see Will weakening enough to begin to believe her and, as she smiled at him, she felt her mind opening to a whole new story. It was one that made such sense she couldn't imagine how she'd missed it for so long.

'Maybe Silas wasn't acting alone after all,' she said, struggling to keep the excitement out of her voice so that they'd be more likely to accept the new idea. 'D'you two remember how I talked about a possible *folie à deux?* What if it wasn't Spike and Silas working together, but Silas and his father? That would make sense of the elaborate alibi that wasn't actually used, and of the fact that the killings happened while Silas was in the air.'

'Oh, come on.' The protest could have come from either man. Karen barely noticed it as she powered her way through every new possibility.

'It *is* possible. We know that, as a child, Silas was terrified of his father and yet longed for his approval.'

'Do we?' said Charlie.

'Yes. Take it from me. But these days Colonel Falconer thoroughly approves of Silas, and Silas acts as his father's deputy.' Karen thought of the day when Silas had ordered her to stay away from his mother and talked as though he were her gaoler. One of her gaolers.

'What if,' Karen went on, 'part of the bonding they've achieved came from their shared loathing of Spike?'

'That's fair enough,' said Will.

'And what if they fantasized about getting rid of him? The fantasies could so easily have hardened into plans and then, eventually, into action. The colonel would have known Silas would need an unbreakable alibi for the murder they were going to commit together, so part of their long-term strategy would have entailed setting one up, preparing the ground just in case they should ever decide to go ahead for real. Then that weekend when Sylvia had finally given them the permission – or excuse – they needed, the old man decided to go for it and told Silas to give his actor the go-ahead for the next day, the Monday.'

'And what about the old man himself?' Will said, glancing at Trench. 'Colonel Falconer, I mean. Did he have an elaborate alibi for the Picnic Massacre?'

Charlie shook his head. 'Nothing interesting. He and his wife were together at home. No one had any reason to doubt it. They're the most upright of citizens, with nothing to suggest either of them would ever commit even a traffic offence, let alone something violent.'

'So no alibi at all,' Karen said. 'She'd never betray him, and she's well enough under his thumb to tell the police anything he ordered her to say, just as Silas did everything he'd been told to do.'

She paused, checked the few facts against all the possibilities, then added: 'Except when something even more powerful prevented him. Like the call from his bosses at the bank telling him to fly to the States that Monday. I wonder why the colonel went ahead with the killing on his own. Maybe he'd gone so far with it in his imagination he had to carry it out.'

Karen flashed a brilliant smile at Charlie, and added: 'It's ironic, isn't it? Without that over-elaborate actor-in-hospital stuff, which they didn't actually need, would anyone ever have listened to me and brought Silas in for questioning?'

'You've got a mind like a liar who never knows when to stop,' Charlie said bitterly, not remotely pacified by her smiles. 'How in this bonkers scenario of a plot to kill Spike do you explain the Sanders family getting shot?'

'One of them must have seen the fake Spike brandishing his sawn-off and tried to call for help. Something like that. Shocked him into shooting. Yes.' Karen was getting more excited as more ideas fell into place, like the disparate ingredients in a mayonnaise finally coming together in a perfect emulsion. She didn't even register his insult. 'The records say only four cartridge cases were found, don't they?'

Trench jerked his head in a nod that expressed more impatience than agreement. He looked as though he had exhausted any tolerance he might once have had. She wasn't going to let that stop her.

'Whether it was the colonel or not, the killer must have taken only four with him and shot the family one after the other, which is why Spike was allowed to survive. If there'd been another cartridge in the killer's pocket, he'd have shoved that in the gun and gone to find Spike and kill him, too. As it was, he didn't have any more ammunition, so the next best thing was to collect the cartridge cases and plant Spike's fingerprints all over them, framing him for the massacre. Which is how it worked out. Charlie, have you got the original DNA reports on file?'

'Yes.'

'Can you check those? Find out which of the other Falconers' DNA is on the coat, the gun, the gloves, the balaclava *and* the cartridge cases. That way . . .'

'Won't help. All the clothes Spike ever had came originally from the White House. The whole family's DNA would be on all of them. The colonel's because the clothes were originally his; Sylvia's because she handled them; Silas, the same. And because the cartridge cases were found in the coat pocket, they have all the same traces. DNA evidence won't help you.'

'Nor will anything else,' Will said, reaching out a hand towards her. 'It's an ingenious theory, Karen, but I can't see how you could ever prove it without a confession.'

'But you do buy it this time, don't you, Charlie?' Her eyes felt hot with the intensity of her need to make him take this further.

'No, I don't. It's barmy. Why are you so keen for Spike to be innocent?'

Out of the corner of her eye, she saw Will twitch. He knew why it mattered.

'I wonder how much Sylvia knows – or guesses. She's clearly terrified, but she must know the real story.'

'Then why wouldn't she have said anything when the son she preferred went down for something he didn't do?' Charlie demanded.

'Too frightened,' Karen said at once. This was easy. 'Too much in the habit of placating her husband, too scared even of what he might do to Spike if she did tell the truth. Or maybe it's just an example of cognitive dissonance.'

'You what?' Charlie looked more obstinate than ever.

'Cognitive dissonance is the term invented to explain the process by which we lie to ourselves,' Karen told him, hoping she didn't sound patronizing. 'Festinger and Carlsmith published a paper about it at the end of the 1950s, I think, showing that the more we've invested in something, the more we lie to ourselves to protect our view of it. Sylvia Falconer's marriage has cost her a vast amount emotionally, so maybe she lies to herself to make the investment seem bearable.'

Charlie scowled, unconvinced and angry.

'Interestingly,' Karen said, 'the Festinger and Carlsmith paper was subtitled "Cognitive consequences of forced compliance".'

'I've had enough of this,' Charlie said. 'I can see it's fun for you to play guessing games full of academic references, but I'm off back to work, fiddling with lost dogs and stuff while the investigation into the body at Freshwater carries on without me, thanks to you.'

He looked around the shabby building, then back at Karen.

'There's no justice,' he went on. 'All you'll pay for this mess is exile from the Island and I don't suppose you'll grieve after that.'

'What d'you mean exile?' Karen said, following his gaze.

He laughed. 'You've made the police look like tits. You've pissed off the Falconer family, wound up Spike to kill the best officer Parkhurst has ever had, and made a complete arse of yourself and your profession. I hope for your sake no one goes public with your antics. I'll see myself out.'

Karen felt hot dangerous furious words cramming her mouth, fighting to get out. She clamped it shut on them all, flashing a glance at Will, who wrinkled his face in sympathy but didn't say anything.

'Before you go, Charlie, will you listen to one of my tapes?'

'Tapes,' he said, with one foot already across the threshold. 'What tapes?'

'I record my talks with Spike every day. And he said something really interesting in one of our early discussions. Wait, while I find it.'

Charlie hesitated and she ran for her stack of mini tapes, each one labelled with the date and time it had been recorded. She couldn't remember exactly which day was the right one. Charlie's exasperation grew as she clicked in one tape after another, fast-forwarding through it until she found the right passage.

'Here,' she said, pausing the tape. 'Listen carefully as I ask Spike who could've damaged Lara if he didn't.'

She clicked the button to make the tape move again. Her voice sounded calm and easy:

'So who did kill her?'

Then came Spike's voice, fast, almost panicky behind the laughter: 'Pa prob'ly, trying to look scary.'

'And you take that seriously?' Charlie Trench said in disgust, just before he stormed out of the chalet.

'What a sod!' Karen burst out.

His engine revved outside. They watched the headlights swing round, lighting up the ugly trees, then they heard the car cough its way up the muddy track. She hoped he'd swerve off the road and get bogged down in the mud.

Will took up his favourite position, standing behind her with his arms wrapped around her waist.

'Don't let him get to you.'

'Hard not to.' She unclamped Will's hands and pulled them apart so that she could turn to face him, knowing Granny was right. Putting your head above the parapet meant someone was bound to cut it off. She could almost feel the blood dripping down her headless neck now.

'If he won't listen and do something to find out which of the Falconers *is* the real killer, what happens to Spike?' she went on.

'Poor battered, brutalized Spike, so messed about that he doesn't know who he is or what part he's supposed to be playing each day. He'll go on carrying the responsibility for someone else's violence, being punished for ever for having the appalling luck to be born to one wrong family and then given over to a second.'

She put her hands on his shoulders and shook him, as though he was an idea she had to get clear of messy confusion.

'I can't leave it like this, Will.'

'I don't see why not. It's not your affair.'

'No one else is going to speak up for Spike,' she said. 'I've stirred up all this mess, made things worse than they were before I arrived. I can't go without at least trying to make it right.'

Chapter 28

The car park at the Goose Inn was empty as it baked in the hot sun. Even the geese themselves were torpid, huddled round their water trough. Karen knew her car would be visible to any new-comer who drove in off the main road, but there was nothing to be done about that. There was nowhere to hide it, just as there was no shade. She pulled down the sun-visor to shield her eyes.

Today was Tuesday, the day when Colonel Falconer had a reg-ular meeting away from the house and also the day of Peg's dutiful three-weekly visit to Parkhurst to see Spike. Karen did not believe the timing could be coincidental. Silas had told her his mother would never be left alone again, but that could have been bluster. Karen hoped it was, and that Sylvia would use today's freedom to visit the Goose Inn in time to give Peg phone cards, cigarettes or messages to take to Spike, as she'd so often done in the past.

Karen shifted in the seat and rolled her head on her neck. If Sylvia didn't come soon, she'd have to get out and shake her legs and arms or she'd get cramp.

The sound of an engine slowing alerted Karen and she looked down at her knees. She didn't want Sylvia recognizing her and being frightened off too soon.

A dark-blue Volvo turned into the gravelled space outside the pub and stopped. Karen didn't move. After a long silence, she looked cautiously sideways and saw that Sylvia was peering into her driving mirror, apparently tidying her hair. Then she applied powder and lipstick to her face. Then she sat back, unmoving.

Was the routine for Peg to come out to her? Karen thought. That would be a right pain.

No, at last Sylvia was getting going. Karen waited until she was out of the car and had turned to aim the bleeper to lock the doors.

'Mrs Falconer?' Karen said, emerging from her own dusty wreck. 'May I have a word, please?'

'Haven't you done enough damage already, Doctor Taylor? I *am* grateful for the way you've helped Spike, but this absurdity of having Silas arrested! How could you?'

'Because I know that Spike did not commit those murders.' Karen watched Sylvia's face for signs of relief or hope or even denial, but there was nothing.

She didn't speak, just stood in all her old-fashioned simple elegance, waiting.

'Don't you *want* to know the truth?' Karen said.

Still Sylvia didn't respond. The sun beat down on their heads. It seemed to have no effect on the older woman, although Karen felt it burning into her scalp, even through her thick hair.

'Is it that you feel Spike's safer in prison than anywhere his father could get at him?' Karen said, ready to try as many stories as she had to in order to break through the cognitive dissonance – or the deliberate lying – that stopped Sylvia revealing what she knew.

'He's not always safe.' Sylvia's voice was quiet, almost as though she were talking to herself alone. She looked right past Karen, still without any interpretable expression in her eyes. 'He's been attacked several times. They can't stop that kind of thing in any prison, even when there's someone like Jim Blake paid extra privately to try to prevent it. The latest horror was the fork in Spike's face. And now Jim's not there to protect him, anything could happen.'

'I heard about the fork in Spike's face.' Karen was so grateful the silence had been broken, she'd have said almost anything to keep the dialogue going. She filed away the reference to Jim Blake and the extra payments. 'And I saw Spike only a couple of days later, before the marks had healed. He didn't seem too bad.'

'But was he in pain?' Sylvia's voice was breathless with suppressed distress now and a little louder.

'I thought so,' Karen admitted. 'But they said when it happened, all he did was laugh, even when the fork was hanging off his skin and the blood was pouring down his face.'

Sylvia turned her head on her thin neck, allowing her chin to droop.

'He always laughed,' she said, sounding almost despairing. 'One of the psychiatrists we took him to in the early days told us that inappropriate laughter is one of the first signs of psychopathy.'

She closed her eyes. Her lips straightened into a fleshless line.

'That's true. Didn't you believe it?' Karen asked, keeping her tone gentle and without any kind of judgement. 'About the laughter, I mean.'

Sylvia's eyes opened. 'How could I not? The doctor was an expert. He knew about all this when we were only fumbling our way to any kind of understanding.'

'But *you* did understand Spike. Your care made good all the damage done to him by his natural mother's neglect.'

Sylvia's beautifully shaped grey eyebrows twitched. She shook her head and put out both hands, as though to ward off a new idea that was even more threatening than the rest.

'You still do understand him,' Karen added. 'So what else do you see in his laughter, Mrs Falconer?'

There was a long pause. Karen waited unmoving. Sylvia chewed her lip, smearing all the carefully applied lipstick.

'That it's his only defence,' she said at last, giving up most of her own. 'But, you know, he'd stopped laughing about the fork in his face long before Jim came to give us his weekly report and tell us about the attack. He worried us when he described the marks on Spike's cheek. They sounded so like the cuts made in Lara's body all those years ago.'

'Have you ever wondered whether it was really Spike who killed Lara and mutilated the body?' Karen kept her voice as gentle and unthreatening as she knew how, but it didn't help.

Sylvia took two steps away, then came back. Her face looked severe, hard even, with all the sadness hidden.

'I do appreciate what you're trying to do, Doctor Taylor, but you're wrong about me and Spike. It's true that I tried to make good the damage, but I failed. We could see it everywhere, in everything he did.'

'What d'you mean?'

Sylvia sighed. 'It wasn't just Lara, you know. When he was very young, Spike used to rip the heads off rabbits.'

'Are you . . .?'

'His father said he actually saw him do it once,' Sylvia said so fast it was clear she couldn't bear the thought of Karen's cross-examining her. 'And all the doctors and psychiatrists we took him to told us that was the typical precursor to violence against human beings. Just like the inappropriate laughter. He fits all the criteria. I wish it wasn't so, but it is. The verdict was the right one. Spike's dreams of a successful appeal aren't realistic. You *have* to believe that.'

'Was Spike punished after episodes like the rabbit decapitation?' Karen knew how delicately she had to tread if she were to keep the conversation going long enough for Sylvia to produce the information she'd hidden for so long.

'Of course,' Sylvia said. 'No one could ignore that kind of cruelty, particularly not once we'd been warned of what it could lead to.'

'And yet he's told me several times that his father never hit him,' Karen said.

'That's true. Punishment was always verbal.'

'He told me once he was sent to his room and kept there in silence. That doesn't sound very verbal.'

'Verbal. Non-verbal. What's the difference? It was psychological punishment, not physical. That's the important thing. Once Fergus had told Spike to go to his room, he wouldn't speak again, and I wasn't allowed to. Fergus's theory was that Spike would learn by being ostracized that what he'd done made him unfit for decent society. He'd spend days alone in his room. I *was* allowed to feed him, to take up trays of basic food, but not to speak.'

'What would happen if you did say something to Spike?' Karen asked and saw that she had hit a nerve.

Sylvia faced her for a second, then let her eyes slide sideways. Too much eye contact was hard for her, just as it was for Spike.

'I never did say anything,' she said. 'I never dared break the rule.'

'Did your husband hit you?' Karen said. 'Does he still?'

Sylvia shook her head. Then she turned to go, moving so fast she tripped over her own feet and fell heavily on her left side. Her skirt flew up around her waist, exposing thin legs in fine old-fashioned stockings. Through the nylon Karen could see a row of neat straight scars. Most of them were white, but a few were still pink and two had the dark-purple rawness of recent cuts.

'Who knows about this?' Karen said, doing her inadequate best to keep the shock from her voice. She bent down to help Sylvia straighten her skirt and then get up from the ground.

'I don't know what you mean.' Sylvia let the hem of her dress fall back to its usual length of four inches below her knees. 'And I mustn't leave my niece waiting any longer. Goodbye, Doctor Taylor. We won't meet again.'

'Don't go. *Please*. You know, if something isn't done to stop your husband, he'll go on causing damage to you – and to other people. You do know about the swimmer, don't you?'

'Swimmer?' Sylvia looked blank. Karen thought this time Sylvia's incomprehension might be genuine. 'What swimmer?'

'The one who died at Alum Bay.'

'There are wicked currents there. I know people have drowned.'

'This one was murdered, and there's been a suggestion from the police that Spike might have killed her and then mutilated her body with cuts like the ones found on Lara's corpse. There may have been other victims, too.'

Sylvia shook her head. She looked very white. Karen tried not to feel any impatience.

She knew how abused and battered wives learned to be passive and in a way to collude with what was done to them because that was the only way they believed they could contain and control the danger they lived with.

'But you and I know Spike never killed anyone, don't we?' Karen said gently.

Sylvia shook her head. Her eyes were closed so they couldn't betray her.

'The verdict at his trial was right, Doctor Taylor,' she insisted. 'Spike lost it after I said all those unforgivable things to him and then he shot all four members of the Sanders family on Chillerton Down. He did do it. And it was my fault.'

'You know that's not true.' Karen felt as though she was fighting for her own sanity as much as Sylvia's. 'However hard it is to admit, you have to let yourself acknowledge the truth. Your husband and Silas are both dangerous men. That's not your fault any more than it is Spike's. I think you've allowed yourself to believe that, with Spike in prison, his father can't use him to hide behind any longer, and so the safest thing is not to say anything to anyone. But . . .'

'I can't listen to any more of this nonsense.' This time Sylvia did walk away and into the pub, leaving Karen to go back to her car and sit in the driver's seat, so frustrated she could hardly bear it.

Sylvia Falconer was a victim, just as much as Spike, and possibly even Silas. Someone had to stop Colonel Fergus Falconer. Otherwise, like all too many men with money and social standing and authority, he would escape not only the law but also the experts who should have diagnosed his personality disorder years ago.

But no police officer would ever arrest him without unshakeable proof of what he was and what he'd done. Karen swore at the memory of Charlie Trench's refusal to believe in her suspicions. If she had one bit of proof, she might be able to persuade him to look for some of the evidence that must be out there. She didn't have the resources to do it herself in a way that would ever make the evidence usable in court.

'Just one piece of physical evidence, or testimony from someone who knows what happened,' Karen muttered.

There were only two people who might be able to tell her the truth. Remembering one of her first visits to Spike, and her conviction that he was hiding something big, Karen fumbled in her bag for the notebook she always carried, found a pen and wrote:

Dear Mrs Falconer,

One day at the prison Spike told me – speaking so casually that I didn't take him seriously at the time – that he thought his father had killed and mutilated Lara.

I think both you and Spike have kept quiet about what you know of your husband's crimes because you are too frightened of the consequences of disclosure. I can understand that, but the lives you and Spike have been living are intolerable.

If you have any evidence of what really happened, please get it to the police. You don't have to give them your name. No one need know it was you. He has to be stopped before anyone else dies.

Karen Taylor

She tore the page from the notebook and took it into the pub. She thought she would never forget the tableau she saw as she pushed open the door.

Peg was kneeling on the floor, pulling at her aunt's hands as they covered her eyes.

'Don't cry, Auntie,' Peg was saying. 'Don't cry. You couldn't have stopped Spike killing those people. It's not your fault. If anyone made him into a killer, it was Uncle Fergus. You know what he was like with the boys. How brutal he was. You *know* how he terrorized them.'

Peg looked round at the sound of Karen's steps and shouted: 'Leave her alone! She's had more than she can take.'

'I know,' Karen said, adding a moment later: 'Mrs Falconer, I've a note here I forgot to give you. It's private, and I promised I would make sure you got it.'

Sylvia took her hands away from her sodden eyes, met Karen's glance, then nodded. Karen knew Sylvia thought the note must be from Spike.

'Don't leave it hanging about, will you?' Karen said.

Sylvia read it and gave it right back without a word.

Chapter 29

The dying stocks and delphiniums lay where Karen had thrown them in the old flower bed under the kitchen window. Their faded petals and slimy stalks had fallen into a messy heap, but they'd rot down soon enough. They weren't litter in the ordinary sense. Karen shook the last of the stinking water from the vase after them, wondering why flower water had to smell quite so disgusting after so few days.

She put the glass vase in the sink, ready to scour it, gagging at the smell that welled up through the open window. Decomposition. It made her think again of all the women's bodies that might lie buried around the Island.

How could she leave without having resolved anything? Her plea to Sylvia had resulted in nothing at all. Charlie Trench still refused to believe the colonel could have had anything to do with any of the crimes. And Silas was free and clear with his airline alibi unchallenged.

Pulling the window sharply shut, Karen squirted a big slug of detergent into the vase and followed it with gouts of clean water. Soon all she could smell was the sickly fake lemon of the detergent.

The fridge had ceased to hum and stood now with its door open, with the ice slowly dripping into plastic boxes and wadded cloths as she defrosted it. The sheets she and Will had used were rolled up in a plastic carrier in the back of the car, along with her luggage and her boxes of files and papers. There was no point laundering sheets here.

But she had swept and dusted every surface, and all the other windows were open to air the place thoroughly. As soon as the water was hot again, she'd scrub the floors.

Even though there was no point, even though she was probably the last visitor the chalet would ever have, somehow she couldn't leave it dirty.

She wished it could be as easy to clean up the mess she'd left around Spike. Without police resources, she had no way of chasing down the kind of information that might force the truth out of Colonel Falconer. And without any more access to Sylvia, Karen couldn't even help her further into whatever confessional impulse she'd felt when she'd described Spike's last visit to the White House. Or get her to talk about those rows and rows of scars on her upper thighs.

Had Colonel Falconer taken a knife to her? Or had she made the cuts herself? Were they part of his attempts to get satisfaction from slicing up beautiful long-faced women? Or self-punishment for each time Sylvia failed to stand up to him and stop him blaming Spike for his own crimes?

It *had* to be old Colonel Falconer who'd dressed himself up in Spike's threadbare overcoat and balaclava and shot the family on Chillerton Down, whether to frame Spike or in a ghastly error on his way to fake Spike's suicide. It had to be. Silas had been in mid-air at the time, halfway over the Atlantic and, with all the anti-terrorist security at the airports through which he'd passed, there was no doubt that the man travelling under his name had actually been him.

Ideas spooled through Karen's mind, truncated, half-finished, trailing one behind the other. What did the colonel's army record look like? Where was he on the day the swimmer was killed? Were there really other bodies here, or on the mainland perhaps, with those neat horizontal slices through their dead flesh? How much did Sylvia and Spike actually know of what he did?

What was it Charlie Trench had said originally? Something about why Colonel Falconer had married 'a girl from the local pub'. He'd been brought up isolated in a cold unloving family and turned to her for warmth and normality. Something like that. Had the coldness been enough to amount to neglect? The kind of treatment that could lead to an inadequately developed pre-frontal cortex and a lifetime's inability to empathize with other people, or to understand and so regulate his own destructive emotions?

Poor Spike, carrying the responsibility, just as he'd carried the pain, learning as an infant to hide it, to hide his need, his fear, his anger because revealing any of them would lead only to more punishment.

Karen was seized with such fury at the thought that she let the vase drop through her soapy hands to crash into the pot sink, breaking into tiny pieces. Mindlessly she tried to tidy them up, then noticed the blood streaming down her fingers, mingling with the white foam and the sticky bits of rotting flower stem.

She pulled herself together, turned on the cold tap and held her hands under it, letting the water carry off all the mess, feeling the sting and bite as it pushed apart the lips of dozens of small cuts. Then she wound a clean tea towel around her right hand and went in search of plaster and scissors.

There weren't any in the house, of course. She'd already packed. Kicking open the front door, she was pulled up on the top step by the sight of a square Tupperware box with some-thing long and dark in it. What had Roderick killed for her this time?

As she bent to pick it up, she saw more clearly. Inside the box were the sawn-off barrels of a shotgun. Using a clean corner of the tea towel to make sure she left no fingerprints or blood on the plastic box, Karen picked it up and carried it into the house.

She banged all the windows shut, picked up her phone, then left the chalet, double-locking the front door.

Up at Reception Point, she wheeled through the stored numbers until she came to Charlie's. He answered in seconds.

'Karen?' he said urgently. 'Where are you?'

'At the chalet. More or less, anyway. Why?'

'You were supposed to be on the three o'clock ferry. I've been waiting. Now it's gone.'

She couldn't help smiling. The one good thing about her last few days here was the return of a friendship they'd wrestled out of suspicion and rage.

'I had been meaning to catch it,' she said. 'But packing up took longer than I expected. And now someone's left me a present of the sawn-off barrels of a shotgun. You need to see them.'

'On my way,' Trench said, sounding suddenly breathless. 'Ten minutes.'

She clicked off the phone and set off back down the track to the chalet, thinking of all the things she would do if she had the power.

She would have sent officers to talk to Peg, who clearly knew far more than she'd been prepared to tell either Charlie or herself. The army might have revealing information, too. They must have records of Colonel Falconer's service; if he had any personality disorder, or had ever shown signs of the kind of violence Karen was sure he enjoyed, something must have been evident then. If so, it would have been reported to his senior officers, even if it had never been made public.

And it would be worth finding out whether Jim Blake had been in the army with Falconer. Plenty of prison officers had had careers in the services. Some kind of connection between the two men could explain why Jim had done so much extra-curricular work for the colonel and even why he might have agreed to break every professional code and arrange Spike's escape.

Karen heard a car coming fast down the muddy track and

backed quickly into the trees, the phone clutched in her sweaty hand. Her heart was pounding suddenly as she had a vision of the colonel guessing what she was up to and coming after her.

But the car that came flashing past was Charlie Trench's matronly dark-blue Ford.

Karen ran after him, waving. His brakes squealed as he pulled the car to a standstill.

'Get in,' he said, without ceremony.

Chapter 30

'Why do you keep staring out at that poxy little Island?' Max Pitton's gravelly voice sounded as though he was on the edge of laughter. 'Is it the thought of your rough-trade policeman? Should Will be worried?'

'Don't be silly,' Karen said as she poured wine into two glasses and handed one to Max. 'You know, there's something to be said for such a late summer if it extends into September like this.'

They were on the narrow slip of a balcony outside her living room, looking out over the sea, and she was wearing her usual cropped trousers with bare feet. Today she had a metallic varnish on her toenails, pewtery and subtle.

'So, if not the policeman, then what is it? You can't be home-sick for the hovel you described in such vivid and disgusting detail.'

'It's the case,' Karen said. 'Charlie Trench tells me as much as he can, but it's not enough. I wanted to be there when they went to pick up Colonel Falconer.'

'Don't be a fool. No police force in the world would let an interested observer anywhere near an arrest as sensitive as that one.'

'I know. But it's so frustrating! Especially now that they're interviewing him. They've got bags of circumstantial evidence. But it's not nearly enough.'

'Circumstantial evidence like what?' said Max.

'Falconer *had* served in the army with Jim Blake and when Jim was invalided out with a smashed ankle, Falconer eased his passage into the prison service. Once Spike was in Parkhurst, Falconer paid Jim a regular sum – a generous sum – every month.'

'There's nothing there that will help, Karen. He'd claim he was grateful for the care Jim gave his delinquent adopted son.'

'I know, but Falconer and Jim can be seen together on CCTV film taken in Cowes between the time Spike escaped from Parkhurst and Jim's body surfaced during the powerboat race. Unfortunately it's only what you might call a fleeting glimpse, so it's not enough to prove collusion – or murder.'

'And *you* can't do anything about any of it.' Max wasn't asking a question, but Karen still felt she had to comment.

'I know. It's almost enough to make me wish I'd gone into the police instead of becoming a psychologist.'

'Don't despair: the prosecution might yet use you for the case.'

'If it ever comes to trial,' Karen said gloomily. 'Which it won't unless Charlie's team can get a confession. The labs couldn't find anything useful on the shotgun barrels, you know. They'd definitely been sawn from the gun that was used in the Picnic Massacre and the Falconer family's DNA is all over them. The scientists have established that much, but given that Spike was wearing clothes that had been hanging around the White House for years when he's supposed to have chopped up the shotgun, that doesn't help. And Sylvia keeps professing ignorance of everything. No one saw her dump the barrels on my doorstep, so there's nothing they can use to make her talk. She must have come incredibly early to escape both Jan Davies and the Elephant Man. I can't bear it, you know.'

'Any news of Spike himself? Has anyone told him about his father's arrest?' said Max, wrinkling his nose as he tasted the wine.

If there were something wrong with it, it wouldn't be Karen's fault. He'd brought it with him. She tasted her own share. It seemed fine, white and flinty with nothing worryingly sweet about it.

'No idea,' she said, just as her phone rang. She reached for it, in spite of Max's disapproval, and pressed the incoming call button.

'Karen Taylor.'

'Karen, it's Charlie.' The familiar voice was rough, as though it had been overused for a long time. 'We're getting nowhere. Falconer's a right slippery bugger. One minute I think we've nailed him and then he's away free again. Maybe there is an innocent explanation for everything. Christ, I hope not. I've staked my all on you, in spite of everything.'

'Don't, Charlie. Don't go soft on this. I *know* it's him.'

'Not good enough. A lot of people *knew* it was Spike. I need you here, feeding me questions to pin him down.'

At last! Karen wanted to cheer. She glanced round at Max, then said into the phone:

'When?'

'Now. The clock's ticking. I'll send a car to Fountain Quay to meet the Red Jet.'

'I'm on my way.'

'Hurry. There's only seven hours left. We need a confession now or it was all for nothing – and I'm ruined here.'

Karen dropped the phone on the chair and said: 'I'm going to have to throw you out, Prof. I have to go.'

He looked outraged, so she explained, even as she rushed about the flat collecting what she needed, even through the closed bathroom door as she peed and then changed into black jeans.

'I'll drive you to the Jets. Come on, Karen.'

They raced to his car. She began to worry about his cholesterol again when he wheezed and panted after less than fifty yards. Almost as soon as they'd driven out of her road they were stuck in traffic.

'I'll do better on foot,' she said, leaning across the gear lever to kiss his plump cheek. 'See you when I get back.'

'OK. And what do I say to your mother-in-law? She's been phoning me every day.'

Karen paused, with her hand on the car door. '"Fuck off" should do it,' she said and slammed the door, free at last, from the guilt and fear that had crippled her for the last ten years.

The colonel sat beside his lawyer. Both were dressed in impeccable suits: the colonel's was of greenish-brown country tweed; his solicitor's, a smooth city suit of dark-grey slightly speckled cloth.

Karen slid into one of the observer's seats, beside DS Eve Clarke, who greeted her with an expression of impatient loathing.

'You've really screwed up now,' she said. 'I hope you're pleased with yourself. Because no one else is.'

'Not going well, then?' Karen said, pretending to be light-hearted.

'Like a train crash.'

Karen put on the spare set of headphones and heard the colonel say:

'This is a farce. If I did not know you were well intentioned and had had the wool pulled over your eyes by that over-enthusiastic, under-trained psychologist girl, I should be making serious representations to the Chief Constable. As it is, DCI Trench, you have one last opportunity to save your career and shut down this absurdity.'

Charlie Trench didn't look pleadingly up at the one-way glass, but Karen watched his shoulders contract and knew he needed her help.

'Ask him to tell you about the cuts in his wife's upper thighs,' she said into the microphone that led to his discreet earpiece. 'They're absolutely straight, each one's about two inches long, and there's a whole series. Some are so old they're barely visible; others are fresh and new.'

'Don't do it,' said Eve Clarke into her own microphone. 'You'll be taking a hell of a risk. And making a bad situation much worse.'

Karen barely heard her, watching the colonel carefully as Charlie Trench put the question. He looked only a little uncomfortable and shot a glance at his solicitor, whose face showed a great deal more anxiety. They put their heads together and whispered briefly, but the colonel shook his head and turned back to Trench.

'I am surprised you should know anything about them. I'm shocked that our doctor should have been so indiscreet, but if he has then so be it. My unfortunate wife has been in the habit for as long as I have known her of dealing with unbearable tension by cutting herself. I understand it is a fairly well-understood syndrome, although I can't say I understand it myself, what. All I can do is pity her, and make sure the cuts are clean and dressed.'

'Ask him why some of the cuts are new,' Karen said into the microphone.

'Some of the cuts are newly made,' Charlie said without a pause, as though he'd thought of the question himself.

He's good at this, Karen thought in relief.

'What has been putting your wife under stress recently, Colonel?' he added.

There was a second's silence, then Falconer burst out: 'How can you even ask that, man? Your officers arrested my son, Silas, on wholly spurious trumped-up charges. You allowed that girl from the mainland to come asking intrusive, damaging questions about Spike, stirring up everything we've worked so hard to forget. And stirring Spike up to kill again. Jim Blake was one of the finest men I've ever known.'

The colonel covered his eyes for a moment. Karen saw that his hand was covered with liver spots. It was shaking. After a moment, he coughed loudly, then brought the hand down, away from his face, which looked suddenly haggard.

What an actor! Karen thought.

'His murder sickens me more than anything else Spike has ever done,' Falconer said. His voice was trembling a little. He squared his shoulders and glared at Charlie. 'Are you surprised the whole thing has thrown my wife back into the unhappiest, most troubled time of her entire life? Of course she's been stressed.'

'Are you really telling me that none of this stress is anything to do with you?' Charlie said, to Karen's admiration.

'How dare you?' The colonel's icily furious voice made Karen's guts leap, sending shivers right through her. She could only imagine its effect on a child, an abnormally compliant, frightened child, and his younger, even more frightened, brother.

This *is* the monster at the heart of Spike's labyrinth, she thought. We have to nail him.

'Now, Charlie,' she said, 'throw in the swimmer and *her* cuts. And Claire Willkins – or at least tell him you've found another of his victims near Freshwater. Ask if Sylvia ever watched him slicing up one of his victims, even if it was only the Labrador.'

'The cuts, Colonel, are too like those on the body of the dead swimmer in Alum Bay for me to ignore them. We've got one of the other bodies, too. This one's near Freshwater. We'll get the rest in no time now. Specialist equipment and dogs are already in operation all over the Island. You won't be able to hide much longer.'

Colonel Falconer did not react.

'The swimmer's cuts are just like the slices you made into the body of your family's Labrador. Lara, she was called, wasn't she? Did you enjoy it, killing her, ripping open the body to take out her guts, then turning it over and cutting those slices into it?'

'Enough!' The solicitor was on his feet.

Damn, thought Karen. It wasn't supposed to be *you* who reacted. Sit down and let us get on with Fergus Falconer.

'Charlie,' she said into the microphone, 'now hit him with something about what he did to Spike, but call him "your son". He's always resisted that. It could just tip him over. Go. Now.'

'You're sick,' the colonel was saying, sounding a lot more modern than the bluff old soldier he pretended to be.

'Maybe,' said Charlie Trench, 'but *I* don't suffer from a personality disorder. You do, though, don't you? Spike, your son, has spent his whole life taking the rap for the things you did – or made him do. Your own son.'

'He is not my son. No son of mine would act as he did. Or commit those appalling crimes.'

'This is not going to work. I knew it wouldn't,' Eve Clarke said to Karen, putting her hand over the microphone. 'We're all fucked now. And it's your fault.'

Karen didn't even look at her. This was no moment for defeatism.

'Ask him about the rabbits,' she said into her own microphone.

'Tell me about the rabbits,' Charlie Trench said, without missing a beat.

'What rabbits? What the hell are you talking about now?' The colonel's face was turning the dark red of raw liver, and a blob of spittle had gathered in the corner of his mouth.

'Ask him how old Spike was the first time he saw his father ripping the heads off snared rabbits.'

'Spike saw you, didn't he?' Charlie Trench said, as though with complete conviction. 'You were ripping the heads off rabbits and he came and watched you. How old was he?'

Sitting beside Eve Clarke behind the one-way glass, Karen watched the colonel's liver-spotted hands seize up into tight fists.

'He was seven, wasn't he? Just before the Labrador incident, and that's why it happened.'

'I don't know what you mean.'

'I think you do, Colonel. Your son saw what you were doing, so you had to make absolutely certain that he could not blow your cover. That's what all this has been about. In that moment you decided it was he who had to be the Island Freak, when all the time it was you.'

'That's *enough*,' said the solicitor. But it wasn't enough. Not nearly enough.

'And your wife knew, too, didn't she? That's why she cut those lines in her own flesh because she wasn't strong enough to tell anyone the truth about you.' Charlie Trench leaned back in his chair, pushing it onto its back legs. 'You know we'll have to bring her in unless you tell us the whole story now.'

But he can't, Karen thought. Part of his personality disorder will stop him being able to tell any story, let alone the whole one.

'She knows everything and we'll find a way to break her . . .' Charlie Trench looked from the solicitor to the colonel and back again in a nerve-stretching pause. Then he added, 'silence.'

'If you go anywhere near my wife without allowing her the protection of our lawyers, who will see that she tells you nothing, I will have you drummed out of the force.'

'OK, Charlie,' Karen said, 'now hit him with Silas. Tell him you're arresting Silas and he'll be charged with conspiracy to murder. Make it clear we know everything.'

Charlie Trench's shoulder muscles eased. Karen could see the movement from where she sat. He took his time slapping his notes in order, while the colonel got hold of himself and sat down again.

'Moving on to Silas,' Charlie said in a tone so calm it sounded almost bored.

'What about him? This has nothing to do with him.'

'Oh, but it has. He set up the fake alibi for the day of the Picnic Massacre, on your instructions, so that he could join you in your expedition to kill Spike and make it look like suicide, didn't he? Then you were forced to do it on your own because his bosses at the bank sent him to the States at no notice. We know all about it, you see, and we have a witness who has testified to the fact that he sent an actor to the hospital as a stand-in.'

He paused, but neither the colonel nor his lawyer said anything. Charlie ploughed on.

'Which makes Silas a conspirator to murder. Penalty for

conspiracy is the same as for murder itself. Life. That's what you've done to Silas: made sure he'll stand in the dock with you and go down for life.'

'Leave my son out of this madness.'

'We can't. Because of what you've taught him, he's dangerous. And we will have to stop him, come what may.'

Karen admired the apparently genuine sadness in Charlie Trench's voice.

'He's up to his neck in it,' he went on. 'And he's not as tough as you. He'll talk. He'll tell us what the original plan was and how the Sanders family came to be shot on Chillerton Down. Got in the way, didn't they, when you went out to kill Spike that day?'

Karen knew she had to keep alert in case Charlie needed more help but she thought he'd probably manage on his own now. This *had* to work.

'You went up there to fake Spike's suicide, didn't you? You knew where he was living rough in that wood and you thought you'd get rid of him once and for all.'

'Don't be dis-gusting.'

'Now talk to him about the clothes, Charlie. Spike's filthy clothes that the colonel must have worn that day,' Karen said quickly into the microphone.

'So you dressed yourself in the scuzzy clothes your wife had taken back from him when she gave him some of your old stuff.' Charlie Trench paused artistically, then added: 'For a man as clean as you, wearing Spike's clothes must've been hard. The smell! But you had to put up with it, didn't you, in case someone saw you. They had to believe they'd just seen Spike.'

He paused again. The colonel sat motionless, looking as solid as one of the sarsens at Stonehenge.

'And someone did see you. At least one member of the pic-nicking family. And when they challenged you, you panicked. Unlike a soldier to panic. You're probably more ashamed of that than killing them.'

There was no response. Charlie pushed on, still sounding as though he believed what he was saying.

'Four picknickers and only four cartridges in your pocket, so once you'd killed them all, you had to think again. You think quickly on your feet, don't you, Colonel? Part of army training, is it?'

Still the colonel didn't move or speak. Karen thought it looked as though he was hardly breathing.

'So you framed Spike for the killings and thought you'd never have to be bothered with him again, until Karen Taylor came over from the mainland and built a rapport with him.'

The colonel's head was tipped forward, with his chin resting against his neck. He looked almost as though he were asleep.

'Did Jim Blake tell you that Spike was talking frankly to Doctor Taylor? Is that why you decided you had to frame Spike for another murder to make sure no one believed anything he told her? Is that why you paid Jim to get Spike out of prison? Were you always planning to kill Jim? Or was it a kind of a spur of the moment thing? Did he turn on you in the end and refuse to join in with the tormenting of Spike? That's it, isn't it? Because Jim liked Spike, didn't he? Your tool eventually refused to do the work you demanded and so he had to be disposed of.'

'I have no idea what you're talking about,' said the colonel raising his head. Now his voice dragged, as though with exhaustion. 'Spike is a mad psychopathic killer with a recognized severe dangerous personality disorder. He should never have been given for adoption. He was always a time bomb waiting to explode.'

'No wonder you're so angry with Doctor Taylor,' Charlie went on, as though the colonel hadn't spoken. 'Beaten by a long-legged blonde beauty from the mainland. Working class, like me. That burns, doesn't it? The great man at the mercy of people who should be cleaning your house and serving your food. People like Karen Taylor and me. That must be a dis-gusting thought.'

Colonel Falconer lost it. Karen couldn't believe that Trench's one piece of minor mockery could crack him when everything else had failed, but it did.

'You shit of an insinuating upstart! You come wiping your filthy mind over my family, suborning my wife, threatening my son and all to get that mad psychopath out of prison again. Yes, I shot those bloody picnickers. Who the hell wouldn't? The child was taking photographs and however well I was disguised in the psychopath's filthy rags, she was making a record that could have identified me. I took the camera so I could destroy it, and then her interfering bitch of a mother had to come crashing into the trees, and then the others. I had no option, man.'

'Well done, Charlie,' Karen said into the microphone and stood to ease her aching muscles.

Only when her legs took her weight did she realize how tightly she'd been clenching them. She almost fell.

Postscript

'So, Karen, are you going to tell me why your husband crashed his car that night?'

She turned to look at Charlie Trench in the half light of this most perfect early October evening. He looked wonderful, posed against the thick white walls of the Goose Inn, nursing his pint of Peg's Special. And he seemed to have recovered all the strength taken by the powerboat explosion and his burns. Tonight he had a steady watchfulness that made her think of his talk of heavy-weight boxing. A big fighter confident of his technique and his fitness must look like this when he's about to go in the ring.

'Why not?' Karen smiled at him. 'You're a good keeper of secrets.'

'Only sometimes,' he said. 'But I'll keep this one for sure.'

'OK. I'd finally discovered what Peter had been up to. I'd been through all his files,' she said, trusting Charlie Trench for no good reason except that they'd been through a lot together and she liked him. 'I couldn't believe he'd just kept them there always at home for anyone to find. They showed it all. The whole fraud. He was an independent financial adviser, you see, and he'd been at it for years and years, taking money from the vulnerable and the persuadable and the worried. I tracked every piece of dis-honesty and sharp practice and I printed off the report I'd written about it all to present to him.'

Karen paused, seeing Peter's furious, greying face and his

juddering jaw muscles, and the way his fist had come at her, aiming at her face, straight between the eyes.

'I told him I'd already sent it to the FSA, the Financial Services Authority.' She stopped talking and waited, just as she had then. Peter had pulled back at the last minute, so the blow in her face hadn't done much damage. She could feel the thump, still, but it hadn't broken her nose or even the skin around it.

'But you were lying?' Charlie said, making it a question.

'I was lying,' she agreed, adding: 'and it's a lie that may have saved my life that night.'

'Yours but not his.' This time there was no question. Charlie stated it as a fact. 'He rushed straight off and killed himself in his car, and you've thought of yourself as a murderer ever since.'

Karen didn't see any need to answer. They both knew he was right.

'Since we're playing truth and lies,' she said, 'd'you want to tell me why Eve Clarke is so proprietorial about you? Did the two of you have a relationship that went bad?'

His crack of laughter was entirely humourless. 'There's more to it.'

'There always is.'

'You don't understand. She's got a sister. Younger. I had a run-in with Daisy when I was with the Met.' His dark face closed up, as though there were shutters being pulled across his eyes and mouth to conceal any hint of a betraying expression.

Karen wondered about his dealings with this Daisy. Had they been romantic? Or professional? Either way, he hadn't got over it yet. She could see that much.

'Eve grew up believing she had to sort out the people her sister messed up. There are plenty of us. The Met wanted me off their patch for a while. Sick leave. Eve heard about it and sent me details of this job. I was too . . . bruised to hold out. She's been looking after me ever since.'

'And driving you nuts,' Karen said, remembering the phone call that had come when she'd been here with him the first time.

Karen was professionally curious about everything Charlie hadn't told her, but she liked him too much to ask for more yet. One day he might tell her the rest. She opened her mouth to say something anodyne and get them both out of the past, but he did it first.

'What's that dead cat in your bag?' he said with an effort that showed how much he wanted to get away from thoughts of Daisy and her sister.

Karen looked down and laughed at the mass of greyish fur balanced on top of her papers.

'Roderick – the Elephant Man – who was my neighbour while I was here has made me a rabbit-fur hat as a going-away present. That's it.'

Charlie began to hum. Karen took a moment to recognize the tune of an old, once-familiar nursery song. Oddly enough it had been Aidan's favourite lullaby when he'd been trying to get her off to sleep when their parents were out gallivanting. She'd have lots to tell him in the next email and somehow she'd get him back to England, if only for a visit. Charlie went on humming and she found the words Aidan had sung so often unfolding in her mind:

> Bye baby bunting.
> Daddy's gone a hunting
> To fetch a little rabbit skin
> To wrap his baby bunting in.

'So, are you off back to your chilly surgeon now?' Charlie said into the silence.

'More or less,' she said, wondering whether she should send Aidan the rabbit-fur hat to protect him through all those bitter New England winters. He'd enjoy the story of the Elephant Man and their peculiar relationship. She dragged her mind back to the present. 'Although Will's a lot less chilly than you think.'

'I'll take your word for it. Shall I drop you at Fountain Quay? I'm going that way.'

She put down her empty glass with regret. The Goose Inn had never seemed more welcoming and cosy than it did tonight, with the ground still exuding warmth and the sky clear enough to reveal a positive light show of stars. The pale waddley shapes of the geese had become less and less distinct as the last of the daylight went. But Will was waiting for her on the mainland.

'Thanks. That'd be great,' she said. 'And we can all get on with our lives. After all that doubt, we got it right in the end.'

'Only about the real killer of the Sanders family on Chillerton Down,' Charlie said.

'And Jim Blake. Don't forget poor Jim, killed after all that devoted work for the Falconers because he knew too much and could've betrayed the colonel.'

'I haven't forgotten Jim. But I wish I thought we'd ever be able to try Falconer for the murders of the swimmer at Alum Bay and Claire Wilkins – or the other women I *know* he buried around the Island.'

'Even though your colleagues from the mainland still haven't found any more bodies,' Karen said without any mockery. 'Are you really still *so* sure that he killed them?'

Charlie shrugged. 'If he didn't, we're back with the idea that there were two psychopaths operating at the same time on one small island. It's as hard to believe as it ever was.'

'Maybe. And what about Silas? Are you going to be able to charge him?'

Charlie shook his head, looking depressed.

'The feeling is that we should count ourselves lucky we've got a confession from the colonel and not push it trying to get Silas for conspiracy.'

'That sounds as though someone did a deal,' Karen said.

'We don't do deals.' A hint of a smile brightened Charlie's dark face. 'But Silas will probably always be the one that got away. I doubt if he'll come back here to the Island. I just hope he doesn't harass his mother – or Spike – or start killing anyone else.'

'It could be that, if he really was involved in planning Spike's death, it was only because of his submission to his father. Without the colonel, Silas may be OK.'

'I hope you're right,' Charlie said. 'Still he worries me less than finding the colonel's other victims. The search has been stopped, you know. If there'd been any sign on Claire Wilkins's skeleton of any slice marks, they might have gone on looking. But there isn't. So there's nothing to link her to the swimmer.'

'Or to Lara the Labrador,' Karen said, remembering their first encounter here at the Goose Inn, when Charlie had shown her the horrible photographs. 'But it's not so bad. Falconer will be serving life in any case. And at his age "life" really will mean life. He's never going to be free again. If he is a serial killer of beautiful dark-haired women, there won't be any more deaths.'

'Sticks in the craw, though. Still, *you* don't have to worry, Karen.' Charlie was making an obvious attempt to sound more cheerful. 'From what I hear you've already got defence lawyers clamouring for your services. You'll be fine now.'

'It's beginning to look like it.' Karen thought of Max Pitton's congratulations and final comment:

'So you see, you don't have to sabotage yourself. Nothing dreadful happens when you win. Go for it now and give it your all.'

'And Spike will be out of prison once the new appeal has happened,' Charlie said, still trying to sound cheerful. 'He'll be due compensation, too, but how will he be able to build a life outside now?'

Karen stood, looking down into Charlie's troubled face.

'He needs years of patient, one-to-one work to make good all the damage,' she said, aching with sympathy for him. 'I just don't know if he'll get it. Mental health is starved of funds, as you know.'

'Can't you help him?'

'My work isn't therapeutic, Charlie. I've already given Sylvia names of all the best psychiatrists in the field. I wish I could say I'd keep an eye on him, but it's not realistic.'

She thought back to the last visit she'd made to the prison, when she'd told Spike what had been happening and how glad she was that he would now get his appeal.

'You'll come to court for it, won't you, Doctor Taylor?' he'd said, sounding far more straightforward than ever before. 'I'd like you to be there with me.'

'I'll try,' was all she'd been able to promise, and she'd seen in his eyes that he knew what she meant.

She shook her head hard to get rid of the memory. She couldn't change Spike's life for him now. And she couldn't have him in hers.

Charlie put his hand on her wrist and held it firmly.

'Karen?'

'Yes. Sorry. I got distracted. What did you say?'

'I asked how Sylvia had taken it.'

'In silence.' Karen glanced up towards the closed and shuttered windows of the pub. 'Peg told me she's gone to the mainland now, and is having some kind of therapy for self-harm, but that's all anyone's saying.'

'No neatly tied-up ends, then?'

'None. There never are in real human messes like this: the ones where it's not enough to be innocent; you have to be lucky, too.'

'I know.' Charlie pushed himself to his feet and stood beside her. 'I'll take you back now. Don't disappear though.'

'I wasn't planning to.'

'We work well together. That's rare. Can't waste it.'

She laughed. 'See you later, then.'

'Sure.'